Readers Love Mic[...]

'Real page turner!'

'The most exciting and imaginative fantasy
novel since the hunger games'

'A fast-paced, action packed adventure you won't
be able to put down'

'Simply Amazing!'

'Beautifully written, the world building is amazing!
Couldn't stop reading!'

'I can't recommend this book (and series) enough'

MICHELLE KENNEY is a firm believer in magic, and that ancient doorways to other worlds can still be found if we look hard enough. She is also a hopeless scribbleaholic and, when left to her own devices, likes nothing better than to dream up new fantasy worlds in the back of a dog-eared notebook. Doctors say they're unlikely to find a cure any time soon.

In between scribbling, Michelle loves reading, running, attempting to play bluegrass and beach treasure-hunting with her two daughters (dreamers-in-training).

Michelle holds a LLB (hons) degree, an APD in Public Relations and is an Accredited Practitioner with the CIPR (with whom she's won awards for Magazine and PR work). But she's definitely happiest curled up against a rainy window, with her nose in a book.

Michelle is represented by Northbank Talent Management, and loves chatting all things book-related at Twitter: @mkenneypr Instagram: @mich_kenneyauthor and https://www.facebook.com/BookofFireMK For further news of events, festivals and giveaways see https://michellekenney.co.uk

Also by Michelle Kenney

Book of Fire
City of Dust

Storm of Ash

MICHELLE KENNEY

ONE PLACE. MANY STORIES

HQ
An imprint of HarperCollins*Publishers* Ltd
1 London Bridge Street
London SE1 9GF

First published by HQ Digital 2019

This edition published in Great Britain by
HQ, an imprint of HarperCollins*Publishers* Ltd 2020

Copyright © Michelle Kenney 2020

Michelle Kenney asserts the moral right to be
identified as the author of this work.
A catalogue record for this book is
available from the British Library.

ISBN: 9780008331108

Printed by CPI Group (UK) Ltd, Croydon CR0 4YY

For Bella and Georgi
from the icy dawn until the fireflies dance.

Astra inclinant, sed non obligant:
The stars incline us; they do not bind us

PROLOGUE

The hunt for *Hominum chimera*

A feral Outsider hunting a feral Insider. There was a rhythm to it. Except *Hominum chimera* was clever, always travelling north of our beat.

We knew from the outset that though there were many ways to track Lake, trapping her would be another matter entirely. Her powerful Nemean lion prints were clear enough; the North Mountain snow made them gleam like ice-dusted runes, while a brave last stand of arid trees, split and broken by her aggressive marking, pointed onwards like wretched ghouls. From time to time, we also came across a scattering of mountain goat tracks, enough to make me wonder whether her volatile chimera nature was morphing again.

But it was always the long black veins of scorching that offered the real evidence. Evidence that, no matter how buried her humanity, Lake still found comfort in being close to Arafel. Close to us.

I couldn't voice the urgency I felt to find Lake, but August seemed to understand anyway. There was something deep within me, some primeval instinct that needed to face her and acknowledge our bond. That she was the key to finally understanding the Voynich was beyond doubt – she was Cassius's alpha weapon of mythical proportions, yet Thomas had somehow bound us with an older connection too. Cassius called it an antidote, a complex protein that would provide some level of control over which of her mythical natures dominated, but I had a suspicion it bore another name, that this was the real legacy for which Grandpa had prepared me.

And I cared. More than I could put into words. Ever since Lake had taken a knife to Max's throat in the tunnels beneath the City of Dust. Back then she looked just another hungry, scraggy child in a dirty headscarf and smoke-grey tunic – no different from the rest of the Prolet children we were trying to rescue. And yet, her veins pumped with a biology more complex than any other creature of Cassius's bestiary. Which made her nature a complete mystery because *Hominum chimera* was also an ancient prophecy. Or curse. Depending on which way you looked at it.

The truth was Lake was entirely unique. And even though Cassius didn't hold the final genetic coding for the hybrid creature, she was clearly a dangerously close match. According to legend, *Hominum chimera* was the mother of all mythological beasts, the one hybrid creature believed to be stronger, faster and more agile than her only existing counterpart. Nature. But while Aelia had always suspected the Voynich of hiding a last secret, it was only when August journeyed to Europa that we all learned of Lake's real potential.

'*There's an ancient myth that* Hominum chimera *is capable of triggering a sequence of natural disasters, culminating in the eternal fire of damnation.*'

August's words looped in my head. An eternal fire of damnation seemed so easy to dismiss as mythological rhetoric, and yet

2

I knew better now. There was something in Lake's serpentine eyes that reached back through the dust of years, to a time when myth and reality were separated by only the thinnest of veils.

Legacy or lunacy, Cassius's ambition had never been clearer. It was all about power to redesign the natural world, and now that he had The Book of Arafel, Thomas's secret research decoding the Voynich, it was nearly within reach.

Arafel was nearly within reach.

All that remained was the keyword to operate the cipher and, if he was looking to replicate *Hominum chimera* perfectly, a certain annotated, aged diagram. It was the same fragile page I'd rolled up and inserted into a certain treehouse dart tube for safekeeping, the last present Max made for me. To get it Cassius would have to slit the feral throat around which it was hung.

I lifted my hand to the precious tiny dart tube. Thomas's clue had been there the whole time, a simple faint abbreviation on the same page as Thomas's *Hominum chimera* sketch.

REQ.

It wasn't until August mentioned its appearance in the tomb frescos beneath the ancient Colosseum that I guessed at its true significance. REQ was an abbreviation for *Requiem*, or *Mass for the Dead*, and a warning, through the sands of time, from the original medieval scribe of the Voynich Manuscript.

Five hundred years later and against all the odds, Thomas had worked out it was also the only keyword to operate the Voynich cipher, the same cipher he drew out on the floor of the first treehouse in Arafel. Our treehouse. I thought of my mother's living area, of the old reed mat that had always covered what we believed to be our ancestor's first crude map of Arafel. Little had we known we'd been walking over the only existing key to the world's most dangerous genetic heirloom.

Now it was a knowledge that burned, in the same way my blood burned every time I imagined Lake's heavy double-lidded eyes peering out of the crevices and caves of the North Mountain landscape we scoured. Ancient, powerful eyes that watched us track and hunt, from the icy dawn until the fireflies danced.

Biding time.

4

Chapter 1

Arafel

Raven was the first to spot us.

I watched her slight figure straighten in shock, as I fell into a stumbling run towards the afternoon shift working among the corn. Twice my exhausted feet slipped on the mountainous shale, making me skid and graze my blistered skin, but nothing could slow me. We'd been walking for longer than I could remember, and our conversation had long since worn as thin and broken as our soles. But in the past few minutes, Arafel had finally reached through the mountain mist like a ray of dawn after a nightmare, and Raven's expression was everything I needed to pull me over the last stretch.

She lifted her hand, and a sharp piercing whistle filled the air. It was the village alert, the same one we'd all learned as part of our shift training, more usually associated with flagging wild animals among the crops than alerting the village to intruders. But not today.

A dozen more figures straightened throughout the large corn-field, and I could read their incredulity even at a distance.

'*Mum?*' I tried to force the word out between my blistered lips, but there was no sound but the rustling of the breeze through the corn.

I was spent. My body knew it, I knew it, even the ground beneath my exhausted feet knew it. *Just a few more steps.* The whisper echoed around my head as the field group convened and stood together to await us. And I understood their hesitation. I knew what a sight we had to present: the disloyal, rebellious girl with two strangers – a gladiator and a Cyclops – for company. But still they waited. And although Mum wasn't among them, dry sobs reached up my throat, racking my body with convulsive pain as I opened the field gate and stumbled in among Arafel's irrigated crops.

'Talia?'

Raven's voice was as sweet as the first rain, and as I barrelled into her open arms I was overcome by her homely scent of apples and cinnamon, warming me a thousand times faster than any knitted blanket.

'Hush, Talia, you're in Arafel now … you're home,' she soothed, her voice distant and strained as my knees buckled.

My vision shrank, but I was just conscious of Bereg's thunderous face as he strode past to confront August and Unus, flanked by three machete-wielding hunters.

I wanted to protest, but there was nothing left – just a few hoarse words that spilled over my cracked lips as the fields receded in a blur.

'Don't hurt them … they're friends.'

***

The days that followed were a haze of delirium. I was racked with pain one moment and incoherent with fever the next, but as the world slowly returned, I became aware of two stone-cold facts:

I'd made it home; Max and Eli hadn't.

And each time I remembered, it was as though I was teetering at the edge of a North Mountain abyss all over again.

August and Unus made swifter progress and became frequent visitors. And if the villagers were wary of my new Insider companions, they guessed my survival was at least due to them in part, and afforded them a cautious respect.

'They want to know if you're feeling well enough for the Ring meeting?' August murmured a few mornings after our return. 'I could handle it myself but your leader, Art, he's quite insistent you're there … needs to hear it from you … it's understandable.'

He was trying to act normal, to be his old confident self but his iris-blues betrayed him in a way they never had before. His pain was visible. There were glimpses that spoke louder than the iron will forcing his Roman lips upwards, or his tone to be even. It was a vulnerability no amount of Pantheonite training or armour could hide, and then there was our own stalemate, frozen in place by the icy North Mountain winds.

I turned to gaze out of the window. It was the end of winter, so the rains were still heavy and frequent, but there was a hint of the new honeysuckle that grew all around the old wooden frame in spring. *A ghost of its scent.*

'Tal?' August laid his hand gently over mine.

I drew my hand away distractedly, focusing on the forest, willing spring to come and chase away the winter that had settled in my bones.

Because I couldn't pretend. Not to August.

And the furrow between his eyes told me he knew. He could sense I was watching the world as though I'd never really emerged from the glass river at all. I could see and hear it all in sonorous detail, I just couldn't touch it. I was isolated – from everyone. And while he did his best to deflect the darting glances and barely contained curiosity, I knew he felt it too. Every second of every day, we were slipping a little further away from each other, and we were both utterly powerless to stop it.

Again and again my dreams took me back to the North Mountains, to the unique magic we'd created in a remote cave, and to what *almost* happened there. The edges of my thoughts darkened with guilt, the same guilt that forced me into consciousness each time. Because of my best friend Max, because of my twin Eli, because of August's sister Aelia, and because of Lake and her guardian, Pan. And finally because the spell binding us in the harsh solitude of the North Mountains had been broken. We could no longer pretend we were at the end of the world, that no one else existed, or that we were the only ones hurt by Isca Pantheon. And while our connection had saved us while we were isolated, it did nothing but scorch in Arafel, where ghosts darkened every corner.

'I'll tell him you need more time,' he breathed.

I stared out at the white oak branches shadowing my window, willing the impossible every time it rustled.

'No.'

I turned back to face him. My head was still hazy with weakness and denial, but in the last few hours one thought had materialized clearly: so long as Max was missing, there was a chance. And while there was a chance, I was wasting time. There was little doubt Cassius was already devising his revenge. After all, we'd escaped Ludi Pantheonares, and set his prized mythological weapon free.

And I'd made too many mistakes to expect any reprieve, but Max deserved so much more. Art needed to know what danger I'd carried through Arafel's door. And Taskforce, special delegation, army … whatever he decided, I was going to be right at the front. *Come what may.*

'I'm ready.'

And somewhere deep in the jungle a lone oropendola bird hissed, stilling the forest briefly.

8

Chapter 2

'Friends, we gather here today for two important reasons.' Art's grave voice echoed through the Ring's flickering torchlight.

'Firstly, to give thanks that the stars and earth have conspired between them, to bring home a much-loved daughter of Arafel. On behalf of everyone gathered here, I would like to offer our sincerest gratitude to Talia's companions who, we can all be assured, have played a critical role in her return.

'Commander General Augustus Aquila and Unus of Isca Prolet, you are most welcome.'

I watched as August and Unus, seated to the right of the Ring platform, nodded in acknowledgement. August's inclination was brief and tight; while Unus's great pudgy head fell forward in confused embarrassment, his one misted eye focused on the rock floor.

My nerves settled briefly. I owed Unus so much. From the moment we met in the strix-ridden passages beneath Pantheon, he'd proven himself a loyal and true friend. He'd saved my life countless times, but more than that, he'd proven real friendship could come from the unlikeliest of places. In truth, Unus gave me hope. He'd also eased into village life easily, proving invaluable in treehouse construction work. And despite a mistrustful start, fuelled by generations of fireside tales, villagers were now starting to treat him with real respect and kindness.

Much more so than Commander General August Aquila, who remained aloof and harder to know. I dragged my gaze back to his proud Roman face, still over-bright from the raw biting wind of the North Mountains, and so at odds here among my people. He'd insisted on sleeping on a mattress outside my bedroom door for the past week, and barely left my bedside during the long silent days. Yet conversation between us had long since guttered and died, overladen with shadows neither of us could ignore. We were lost. Not only because his presence forced me to face the absences, but also because it meant accepting who we'd become, that the constellation that had aligned over our snowstorm cave had faded.

Our snowstorm cave.

I couldn't think about what we'd done, of how we'd nearly given in, despite everything. Despite everyone. Every time I closed my eyes I was haunted by a memory of us lying together, the flickering flames shadowing our skin as if inking our shame there. *How could we have forgotten the others, even for a moment?*

August's eyes narrowed, reading me, as I dropped my eyes to my feet. The memories were corrosive. He could feel it too – I could tell whenever we made the mistake of catching each other's gaze.

And the irony nearly consumed me – I'd spent a year feeling like a ghost girl with Max, and now I'd give anything to go back there. Not because I was happier, but because those feelings were so much easier than this caustic pit of guilt. The knowledge that Max, Eli and Aelia were lying pale and lifeless within the glassy Dead City river. Because of me. While I was still here, beside two Insiders instead of my childhood companions, and expected to explain their absence in a way that made it bearable. *What could be more impossible than that?*

'Secondly, in accordance with Arafel tradition, when one of our community has been reported missing or compromised, we gather to hear the facts and decide on our collective response.

'Action or inaction, Thomas's principles stand as firmly today as they did two hundred years ago. An Arafel hunter believes in natural order, respect for his place in the forest, and taking only what he needs to survive. But if the circle is broken, particularly by forces outside of these four walls, it is up to the rest of us to decide whether to meet that betrayal with earth – or fire.'

I looked up at Art, Thomas's wisdom echoing around the rock walls. He looked older and more wizened than ever before, and though our return had been celebrated with a whole roasted lamb and two kegs of elderberry wine, I could also see how it changed everything. *I'd changed everything.*

Cassius had broken the circle, but I had too. I'd brought Insiders here, to our most precious secret valley home. I'd violated the most sacred of rules, and I didn't need to look around the room. I already knew fear and suspicion would be etched into every single face, all at my hand. I wished Mum was beside me, that I could bury my face in her familiar scent and comfort. But she was seated at the back, shelling peas as though it were just an ordinary harvest meeting, safe inside her own quiet oblivion.

So I locked my agitation inside my knotted fingers, because there was still Max, and that meant there was nothing I could do except tell them the stone-cold facts, and hope the people I'd always called my family didn't end up hating me.

'Talia … Commander General Augustus Aquila … Unus of Isca Prolet, I ask you to relate your journey and experiences with us now, omitting no … difficult details, so that we might arrive at the best course of action for Arafel.

'The Ring platform is yours.'

My chest tightened, and I climbed the wide stone steps, feeling as though my legs had grown as dense and heavy as the rock surrounding us. I'd never felt more alone in the world, and yet there was nowhere to hide either. I'd been dreading this moment, finally facing Art, Max's family … and Mum. Although she'd stopped asking after Eli, I was all too aware that didn't mean the

11

truth had reached through the mist separating her from the rest of Arafel. If anything, I was probably about to push her further away.

I turned slowly and surveyed the waiting crowd, recalling the last time I'd stood here – appealing for help to rescue the Prolet insurgents. I'd chosen my own path anyway, and could already see the doubt in their eyes.

Why were they even listening to me? I'd acted rashly, spent innocent lives, and exposed Arafel to danger.

The air was sombre and suspicious, I closed my eyes and Pan's pale face loomed out of nowhere. It was the moment before he stepped into the writhing mass of basilisk, a moment filled with both fear and courage. Human attributes blazing in a creature of Pantheon.

He'd sacrificed his life so Max and I stood a chance of finding and protecting Lake. From Cassius, from the world and from herself. And now Max was gone, which meant the responsibility was mine alone.

It was time.

It was nearly an hour later when we finally finished relating our story. Mum had shelled peas consistently throughout, and the cavern was eerily quiet.

'We tried everything.' My voice sounded brittle in the echoing space. 'We took them to the Oceanids, hoping they would do what they did for myself and the Commander General … hoping they would bring them back … somehow?'

My voice was growing thinner, an invisible fist closing around my throat.

Could they tell I was just about the worst human being alive? That I was the type of girl likely to give in to her darkest desire, even when her best friend was missing and her brother not quite cold in his watery grave?

'They didn't,' August finished for me, 'or more likely, they couldn't – not in the time we needed them to.'

His words met with ominous silence, before the uproar began. I was conscious of time slowing, of the mood turning as faces I loved twisted beyond recognition. Until now there had been whispers and conjecture, still laced with hope, but now their worst suspicions had been confirmed there was only pain. And honest-to-God fury.

'These ... Oceanids of which you speak ... dare we hope they may yet return Eli and Aelia?' Art's face was grave, his eyes straining with grief.

A poignant silence hung on the air before August shook his head. 'From experience, and what I understand of how the Oceanids work – their therapies either work swiftly, or not at all. So ... tempting though the thought is, it is better not to nurse unrealistic hope.'

'Then I think we have our answer!' Bereg roared from the back of the crowd, his affable face over-red and raw.

Loud voices bayed their support, their faces leering as unbridled fury pierced my skin like barbs. And for a fleeting moment, I could almost believe I was back beneath the flashing screens and bloodthirsty crowds of Ludi. *But how could I blame them?* I'd breached village protocol by taking off with Eli and Max in the first place, and I'd breached it again by bringing back two Insiders, instead of two much-loved sons. And August's defection and Unus's efficiency with whatever he turned his hand to were no recompense for the biggest danger I'd carried right into the heart of our home. *I was a Trojan horse of the worst kind.*

'There are others!' August's authoritative tone rose above the din, quieting it momentarily.

'There are other Outsiders – communities like you – in isolated locations across Europa. The fate that befell Eli, Max and my own beloved blood sister, Aelia, was beyond our control. You must believe what Talia is saying – we did *everything* we could to save them.'

I stared at the floor, acutely aware he was still doing it.

13

Protecting me by trying to turn the tide, saving me when I least deserved saving. *Didn't he get it yet?* There was no reprieve from this. I deserved it all. How could there be any light when the blood flowing through my veins was dark, like Cassius's?

Black to black, dust to dust.

'Believe me, I understand ...' his voice faltered momentarily '... how you are feeling right now. But there is a darker day than this yet to come.

'Max, Eli, Aelia ... they are just the beginning. Cassius is coming for Arafel; he is coming for each and every one of you. And the reason I know this is because I was a Commander General of Isca Pantheon's Equite forces, and a senior member of the scientific team for too long. Cassius will not rest until every last Outsider has been eliminated.'

A muted gasp swept across the belligerent crowd.

'You want revenge on your sons' deaths, but you would do better to save your energy for those who are still alive. If you march on Pantheon as you are, you will join Max and Eli before the sun goes down. To stand even the remotest chance of bringing Cassius's Civitas down once and for all, you need strength, speed and numbers. In truth, you need every last Outsider on this earth standing beside you.

'And I know where they are.'

For a second it was quiet enough to hear the faint call of a lemur outside. And then fresh pandemonium broke.

'He must be lying ... It can't be true! Where are these other Outsiders? We would know of them. Do they look like him? It's obviously a lie! How could an Insider know this? We would have known before now!'

'Silence!' This time it was Art's command filling the space, and every pair of eyes levelled with the elderly man charged with making sense of it all.

'If all of this is indeed true ...' he exhaled raggedly '... it is both a dark and wondrous day. We have lived with dreams of finding other communities like our own, but ... how do we know they will be friendly or even receptive to helping Arafel?'

'You don't,' August returned baldly. 'We don't ... at least not yet. But I can tell you they are more like this community than they are different.'

His tone grew gentler as the Ring hushed with new respect. 'I've no idea how many individual communities there may be scattered across Europa. But my own Pantheon mission encountered one that had adapted to a similar climate, and where there is one there must be others. It's vital to remember that while their Outsider DNA may be as original as any of yours, their culture will likely be very different ... We would all need to tread cautiously.

'Any community that stands beside Arafel will be unpredictable and a risk, until we know otherwise.'

I scanned the faces in the crowd, which had morphed from hostility into something quieter, a grim unified determination. It was a real turnaround, and I knew if it wasn't for his intervention we would be facing a very different scene now.

My eyes flickered back to meet his. The lanterns were casting shadows across his tapered cheekbones, his dark eyes were hollowed, and the tiny muscle beside his mouth was twitching as though he wanted to say so much more. And yet, even though he'd saved me from clear ostracization, and provided my people with the most fragile of new hopes, I still couldn't feel anything.

I swallowed, trying to recall my father's face. I could just see a hint of his smile, and his hunched back as he pored over the old-world maps in his treehouse study, ringing all the valleys in dark red. He would have been euphoric to know his belief and years of work weren't in vain.

August pulled his gaze away abruptly.

'You need to gather a *legatio*, a deposition to locate new communities quickly and appeal for their help. There is no time to waste. I am willing and able to lead this legatio – in Arafel's name.'

15

There was a murmur across the crowd as Art nodded, visibly relieved. August already knew where to locate at least one other community, and that whoever travelled as embassy had the huge challenge of rallying them to our cause. He had a natural authority and had just demonstrated his powers of persuasion. There was no doubt he made the perfect choice.

An Insider rallying feral communities to an Outsider army.

It was a bittersweet outcome, and though it was clearly fraught with danger, there was no way back. I'd hurt them all, my own family included, and while August had provided some hope, it was merely a glimmer of light amid the gathering storm clouds.

A war was coming, and my peace-loving people had eyes the colour of revenge.

What, in the name of Arafel, had I started?

16

Chapter 3

The scar on his face glistened in the sun, while his eyes belied his words. Leaving words.

'You know I have to do this. It gives the legatio a chance. I know where to go. I can lead them – it's what I'm good at … Tal?'

Hopelessness, then worse, hurt fleeted across his face as I gave him nothing back. But how could I when emotion was the cause of so much.

'Feral means free, remember?' he whispered. 'That's worth something even if you let go … of everything else.'

I stared at the spring grass surrounding my leather-soled feet. It looked so fragile and swollen with monsoon rain. There were no dark veins or dust-choked roots. It had no idea of the shadows creeping closer every day. Unlike Augustus Aquila, standing less than a metre away, in my forest home, trying to save any part of us that was still salvageable.

Why didn't he understand? How could he stand there, alive, thinking of us when we'd watched so many others sink to the icy depths of the glass river … the icy depths.

'For all Oceanid revivals there has to be a payment of sorts: either a trade of treasure or promise of recompense …'

August's words never felt more poignant.

Was that it? Had August and I paid the ultimate price? Could our revival have cost us ... us?

I swallowed, trying to force thoughts past the rush of blood in my ears. Why would the Oceanids demand such a payment? Yet it would explain so much.

'The Oceanids are loyal to no one but themselves.'

That they helped us was indisputable, *but to what purpose?*

Thoughts tumbled through my head, confused and overlapping. I gritted my teeth. It had to be a purpose bigger than us altogether. *Was it to make us strong enough to finish what we'd started? To lead the war?*

'It was real for me, Talia.'

And it seemed as though the branches around us leaned in to catch his whisper, and cocoon it within their scrolled leaves.

We both knew the dangers of the legatio meant his return was against all the odds. Leaving nothing. An enormous silence, when so much had preceded it. Which was why no more words made it into the dead air between us.

After all, what was there left to say if we'd already traded it all?

Chapter 4

Two months later

I tensed, Harlo's slingshot taut and short in my hands. The catapult was larger than my old one, and made of a hard wood I didn't recognize. Harlo called it camphor when he relinquished it, but a borrowed slingshot made of foreign wood was only the beginning. Arafel had been slowly changing since the new Outsiders started arriving.

Ida's soft whistle perforated the humid air. I peered through the thick foliage and spied her blue-inked skin gleaming through the giant yuccas a little way off. Lifting my hands, I hooted twice by way of response. Birdcalls were a useful method of communication when the Elders weren't around to disapprove. They were simple and uncomplicated, which suited us both.

I retrained the slingshot, as a warm breeze rustled the foliage cocooning me. Ida was a Komodo, one of the first Outsiders to arrive, and a formidable huntress, even among her people. I caught the rise of her hand, just enough to say she'd heard, and nodded once. It was always enough.

The arrival of her tribe had stopped everyone in their tracks. Flanked by lizards the size of small ponies, and with midnight bodies and long plaited hair, they looked more like gods and goddesses than flesh-and-blood Outsiders. They were also a people of very few words, and though it was the same Outsider community August had described before leaving, their actual appearance had turned our quiet village into a place I no longer recognized.

August. I exhaled slowly, forcing his image from my mind. It was how I'd survived, volunteering for every possible shift and spending all my days in the outer forest, away from everyone. Denying it all.

I tucked the slingshot into my leather rations belt and climbed higher.

The Komodo tribe were some four hundred in number, and brought whole families of naked, inked children with them. Within a single day the outside forest had looked and felt like an entirely new world. They set up ad hoc camps, cut down mature trees for shelter and baited large food for their unusual guard – the dragons, who were also the tribe's symbolic alter ego.

The Komodo dragon lizards tested everyone. The huge, lumbering reptiles were constantly hungry and aggressive, particularly to children, so Art insisted they were herded into pens in the outside forest. It had sparked the first real confronta-tion. The tribe were unwilling to be parted from their reptilian family, and unable to return to their Europa home without stock-piling provisions from Arafel's forest.

Art called an emergency Ring, and counter-proposed bringing the newcomers into Arafel, where food and shelter could be shared and a war strategy agreed. The lizards would remain in pens, while the tribe would have the protection of the North Mountains instead.

There was a long, heated meeting but the motion was eventu-ally passed, and there was no doubt it was a good compromise. The tribe moved into the village, while the lizards stayed in the outside forest, and if they mourned their separation, the pens were built sufficiently close to the river stepping stones to ensure any lovelorn tribe member didn't have far to go.

The simple truth was, we were all acutely aware that the Komodos' arrival was a powerful show of solidarity and support – and that harmonious living was essential if we were to stand any chance against Cassius.

Yet the new integrated living brought sharper edges to Arafel none of us could ignore. While the tribespeople were an undeniable asset to our hunter army, their physique an easy match for any Pantheonite gladiator, it was less clear whether the outside forest could keep up with their significant drain on resources. It wasn't helped by the fact the tribe were focused ground hunters, and preferred to work alone when it came to securing a kill, which was too often outside our regular village shifts.

Another muted whistle reached through the undergrowth, the warning call of a green turaco. I scanned the bushes, but couldn't see Ida. It didn't matter; the call was her warning to keep my distance, that she had a scent or a lead. Today, I was content to oblige. I scurried up a few more branches and lodged myself in a fork.

Everyone knew the new rate of consumption was unsustainable. Our stockpile of grain and pulses had depleted at a frightening rate, even though the Komodo tribe's diet was predominantly carnivorous. Their survival philosophy was different to ours too. While we tried to strike a balance with nature, their approach was territorial. Food was there for the taking, until it wasn't. Then they moved on. Art and the Council remonstrated, pointing out that their approach wouldn't work within a fixed community like Arafel, but there were still too many unofficial dawn raids to number.

At times, the differences seemed bigger than the similarities. While my people had long, sculpted limbs, adapted for swift passage through our forest trees, the Komodos had developed a muscular physiology that almost matched that of their dragon

21

friends. The tribe had also travelled their lands nomadically for more than two hundred years, while Arafel had been our home since Thomas's discovery. The Komodo considered hunting to be a right, while Arafel people considered it the blessing of a healthy forest.

And yet, there was one binding commonality that put us all squarely on the same dirt ground. The Lifedomes of Isca Pantheon. Their ancestors had also passed down myths about the Great War, how the Lifedomes were supposed to be a refuge before the trapped population realized they couldn't leave. It explained their swift arrival, their unquestioning solidarity and was the first sign the legatio might actually succeed.

I reached out to pick a few rare bunches of ripe blueberries and add them to my foraged roots and oranges. I'd only discovered two other blueberry bushes in the outer forest before and they'd quickly disappeared. Max would be impressed with this particular crop, especially now the outside forest was supporting so many more.

I popped one into my mouth, before dropping the rest into my bag. While the Komodos were the first to arrive, they weren't the last. Less than three weeks after their arrival, two more Outsider communities arrived. First there was a pale-skinned, northern hemisphere tribe calling themselves Lynx – they didn't say why but I had a feeling their green eyes and shy, nocturnal habits had something to do with it – and they were swiftly followed by a large party of peace-loving Eurasians. While the Lynx had built a life hunting fattened seals and ice-diving for fish, the Eurasians were much more like us – forest dwellers with farming and pottery skills. And it seemed each new arrival built new pillars of hope, yet August was never with them.

Another turaco warning call whistled through the leaves, followed by the swift and soft impact of an arrow about ten metres away. Seconds later, Ida's athletic form crept through the clearing below. I watched as she retrieved her arrow from a twisted baobab root and swiftly cleaned it, before melting back into the trees. Hunting was often like this now. The forest animals seemed to understand they were under greater threat, and that the old balance was shifting.

It was a permanent heated agenda item at the open leader meetings. Art's diplomacy and leadership were tested more than ever before, and for the first time since Thomas's days, a penal code was resurrected. The Council called it a temporary measure while communities grew and integrated. But we all knew it was a by-product of the new conflict that was unlikely to disappear, and while the Ring had been nominated as a place where disputes could be resolved – the village grazing field stood in for those who couldn't wait.

It was Raven who suggested using Arafel's story nights as an opportunity for communities to exchange stories and history. There was plenty of scepticism at first, but the evenings bred a little ease as we learned about our new brothers and sisters. And each new community arrival meant one certainty to me: August was still out there, *still breathing*. Which somehow still eased my own.

A spotted tiger beetle scurried across the dirt floor before disappearing beneath a pile of large maple leaves. There was a momentary lull, before the telltale rustle, and a young corn snake slithered out looking satisfied. I watched unmoved. It was the way of the forest, from the smallest to the largest. Each and every species had its natural predator and check – all except, it seemed, for Lake.

I pictured her vast, scaled head and grey spiny body as I swung myself up between the thick fringed leaves of a papaya tree, intent on reaching the fruit weighing down the topmost branches. Her existence had been harder to explain to the Council.

'Lake is believed to possess extraordinary strength, speed and agility. Cassius intends to recapture and use her against us.'

The Elders were still reeling from August's bombshell about

outside communities, when I shared the news that an unstable draco-chimera was also living among the mountainous peaks above our quiet valley. And their initial scepticism was rapidly replaced with palpable fear, even though I was careful to provide only as much detail as they really needed.

'I've kept Lake's chimera coding safe,' I whispered to Grandpa, touching the tiny dart tube resting against my chest, just to reassure myself it was still there.

It was a small consolation, but one of the few I still had. Grandpa had entrusted the legacy of the Book of Arafel to me, and the circle of knowledge had grown so much since then. I had to trust that protecting the genetic coding of the Voynich's oldest secret, as well as Thomas's original cipher, would thwart Cassius, until the day he brought his war.

And found an army of freshly trained Outsiders waiting.

One of August's key instructions, before he left, was that training and weapon instruction should take place in the outside forest. It was also where a skeleton shift of Arafel hunters, Komodos and Lynx warriors kept careful watch on the fringe of the forest every day. If there was to be a battle, it would be in the outer forest, away from Arafel, our home and the only real retreat we had. And there was no doubt we had a formidable Outsider army now with a wide range of skills and weaponry.

Training was intense and overseen by Bereg, Ida's father, and a sharp Lynx captain called Marta. I assisted where I could, describing Cassius's creatures and training some of the younger recruits in darting and knifing, but I escaped to hunt and forage whenever I could. It was the only time I got to escape, and pretend.

Somewhere above my head a lemur called a warning as a green lorikeet swooped low. I lowered my borrowed slingshot and watched its silent dive towards the forest floor, before it flew up and out of sight. There were still some compromises I couldn't make, though we were trying to widen our diet as much as possible.

I leaned back into the fork of the gnarled papaya, and reached into my leather rations bag. It was still there, my lucky apricot stone. I withdrew it and rolled it around in my fingers, drawing some comfort from its mottled, wizened surface. It reminded me of the stone I'd rolled into the cage of the little apricot monkey; a seed from the outside world offering comfort and hope through the bars of Isca Pantheon. It was a promise I was determined to deliver.

A young monkey swung through the cedar branches opposite, and Ida's turaco call followed. I frowned. We were asking the other outside communities for so much, but there were rules about the infant animals.

At the same time, a series of thin branches snapped in the bushes directly below me. *Medium-sized … bold given its proximity … wild boar?* Years of hunting had equipped me well when it came to assessing a potential meal and I focused on the bushes intently. A single bigger kill would keep everyone happy.

I drew Harlo's slingshot back, my eyes narrowing as a swift silver blade suddenly flew through the opaque sunlight beneath me. A hoopoe cried its warning seconds too late as the blade impacted softly halfway up a neighbouring tree, while my intended quarry rustled away through the undergrowth.

Scowling, I watched as Ida's different target swung through the low branches, screeching its distress. We'd made our feelings about young monkey meat clear, and while it was a Komodo delicacy, the forest couldn't sustain the rate at which the tribe wanted to feast on them. Instinctively, I leapt into action, running swiftly through the neighbouring trees until I reached the baby bonnet macaque, which seemed frozen to the cedar trunk above the gleaming blade. My arrival startled it back into life, and it scurried swiftly up to the topmost branches, where a mature macaque chattered her relief.

Satisfied, I yanked the blade out of the trunk and dropped to the ground, just as the low grunting of a confident predator filled the air. I swung up into the nearest fork and swivelled to glance at the snorting creature, which was only a stone's throw away. It had to be the same wild boar, and by the way it was squaring up to me, a hungry adult male.

'First rule of the jungle: never hesitate or show doubt.'

Bereg's training was entrenched in us all and his voice echoed through my head. Stealthily, I levelled Harlo's slingshot just as a second flash of silver flew past and buried itself in the boar's neck. It dropped forward onto its knees, eyeing me reproachfully, before collapsing in a growing pool of its own dark blood.

The bushes parted a moment later and Ida, clad in a leather sarong and beaded tunic top, strode past me, her long plaited ebony hair glistening in the iridescent light.

She reached down and placed her palm over the animal's forehead as a mark of respect, before retrieving her knife and tucking it inside her leather waistband. Then she shot me a questioning glance, the painted seasons on her forehead and forked tongues around her oaken eyes crinkling with satisfaction. I swallowed my frustration and nodded; it was a clean kill and we were all hungry.

Together, we strapped the boar onto a short length of hickory using a mixture of rudimentary signing and gestures. It hung there, unprotesting, and now that I was closer I could see why it hadn't run when it could. It was starving. I suppressed another frown as Ida lifted her trophy over her strong shoulders and melted back into the bushes. Then we set off at hunting pace, and I took my last forage into the trees among the leaves and birds.

The Komodo knew how to ground-run, even wearing a kill, and I had to concentrate to forage while keeping her dark silhouette in sight. A lone hoopoe's echo rang among the branches as I ran down a twisted kapok branch and leapt into the tree opposite. It was an easy leap, and one Max and I used to navigate without blinking.

I set my teeth, refusing to let the memories consume me, as two fat pheasants ran out of the bushes below. I raised my slingshot instinctively, and within a heartbeat they were still. Relieved, I dropped to the forest floor and grabbed their scrawny legs, just as Ida pushed through the bushes. I held up a count of two, and it was her turn to nod, her lips parted in a garish smile that displayed her impressive Komodo teeth chiselled into tiny points.

Deftly, I strung the pheasants to my tunic belt, alongside my leather rations bag. It was full of wild roots, blueberries and the small papaya. The wild roots would provide an alternative stock to our usual cultivated vegetables, and now there was the boar and pheasant. It had been a good early shift. The sun was glinting through the dense foliage, casting longer shadows across the forest floor, which meant it had to be approaching breakfast time. I gesticulated at the sky and Ida nodded.

We set out again, two hunters from different communities bringing food to share. It was progress, I told myself as a jaybird darted low in front of us, dropping the remainder of its meal onto the forest floor.

In a breath, the jungle melted away, and I was free-falling towards the glass river with its slow snaking arms and muted starlight. My eyes closed briefly and I willed it to consume me, to take me back to oblivion. But the jungle loomed back anyway with its coarse sunlight and unapologetic life. I was conscious of a rush of disappointment, before a cool palm on my cheek. I longed to fold into it, to take the comfort my silent friend offered, but I'd learned the hard way that caring led only to pain.

I quickened my pace. We'd stayed too long today.

Chapter 5

'Astra inclinant, sed non obligant.'

August's whisper was barely there, but his pain was as clear as a monsoon moon.

I tried to resist the dream but it fought back, tightening its hold, and trapping me inside my own memory. I told myself that I would wake soon, that I should focus on breathing, but each inhalation drew nails over my lungs. Raking in and raking out. Shouldn't it be easier than this now?

'The stars incline us ... they do not bind us,' I whispered, a hazy echo of Grandpa's wisdom reaching through.

August watched me, his silence saying nothing and everything all at once.

'I am not bound by this,' I repeated, staring at my aching, blistered fingers as clearly as though we were back there.

I was bluffing though.

We both knew it. It was the thing that always undid me, his unerring ability to read my thoughts, no matter how hard I tried to block him out. I fixed my gaze on the flames, feeling none of their warmth. We'd come so far over the mountains together; and yet the distance was growing.

If August hadn't gone to Europa, if I hadn't asked Max to

28

save Aelia, if we hadn't run after the Prolets, if I'd stayed with Eli …

The charges went on, the guilt was asphyxiating and yet every cell of my disloyal body wanted to steal inside his battle-worn arms. To let him take me far away from the perishing mountains, Isca Pantheon and everything we knew.

I stretched out and let my fingers rest over his as I stared into the dancing flames. I didn't need to look at him to know the fresh lines the North Mountains had etched in his face. He didn't need to know how his vulnerability weakened me, and made me remember the first time I saw him look like that back in Aelia's cave in Isca Prolet. That time.

His fingers closed over mine, and even though it was a dream, I could feel their question as clearly as though he'd whispered the words.

Unus had ventured out for firewood, and was likely to be a while given the sparse mountain shale. And this tiny mountain cave tucked away from the harsh, unforgiving elements had created a brief reprieve none of us had expected. It was precious time together, perhaps the last we would ever have.

Suddenly I felt like the naive girl he'd smuggled into his rooms in Pantheon. Trapped, uncertain, doubting everything he said and yet wanting so much to believe him too. His eyes crinkled as a ghost smile played across his lips.

'I think the stars bind us more than we know.'

His whisper made me shiver.

'And I would have given up a long time ago if it wasn't for you. Your kind have a feral hunger for survival that my … Pantheonites … have long forgotten.'

'Kind? Since when did you start getting fussy about a couple of chromosomes?'

His eyelids lowered briefly, but I could see his iris-blues were dulled. It terrified me. I could just about cope with anything but his mental defeat. The void loomed as he stared down at his noble

29

hands, designed for Equite service, not the precipitous North Mountains at the start of the stormy season.

'We are who we become,' I added. 'The only legacy that counts is the one we leave behind.'

'Unless we happen to be the last guardian of the Book of Arafel,' he responded with a glint of a smile, 'then it's just a simple matter of fulfilling ancient prophecies, and going down in history as the girl who saved the world.'

I rolled my eyes at him, suddenly aware he was moving – getting up and settling back down. Behind me. I stiffened as he reached his arm around me, pulling me tight in a way that said everything. It was the closest we'd been since waking up beside the glass river in the Dead City. And it prompted a river of gold to chase my veins, dazzling and beguiling gold that carried me away from the perilous mountains to a place where pain was a stranger. I mumbled something, unintelligible words, but they lacked any kind of commitment. My body was winning a very short race. Some legacy I was turning out to be.

'What are you thinking about?'

His whisper made the hairs at the back of my neck stir traitorously.

'Failure.'

The word danced among the flickering flames.

'What do you think is going to happen?'

I wasn't even sure I'd spoken the question aloud.

'To us?' he breathed, drawing a finger down my cheek and awakening the elephant moths I'd thought long since flown.

'To them,' I amended, when I could trust my voice.

The only sound was the crackling of the scarlet flames we had nursed to life minutes before, before he exhaled raggedly – one breath that told me that he too was holding the world inside.

'Perhaps, if they're lucky, the same that happened to us? But they were so …'

I nodded, recalling the slow, agonizing moment Cassius's arrow had buried itself at the top of Max's spine, and the strange waxen sheen on Aelia's skin. I'd known the truth even before Grey arrived. Yet the Oceanids had revived us …?

'Octavia once told me, the harder the revival, the higher the price.'

I twisted around to find August's swarthy, windburned face only millimetres away.

His words whispered through me as I stared upwards into the face that had challenged everything since the day we met. He was Octavia's blueprint, one of her first experiments, destined for the highest office in Isca Pantheon, and yet here he was, lying beside a feral Outsider. Offering what little comfort he could. What alignment of stars had created such an alliance? And were we really free of them in the end?

His military tunic was undone at the neck, revealing honey skin, and the glint of his Equite mark just snaking over the curve of his shoulder. A slow flush crept upwards from my neck that had nothing to do with the fire. How could he make me feel this way, despite everything?

'Price?' I repeated.

He nodded, his eyes burning into mine in a way that made the cave recede.

'For all revivals the Oceanids demand a payment of sorts: either an equitable trade or promise of recompense.'

I swallowed. They'd kept my old slingshot, but I knew that wasn't what he meant.

'Then what did I … we …?'

'Promise or give in exchange?'

There was a heavy silence as we both weighed the enormity of the suggestion.

'I'm not certain … but as the other legends seem to be holding true …'

I struggled for breath. I could feel the dream loosening its hold. His words conjured up an uncomfortable, distant memory. A dark promise, uttered deep within the depths of the icy waters, yet just as binding as if it were echoed from the top of a sun-drenched mountain.

'Lia and Eli … they wouldn't want us to give up Tal.'

His raw dark blues were emptying into mine, saying everything in case there was never another time.

I nodded again, a rock in my throat, as he gently traced the exact spot, his touch somehow relieving the constriction. And for the first time since leaving the Dead City, I allowed my thoughts to settle on home and whether I would ever see Mum again. The thought raked through what was left inside, making it soft and raw.

'It wasn't your fault.'

His whisper burned through me, like the first sun on ice-white snow. I opened my mouth but my voice, like my grief, was empty. And that was the moment. The moment I was guilty of wanting to forget – more than being unable to forget.

I slipped my fingers inside his open tunic collar, and let them rest against his insignia, burned into his golden skin. Her mark, just tangible beneath his warm skin, the ring of jellyfish protein that announced his modified DNA status to the world. It was his gateway into Octavia's elite club, and the mark of the damned. And yet he couldn't be any less hers now.

'We have a saying in Arafel,' I whispered, 'that one feral heart can only be well met—'

His lips were against mine before I could finish, and if there was ever any doubt that our journeys were meant to cross, it was answered here and now, while the mountain storms raged. Our need became a heat that blurred the freezing night, and a belief that somewhere there was a parallel world where two people could travel their own path beneath the stars that guided them. And as I dug my fingers into his shoulders, his touch misting every ache and pain, I knew this was where it had all been leading.

That the mark we were making was one last act of defiance, proving free will was always the real legacy anyway.

Chapter 6

The moonlight was illuminating the floorboards like an old-world piano. I rested back against Grandpa's willow chair. This had always been my safe place: my back against his legs, my cheek against his knee. Tonight though, I could only rest my weary head against his empty seat, and watch the night alone.

The insomnia was consistent at least, and when I did sleep, there was no Max to wake me from the vivid North Mountain dream that had returned these past few weeks. A barn owl hooted a few trees away. Somehow it seemed to know that the worst part was waking to a shame so intense I could barely force any thoughts past it.

I'd taken to sitting in Grandpa's study when sleep eluded me. Partly so I didn't disturb Mum, who was a light sleeper, but also because it was the one room that could offer some comfort. There were too many memories elsewhere – my window was too empty; Eli's makeshift animal nurseries still swung from the beam in the living room; and Jas's bed was neat and cold. I thought of the moment Eli had brought Jas home as a tiny, abandoned snow-leopard cub. The two of them had an unbreakable bond and she'd grown up to become one of the best and most loyal watch-cats in the world, even finding a way over the Mountains to

Octavia's research centre in the Dead City. The moment she saw him incarcerated inside the canister haunted me, as did the moment she squared up to Brutus, a molossus hound more than four times her size. *Where was she now?* I closed my eyes.

Only Grandpa's room offered some semblance of peace. He was gone but his scent still pervaded the enclosed space, and if I closed my eyes tightly, I could hear his whisper.

'Come what may, nature finds a way … We take what we need to survive, nothing more, Talia … All life has its place within the forest, including us …'

I contemplated the flickering floor, trying to forget the dream that left too many aches in places I never knew even existed. It was nearly three months since August left with the legatio, though my head seemed determined to replay that night above everything else. It was taunting me, lest I forget the consequences of letting myself feel anything. I could only be grateful that Unus had returned to the cave with armfuls of firewood before we'd had time to give in completely. I flushed at the memory, at the way we'd pulled apart, aching and sober, before he shuffled back inside our tiny cave.

I'd considered disappearing. And yet I was the last carrier of Thomas's biological control, which both isolated and trapped me simultaneously. I was different, and not Eli different. Even though my twin had also possessed Thomas's bloodline, Cassius had already hinted the control wasn't as effective in the male line. Which left me.

By Thomas's own hand I was no longer an Outsider or an Insider.

I was tainted.

And inexorably linked to the mother of all mythical creatures, a genetic hybrid far older than the Roman civilization and with the soul of a young girl who'd never seen the world. Lake's double-lidded serpent eyes flickered through my head, and I knew she was searching.

Did she know she had the power to change everything?

August had made me promise I wouldn't look for her without him. Even the lower slopes of the North Mountains were treacherous, without happening across an unstable chimera with a chemical attraction to my blood. And yet, he must have known I couldn't *not* try. I was drawn to her, as I knew she was to me. A darkness, like Cassius himself, had been poured into our cells. *I could feel him growing closer, like the night, crossing my sun. Dark to dark. Dust to ...*

'Talia?'

Mum's cracked voice broke the still air and I raised my head to spy her fragile frame, silhouetted in Grandpa's doorway.

'It isn't dawn and you're not on shift. Why aren't you abed, child? You should sleep. The day's long enough for us all ... long enough ... I'll wake your brother – he'll know what to do ... Eli?'

She shuffled away, and the knot in my stomach tightened. She'd been anxious for a while, but Eli's death had hit her hard and most days it seemed as though she lived in a world that had died along with Grandpa and Eli. I'd stopped trying to wake her. What point was there in making her live a reality she hated? And truthfully, part of me was jealous of the escape she'd created for herself. Leaving me out in the cold.

Her bedroom door creaked closed again and I sighed in relief. She'd get up again in a couple of hours and have forgotten she ever saw me.

Quietly, I climbed to my feet. The night air was warm and the forest was sleeping, which meant there was no one to convince I was the same old Tal. I slipped through the open doorway and stepped across towards the trapdoor that opened into the forest below. Our home had provided shelter to generations of my family, yet tonight it was too full of ghosts. With a final glance at Jas's empty bed, I swung down to the forest floor and paused. It was one of my first lessons from Grandpa.

Listen to the forest, Talia. Sense what kind of mood she's in.

35

But it was one of those nights. Ambivalent.

'Tal …?'

I hesitated, cursing under my breath.

Unus's stilted voice was unmistakable as it reached out from the gloomy trees. His was the first shelter of its kind in Arafel, a floor-house, although more had been added since the arrival of the new Outsiders. It was where he spent his nights, as no tree-house could be expected to support the weight of a ten-foot Cyclops, and until now I'd taken comfort from his proximity.

'Tal, no sleep?'

He shuffled out across the milky clearing, care written all over his one-eyed pudgy face. He still looked so out of place in Arafel, and yet his skin had developed a warmer glow over the past couple of months, which suited him.

'Yes … no … I just need to … to be …'

'Alone?' he finished, dropping his club hand.

I nodded, the old rock in my throat preventing any words from escaping. I didn't deserve any sort of comfort, not even the shoulder of a best friend.

I forced my feet into a run, and was among the topmost branches before I could think. Not pausing to look down. Not allowing Unus's kindness to turn into self-pity. And hoping so hard he understood. The forest stroked my cheeks with early summer, and showed me the swiftest path. I still hadn't grown used to running without a shadow, but when I finally glimpsed my destination my thoughts were calmer than they had been in a long while.

I dropped as the trees thinned, calmed by the way the silver fingers of the bathing pool beckoned through the shadowy branches. The lake had always held a special significance. Ever since the day Max had frozen behind the cascading waterfall, paralysed with fear. It was the only time I'd known him to need help, and Eli and my acrobatic rescue had prompted our lifelong mantra.

36

Even now, as I watched the white water being swallowed mercilessly by the wide black lake, I could hear his grudging admiration.

'*What took you so long? Why run when you can fly, hey ... crazy apricot-queen!*'

My smile tightened as I stepped through the cool night grass towards the water's edge, remembering how Max and Eli would race to be first in the water, naked and sun-kissed. I'd felt no shame watching their fresh-toned, youthful bodies glimmer in the dappled forest light, until our expeditions to the lake became known to Mum.

'*I don't mind the swimming, but wear your slip and change separately.*'

She never explained why, but it was the first time I realized things were changing.

Tonight though, I just wanted to be a child again.

I cast a look around the shadowy trees, which were rustling as though they too were reminiscing. The water was opaque and strangely inviting. It would help me forget – at least for a while.

Swiftly, I stripped off until the only thing warming my skin was my memories. I wasn't cold but the anticipation of the swim was real now, and something else besides. There was a ritualistic feeling to what I was about to do.

I stepped across to the edge of the dark rippling lake, and looked at the waterfall spilling silver life into the void. Our distant voices reached across the water as clearly as though they were here now.

'*I can't move! It's not funny ... One of you needs to climb up.*'

It was one of the rare occasions I'd heard real fear in Max's voice – that and the time we ran into the Minotaurus in Ludi Pantheonares. I closed my eyes briefly. The desperation in his forest-green eyes had pierced deeper than the Minotaur's horns ever could.

'*Now, Tal?*'

But I hadn't let him speak, and that was how he'd met Cassius's

37

arrow, thinking I didn't care when nothing could be farther from the truth.

I gritted my teeth, forcing myself past the raw memory, and back to the peace of this childhood place.

'We could always leave him there … do him good to need us for a change.'

I recalled Eli's nudge and wink as we realized Max was stuck. He always considered Max had it too easy. Life had tipped the scales in his favour, whereas Eli, silent from birth, had to rely on his twin sister for everything.

And I'd never underestimated my animal-whispering brother – yet he'd surprised me more than anyone. He'd sensed the griffin's weakness in the Flavium, and brought the ravenous vultures when we most needed them in the cathedral.

All while possessing the gentlest soul I'd ever known.

I gazed at the spray bubbling up around the edge of shadowy water. I could see him signing now, teasing Max and winking at me.

'C'mon … I was only kidding … We'll be able to reach him more easily from the top.'

And I was there too, eyebrows raised and with a wide grin. Always so much older than my thirteen years, and usually the peacemaker. Back then I hadn't realized the conflict between Max and Eli was so complex.

I dipped my toes and created a ripple of my own. It was curved and symmetrical. Like a story. And as mysterious as the night around me.

Carefully, I waded out into the black. Its still cool penetrating my skin, and soothing the rise of emotions there. I breathed out slowly. This felt good. I could imagine Max and Eli diving beneath the cool night water, almost feel their warm smooth bodies gliding past mine. I thrust my arms forward and let myself slide into the water, kicking my legs the way my father had taught me. The water lilies felt like tiny arms, reaching out to caress my limbs. I sank my face further into their soft tendrils, which hooked around my ears and toes, securing me in their dark world. And although I knew I was too deep to touch the bottom, and there was a strong undercurrent near the cascading falls, I didn't feel threatened. Not by the black, not by the depth, and not by the tiny hands all over my body. Touching me, healing me.

I had no idea I'd floated out to the centre of the pool until the noise of the falls forced me to open my eyes. And for a moment I was unsure whether I'd slipped into a dream world entirely. I kicked out with my arms and legs but they felt oddly heavy. The moonlight was playing with me, darting with the tiny silver fish just beneath the surface of the lake. Only it couldn't be moonlight, I fathomed, because the moon had gone behind a cloud and the light was beneath me. Shining up. Not down.

Which was when I saw I was surrounded.

Not by the lilies or any kind of plant life, but by eyes. Huge black ovoid eyes, and strong iridescent tails that had stolen the moonlight and painted it into their scales. There were too many to count, touching me, immobilizing me. But for some reason I wasn't scared. Because I knew them. *And last time they'd taken away all the pain.*

'Oceanids,' I whispered into the night air, closing my eyes and submitting to the fate of the hands completely. Perhaps this was the end, perhaps it wasn't. What did it matter?

Then a moment of clarity.

'Oceanids?' I repeated with more conviction, striking out in vain.

'Where are you?' I struggled, as the hands suddenly became stronger, pulling me. Downwards.

Reality flooded my frozen body, filling me with fresh, choking fear.

'Where are you? Eli! Aelia!' I yelled between mouthfuls of icy water.

The Oceanids are loyal only to themselves ... They're the only

39

chance we have left,' August whispered as we watched Eli and Aelia slip beneath the glass water.

But how could the Oceanids be here in the middle of Arafel's forest? And why would they come now?

I was losing. The water that had seemed so calm and inviting was blurring my sight and stealing my breath. I tried to kick but the ovoid eyes were taking me down, despite my fight. Was this what it had all come to? Some kind of ceremonial drowning because I'd failed on the prophetic journey they'd envisaged?

Then just when the outside world began drifting away, I rose from the surface as though snatched from the waves in a storm. My chest tightened as I bent over to retch and rid my lungs of the black water, and only then did I snatch a glimpse of my rescuer. It was dark, but I knew him. Somehow.

I reached up to touch his jaw, before jerking my fingers away again. He was icy, angular – and one of them. He lowered his gilled head to focus his ovoid eyes directly on mine, his white chest rippling like sand dunes in the emerging moon. His nape-length hair hung like tendrils of bladderwrack, while the ivory-white shell strung around his neck proclaimed his regal status as loudly as a bugle.

'Talia.'

His whisper filled the air, though his lips were sealed. Then snatches of eerie forgotten music reached through the water as though from the depths of an old shipwreck. It was the same soft and haunting music I'd heard in the tunnels when I was so close to death. Back then I thought it was the call of heaven; now I knew it was the pull of the underworld.

'Eli?' I forced through numb lips. 'Where is he?' My voice came in gasps, fierce and uneven.

He stared down intently, allowing me to glimpse him. Eli, reflected in the black ovoid surface of his fathomless eyes. He was smiling, holding out his hands towards me or to another. *To the one holding me now?*

I stared, dumbfounded, feeling a spark fire within me.

'What have you done with him?' I raged, pummelling my fists against his rock-hard chest.

His gills opened, releasing a soft outpouring of freezing mist that stopped me in my tracks. I stared into his black eyes, praying fervently they would show me again.

'You know me, Talia. I am Prince Phaethon, Son of Clymene.' His whisper clung to the air. 'I come to you in peace.'

My mind was whirling through the pages of Grandpa's book of mythology, until it reached the page I was searching for – heavily inked with a dark, stormy ocean, and eyes that watched as you read. A memory stirred, and Grandpa's voice whispered through the trees.

Clymene was an Oceanid nymph loved by the sun god, Helios. Together, they had seven daughters and a son, a prince named Phaethon, who was killed when he tried to drive his father's chariot of the sun across the sky, scorching the land and its people for all time.

'Phaethon?' I echoed, my frozen lips barely able to form the word.

An intense stare was my confirmation.

'Eli ... my brother ...?'

The water stirred around us.

'He is safe ...'

I exhaled, feeling the fractures in my heart flood with fresh pain, forcing open the scars.

'Then where is he?' I burned. 'Is he here? Why can't I see him? And Aelia!'

'You brought them to us with barely any life. But we accepted them, as we accepted you and the Commander General ...'

'Where are they, Phaethon?'

And then I glimpsed it, buried in the place where things are supposed to be forgotten.

A huge rambling city, concealed by an underwater garden, its bioluminescence gleaming like a million candles.

41

It was a world I'd chosen to forget. My breath rattled the cool night air, and the shapes beneath the black water darted faster and faster – as though they knew it too.

'Now you claim a right, despite this world doing all it could to end them,' his ovoid eyes challenged, showing a glimpse of Eli and Aelia's pale, waxen faces as they slid into the glass river, 'so, my question to you is, what will you do for my kind in return?'

His imperial face was as still as stone, the strength coursing through his arms as old as mountains.

For all revivals the Oceanids demand a payment of sorts: either an equitable trade or promise of recompense.

I tried to steady my breath. Hadn't August and I paid the heaviest price already?

Fresh zeal flooded my veins.

'I can pay,' I forced through gritted teeth. 'There can be a trade. Give them back; give Eli back. Stand beside us against Cassius – and I will pay in blood. For the Oceanids, for the Prolets, for Arafel, and for every last misbegotten creature who has suffered at his hand – I will watch Cassius draw his last breath before burning his dark heart until there is nothing but dust.'

Another memory stirred, only this time it was Atticus pleading with me to spare his father's life in the cathedral. Was it prompted by Phaethon? Some kind of test?

'This time I will have no mercy,' I swore.

'Find *Hominum chimera*.'

Prince Phaethon's words faded into my skin as a myriad of illuminations reached up through the water. I stared down, glimpsed them floating somewhere between sleeping and waking, their hypnotic lullaby growing louder all the while. I could see they were coming, all of them, a thousand pairs of fathomless eyes powering towards me and reaching for my innermost thoughts.

It was beautiful, terrifying and magical in the way only ancient worlds understood. I wanted to sleep, to let their bewitching song engulf me, to take me to them. Perhaps never to return.

42

But instead the surface broke one last time and a familiar silhouette reached out of the water beside me. A gentle face, grey-blue eyes and longish sandy-brown hair. He smiled, and for the first time in months, I was conscious of a knot releasing somewhere deep inside.

Chapter 7

I was alone. Save for the rustling trees, and the ground beneath me which was as dry as a bone. For a second I stared upwards at the protective canopy of branches, entwined over my head as though to protest, *'She's one of us ... a land creature ... not of the water.'*

Adrenaline fired my limbs into action and I bolted upright, a million thoughts misfiring. I could see the silvery gleam of the lake through the trees, yet somehow I was dressed again – and as dry as though I'd never been swimming at all.

Was it all a dream?

Then I heard a rustle in the jade grass beside me. I turned slowly, still caught in the web of my dream.

There was a man asleep next to me. My breath stilled. *A familiar, missing man.*

My breath caught on a painful cough as I reached out. It was him. *My brother.* Lying asleep beside me as though it were the most natural thing in the world. His skin peachy and perfect. Arafel perfect. As though we'd never lost him at all.

For a moment it was as much as I could do just to sit there, drinking in every tiny contour of the face that was so like my own, and had yet been so difficult to picture these last few weeks.

Then at last, I smiled. Not gratefully. But blissfully. A real smile that broke through the walled-up fissures of my heart and reached into my cheeks to make them stretch until they ached.

It really was Eli. Glistening and whole, as though he'd never known Pantheon, Cassius or the research facility. And then he was opening his grey-blue eyes, and rolling his head towards me. Fixing me with his gentle smile, and healing me in a way no one else could.

He raised his head in bewilderment as I reached for his hand. His fingers were a shade of field-gold just before harvest, and I recalled how pale he was when I whispered my goodbye. The thought sobered me faster than if I'd plunged into the river myself, and I threw my arms around him with a sob.

'I'm OK, I'm OK,' he soothed as I held him fast, uncertain I would ever let him go again.

He looked the same, felt the same, and yet his eyes glinted with the light of another world and its secrets. And he was alone. My heart ached for Max and Lia, but it only made me hug Eli harder.

'Where have you been?' I whispered finally.

Chapter 8

There was an iridescent mist bathing the mountains today. It swirled around my strapped ankles like tendrils of heaven reaching down to soothe the warm, dusty rocks. It was the sort of day we used to enjoy in the fields. The sun was a blur of spring warmth, affording the workers a degree of respite from the usual searing heat. But the mountain mist was also deceptive, ready to lead any hunter to his swift demise given any lapse in concentration.

Unus paused to kneel beside a scorched Venus flytrap. We'd passed this way a few days ago, when the plant was green and budding.

'Close,' he pronounced with difficulty.

I nodded briefly, gesturing up the trail. Unus followed my gaze, his single pale eyebrow forked and anxious. We all knew why. Lake was roaming closer to the village with each passing day, and whether she was friend or foe, we had to find her.

Eli frowned. Art and the rest of the Council had heralded his return as nothing less than a miracle. There was a full day of celebration, and while my jubilation was no less real, it was shadowed too. My twin was back, but there was a new quietness about him, as though he carried the weight of the ocean inside.

46

I recalled his image smiling inside Prince Phaethon's eyes, and I couldn't help but wonder whether it was more significant than I had first realized. Once I mustered enough courage to ask about Aelia too, but he only shook his head. I didn't press him – I knew the answers would come in their own time.

And Mum's reaction was worth all the unanswered questions in the world. She was still fragile, but hadn't stopped smiling since Eli followed me into the treehouse that morning. She glowed as though a thousand sunbeams had coalesced inside her all at once.

'I knew you'd come home … I said you'd come … I knew you'd come home … I said you'd come,' she repeated.

But no one stopped her.

And if Eli's return had provided some semblance of hope, Prince Phathon's deal had provided a grim focus. I wasn't ignorant to the irony of a mythical prince with an Oceanid army at his fingertips, challenging a feral Outsider to rid the world of a monster, but knew enough to understand there were rules. It had been my legacy from the start after all. I could only hope our deal would stand, and the Oceanids would stand beside us when we needed them. I glanced at my quiet brother. Perhaps we stood more chance than I realized.

'Tal … look?'

Unus paused again and threw a long look around, before returning his attention to his feet. Eli and I caught up to find him staring at the mangled hindquarter of an ocelot, strewn across the shaley path. It was clear it hadn't died from natural causes. I glanced up into Unus's blue eye, barely visible beneath huge flushed folds of squinting flesh.

'It's fresh,' I confirmed, racking my brains for any other animal that may have had the power to rip a body apart in this way.

Only a larger mountain cat would come close, and those I'd encountered would never leave half a carcass for another creature to finish. I turned the unfortunate animal's remains over and something hard and ivory rolled away. Frowning, I picked it up and held it aloft, so it glinted in the sunlight.

'Looks like someone is losing their milk teeth,' Eli signed.

I stared in fascination. It was about the size of my fist, ivory-white, and tapered to a perfect razor-sharp point. Carefully, I reached out and tapped the tip of the tooth on a spiny cactus plant. Instantly its tough exterior skin split open, spilling its soft pulp and inner juices down over its spiny prickles until they pooled at our feet.

'Bigger teeth … bigger draco,' Unus remarked, his eye stretching as round as a rice bowl.

I frowned, assessing the steep mountain pass. 'Which is why we can't wait,' I muttered, refusing to think about the promise August had extracted before he left.

The higher we climbed, the steeper the trail, and the more frequently we needed to rest. We reached the mid-peak summits without too much trouble, and though we were still within a few hours' hike of Arafel, the air was noticeably thinner. There was also less animal life the higher we climbed, while mountain shale grew more crumbly underfoot. I fought to suppress the dark memories pushing to the forefront of my mind, and focused instead on the stark cries of the golden eagles circling above our heads.

Within a breath, I was back in Isca Pantheon with August, looking down on the main dome floor as Octavia's regal two-headed eagles dived past.

'The haga are two-headed – it's a Roman thing,' he joked.

Gritting my teeth, I spun on my feet and looked for Unus. He'd dropped a little way behind. His face was flushed, and his usual lumbering rhythmic pace had slowed. I glanced at Eli anxiously.

'I don't think Cyclops' circulatory systems are designed for altitude,' he signed. 'Anyway, it's well past midday … time we turned back.'

He met my rigid look warily. He could sense that another sleepless night was one too many. I had to find her, even if it meant staying out all night.

'Tal, I promise … we'll come back tomorrow.'

His signing was almost persuasive, and then an ominous shuddering stopped us all in our tracks. It was chased by a barrage of sharp stones raining down on the pathway just ahead of us. Small avalanches of slippery mountain shale weren't unusual, but something told me this freshly dislodged debris wasn't due to the variable weather. We jumped back as another torrent of hardened topsoil and shale cascaded down. It was closer this time. Unus shuffled in front of us protectively, but I could feel his fear. A Cyclops was stronger than ten men, but pitching brute strength against a hormonally charged adolescent *Hominum chimera* wasn't likely to end happily.

'Wait here with Unus!' I signed to Eli, knowing Unus's wheezing would slow them both for a couple of minutes.

Then without waiting for a response, I turned and flew up the edge of the falling debris as lightly as I could. The trail was lined with boulders, their narrow crevices providing scant protection for the mountain's hardy plants. Occasionally, foragers would bring a basketful back to the village for Raven to use in herbal compresses or medicines. Today though, my eyes were trained on the jagged mountain path that disappeared up ahead. I'd seen this mountain's summit once before, could just recall the haze of shaley paths and treacherous passes I'd pushed to the back of my mind. We had every reason to turn back – except the air was filled with the faint scent of smouldering ash.

With blood thumping in my ears, I continued upwards until the trail met a near vertical, creviced wall. Scanning the rock, I spotted a shelf about five metres above my head. It was a short easy climb providing the rock was stable. There was no time to waste, and I scurried up the jagged surface as swiftly as I dared, so conscious Eli and Unus would catch up at any moment, just when she was close at last. *Dark to dark.* I gritted my teeth, unable to deny the truth clawing up my throat with each hand and foot hold – she knew I was near too.

I peered over the top cautiously, and was surprised to find a wide, barren mountain shelf, lined with piles of fallen rock and shingle. It looked barren enough, but somehow I knew it wasn't. There was a waiting in the air, an anticipation of the kind that forces every nerve to strain beyond comfort, and today it was because of the looming black cave set about twenty metres away to my right. A cave that looked as black and uninviting as any of Pantheon's tunnels.

And though it couldn't conceal any strix, I knew that Lake in draco form could incinerate one hundred of the mythological flesh-eating birds with a single, violent breath if she chose.

I crept forward, aware the eagles overhead had quietened, as though they too were able to sense a menace reaching through their spiralling thermals. I wasn't sure what I was hoping to achieve. I was hopelessly ill-equipped to challenge Lake in any form. She was the most successful of all Cassius's trials – brutal, powerful, and more than capable of reducing a girl from the forest to dust – and yet, my leather-clad feet kept on stealing forward anyway. I just had to gaze into her yellow, double-lidded eyes, and know she felt it too.

Then I glimpsed her, or rather I glimpsed her breath, hanging on the cool air just outside the cave. I froze, my chest tightening. I hadn't set eyes on her for more than three months, when she unwittingly helped us escape the research centre by incinerating it. August and I had only escaped by squeezing inside one of the life-support canisters, but her abject fury had imprinted on me for ever. There was no doubting the astonishing myths about *Hominum chimera*'s strength and abilities were not to be dismissed. She possessed a nature that was different to every other creature I knew, natural or otherwise.

'*There's an ancient myth that* Hominum chimera *is capable of triggering a sequence of natural disasters, culminating in the eternal fire of damnation.'*

It was spine-tingling, a tale worthy of Grandpa's book of mythology, beyond probable – and yet wholly believable too. I could sense her truth, as she could sense the difference in me. And that was my best hope, her instinct for our blood connection – and what it truly meant.

'Lake?' I called, watching tendrils of steam slowly float away in the early spring sunshine.

I pressed my teeth together. My voice sounded surprisingly steady for a forest girl approaching a legendary chimera, who was probably hungry too. Momentarily inspired, I felt in my leather rations bag for whatever food I had remaining – some smoked cheese and a hunk of rye bread. It would have to do.

I threw the meagre offering into the mouth of the cave, and backed off warily. There was a thick silence before a heavy dragging, then a savage burst of steam followed by silence again.

I hesitated, as the shadows inside the mouth of the cave appeared to dance and cavort. Somehow I knew she was looking straight at me, while making short shrift of my meagre offering. Her double-lidded liquid amber eyes were narrowing, contracting and assessing – was I predator or prey? *Or something else entirely.*

'Lake … it's me, Talia,' I offered steadily.

My legs felt oddly weak, and there was a strange creeping cramp spreading out from the pit of my stomach. I forced myself to scramble up onto a large flat boulder anyway. I had to face her now, before I lost my nerve completely.

It felt better being higher, although I knew Eli would say I was breaking cardinal rule number one: always present yourself lower than the animal you're trying to pacify. Somehow though I knew it wasn't the right way for me and Lake.

'You have to remember me? Max and I? We came to find you from Arafel …? You were hiding with Atticus and the Prolet children beneath the Dead City? Remember? We were with you

51

– in New Arfel – when you were taken – by … Cassius's aquila?'

Then there was another violent projection of steam, the colour of Bereg's mulberry wine, and then a raking noise – the sound of heavy claws digging into a hard rock floor. Every cell of my body tightened. She recognized Cassius's name. There was hope.

'We followed you to Pantheon, to try and rescue you! Max and I were forced into Ludi Pantheonares to face the Minotaurus. And we only escaped with Unus – the Cyclops' help … I was injured but we managed to escape through the tunnels beneath Pantheon only to be hijacked by Cassius and his guards at the cathedral. There was a fight, Lake. We lost … so many.'

'… Tal!'

Unus's voice broke my concentration, and somehow the warning note in his tone told me exactly what to do. I dropped and flattened out on top of the boulder, just as a burst of searing red heat passed over my back with scarcely a gnat's length to spare.

Instinctively, I rolled away and slid down into a crevice as a second burst of her fury enveloped the entire side of the boulder. From my sheltered position, I could see only Unus and Eli's incredulous expressions, but they were enough. I took hold of the stone edge, and pulled myself up until finally I had a clear view of the spiny-tailed mythological legend dwarfing the dark hole behind her. It was Lake.

And she made the mountain look feeble.

Clearly draco-chimera adolescence involved huge growth. Although her five metres had already seemed big at the research centre, now she had to reach at least twenty metres into the sky, and I couldn't even see the tip of her tail, which disappeared into the darkness behind. She was still ash-grey with spiny titian scales, but they'd tapered into menacing arrow-points that stretched all the way down the back of her thick, muscular back and hind quarters.

I swallowed the rock in my throat, mesmerized by her new adolescent appearance.

New veins of regal purple traced a visible path from her neck, all the way down her torso and into the tops of her powerful forelegs. But it was her double-lidded honey eyes that stole all my attention. They were older, hungrier – angrier. But they were still eyes that didn't belong on such a vast, serpentine creature. They were hers. Lake's eyes. And they were eyeballing me intently.

'We came to look for you, Lake!' I entreated, as she opened her huge scaly jaws and spilled her rage into the chilled mountain air.

'With Pan! We came with Pan!' I added hoarsely, my eyes streaming.

An eerie, smoky silence suddenly filled the air. Lake paused, lowering her great spiny head so it was level with the top of my boulder. And it could have been her proximity, or the late sun glinting off the shale, but I fancied there was a reddening to the underside of her amber eyes, almost as though she associated the name with pain.

'He traded his life to save us … so we could come and find you,' I whispered.

Her purple scaly nostrils vibrated with barely contained aggression, and this time I could tell she was listening, that somewhere in her hybrid, mixed-up mind, she remembered.

'Pan knew about our blood, he knew we shared a connection,' I begged, my throat feeling like razor blades. 'Lake?'

I extended my hand, but a familiar rumble filled the air before I could finish, and as Lake swung her thick leathery head back to identify the source of the noise, my heart sank.

Unus and Eli had caught up, and were clearly intent on distracting Lake from incinerating me. I scowled furiously, shaking my head, but it was already too late.

Lake wasted no time in swinging her huge reptilian body around, her heavy thrashing tail sweeping across the top of the boulder and nearly taking my head off in the process. And as I bolted out from behind her, I was conscious of her titian spines flushing with deep scarlet blood, staining their dark jagged points cruel and hard.

'Move!' I bellowed, sprinting across the top of the rocks.

She settled her gaze on Unus, her eyes narrowing to slits, and opened her brutal jaws to reveal violent canines, designed with one purpose in mind. In that split second I understood. She was the mother of all mythical creatures and here was one of her kind, actually daring to challenge her. And while Unus possessed the strength of ten hunters, he was still paltry defence against an adolescent *Hominum chimera*.

'Get down … Unus, get down!' I yelled, flying towards them as Lake closed in from the opposite side, the ground shaking with her every colossal step.

Eli was trying, heroically, to force Unus to his knees, but I could see he was struggling.

I scowled as a snippet of Aelia's medical knowledge floated out of the whirlwind in my head.

Cyclopean arteries and limbs are especially thick; they have low blood pressure and are pretty inflexible …'

'He can't … Lake, he can't kneel!' I yelled, just as she reached forward with one of her powerful, regal claws and knocked Unus flat onto his back.

He landed with an almighty crash, his face swiftly staining purple as breath deserted his ill-designed body. He looked up in utter bewilderment as I ran out in front of his plate-feet, and spun to face Lake's wide-open jaws.

'No!' I yelled furiously, throwing my arms wide as she teetered, before swinging her colossal weight back.

And in that moment I don't know who was more amazed. Lake, because I'd dared to defy her – or me, because she actually listened and reacted.

Eli stepped in beside me, calm glued to his face, as Unus recovered enough to start slowly dragging himself backwards. But Lake's surprise was short-lived. And as reality returned, her giant head sank once again towards the ground, jowls drawn back in ugly contemplation, haunches high and arched. The frenzied look was back in her double-lidded eyes, and even though Eli had begun to sign, they were locked on me alone.

'We aren't here to hurt you, Lake,' I forced out, so conscious of our vulnerability, and yet determined to reach the little girl inside, wherever she was. 'We've come to help, and to ask for yours in return. Cassius is raising an army, waging a war on the outside ... and we ... Arafel, the Outsiders ... we need your help.

'You are *Hominum chimera*, mother of all mythical beasts, and the most ancient of all creatures described in the Voynich. But you are also Lake, a loyal friend with the bravest, truest heart I've ever known.'

She tilted her head so suddenly, Eli and I had to jump aside to avoid a sharp stream of boiling acrid steam.

'Cassius wants to control you,' I continued stubbornly, 'to use you as a weapon to change the outside world. But there is another way. A way to live freely, to live the life you deserve on the outside ... Help us, Lake. Help us stop Cassius, help us free the Prolets – your people ... and Max.'

I finished on a whisper, and though Eli was signing fast, translating my words as swiftly as I spoke, I could tell she was so different from Brutus, the griffin and the vultures. Because for once, the only control in the world was standing right beside him.

And I knew Lake understood every damned word, and not because of anything she was doing, but rather because of what she wasn't doing. Her giant scaled head was still angled to one side and though her honey eyes were blazing, there was something else too.

She was listening.

Somehow it was working.

Just as a new sound cut the air, a groan I only half-recognized as belonging to Unus it was so shot through with shock. In that moment we all shared the same instinct – *draco*, *Cyclops* and Outsiders alike – to turn our gaze upon the valley at the bottom of the North Mountain slopes. *Towards Arafel.*

And I barely acknowledged Lake's last violence as she shook out her draco wings, each one the length of three stallions, and thundered off the mountain shelf – because my sights were locked on a serpent much closer to home. A serpent that took the last of my hopes, and crushed them to ash before my darkening eyes.

Arafel was in flames.

Chapter 9

I felt only the scorching jaws of a dark curse. As acutely as though it were slowly gorging itself on my own feral heart. Raw and bloody, bite by bite.

Instinctively I slowed as the charred skeleton of Arafel's forest rose up before us like a giant desiccated spider; its appearance as alien as Pantheon's Eagle aircraft disappearing over the North Mountains peaks.

Eli and I picked our way, among the handful of survivors on the outskirts of the village, in silent shock. The Eagle Stealth Sweepers had dived silently and without warning, using laser fire technology to obliterate most of our forest home within seconds. No one heard them coming, and for most, there was no time to escape their individual treehouse furnace.

The air was dead, broken only by the splitting and cracking of disintegrating trees, hanging over what was left of our home village like a funeral shroud. As we entered the village community area, a handful of disparate people emerged from different directions – Komodos, Lynx, Eurasians and my people – their faces as mutilated as the landscape surrounding us. No one could give voice to the sudden and absolute devastation shattering our village home. It was too much like admitting it had happened; that somehow we had to process this horror.

There were bodies everywhere, people and animals, limbs entwined, as the laser fire had prompted that most human of responses. Raven and Mathilda lay face down by the grazing ground gate, cut down in a desperate attempt to set the grazing animals free. To give them the fighting chance Cassius had denied them.

And an ocean of blood was staining the earth beneath our feet.

The ground was sodden, rivulets converging and painting my feet with the fate of so many innocents. My mind recalled the moment we glimpsed the vampiric eyes of the basilisk in the Isca Prolet, watching and waiting. A single drop of the basilisk's acidic venom had reduced the ironmonger's tool to nothing but a pool of molten metal. It was just the same now, only the acid was Cassius, and the molten iron my family and friends, children and animals alike. Nothing and no one had been spared. We were staring at a massacre.

Eli regained himself first, breaking into a run that blurred into the splintered trees within seconds. It pulled me back into the moment, into conscious thought, and I flew after him, not needing to ask where he was headed.

I tried to keep my eyes focused on the unrecognizable ground in front, conscious only of a dull thump in my ears as I sprinted. The communal buildings were just a series of dusty, blackened rises, their top layer already scattering to the wind. And as I willed the violence and destruction to blur behind my eyes, I was already aware of a muted resemblance to the Dead City.

We entered what used to be the perimeter of the forest at a speed neither of us knew we possessed, but were then forced to slow. Because nothing was the same. And where before there was a network of treehouses, now there was only chilling, empty space. It was as disorientating as it was devastating. Most of the outlying homes had stood no chance against the intense heat of Cassius's weaponry. My chest strained as though a vortex was growing inside, a whirling gut-slicing vortex. If I even gave an inch, there would be a storm to pay.

With no trees left to run through, we were forced to keep our path on the ground, circumventing any ominous smoking remains. I kept my gaze locked forward, pushing my feet until we reached the scorched embers of Art's treehome. It was where the Council held meetings on the last working day of the month, a tradition Grandpa started when he was Village Leader.

Now I could only stare at the twisted blackened remains of a tree stump, with bile burning up my throat.

We stood together dully. There was unrecognizable debris, and the same oppressive smoke everywhere. The guilt of survival volumed up from my core, threatening to swallow me whole as I turned slowly, trying to force my clouded brain to work.

Then a voice, calling through the smog. It was a familiar voice, from behind the remains of a Norwegian fir. Blindly, I ran towards the sound, and skidded to my knees beside a trapped, skewed person. And even though she was covered in blood, and my senses were suffocated, I knew her instantly.

'Ida,' I whispered.

She turned her glistening head, only now the tongues dancing around her fading eyes were choked with dust.

'Tal,' she whispered with the glint of a smile, as I pushed my arms beneath her soaking back and pulled her close.

Then she closed her proud Komodo eyes and breathed her last.

I cradled her tightly as though that could make a difference. But I was too late, far too late. It was only when Eli took her shoulders to lower her that I realized her legs were skewed because they had been severed by the indiscriminate laser fire. Numbly, we straightened her so the division was barely visible. Then she lay there, with as much dignity in death as she had in life, and I watched as the scorched ground darkened around her body, as though it too knew it wasn't her time, that this warrior belonged to the sun.

A quiver of her pared hand-darts rested against her still hip, and gently, I reached out to unhook the small weapons she always used with such accuracy. Each one had an immature Komodo tooth set into its tail, weighting it precisely, so it flew with the tribe's honour.

'I promise,' I breathed, placing my palm over her cooling forehead the way she used to mark respect, before pushing to my feet.

Then we flew as though our feet could defy gravity. And as the desiccated landscape blurred, all I could think was that if the Eagle Stealth aircraft had reached our white oak, I'd failed Mum in the same way I'd failed Grandpa. And that hurt was just too much for any one body to contain.

Eli pulled ahead of me, his longer legs giving him the edge over the charred ground. We hadn't spoken on our flight down the North Mountains, leaving Unus far behind on the slopes, but I knew we were both thinking the same thing. We'd left Mum when she needed us most. She wouldn't have understood what was happening, and she wouldn't have had the wherewithal to run if there had been chance to escape. The thought stole my air, making my feet leaden as the silent forest blurred like a monument to itself.

Then, suddenly, our feet were plunging into denser foliage, and I found myself holding my acrid breath until it hurt. Our treehouse was the first to be built in the middle of Arafel's forest, whereas most of the newer treehouses had been built nearer the village centre, where the laser fire had been concentrated. *Dare we hope?* The foliage was definitely greener, though the indiscriminate path of laser fire was still visible. It was the tiniest ray of hope, but I clung to it fiercely until Eli slowed in front of a familiar willow bough.

My chest thumped painfully as I approached, my brother's

silhouette looming through the dust like a dark angel. And then we were back, standing at the edge of our clearing, staring up at the old white oak that had sheltered Thomas and our ancestors through the worst storm mankind could devise.

It was still there.

Or at least most of it was. One of the large supporting boughs had been split off by passing laser fire, leaving the edge of our living room exposed, *but the rest was there*, its silver-white bark a beacon of hope among all the grey.

'Mum?' I whispered, my eyes streaming. 'Mum?'

My anguish exhaled forcibly as I scrambled forward, willing myself up there, willing Mum to be OK. Before a sudden, bruising grip on my upper arm yanked me back into the foliage.

'What?!' I hissed as I regained my balance, only to find his other hand clamping down hard over my mouth.

Then I saw his expression. He was staring straight ahead, and there was something in his fixed stare that flooded my limbs with fresh dread. Yet I couldn't not look. I forced my gaze to level with his, and scowled through the eerie, particle-choking air.

And then I understood. Because she was there, just past the dust and devastation, just beyond the shadow of our treehouse. *Mum.*

Mum was standing, unprotesting, as some kind of metal frame box closed around her, a box connected by a glinting silver cord to the open underbelly of an Eagle aircraft.

They were taking her.

The words repeated dully in my head before reality bit back. Then cold fury snaked through my limbs and I fought like a caged medusa to show I didn't care, that I knew he was trying to save us, but that it didn't matter any more. There was no way I could stand here and watch them take her the way they took Grandpa. I had to try to stop it. And somehow, whether it was a moment's weakness, or some brief understanding that there was no survival worth her loss, his hold loosened. It was all I needed and I was away in a flash, pelting past our treehouse, across the open ground and towards her.

'Mum!' I grated hoarsely, as the cage swung just out of reach of my gut-twisting leap.

I landed in a heap before turning my burning face skywards.

'Cassius!' I bellowed into the air. 'Fight me! You goddamned son of a cowardly death-adder bastard! Do you hear me?'

Panic was clawing up my throat, blinding me as Mum's frail figure grew terrifyingly smaller.

'Or are you too scared to face me after the cathedral? Cassius …!'

A second grill was over my person in a breath, and it was only then that I realized the metallic frame was lined with a transparent material. It was a fortified box, much like the canisters in the research centre, and it sucked me in with intense force. Stealing my breath. Dulling my consciousness.

'Mum,' I moaned desperately.

And as my senses dimmed, I was vaguely aware of a broken face far below, of a dark hole looming closer, and the mechanical clatter of a hatch closing. Then there was motion, but it didn't matter because through my dimming eyes I caught a glimpse of her. Beside me. And whatever she was facing, I was right beside her. Facing it too. Grandpa's eyes blurred before mine, he was smiling so sadly.

'I tried,' I pleaded, as the world dimmed to a faint pink spot, and all I could think was that, sometimes, winning wasn't about fulfilling prophecies or defeating monsters.

That sometimes, it was about knowing when to lose.

Chapter 10

It was the always the whirring that came first. Like the chirruping of a mechanical grasshopper, an alien sound compared with the soft hum of Arafel's forest.

I wasn't awake. I knew that. But I wasn't exactly unconscious either. It was a blurred world somewhere between. Like a forced daydream from which I couldn't fully awake. And there were voices, thin laughter, before a thundering in my ears, like rain on metal. Then my arm was pressed hard, and a darting pain invaded my wrist, swallowing me whole as a succession of hollow clicks and footsteps faded to the edges of my dreams.

***

'Who are you?'

The voice was probing, disturbing me from my sleep. *Who was I?* Why wouldn't they leave me alone? *Who was I?* Couldn't they see I was tired? *Who was I?*

There was a sharp pain in my head, making me groan.

'I said ... who ... are ... you?'

It was her, the one who talked. She had a reedy voice, reminding me of someone I knew once. But it was so long ago. And her shadow clung to her like a Valkyrie.

'How much did you give her? She's comatose! Repeat the prompt.'

Another sharp pain in my head.

'Tell me who you are and the pain will stop.'

Who was I? The pressure of thinking was almost as painful. I had to be someone didn't I? And then the faintest scent ... forest honeysuckle ... like Mum's hair.

'Tal ...' I whispered.

It was the only word that came to mind through lips that no longer belonged to me.

Silence.

'I thought you said she was batch 3,067?'

The reedy voice rose. Like a lemur's warning. And I knew I'd given the wrong answer. My confusion was brief, as my arm was claimed by another hard clamp and sharp, darting pain.

And this time I felt my veins sag in response.

***

There was no time. Only the dull acceptance of just being. And there was no memory or care, for which I was oddly grateful. I wasn't cold. Or hot if it came to that. I just was.

And if there was a feeling of *elsewhere*, a low-level knowledge that I wasn't quite where I always had been, it was swiftly swallowed by my floating existence, a squeaking of trolley wheels, clipped voices and fading lights.

***

'What is your name?'

It was a repeated stimulus, and one I'd learned to respond to quickly to stop the pain.

'MMDCL,' I whispered. '2650,' I repeated under my breath.

'Louder!'

'MMDCL,' I repeated.

The pain came anyway. Just less intense than when you got it wrong. It was the game – you had to learn the rules.

And then something new.

'What is the keyword?'

White. Undefined. Floating. White.

'Did she say something?'

'No, she's fried, I think. She was given batch 3,068 too. Her blood was the critical part. He's got a vat full of that now so he authorized the new order code.'

'... which also has an expiry time against it, so if you don't mind?'

'What is the keyword? If you do not respond there will be pain.'

The voice paused to send an intense searing dart through my head, as though to confirm the point.

Something like a whisper passed over my lips, but even I couldn't recognize it.

'I repeat. What is the keyword? You have until the count of three to tell me or the pain will come again.'

'One ...'

My breathing escalated, and my body felt too tight as I fought a tidal wave of fear.

'What is the keyword?'

It was a familiar question, and I knew the answer. Didn't I?

Keyword? A key to operate it ... to make the code work.

Images floated randomly around the edges of my consciousness, like stepping stones to the answer. I focused harder, the muscles in my face quivering with effort, trying to draw them in with an invisible net. Then one floated close, just within reach. It was a yellow page, a hand-drawn image of something I recognized. There were parts of animals, all joined up, and scrawled across the top were three faint letters: *R-E-Q.*

I reached out … I was nearly there … just as the vice reached again and it all dissolved.

This time the pain snaked down my spine and radiated out through my ribs and limbs. Dragging all my breath into the black. Into the void. And temporary bliss. Only to crash me back into grim reality without warning, tearing up my limbs and splaying each nerve with a searing intensity. My body buckled as I sucked in a gasp, lifting my head and feet simultaneously into the grey air. I moaned as the room spun around me like a vortex, a white vortex concealing the answer. Shimmering.

'This is your last chance! Tell me the keyword or …'

'R-E-Q.'

The soft sounds emptied through my lips as though carried by my last breath.

'What? What did you say?'

'R-E-Q,' I repeated, their echo merging with my failing heartbeat.

'… Requiem …'

***

The ceiling was different. The smooth white had been replaced with red ravined rock that was familiar somehow. My head strained. I knew this place. *Think.* But it was all so hard.

'Your daily supplement, courtesy of the Emperor,' one of the uniformed ones bawled. 'Long live Imperator Cassius!'

He was tall, dressed in some sort of military uniform. It looked Roman. *How did I know?* His gleaming helmet was decorated with a silver eagle inscribed with four words: *Senatus Popules Que Romanum.*

'*The Senate and the People of Rome,*' I translated effortlessly.

How did I know?

A bright blue feather danced away on the top of his helmet, snagging my attention. *Like a peacock!* A sudden irrational chuckle rose up my throat.

Stop. He was looking at me. Stop.

'MMDCL!'

'MMDCL!' he bellowed again.

It was my number. I liked it. But there was no mistaking he was eyeballing me.

I shuffled forward, bare feet, dirt-brown, shackled. I frowned. Something was wrong.

'Were you smirking?' the tall one leered.

His pea-head was even smaller up close, and the feather was still dancing. *Peacock*. A bubble of hysteria threatened to reach up my throat, to betray me. I sank my head lower, staring at my wrong feet.

'Look at me!'

My head was yanked upwards, and a pain jack-knifed through my body as I struggled to retain my balance. My body felt awkward, stiff like sandpaper. The rough grating of sandpaper. *The thought was oddly comforting.*

'Did … you … smirk?'

I looked into his yellow eyes, flecked with scorching-hot, dust-choked red. Like blood. A river of blood beneath my feet. The shudder in my heart fanned out to my face. He saw.

Then came the violent blow, like all the weight being pulled from my body at once, leaving just a shadow to fly across the tunnel. Red ravined rock reached out to meet me, to catch and cradle me with its bony fingers. There was a crack, and I was dimly aware of another pain towards the back of my head.

The peacock was towering above me, a sickening grin spreading across his sallow face. Then more faces all around, their bodies pressed back against the rock face. Different ones, some animal, some more like me. But all pale, thin, and scared, looking at me. Nothing written there, except defeat.

'Not so funny now, eh? They said you needed two batches. Seems like a waste to me. Some things the chemicals never fix, so what's wrong with a bit of old-fashioned persuasion … Seems like fair play after all the trouble you've caused!'

67

The walls twisted to the side as I was yanked from the floor, and I was conscious of something wet running down my neck.

It made a tiny hollow dripping noise as it hit the floor.

'She's cut, Dimiti!' a gruff voice interrupted.

It was another one of them, with a huge muscular hound standing beside him. Disinterested.

The peacock flicked me a hard look, a metallic nosepiece trying to conceal his broad nose, dusted in dirt.

'Orders were to treat her the same as the rest, but no injuries. There'll be hell to pay now,' the gruff one complained. 'He wants her alive in case they need more of that stuff you're so keen to spill. I ain't having no part of it. Livia will ...'

'Livia ain't gonna find out,' the peacock snarled. 'Is she? I was just having a bit of fun. Can't a soldier have any fun any more?'

He looked down at me, and something in the glint in his eye made me tighten every muscle I possessed. Then he craned further, and all I could see was the bobbing feather.

And I shouldn't have smirked, I really shouldn't have smirked.

The ravined walls lurched again as he threw out a lightning blow that made me double over. My shackled feet staggered backwards, trying in vain to maintain balance before I hit the floor again, and this time I was racked with pain.

'Perhaps a night in the sweatbox will make you rethink, eh? No room for any of your tricks in there either ... You're one of them now, d'ya hear me? ... Prolet scum!'

He dragged me up and shoved me again, in the direction of a dark recess in the wall. There was something familiar about it, but my throbbing limbs were too consumed to do anything but comply.

He pushed past me into the snug entrance, his strutting walk matching his dancing feather. My veins clouded, and I held my breath, willing myself to float away.

'You are numero MMDCL. Your purpose is to obey. Your allegiance is to the Emperor Cassius. All hail the Holy Emperor and Imperator Cassius. All hail the Empress Livia.'

68

I felt sure the words must be imprinted on the backs of my gritty eyeballs, and I exhaled with relief. I could remember them. So long as I could remember the words, the pain would be short-lived.

I shuffled inside the recess, barely daring to lift my gaze. The small space was lined with stained hammocks, while a yellow guttering lamp, suspended from the middle of the low rock ceiling, creaked as the peacock picked his way through dirty, abandoned metal mugs. The air reeked of putrid vegetables, stale breath and something else I couldn't quite identify. It was rank, and I held my breath. I didn't want to be in this place.

A shape shifted in the corner. It was another one of them, sleeping, his shadowed face relaxed and carefree. My eyes fixed, though I knew I shouldn't be looking. The hilt of his Diasord glinted when the lamp was knocked by the peacock's helmet. It continued to rock awhile on its rusted nail, throwing a strange jaded light around the small space. Its creaking protest disturbed him. He inched open one eye. One green eye, which shone like the sun through the branches of a willow tree. *Why weren't there any trees?*

He opened his other eye, and I dragged my gaze away. I didn't need any more trouble. No more looking – it only ended in trouble. And more pain. He was on his feet now. And he was staring back. *Don't look, don't look.* He was taller than the peacock. My eyes dropped to his feet, feet as brown as my own, enclosed in gladiatorial sandals, not Roman boots.

'Remember this?'

The peacock's face loomed large in front of my own, a large rusted iron key dangling.

'Now … move! Maybe a couple of days in the sweatbox will help you remember you're nothing but Prolet scum.'

Then they were gone. And I was in hell again.

***

There was a rhythm to it, the regular thump of the laundry drum, announcing its benign interest in the world. And there were six of us, closely guarded by a satyr, emptying the laundry trucks and reloading again. I knew it was bedding, though it wasn't mine, and the guards occasionally barked a reminder. It was always this routine for me, laundry followed by the medical research unit. A little different to everyone else. I'd learned not to ask why.

'It's falling!'

A young girl with white hair and a hunched back cried out as one of the overladen laundry baskets tipped over, emptying its soiled contents onto the floor. The satyr growled and stepped forward, his Diasord high and ready to strike.

Her muffled shriek filled the air as it brought three heavy thrashes down on her head and shoulders, the force of his blows moving closer and closer to the floor. He drew back, and she tried to climb back onto her feet. We all knew lying on the floor brought only further, unwanted attention. I took another load of washing in my blistered hands. Nobody wanted the sweatbox either.

White to white, detergent, dial, red button.

I glanced back at the cowering girl, her dress split across her shoulders revealing unusually dark, pitted flesh. A sickly grin spread across the satyr's face, before I looked back at my half-loaded laundry.

White to white, detergent, dial, red button.

I'd seen similar skin before, just couldn't remember where. Not here. Somewhere else.

I started unloading another truck before the attention turned to the rest of us. The girl stumbled as she tried to lift the fallen laundry cart, and the satyr let out another roar of rage. I gritted my teeth as he bent down, muscles rippling, and lifted her up by the scruff of her neck, as lightly as though she were a feather. Then he smiled. It was a slow smile of sadistic pleasure, while she hung there, white and shaking. Then he pushed the tip of one of his black pointed nails into a tear in the back of her thin tunic. The split revealed the extent of her leather back. It was scaled into thin hard points like a desert lizard – while her long white hair hung around her pale face like a midnight waterfall. *What waterfall?*

He smiled again before turning and lumbering from the room, the girl clamped to him like a weak fallow deer. I frowned. There were no deer.

The five of us remaining turned back to our duties, knowing we wouldn't see her again. This happened to the ones who disappointed the Imperator. They were fed. To the big, clawed birds. After the satyrs had their fun. An odd feeling flitted down my spine and across my aching back. *Strix.* I'd heard the name somewhere once, but though I could picture one perfectly in my head I was sure I'd never actually seen one. Except perhaps in my dreams.

I turned back to the laundry, and the girl's leather back floated to the forefront of my mind again. I tried to push it back. This was what they warned us against – thinking too much. Conscious thought was prohibited they said, against the laws of Pantheon. Disloyal to the Emperor Cassius and Empress Livia.

But of who or what did she remind me? Her image was stuck, like a determined flame on a dark night. And I couldn't move it, despite the fear flooding my head and threatening to extinguish the thought for ever. It was the glimpse of her back. And now there was something else: a word. *Or was it a name?* Now the need was so intense I could barely control my breathing. I closed my eyes and the throbbing sharpened while snatches of forgotten conversations whispered through the void.

'I thought you said she was batch 3,067.'

It was a name.

'Is she still fighting it?'

Just a short name.

71

'This should be enough to dissolve every last synapse in her cerebral hemisphere.'

And then a break in the fog, just enough for a glimpse of the letters.

... L ... a ... k ... e ...

I sucked in a breath, and it felt as though the room was being shaken by the most violent earthquake.

Lake?

And in a blinding flash I was back there, standing on the crumbling mountain shelf, staring up at Cassius's most volatile of ancient re-creations: *Hominum chimera.*

I gasped again as a volcanic pain erupted in my head, claiming my nerves and trying to block the synapses. It hurt so much my heart was hammering like a trapped leveret, sending shock waves through my heaving body.

The others were looking at me now. Blank faces, frowning. Had I made a noise? I forced my gaze down. Breath shaking. Bare feet. There was another flash, and they were leather-soled.

Running beneath the sun, leaves in my hair and a shadow at my back ...

Arafel ...?

The whisper was so loud it could have been uttered by one of the pale faces staring at me.

Frightened leveret faces, watching and waiting for the hunters with their bloodied knives. Who was next? Arafel?

I staggered and collapsed to my knees, my head in my hands. The pain was coming in intense waves now, fighting to stop the memories that had been severed into raw, quivering parts from firing with life. I moaned and squeezed my temples, trying to make it stop and go away.

'What are you doing? MMDCL!' one of the laundry operatives next to me hissed.

He grabbed my arm and tried to pull me to my feet. I looked up into his small angular face, his dark hollowed eyes pleading with me to get up while the rest stood around gaping. Pale hollow-eyed faces, devoid of all conscious thought. *Weren't they?* I gripped his forearm, pulling him closer. He was familiar, I was sure of it.

Then a scurry of panic around us. There were footsteps coming down the corridor. *Louder. Closer.* The satyr was returning, and all the while I was trying to complete the memory. To force the spark across the void. I gripped harder as he yanked back in terror, trying to loosen himself before it was too late and then I saw them. *Feathers.* Barely visible above the collar of his laundry tunic.

There was a flash of colour behind my eyes, before a pressure around my crown as though I'd just fallen from the top of the world. I shook my head, trying to clear the nausea.

'Therry?' I whispered, just as the doorway darkened with a broad shadow.

He blinked, wresting his arm away as he schooled his face back into the mask they all wore. Dead eyes. Workers.

'*You are numero MMDCL. Your purpose is to obey. Your allegiance is to the Emperor Cassius. All hail Emperor Cassius and the Empress Livia.*'

The words echoed in my head as, second by second, my thoughts crystallized. How often had I said them? What had happened to me? *And under what veil of a black moon had he crowned himself Emperor?*

I blinked up at the looming satyr, my raw gaze taking in his narrowing red eyes, and that slow malicious smile. Shakily, I clambered to my feet, trying to hide it all. But every cell of my body shook with fresh knowledge, old voices and painful memories, all clamouring to be set free. Nothing and everything was wrong. It was as though I'd just awaken from a nightmare, to find myself in a worse reality, and I had no idea what my next move should be.

Therry shot me a darting, terrified glance. His was the one

other heart beating faster than the rest in this deafening room. I could feel it – he knew too. Somehow, the young Prolet rebel I'd last seen in the Dead City, had survived the mind-numbing effects of the vaccine. But it didn't matter. It was too late for masks or questions now.

The satyr peeled its thick black lips back in a hideous grimace of delight as it reached towards me, and all I could think as his malicious fingers closed like a vice was that I'd committed the most heinous crime of all.

I'd forgotten Mum.

Chapter 11

It was odd. Firstly, I was free. *Sort of.* At least, I wasn't shackled to anything – machinery, bleeping medical equipment or line of shuffling Prolet slaves.

I was just me. Inside a white room that was completely empty save for a bed and a waste pan. I was certain because as soon as I regained consciousness, I searched the room, inch by clinical inch. And I knew I was being watched too, from the other side of the wall. I couldn't see them, but I hadn't grown up in a forest without developing an innate sixth sense for all life around me – through trees thicker than walls.

I knew it was vital not to let them glimpse my fear; but the memories had returned so fast, fragment by fragment, breaking and mending me simultaneously. And I struggled for breath every time I recalled the moment Eli and I had arrived back at Arafel, its razing seared into my head.

Then there was Mum, taken by the Eagle Sweeper aircraft, despite my best efforts to save her. Her bewildered face turning to me in the next canister, relief in her grey-blue eyes before oblivion stole her away. Where was she now? Had I played into Cassius's hands by giving up the keyword? Would the world now pay for my failure?

Were any of the others still alive? Max, Lake, August ...

Our parting had returned with crystal clarity, together with so much shame. I'd denied there was anything left for us, because ignoring his pain ignored mine too. Yet somehow, my slow recovery from the vaccine had unfrozen other feelings too, feelings I'd convinced myself we'd traded with the Oceanids – now I wasn't so sure.

Had he returned from the legatio? Was he even alive?

My inner fear tolled as clearly as the old bell above Arafel's peace hut. The only time it ever sounded was to herald the onward journey of another soul, and the thought that small sanctuary might no longer exist carved a chasm the size of the North Mountains in my chest.

But I knew better than to let them see – it would simply make me less interesting. They'd vaccinate again, and who knew what long-lasting effect or damage it would have this time. Or whether I'd survive at all. I surveyed my scarred arms and legs, an impressive tribute to the torture I'd endured, and swallowed the ready bile in my throat.

I needed to stay focused, especially now I remembered giving up the keyword.

The realization had felt like the slow descent into a nightmare. I'd given up the final piece of information Cassius needed to operate the Vigenère cipher encrypting the Voynich. And if that wasn't enough, Max's tiny treehouse dart tube no longer hung around my neck, which meant he also had Thomas's coding for *Hominum chimera*. Now he had everything he needed to decode every hellish creature within the Voynich, for his grand purpose. *To redesign the living world.* And all because I thought I could fight every last Insider to rescue Mum. A lone feral girl.

I fought the heat behind my eyes. I'd betrayed everyone, brought death and destruction to Arafel, and now I'd handed Cassius the key to re-creating every mythological creature described in the Voynich. I'd failed in the most epic way possible, except perhaps at surviving. It seemed I was adept at that.

I gritted my teeth. The bright, dazzling walls were moving again. I could tell even though the movement was soundless. The fourth wall slowly faded away to reveal a view of Pantheon's main dome floor. It was one of his games. Only the beasts unleashed were all inside my own head this time.

I stepped across to the fortified glass, the view reaching up to taunt me the way it always did. It was Cassius's ego breathed into life, the tiny marble heart of Isca Pantheon, its Romanesque streets stretching out and converging like the picture of a perfect classical city. It had been Octavia's dream, yet Cassius had proven more than ready to step into her vacant throne, adding his signature with more lavish temples, state buildings, amphitheatres, and rising up to the north of it all, the oppressive Flavium.

I rested my forehead against the cool glass, and stared down at the pristine lines, bustling with life – happy, ignorant life without a care for anyone else. It hardly seemed possible after the chaos Max, August and I had delivered right into its heart, little more than a year before. But now it seemed as though that day had never been.

I wanted to smash my fists though its neat streets, to unleash turmoil through its streets and finish what we'd started. To reaffirm what it meant to be feral and free.

But right now I had only one weapon left against the iron throne of Pantheon.

'Who are you?'

I fixed my gaze on the sky train. There were more stations under construction serving a new domestic tower, thanks to a small army of Prolets. Clearly the re-established autocracy was burgeoning with health. The sky train pulled into a station opposite my glass wall, and three carriages of smiling Pantheonites disembarked, completely oblivious to my presence.

I'd given up trying to attract any attention. My cell had to be completely insulated and invisible to all except those watching me. I focused on the train instead. The carriage shells were alive with bright moving pictures, and this one flickered with Cassius's arrogant face and two-metre-high words:

'Emperor Cassius is building our new-world future: honour, valour and allegiance. Long live the Civitas!'

My lips twisted scornfully. It was almost entertaining, the way Cassius believed his own rhetoric.

The planetary media system that lived among the haga descended regularly to remind citizens how he'd single-handedly rid the outside world of our weaker DNA, as though we were a viral scourge or vermin. But it was always the images that held attention, clear proof should Pantheonites be in any doubt as to the sincerity of his words. They were images I knew by heart now – Arafel burning while tiny people and animals ran for their lives, a close-up of a long line of Eagle aircraft soaring low in the only valley home I'd ever known, and then clouds of fire and smoke billowing up like hell itself had been unleashed. I forced myself to watch every second until the anguish built its own second skin over my heart.

'The threat from the outside world was critical,' the vitriolic propaganda reminded on a loop.

'Poisoned by radiation and soil toxins, the substandard specimens bore little resemblance to the advanced species we have become in Isca Pantheon.

'Our recent insurgent episodes have highlighted the need to control and eradicate this rising pestilence. Thanks to the targeting surveillance of our Eaglecraft squadron, our mission has now been accomplished.

'Isca Pantheon is, at last, safe from infiltration and infection, and together we will build towards a new Civitas, a future that observes the core pillars set out by our ancient forefathers: honour, valour and allegiance.

'Long live Isca Pantheon! Long live Imperator Cassius!'

78

And they accepted it all. Almost as though their indoctrination was as much a part of them, as our feral nature was a part of us. Almost.

Two tall Pantheonites stopped to exchange pleasantries, laughing as though entirely immune to the bloodshed that had just played out across the retracting screens. I still wondered at their indifference. We'd all started from the same place, only two centuries ago. And yet our differences were scored into our cells, as though Octavia and Cassius had cut out anything resembling a conscience or free will and stitched them back together again.

Frankensteins … Pantheosteins.

My top lip curled. To think they now represented the future of the human race was as nauseating as it was terrifying.

A laundry train rumbled by, and I thought briefly of my Prolet shift. *Therry? How had he avoided the vaccine?*

'Who are you?' the patient, anodyne voice repeated behind me.

I was used to it. They came to monitor progress, which was precisely why I was determined to give them none. It kept them guessing, and made me more interesting while I devised a plan.

'You cannot hide anything from us, including your ability to void the vaccine – twice. This is a unique result and of interest to us. Cooperate and we will put an end to your isolation.'

'What if I like isolation?'

My voice was stony. Challenging. It was all I had.

The voice sighed. 'You know we have ways of making you talk, Talia … but I'd far rather we did this the easy way.'

It was the same white-coated scientist every day. He hadn't hurt me yet, but I knew it wasn't an idle threat. The pain I'd endured before was seared into my mind, and yet there was a reason I hadn't been fed to the strix like the leather-backed Prolet girl.

Voiding the vaccine had rendered me important enough to be kept under surveillance, while the destruction of Lake's only living control was clearly too much of a risk, even for Cassius.

It didn't matter. He'd already stolen everyone I loved, so there was nothing and no one left to lose.

Which of course, they knew.

***

It was the same soft lullaby she used to sing when Eli and I were small. I opened my eyes slowly, convinced it was the small round box in the corner of the room again. It was a box of dreams and nightmares. Sometimes the scents and sounds of the forest would drift from it, and there was a precise spot three paces in front where I could just detect the subtlest scent of wild honeysuckle. That was always before the new test though.

First there was the soft wisp of stinging smoke, followed by a dry acidic burn. Then the room would slowly fill with the sound of crackling flames, falling trees and muffled screaming until I was back there again on that last day when the Eaglecraft came. I tried to pace myself, to tell my streaming eyes and burning throat he was trying to break my standoff, but I was always close to breaking point when it disappeared, leaving a hollow silence and my own straining breath.

Even I had to hand it to Cassius. The new personally designed torture was harder to withstand than the moving images, and came without warning, day and night.

Which was why I didn't open my eyes when I first heard her. I was sure it was just part of another test. And when I did open my eyes, I still didn't quite believe what I saw, even though it was her silhouette, standing in front of the glass and looking down onto Pantheon.

'Mum?' I managed hoarsely, barely recognizing my own voice.

She turned then. And suddenly it was as though the last angel in the universe had come for me, and I didn't even care what they might glean from my reaction. *She was alive ... Mum ... My mum ...*

80

'It isn't so bad,' she responded softly, with a smile.

Her smile!

I was across the floor faster than I had moved in too long, shocking my stiff limbs into action. I barrelled into her waiting arms, my energy forcing her to take a step back with a laugh. And it was her old laugh, the one from before.

'Mum, Mum, Mum ...' I half sobbed, half pleaded into her fragile neck.

She was warm, and smelled the way she always did, as though she'd just stepped from a bath scented with cinnamon and honey. It was so intoxicating and I closed my eyes, despite everything.

'Please please be you,' I wished fervently, not daring to lift my eyes to hers for fear of what I may read there.

'It isn't so bad,' she repeated again, stroking my hair in her old familiar way.

And while I wanted nothing more than to remain there for ever, cradled among an armful of old memories, I knew I had to face reality. Slowly, I lifted my heavy eyes to look at her. She was gazing straight ahead; detached and unemotional. I knew it didn't make sense for it not to be just another of his twisted games – and yet I couldn't not try either.

'Mum?' I whispered. 'It's me ... Tal.'

I watched her grey-blue irises, the same hue as Eli's, dilate and retract. I prayed there was enough left – that Pantheon hadn't extinguished a flame that had already been guttering anyway.

'It isn't so bad,' she repeated again.

'Mum! Please ... it's me Tal ... Mum, look at me ...!' I urged intently.

There was a long silence before she opened her mouth, and for one tiny moment, I thought I'd broken through.

'It isn't so bad,' she repeated again, staring across the room.

I followed the direction of her gaze and only then realized she was talking to the box, high up on the wall. And my hopes began to crumble like the trees in my dreams.

'Look at me … look at me, Mum!' I demanded, pulling her head away and forcing her eyes to connect with mine, conscious all the while that they were watching.

Her eyes were dilated and unfocused, their colour – which had always reminded me of the bright grey pebbles in Arafel's stream – faded to stone. My gut twisted sharply. I'd suffered physical and mental torture, but this was different. Mum had already been so weak when we'd arrived, and now they'd stolen whatever was left. Arafel was a ghost, and who knew whether I would ever see Eli, Max, or August again. They were gone, all of them, and now Mum was gone too. For what? To satisfy the ambitions of one delusional man.

A burning-hot serpent of rage suddenly writhed up from my stomach. I tore myself out of Mum's passive arms and pelted towards the white box. It was a cold, inanimate representation of all that I hated, barely worthy of attention. Let alone hatred. Yet it was all there was, and the closest thing to Cassius in the room.

I leapt as though I was bridging the widest tree jump, caught hold of the top of the white box, and brought my feet up sharply to puncture the black square at the front. It crackled ominously, before a loud fizzing and deafening alarm consumed the tense air. Then I dropped like an animal, and stared down at my heels. They were streaked red, like the flames dancing through Arafel. Like Ida's legs the moment she died.

Mum had sunk to the floor, cradling her head, while the wall to my right flickered from white to transparent, revealing a line of seated people with startled faces. My lips twisted. They weren't feeling so superior now. I threw a look at the sealed door. I had a minute, maybe two if I was lucky.

I sprinted back to Mum who was cowering like a child, and started pulling her across towards my bed. She resisted, shaking like a leaf, and my heart lurched as I pushed her to the floor and, using all my strength, slid her into the slim gap beneath my bed.

I followed in a heartbeat, and somehow we both ended up cramped into that tiny dark spot, the only place they couldn't see.

With trembling fingers, I yanked up my tunic and pointed to the jagged white scar that ran up my calf, just visible in the light. It was the same scar Therry had asked about all those months before in the buried bathhouse beneath the Cathedral of Isca. I'd told him I'd fought a tiger, and his childish brown eyes had lit up with excitement. It seemed so long ago.

'Remember this, Mum? It was the day Eli and I took Dad's scythe to build a den. You were so mad with us you made Eli stay in his bedroom for a whole day!' I whispered. 'I got hurt, and was so scared you'd be mad at me, but all you did was cry and hold me tight. We had a whole roasted chicken and an apple pie for dinner. Do you remember … you have to remember … Mum?'

Her brow creased in heavy concentration and the pebbles glinted before something else crept in – a flicker of recognition.

My stomach contracted involuntarily, releasing what felt to be an entire colony of butterflies, which fluttered up against the inside of my ribcage.

'Tal …?' she whispered.

'Yes! Yes! It's me, Mum … Mum,' I responded, throwing my arms around her frail shoulders and pulling her tight, revelling in the sensation of her fragile embrace.

She was back, for a few glorious seconds, she was back.

'Mum, you have to listen!' I forced her to look at me again. 'They'll be here any second. You've been vaccinated, with a chemical that closes the mind.'

There was panic in her eyes and I tried to soothe her.

'But you're stronger … we're stronger because we're Outsiders. Cassius is trying to control us all, but his vaccine isn't enough. You remember, Mum … you remember me … Eli, Max, Arafel?'

I didn't mention its destruction – I still didn't know how much she saw – but I'd said enough anyway. She stared at me and finally, the gleam was back, sunlight picking out the stones in Arafel's stream and the shadow of a world she'd been forced to forget. And as it loomed to the forefront of her eyes, her face darkened with inevitable pain.

'Eli?' she whispered.

'Yes yes, Eli! And Jas and the forest … home, Mum … Arafel.'

'But they said … it's not so bad,' she faltered, trying to mesh two worlds that should never have met.

I placed my hand across her mouth as footsteps entered the room.

'They lied. It is very very bad. You are Eoiffer Hanway, descendant of Thomas Hanway. We were both taken from the forest. By Cassius and his Eaglecraft. And now they're trying to make you forget, the way they've tried to make me forget. But *they* forgot, Mum. They forgot we're Outsiders … and feral means free!'

My last words turned into a gritty yell, as my ankles were seized and I was dragged roughly out into the harsh white light. I fought it but I was no match for two burly Pantheonite guards.

Mum's forcible removal was much harder to take than mine. Her eyes shuttered as soon as she was faced with the scientists, and the sight of her white tunic crumpling up around her thin white thighs as she was yanked out enraged me more than the guards' tough grip on her arms. We were both forced to our knees, and she dropped her head in instant servitude. I glanced at her profile swiftly. Her top lip was twitching, the way it always did when she was angry.

A flame of hope soared through me. She was still in there. Still with me. And I had to protect her.

'Do what you like!' I fumed, thrashing wildly. 'She's no mother of mine any more! She doesn't remember, unlike me … I remember everything! Arafel, August, Max, Aelia, Pan … how your lasers murdered innocent children and people, how

84

you've tried to rid the world of every last Outsider so you can repopulate it with a species that doesn't even resemble itself any more!'

I could see Mum trembling, and prayed she understood.

'I know I wouldn't be here if Cassius didn't need something else from me!' I stormed. 'So you tell him I'm ready, but I will negotiate with him – and no one else!'

I watched Mum lift her trembling hand before dropping it again, and I exhaled silently. If they believed she was still under the vaccine's influence, they would leave her alone.

A tall thin scientist with flint eyes and a nose like one of the North Mountain peaks stepped forward, his shoes clicking ominously on the hard white floor. The rest of the guard shuffled back in response to a small dismissive wave of his hand.

Eight burly guards to protect one scientist against two unarmed, barefoot women. Curious math that only confirmed I was still considered a threat. I eyed him baldly, not bothering to hide my disgust.

He considered me carefully before tapping the identifier strapped to his wrist in a way that took me right back to the day I'd run into August in the forest. It was the day Cassius took Grandpa and Eli, starting everything.

I closed my eyes briefly, hiding the flare of pain.

'Congratulations, Talia, you've passed,' he offered, scribbling something in a thick file.

I leaned over and spat, with perfect aim, on his shining, clicking shoes. Mum's eyes flickered with disapproval and I smothered a brief smile. She was still definitely still in there, and they thought we were rabid vermin anyway, so I might as well enjoy the perks. With satisfaction, I watched a drop of drool run down the black gleam of his boots, ruining their perfect lustre.

'That's what I think of your tests!'

'Positive affirmation,' he murmured, eyeing the top of his boot with clinical interest. 'Affirmation of your identity, and ability to react to environmental stimuli. Atypical behaviour for a vaccinated subject.'

I spat again, onto his other boot this time. It landed in the centre of his shiny toecap and I eyed my aim in admiration.

He paused to look over the top of his file, distaste wrinkling his nose.

'You interest us, Talia. You've voided not one but two vaccines, at successively higher dosages and, given a variety of stimuli, there is clear evidence to suggest you have managed to restore to factory settings. In short, you have shown a demonstrable immunity to the vaccine. Yes, you are quite fascinating …'

'Could have told you that without all the brain-frying,' I responded.

He turned to regard Mum, who was still cowering on her knees beside me.

'She's useless – she remembers nothing,' I repeated, hoping my biting tone hid my fear. 'And what has Cassius done with Max?!'

With one ferocious effort, I yanked my arms out of the guards' pinioned clamp and clambered to my feet, pain jettisoning through my limbs as they returned to life.

The scientist narrowed his gaze, tiny Roman lines furrowing his high forehead, before pursing his lips and scribbling again.

'Your mother has proven to be a little disappointing, considering her blood link. Her weakened mental state made her a void test subject of course, but extra Prolet hands are always useful, as they say.'

He eyed me intently.

'As for … Max, did you say? I'm sorry, I'm not sure …?'

One of the dour-faced guards smirked. 'He's that new one that came in a few months back. Was on the gladiatorial guard before he became the new Ludi favourite … enjoying a spell in the morgue now I suspect.'

I scowled as he grinned maliciously.

'On the gladiatorial guard …'

His words echoed strangely in my head, and suddenly I was back in the Prolet cave with the creaking lantern and dirty mugs, standing opposite a golden sleeping knight. A Roman knight wearing gladiatorial sandals, and with feet the colour of the sun. My body tensed as though shot through by lightning.

Could it have been?

'... *enjoying a spell in the morgue now I suspect ...?*'

My brain slowed, refusing to acknowledge the words. He couldn't be dead, not after everything. The guard shot me a piercing look, and I knew in a flash it was him, the same peacock who'd knocked me to the ground and locked me inside a cell no bigger than one of Bereg's meat-smoking boxes.

I stretched my fingers, like a cat flexing its claws, as I recalled the brutal way he'd handled me. It was little better than the waste they emptied down their latrines, the same way most Prolets were treated here. My unflinching gaze travelled down his sweaty forehead, hooked nose and sour smile, which faded slightly as I made him a silent promise. His rough hands had more than availed themselves of my fragile state, and even if I was the last Outsider standing, he was going to learn what that actually meant.

'We all had our orders,' he muttered gruffly, almost as though my intent was written across my face.

'*Finis.*'

I didn't need to speak Latin to understand the scientist's clipped tone.

He closed his file with a small, almost regretful nod, and stepped back to allow two guards to seize my arms and twist them up behind my back. I steeled myself as tiny beads of icy sweat broke out along my forehead, making me shiver despite the warmth of the room.

'My report,' the scientist added, passing his papers to the front guard, 'don't lose it.'

'They won't need it!' I hissed as I passed Mum's kneeling profile.

And it may have been my fancy but I sensed the tiniest lift of her head as I passed, as though she understood I was protecting her the only way I had left, that she understood.

It was the hardest thing, leaving Mum again, but her survival depended on my indifference, and there was only one real way to rescue her now.

Cassius had the cipher, the keyword, and any moment now, final evidence of my vaccine resistance. I was one of the last living threats from the outside world, and he'd had every opportunity to finish me. Yet, he hadn't. Which left only one thing between us unexplained.

Our dark blood.

I gritted my teeth.

It divided and connected us in a way neither of us fully understood. But somehow it was enough to make him hesitate.

And that was all I needed.

Chapter 12

It was the closest I'd come to direct confrontation since arriving in Isca Pantheon. And I could imagine only too well how Cassius was relishing news of my vaccine resistance and outburst.

We descended by sky train, taking the last carriage reserved for Prolets and prisoners. It smelled of stale food and dirt, but I was out of the clinical box that had incarcerated me since I'd awaken, and the rush was intense. I closed my eyes briefly recalling Mum's small hunched figure, praying she had the mental strength to keep her new awareness to herself. At least until I found a way forward.

The colossal structures growing towards us as we descended did little to allay my nerves. I surveyed the city in silence. There was no denying Cassius had been busy, using his army of Prolet slaves to build and expand; but there was something parasitic about Pantheon's appearance now, almost as though it was sucking the lifeblood out of the earth below it in order to spread.

New Romanesque temples adorned each corner of the Civitas, each embellished with intricately carved gods and goddesses. There was Venus with a small Eros beside her; Minerva beneath a carved gleaming sun, her wisdom depicted by the rays above her head; Vulcan wielding a huge blacksmith's hammer; and

Apollo with his bow and arrows held high, proclaiming his undying loyalty.

I stared around, feeling Arafel's ashes shrink to less than the eye of a needle. This wasn't so much world-building as deity-making. And stretching up out of the centre of the civic lair was a new alabaster statue, twice the size of the rest. His flamboyant uniform and flattering likeness made him unmistakable; Emperor Cassius, Imperator of Isca Pantheon and Protector of the New Order.

A wave of bile threatened my forced calm. It was the work of an esoteric madman. Even Octavia had never placed herself so clearly among the gods. I would have laughed, if it hadn't been so chilling. Less protector than predator.

We exited the sky train, and the guards took an easterly route through the outlying streets towards the grotesque statue leering over the city skyline. I forced my eyes to the streets, which were alive with smiling Pantheonites, all vying for a glimpse of the Civitas' newest criminal or victim. One and the same in Isca Pantheon.

I returned their looks defiantly, challenging them to remember me. The feral girl. Still alive, despite their tyranny, ignorance and annihilation of my home. They stared with fear, curiosity, and occasionally something else I was wary to identify.

'Look, Mama, it's the Outsider!' a young Pantheonite girl exclaimed before finding herself bundled away by her crow-beak mother.

'Yes, the Outsider. Free! The way you should be,' I yelled after her retreating form.

A guard's hand clamped over my mouth, while a Diasord was pushed into the small of my back.

The child twisted to look back and I winked with a confidence I was far from feeling. But the fact she recalled my identity mattered; it meant I wasn't forgotten. Not yet. She threw a brief smile, her pigtails dancing and chestnut eyes brimming with questions, and for just a second she reminded me of Faro. My mind dragged up the last image I had of her lying limply on the cold tower floor, freckles paling. My chest tightened with the sudden memory, and I pushed my head higher as we marched on.

The streets widened into stately plazas, with gleaming stone pavements and young trees trapped behind railings. Briefly, I wondered which part of the forest had been raided by Sweepers, and how many other animals and plants had been sacrificed in the process.

Then just as we turned a corner into one of the wider plazas, an all-too-familiar whirring noise reached into my thoughts, stalling everyone in their tracks. The low drone of voices gave way to an ominous silence and all eyes swivelled skywards as the planetary system in the domed ceiling cranked into action. Several planet-shaped units started towards the floor as crowds of Pantheonites pressed back against the clean white walls of their city, leaving the alabaster statues devoid of company. And I could almost taste the air, as it fell in folds of muted fear.

Now I was on the floor, it was also clear how much the planet system had grown. What had started out as half a dozen planetary screens in Octavia's time, was now a complex network of control that reached into every square throughout the main city centre. I scanned the sky with foreboding. I understood enough to know the planets carried the moving images, the ones that spun destructive lies about the outside, and Cassius's claim to authority. I recalled August's ashen face in the research centre when he also discovered his own propaganda for the first time. I had yet to come across a weapon with so few teeth and claws, and yet could shred a person so swiftly.

One of the dark spheres slowed to a halt three metres above our square, and gleamed oppressively at the small crowd gathered beneath. Then there was another clicking sound as it spun over to reveal a flatter side, and I readied myself for the film I'd watched daily from my white cell. But instead there was a fanfare of new triumphant music, which set the faces around me twitching with anxiety. Today was clearly different.

'Citizens, this is a historic day! A day for our Civitas to remember …'

As his smooth, acidic tone gripped the square, the screen suddenly flickered and projected a larger-than-life human image. Startled, I took a step back to find a Diasord still pinioned against the small of my back. I gritted my teeth and forced myself to look up.

The flickering, technicolour image towering above us – as real as any flesh and blood – was perfect Cassius down to every single tiny detail. Except this Cassius was taller, broader, swarthier, and enhanced in every way to confirm his imperial status. He was dressed from head to foot in royal purple, a gleaming crown on his head and ceremonial mace in his hand, while beside him slathered a hound that had become nearly as familiar to me as Jas. *Brutus*. It was all played to perfection. A scene of which Nero himself would have been proud.

I recalled the man who'd slithered away like a snake over the ancient cathedral stone only months before, and contempt coursed through my body. Arafel would still exist if I'd remained deaf to Atticus's plea, and finished him when I had the chance.

I can pay.

My promise to Prince Phaethon loomed at the forefront of my mind.

Give them back, give Eli back … stand beside us against Cassius – and I will pay in blood.

'I'm coming for you,' I whispered so quietly no one else could hear.

Just as a rough hand gripped me by the scruff of my neck, forcing me to my knees.

'Afford your new Emperor some respect!' the peacock hissed against my right cheek.

As my face hit the dirt, I saw the crowds of Pantheonites dropping to their knees, a show of absolute deference to the Emperor, and a streak of defiance claimed my taut body. Didn't they know it was impossible to get lower than a death adder?

Pushing back, I jumped to my feet. I had nothing else to lose, and the young girl's words were still burning in my mind.

'Look, Mama, it's the Outsider.'

What was the point of being the only Outsider, and behaving like everyone else?

'I defer to no Insider!' I yelled, watching a sea of eyes around me shrink with horror.

Perhaps the chemicals charging my veins were having some counter-effect, I thought as my rebellious tone rose above Cassius's voice. I'd never felt more feral in my life.

'Can you hear me, Cassius? I defer to no Insider, let alone an old yellow-bellied snake purporting to be a man!'

The blow that followed muted the guard's hissing diatribe, and I was almost grateful for the bitter taste of iron that filled my mouth. It was real, unlike the city and people surrounding me.

I was hauled back onto my knees as the world returned to monochrome.

'... historic for two reasons ... Firstly, today we announce the completion of our most glorious Temple of Mars in honour of our new Civitas. It is a symbol of our glorious future, since the vanquishing of the Prolet uprising led by deserter Augustus Aquila, and it will not be tarnished by those who have betrayed our honour.

'Moreover, today we are celebrating the glorious enlightenment of an entire generation. Rejoice, my Roman compatriots, and join me in celebrating one of the original aims of the Biotechnical Programme, the final translation of our most precious ancient Voynich code!'

The crowd erupted as something wet dripped down my ear, and then the image flickered again. This time Cassius was standing on the wide steps of what looked to be a Roman temple, the crown upon his head alight with golden flames, and a precious book cradled in his hands.

There was a succession of stifled gasps and I knew instantly it was the Voynich, the book I'd vowed to burn on a funeral pyre. It might be filled with ancient myths, but now I knew its secrets were a legacy of fire, better turned to ash than flesh and blood.

As we watched, the coding floated out from the book and curled into thin snakes around his head, moving faster than anyone could watch, a medusa in a scientific world. It seemed more than fitting that his alter ego was a creature famed for calcifying veins.

'The final translation of the Voynich is a glorious moment, and we will be remembered as the Civitas that built a new-world order! Now we can re-create glorious creatures that were victims of man's weak folly – ancient glorious creatures that once graced a richer earth.

'With an army of beasts at our command, we will rule as our ancestors did, with honour, valour and a knowledge that a new era has dawned. The era of Imperator Cassius, last of the Constantinian Dynasty, Protector of Isca Pantheon and Conqueror of the outside world!'

A shocked whisper ran through the crowd as the coding vibrated, firing Cassius's opal eyes with a glittering ruby shadow. The effect was mesmerizing and oppressive. He looked every inch a powerful new god of the underworld. Deity-worthy. Then the coding snapped back towards his head before breaking free like a cloud of silent birds. And yet it was his smile that stilled me.

It was overlarge, his teeth bared like a wolf in Roman clothing. *Too wide, too sharp, too bright*. It was a smile of victory – over me, over Arafel and over all Outsiders.

I swallowed, feeling the tip of his teeth press into my jugular momentarily. It had to be my imagination, and yet the impression was so real I had to fight the impulse to lift my fingers and brush it away.

Finally, the image flickered and disappeared, sending the planetary system whirring into action above our heads. They retracted swiftly, straight up into the Dome's natural atria where the hagas wasted no time in voicing their own raucous reception.

And as though Cassius hadn't just promised the complete obliteration of the real, outside world as a new Dynastic Emperor-God, the crowd turned to resume their day, shopping and exchanging pleasantries. It was silently, breathlessly terrifying. Their determination to ignore the single biggest threat to their everyday existence. How long before Cassius decided they were inferior too and designed a new species of Pantheonites, together with bigger, stronger, smarter creatures – more teeth, more claws, greater intellect ... Where would it all stop?

Did they not realize they were in as much danger as the Prolets?

My thoughts clouded painfully. Although I'd glimpsed Therry in the laundry, I'd not seen any of the other young Prolets we found beneath the ruins of the Dead City since I awoke. Their pale, gaunt faces flickered through my head and I clenched my teeth, praying some of them were still alive, that there was still time for me to turn it all around. Somehow.

'Isn't that the feral girl? Didn't the Minotaurus ...?'

'Sssh! The Cyclops broke its neck ... But who'd have thought she'd survive?'

'Survival is what Outsiders have been doing for two hundred years!' I threw as the young Pantheonite women passed by. 'In the real outside world, not a gilded cage!'

They looked around my age, dressed in long silken togas and with head jewellery shaped like oversized dragonflies. They paused, shocked that a feral prisoner would understand, let alone respond, before moving swiftly on. They didn't look back.

There was another sharp blow to the small of my back, and I staggered forward, feeling my courage falter momentarily. I was barefoot, in a white laboratory tunic and heavily guarded and all they saw was the feral girl. The last of her kind. I represented a dying world and I could sense the curiosity and fear in the eyes of all who rested on me.

How could I possibly be enough?

Bereg's training reached through the dust.

Fear is simply a matter of perspective, Talia. Make a move, change the light and the hunted becomes the hunter.

I gritted my teeth. I had to be enough.

We'd arrived in the biggest square, having circumnavigated Cassius's towering statue, which looked even more grotesque close up. His hard, sculpted eyes seemed to look in every direction at once, despite their lack of life, and I worked hard to suppress a shudder as we marched past.

'The Temple of Mars ... All hail the Emperor Cassius and the Empress Livia!'

The peacock's reedy voice rang out as we paused at the bottom of a set of wide, formal steps rising to an imposing temple porch, with too many thick columns to count. The columned front disappeared back into the formal temple entrance, guarded by four armoured gladiators, and huge stand-alone burning torches wafting some sort of bittersweet oily scent towards us.

Mars, the God of War?

I swallowed to contain my nausea.

The Romans revered two types of gods, Talia – those they believed created the universe in all its glory, and those they were forced to worship on pain of death. They called them Emperor-Gods.

Grandpa's words fitted so neatly. It was the most perfect prop-aganda for any psychotic dictator obsessed with redesigning the world.

Cassius was the Emperor-God kind who destroyed threatening communities and deciphered ancient texts; the kind who bred an army of ancient creatures to protect the Civitas. Cassius was a benevolent Emperor-God, unless you wanted a real life and freedom.

I stared back at the new Temple of Mars, glinting in the

powdery light and surpassing all else in its wake. Each of its monstrous pillars, each nearly the width of the Great Oak, reached high to meet the pitched roof while the porch was adorned with a whole array of gleaming Roman sculptures. I didn't need a closer look to know most were sycophantic dedications to himself.

And behind the imposing temple, like a silent bodyguard, was the shadowy profile of the Flavium. My throat constricted. Arrogant Cassius had made his lair right here in the centre of his web, like a synthetic emperor insect, cocooned among his workers.

'All hail the Emperor Cassius and the Empress Livia!'

The hairs prickled on the back of my neck. The guards were moving.

The heavily armoured gladiators started down the wide steps, their Equite insignias catching the bright light of the faux sun high up among the hagas. I stared at the black-crested eagle on the swag of their military armour, and caught my breath. *The ancient aquila.* These had to be soldiers of the second Augusta Legion, August's Legion, and as two of them descended I thought I caught a glimpse of a faint scowl beneath a visor.

Was it one of August's soldiers?

The soldiers saluted with perfect timing, forming a closed guard with the peacock and another behind me, before marching back up the steps towards the gaping black archway at the rear of the temple porch.

I focused on the neck of the Equite who scowled as we moved.

'Commander General Augustus Aquila would be so proud.'

My words were quiet but unmistakable.

His shoulders tightened as we approached the arched entrance guarded by two burning torches as tall as Unus. There was a moment of darkness and then we passed into one of the largest stone chambers I'd ever seen in my life. I suppressed a sharp gasp, as my gaze took in the richly coloured swathes of fabric surrounding us. Gold and silver hangings drooped from the

97

ceiling like scrolls from heaven, while every wall was adorned with intricate, exquisite frescos.

The Equites didn't pause but made their way diagonally across the large echoing stone chamber, while I absorbed the ornate surroundings in disbelief. The rich frescos were scenes of perfect, idealized Pantheonite life.

There were temples, carvings and fountains, starry constellations and opulent tables laden with perfectly ripened food. Victorious gladiators played the roaring Flavium crowd, heads of mythological beasts dangling from their strong golden hands while more beasts feasted on rebellious Prolet corpses.

Smiling Pantheonites sat around in large family groups, laughing and feasting, looking towards a ceiling fresco of Cassius, his arms outstretched and a crown of gold laurel leaves tapering into tiny burning torches. A laughing Mars, the God of War, leaned in conspiratorially, while Vulcan, the God of Fire, watched and smiled.

My eyes lingered on Cassius's onyx eyes. The artist had captured them perfectly and their cold unflinching stare was unmistakable, even in a fresco. My strength wavered. It was all so warped and narcissistic. Who could fight a deity without a real army to bring down his lies? Here he was promising an Arcadia, when he'd obliterated the real Eden lying beyond Pantheon's walls. He was a craftsman in terror and manipulation.

'The Commander General Augustus Aquila is dead.'

I stiffened, shooting the Equite in front a narrow glance as he led me towards a smaller torch-lit entrance at the back of the antechamber. He marched on as though he hadn't muttered anything at all, while the remaining guards remained silent, their gazes locked straight ahead.

We were approaching a second stone archway, lit by a pair of fire torches and topped by a golden cage. There was a pure white dove and a black crow, suspended just high enough above the flames to escape the heat. Their fate was clear and I averted my eyes, unable to look at them. For some reason, their incarceration in this place was almost worse than my own.

'Appeasing gods of the under and upper world?' I muttered. 'Cassius *is* hedging his bets.'

'You would do well to hold your tongue,' the Equite in front hissed, turning his head to the side. 'The Emperor needs no prompting to make another sacrifice. He likes the feral ones best!'

I suppressed a retort, and tried to imagine his face without the ornate Roman helmet and solid nosepiece. A murky image flickered through my mind. *I knew him ... I was sure of it.* And then suddenly I was back there in the moonlit cathedral, the night of the battle of the vultures.

'Grey?' I whispered, my head filling with a barrage of violent images.

A muscle flexed in his cheek, but it was enough.

'It is you, isn't it? I left them with you ... in the cathedral. We found Aelia, but Max ... he was in the guard! Where ... is he? Where's Max?!'

My words came in punctuated breaths as I recalled the peacock's malicious fist reaching out, the crack as my head hit the red stone floor, and being forced into a claustrophobic rock cavern. Before seeing *him*. The gladiator in sandals. *Was it him?* My memory swam, but my senses screamed with accuracy. He was resting, then casting a cursory, indifferent glance over me. Forest-green eyes, cold and unknowing.

It was Max; it had to be Max. The whisper ran through me like a river.

And then the peacock leering again ... saying *Max was dead?*

All at once I knew what the forest animals felt like when barbed and caught in a trap. Pain flared through my veins and I struggled to take a breath.

'Ssssh!'

Grey spun and squared up to me, as the three other guards looked on, fear twisting their faces in the torchlight.

99

'Do you want to put us all back in the Flavium?' he hissed. 'The girl was dead already, OK? There was nothing I could do. The guy … what happened to him was … unlucky.'

'Unlucky?' I echoed and suddenly it seemed the most inadequate word in the world.

'I trusted you!' I threw out vehemently. 'August trusted you! Max fought beside you! And you let that twisted snake take them! Where is Max? What did Cassius do to him?'

Suddenly, the gnarled stone in my chest ballooned upwards and outwards, like a fossilized seed that had finally found water. My mind crowded with Max's lopsided grin, his rough fingers offering his tiny treehouse dart tube, his shape foreshadowing mine as we flew through the trees, his arms holding me through all the difficult nights, and then that moment in the ruined cathedral, when I asked him to save Aelia. He was always so ready to be a damned hero, always the strongest of us, before the arrow impaled his spine. Piercing him in the most cowardly way, so unworthy of a son of Arafel.

He'd trusted me, run with me, sprinted headlong into danger. For me. And all I'd given him was pain, indecision and half a girl. A ghost girl. For what? So that he could end up here, like some soulless tin soldier, ready to do Cassius's bidding come what may.

The guilt was a tight choking vice, crawling into every pore and cell of my body and whispering how much I'd let him down. How much that moment had cost.

'Call yourself an Equite? A soldier worthy of that noble Aquila insignia?' I forced out, my raw whispering carrying eerily down the stone passage, but I didn't care. 'You don't know the meaning of the word! You're nothing but worthless cowards, all of you!'

'Silence!' the peacock hissed, reaching out to close his hand roughly around my throat and squeezing with such ugly pressure the corridor spun like a leaf caught in the wind.

'Dimiti, let her go!'

I was vaguely aware of Grey's hoarse fury, of his hand gripping the peacock's forearm and forcing it up, so he relinquished his hold.

I sprawled on the floor, the leather straps of their booted feet swimming before my eyes. Eight large Roman boots, versus my tree-flying soles. It shouldn't be a contest at all. Dazed, I pushed myself up, catching sight of a hazy outline of my reflection in the polished marble floor. It was the closest I'd come to seeing myself in weeks, and the hollow-eyed girl staring back seemed so out of place in these surroundings.

I fought to recover my senses, conscious this was my last chance. Not that there was any real decision to be made – backwards led straight into a battalion of armed guards, forwards led to darkness and Cassius. But I was damned if I was entering as a prisoner. Not while there was breath in my body.

I rolled as though my life depended on it, jumped to my feet and launched into a full sprint. My legs felt stiff and disjointed, but every stride stirred my blood a little more.

The corridor echoed with ugly curses and the guards gave chase instantly, but my tree-running years gave me the advantage and although I was headed only into the serpent's lair, I felt freer and stronger than I had in a long time. Whatever Cassius had planned, I was meeting him as Talia Hanway.

Chapter 13

The long echoing corridor offered only brief respite before it rounded into another vaulted ceremonial room, twice the size of the entrance lobby. My steps slowed as I passed between a dozen white flame torches, each one slightly bigger than the former, sensing eyes watching me from the shadows behind the room's wide pillars. I stole forward like a silent cat, too vulnerable without my slingshot or dart tube.

'I've been waiting for you, Talia.'

I tensed, feeling as though my air had been poisoned. It was a voice I'd come to associate with hatred and violence, a voice that haunted my nightmares and had stolen nearly everyone I loved. My blood darkened as I lifted my head high and stalked out to the centre of the empty floor, my bare feet padding like a forest animal's.

'And all alone? How extraordinary that an unarmed feral girl should be able to outwit four of my guards so easily ... but then, you always did like to make an entrance, didn't you?'

My eyes alighted on his sardonic figure, reclining on a luxurious settle in the middle of a podium bridging the top half of the ceremonial room. It looked to be some sort of dais or stage.

We locked eyes momentarily before I looked around slowly

and defiantly. He'd mown my people down in cold blood, and I would rather die now than give him any idea of the fear dousing my veins.

I returned my gaze to him, and watched, as he reached out and selected a plump, ripened grape, before proceeding to peel it slowly and deliberately with a sharp paring knife.

'Let's just say I prefer my own company,' I returned baldly.

He leered across the space, with barely concealed excitement. He'd been relishing this moment, and I could tell my calm irritated him. He scrutinized me, closing down the days that had passed since we were in his room. Alone. When I was powerless and his to malign. I'd hated him then, and I hated him now. Some things didn't change.

I set my jaw. Refusing to let him know how he unsettled me.

Silently I looked across to the woman beside him and fought the memory of the Flavium archway collapsing, of staring up through scattered debris and choking dust at a baying crowd – and her triumphant face.

She was young yet mordant, her dark hair pulled back in a tight spiral and every contour of her body clad in rich purple Pantheonite regalia. She was reclining as well but I wasn't deceived. Every line of her body was alert, and her expression was dark and sour as uncorked wine. If anything, she was more dangerous than Octavia or Cassius because she wasn't clouded by revenge. She was interested only in hard science and her preying eyes missed nothing.

'Livia … what a pleasure.' I smiled sardonically.

Max? Cassius insisted he join a special investigation project, back at base.

Her last words danced between us as though she had just spoken them aloud, rather than at Octavia's research centre. Her face twisted momentarily, and I knew she was recalling them too. That she'd used them, like weighted darts, for maximum impact.

Then a strange, sonorous cry interrupted the moment,

103

diverting my gaze to a golden perch to the far right of the dais where a small winged rodent returned my regard without blinking. It was no bigger than a rabbit, with a reptilian snout, spotted front paws and a pair of small downy wings that it kept fluttering in a vain attempt to escape its chains. The tiny beast lifted its small crested head to the air, and released another cry that grated against my nerves. It sounded disturbingly like a shrill human scream trapped inside an oropendola's hiss, and when it turned its attention back on me, its rust-coloured eyes burned with confused fury.

I sucked in a sharp breath, reality dousing my limbs.

More chimerae? It didn't look like Hominum chimera, *but hybrid species trials had to be Voynich work.*

'Where is he?'

My voice was surprisingly steady, and Cassius's opal-black eyes narrowed to slits. He reached for another grape languorously, torturously, but it gave me the opportunity to assess my space the way I would in the forest, and right now they were telling me this lair was full of secrets.

The chamber was no less ornately decorated than the outer frescoed room, and fortified by a ring of stone-white pillars. But this one smelled different, and I knew why instantly. Beneath the heady aroma of burning lavender oil and sweet, overripe fruit was a scent I knew as well as I knew the forest. It was the scent of animal life. And as if to answer my thoughts there was a swift flurry of movement among the shadows beyond the pillars – a heavy dragging sound, accompanied by a soft hiss that pushed me onto the balls of my feet.

Cassius glittered as I shot a look into the gloom. Long rectangular shapes lined the dark walls, shapes that looked too much like the animal tanks and cages in the main laboratory.

What could possibly be so special that he'd brought them here for his personal observation?

I knew, of course. Even if I hadn't seen the tanks, the small double-lidded chimera shrieking its protest to the vaulted ceiling had already confirmed my suspicions.

I'd given him the last part of the jigsaw: the keyword. Requiem: Mass of the Dead. Cassius now owned every ancient genetic secret within the Voynich. And the Cassius in the square, wearing the crown of flames and proclaiming his own divineness to all Pantheon was closer to his ambition than ever before, because of me.

The words floated around my head, whispering their poison. *I'd failed.*

And the translation of the Voynich meant only one thing: each of the tanks in the darkness was a golden cage containing a golden prize.

Voynich prizes.

Cassius stood up and clicked his fingers, reading my expression with a rancorous smile. He was revelling in my discovery of his menagerie, and intended to take his revenge as slowly as he could. At his command, torches on the back wall faded up until we could see clearly. I sucked in a breath, not wanting to give him any satisfaction, but unable to drag my eyes away all the same.

Two long back walls of his chamber were lined with perfect, concentric cages – occupied cages – and the creatures staring out at me now left nothing to the imagination. There was a complete nursery of *perfect, miniature, mythical creatures.*

I scanned them swiftly, trying to make sense of the assortment of bodies, limbs, hooked claws and bared teeth. There was what looked to be some kind of achlis, the size of a roe deer with a distorted oversized mouth; and two identical snow-white caladriai, with gleaming pink eyes that bored right through me. I recalled enough of their legend to know they were designed to be carriers of illness, healers of sick people by drawing illnesses into themselves. Somehow, I imagined Cassius had such a purpose in mind for these. An infantile faun nestled in the corner, eyeing me with interest, while beside it, clinging to its bars with tiny pale hands was a dwarf silenus, complete with miniature horse hooves and immature tail.

'Pan,' I whispered, catching my breath painfully.

Next to the silenus, a tiny owl peeped dolefully. It was scuffling in the shadows of its small tank, and sounded just like the night-birds Eli suspended in the nursery baskets from our treehouse living room. But the rat-owls or strix herded into Ludi Pantheonares couldn't have been any less like the forest creatures I loved, and I had no doubt the pitiful creature was destined to grow into some abomination.

Then, next to the owl, was a final tank. Black. Silent. Still.

Why did the silent tanks always scare me the most?

I reeled as the full impact of Cassius's ambition reared its brutal head. It was a form of dark and chaotic mitosis; a monster breeding a new pack of monsters to change all that was natural and untouched in our world. He'd already reduced Arafel to little more than ash. But a second apocalypse was waiting right here in this room, watching me as it stole breath from the natural world to grow.

I saw the flames consuming Arafel all over again. There would be no more trials, no more genetic defects and hesitations. Cassius had the blueprint for an army of mythical creatures, creatures with which he intended to repopulate the world, and the destruction of my home was only the beginning.

I had never been more aware that only a series of golden grills separated my world from the seeds of carnage.

The Voynich could change the face of the earth.

Grandpa had predicted this, and his words had never meant more. Eli's pale face flashed through my head and I sucked in a raspy breath. I hadn't even looked back when I ran after Mum. *Where had he run? Had he survived? And what of any remaining Outsiders?* Cassius would obliterate them all, build a thousand Lifedomes and introduce this growing menagerie to a macabre new world he could control. Which only left one burning question.

Why was I still alive?

I spun around to face them both, vitriol coursing like wildfire. My blood was the only known control over Lake, but he had to have a ready supply of that by now. Which meant there was still something else. And that was my one remaining hope. One I intended to use to its fullest advantage. Bluff or not.

'Where is he?' I repeated, louder, stronger. More feral.

'Ever direct and to the point, Talia. Even when you were unconscious, you had that wilful expression. A surprise really. I would have thought the … removal of your home and foolish Outsider friends would have checked it … just a little.'

He'd left the dais and was headed towards me, his black gladiatorial uniform glinting with a thousand cruel edges. He was assessing everything, and though every cell recoiled at the thought of being unconscious and vulnerable in front of him, I forced my feet to stay their ground.

'Oh yes … I paid you a few visits while you were being batched, but call me old-fashioned, I didn't really enjoy the one-sided nature of our conversation … Even when you were persuaded to give up that which you held as most precious in the world.'

A flash of memory. Searing pain, poised on the edge of a looming black void, murmuring a word, giving up the keyword. Out of fear, self-protection … and weakness.

I felt myself grow pale, and my gaze lowered as he moved towards me. I was so ashamed I could run, run and keep running for ever. And he knew.

'Oh yes, Talia, you gave me the greatest gift of all. All for the love of one human, and rather a squalid example of one, if I may say so. At least the gladiator has his uses.'

I froze, before slowly raising my stubborn chin. Cassius could taunt me all he liked, but no one insulted my mother. *And he said 'has'.*

He paused to look back at Livia, relishing every second of his

107

own performance, and yet clearly confused by my consistent refusal to cede to him and beg for my life.

'And do tell me,' he added, 'what has a girl with presumably no weapon of her own, save for her bare hands, done with four of my most able gladiators? They are, presumably, still alive? Or do I need yet another household reorganization?'

His voice rose dangerously and sure enough four uniformed gladiators, including Grey and the peacock, shuffled into view. They had to have been waiting in the corridor, putting off an appearance unless it was absolutely necessary. Their pale fearful faces flickered in the torchlight, but I quashed any feelings of pity; they'd had their chance.

'Ahh, how nice of you both to join us at last, and what a shame you can't stay. Throw them to the dogs.'

It was a simple command, but one loaded with finality as twice the number of guards melted out from the gloom beyond the pillar on the opposite side of the room. I swore under my breath. I should have known Cassius would have an army in the shadows, waiting to do his bidding.

I pushed up onto the balls of my feet, ready to use the brief disruption to my own advantage. To look for escape. And then sank back down again. Standing by and letting four grown men be torn to pieces by molossus dogs twice the size of forest wolves was too much. Despite everything.

'Really, Cassius? Still needing to prove your control by spilling innocent blood? Guess lies and propaganda will only do so much, huh?'

The words were out of my mouth, whether I wished them free or not.

Cassius turned back, the furious twist across his features saying everything. We were back in his room, hunter and prey, only I wouldn't play my role and I'd called his bluff in front of his men.

'Tell me, when did you rise above the rank of vermin in this Civitas?' he snarled. 'You're nothing but the dregs of an under-race that is very nearly exterminated. We have never been closer to re-creating a species worthy of inhabiting this recovering planet, unlike your kind who did nothing but drive it to the brink of destruction!'

My eyes narrowed, despite everything. This was the closest I'd come to unpicking his real motivation. Apart from warped, narcissistic 9-ambition.

'Yes!' he hissed stepping towards me. 'I know you always believed it was about the science, that there was no moral purpose to my work. And you stand there, with your ignorant, wilful belief that Nature got it all right.

'Have you never considered there could be a better creator? Why leave it to the whimsical nature of natural selection and archaic food chains? What if it was always waiting for mankind to seize the day, and redesign a more efficient new-world order?

'Why wouldn't we know best? We have the most advanced brains of any animal species, and now we have direct experience of how much chaos and destruction that species can create. Why wouldn't anyone with brilliant science at their fingertips change it all?'

He was close now, and entirely absorbed in his own rhetoric.

'You see, Talia,' he breathed more softly, 'Thomas was absolutely right about one thing – the outside world *is* recovering.'

I started at Cassius's candid admission of something he had always denied so vehemently.

'It's just recovering with the wrong sort of life.'

He paused to laugh, a sound that soured every living cell in my body.

'You don't need to look quite so tragic, beautiful Talia.' He tipped his head to one side as though analysing a laboratory specimen. 'You see my plan makes absolute, scientific sense. Original, Outsider DNA – your DNA – is full of genetic weakness. Cells are loaded with memories that foreshadow life, and taint it. Conditions and fears that were experienced by your ancestors have the ability to scar your genetic memory, and control your present life.

'But with the help of our new Biotechnology Programme, we are creating individuals unfettered by hereditary conditions and weaknesses.'

His eyes were alight with feverish delirium, while his voice was shrill with passion. From the corner of my eye, I watched Livia stand and begin descending the steps towards us.

'And now I have succeeded where Octavia failed. I will be known as the Imperator who deciphered the Voynich, and the hand that sowed the seed of a new world stronger than anything before. It will be a world of order and structure, of hierarchy and control. A world that will never descend into the Great War chaos the originals wrought upon the earth.

'My new species will be a worthy inheritor of the outside world, and they will look to only one Emperor-God for guidance and protection.'

Livia was approaching now, stepping quietly across the floor towards Cassius, her expression giving no more away than it ever did. She placed her cool hand upon Cassius's forearm with practised ease, before looking back at me with duplicitous eyes. And suddenly I glimpsed the real power balance between them.

Throughout the ages, crowns have been seized and overthrown, but for real power look to the ones behind the thrones, look to the ones who mop their brow.

Grandpa's wisdom had never been more apt. She was playing Cassius, biding her time, I was sure of it.

'Guards!'

Livia's cool tone echoed around the space. It was a voice that offered no hope of distraction or second chances.

I ran my eyes around the space for something, anything I could use to stall the moment. The tiny chimera lifted its head in disgruntlement, and released another shrill cry as two more guards stepped out from the shadows.

Then I stilled. Not because of Cassius or Livia, but because of the unmistakable gait of one of the athletic guards looming closer with every step. And for a second the world drained away, leaving just the two of us in this vast soulless room.

He was dressed like every other gladiator, and his striking black helmet visor was shuttered down, leaving only a pair of forest-green eyes and strong jaw on view. But it was a stubborn jaw I'd fought too many times not to recognize now.

'Max,' I whispered hoarsely.

My lips formed the shape of his name woodenly, out of practice. And the breath that escaped me was barely a breath at all, more a ragged expulsion of every flickering hope I'd clung to since awakening.

I'd suspected his presence in the Prolet cave, wanted it to be true even, but it was all so dreamlike I hadn't fully believed it. *I'd watched him fall, an arrow in his spine.* Yet here he was, standing before me. Free and working. For Cassius.

He didn't flinch, even when my eyes caught his. The jade luminescence that had always spoken of Arafel, of the whispering trees that had wrapped their sheltering arms around our home, had gone. In their place, only a dulled moss-green existed, observing me with little interest before looking away again. Who was he?

Barely blinking, barely alive, barely Max.

A cry, like that of a speared bird, escaped me. Incarceration, injuries, even torture I could have taken. But not this. Not a Max drained of every living memory that made him the boy I remembered, that made him one of the last real Outsiders.

'No!'

I reached forward and grabbed his helmet, trying to force his visor up and unmask him.

'Max! It's me, Tal! You have to remember! Do you hear me? You were in the fight in the cathedral. You ran with Aelia … and you were shot in the back … by this man, your so-called Emperor!'

111

My words made a fierce, sibilant sound as I forced them into the vast space, but Max only jerked away, leaving me clutching dead air.

An eerie, curious laugh filled the air.

'The power of science to salvage a body and control a brain. It's breath-taking isn't it?'

I turned my face towards Livia. She was much younger than Octavia had been, but her ambition was already written into her soft features, hardening them and creating a veil over her view of the world. Like a cloak of smoke. Like the burning grey embers of my forest home.

Grandpa, Faro, Pan, Eli, Aelia, Mum. Arafel was little more than ash; the last Outsiders were being forced to work with Prolet slaves … She didn't get to steal my best friend too.

Before I could help it my foot was punching high, landing in the middle of her chest with impressive accuracy and speed, even for an Arafel hunter. I watched with real satisfaction as she staggered backwards, winded. Instantly Max and the other guard seized my arms, twisting them behind my back and upwards, making me double over in pain.

'You sold your soul and for what?' I railed as Livia composed herself, her pale forehead veined with shock.

'You and Cassius steal life from the world,' I gasped, 'and you warp and malign until what you hold in your hands no longer resembles anything that should be breathing.

'Don't you get it? What makes the outside so unique is its *imperfections*, its persistence and resilience despite the odds. Life that bears no resemblance to itself has no more guarantee of sustainability than any of us. Every time you change the DNA – a cut here, a morphing there – you tamper with all the fine checks and balances nature has taken millions of years to know.

'You say you are giving the earth a future, but you are decimating it, cell by cell, and in the end what is left will rise up in an army of shadows and consume you!'

My fury spilled into the air, and for just a moment there seemed to be a real silence of consideration. Before slow, languorous laughter.

I jerked my head around, despite the spiral of pain claiming my twisted arms. Cassius had reclimbed the dais steps, and was unchaining the yellow-eyed chimera that arched its back with a delighted screech, before scrambling up his arm to perch on his shoulder. He turned to face me, his eyes emotionless, like dead embers.

'The problem with spirited speeches, Talia, is that they so often overlook basic facts. You see, Livia knows only one creator. Me. She is a product of Pantheon, and one of our most successful projects. Her natural home is this dome, and her DNA was modified at fusion point … like Augustus before he went rogue. Livia's test group has been much more successful, and she's unlikely to be voided. And that's my point.'

I didn't miss the shadow flitting across Livia's face as he paused to caress the tiny chimera, which shuddered before fixing its eyes on me.

'Only those who meet a precise and exacting genetic premium will be selected for repopulation outside. The rest will live a useful life here, supporting our primary Biotechnical Programme function – the pursuit of perfect DNA.

'You must understand, the Great War made three things very evident: who remains is as unfit to populate our earth as who preceded it. Rogue life is … irritatingly persistent, and never learns. And what other species is stupid enough to kill the very planet on which they depend?

'The civilization I am building will aspire to so much more. Imagine, a world where your genetic blueprint is your only passport. No more disease, no more war, no more defects or weaknesses. A gene pool that will be strong, valiant and uncompromising. Like Atticus, my son, who has lately sworn blood allegiance to Isca Pantheon, and will lead the repopulation when we have confirmation that the outside has been thoroughly cleansed. 'Even you, a feral Outsider without hope of ever experiencing such power, has to appreciate its utopian ambition.

'And I will be its author.'

I clenched my nails into the palms of my hands, despite the burn up my forearms from the guards' twist.

It was the first I'd heard mention of Atticus since the fight in the cathedral, since the moment he'd chosen his father – despite everything.

'What of the others?' I growled, refusing to listen a second longer.

I'd glimpsed Therry in the Prolet workforce, but nearly sixty young Prolets had escaped Pantheon into the old Roman tunnels. The giant desiccated spider that was Ludi Pantheonares flickered through my head, and I tensed.

'What did you do with the rest, Cassius?'

My question hung in the air as he picked a grape and held it up to the hybrid reptile perched on his shoulder. I watched it carefully. It was only a juvenile but anyone could see it had the potential to be huge and powerful.

'Always chasing after the underdog, Talia,' he sighed, replacing the chimera on its stand and making his way slowly back down the dais steps. 'It makes you so weak and predictable.'

'But if it will appease you, the Prolet children are back where Prolet children belong, after revaccination … and a little distribution.'

I baulked as nausea climbed my throat. I had no doubt *distribution* translated as Prolet slavery or live bait for his menagerie.

'Max?' I ground out next, determined to know the whole. 'What have you done to Max?'

And even though he was the one holding me, twisting my arms so tightly I could barely breathe, he didn't so much as flinch or acknowledge his name. *Why hadn't he resisted the vaccine at all?* A cold sweat broke out across my neck and shoulders. I couldn't let myself think of a world where he never came back.

'Ah yes Maximus – you should be proud, Talia! He is proving exemplary in the Gladiatorial Training Programme. It seems certain Outsiders can be of use, once vaccinated of course. His will be a … particular honour.'

I twisted to look up at Max's inflexible profile. His golden cheek was tight and unflinching, and his familiar frame, honed by years of work as a treehouse builder, fitted the proud Roman uniform he wore like a glove. And yet he might as well have been wearing his death shroud.

A wave of wildfire ripped through me. August was gone, Mum barely knew me and now Max was just an empty shell of the best friend he used to be. All the memories, visceral building blocks that defined me, were crumbling to grey ash – like Arafel.

It was enough.

'Let's see exactly what blood to blood means,' I seethed, channelling all my remaining anger into one swift downward movement. The burn was agony, given the iron clasp around my forearms, but it worked.

Wit and timing can be victors over strength, Talia.

Grandpa's words whispered through the chamber as I dived between Cassius and Livia, and sprinted towards the dais.

'Guards!' Cassius's voice rose in irritation.

He knew all the exits were blocked, but I wasn't looking to escape. That was what he expected, and he already thought I was predictable.

I was on top of the dais with a single leap, and sprinting towards the golden stand, conscious I had only a few seconds' advantage. And although Max's footsteps fell in behind my own like a shadow, there was no sense of comfort to their rhythm this time. I reached the stand and made a grab for my intended quarry – the infantile chimera, its tiny wings outstretched in furious objection as my hands closed around its scaly neck.

'What precisely do you think you can do with it?' Cassius's

voice rose in irritation. 'We have its DNA, replicated and stored hundreds of times over, and now I have the correct coding for *Hominum chimera*, there are no secrets left, Talia!' He turned to the guards. 'Seize her! Use the force you need but don't kill her … not yet!'

I glanced at him, his black eyes flashed with rising anger.

My blood was the only reason I was still here, and yet with Pantheon's technology it was clear Cassius could synthesize it ten times over. *So why keep me alive?* Unless there was something about it that couldn't be replicated. And all at once I knew that was exactly what it was.

I thrust my wrist up to the tiny complicated creature's mouth. It latched on instantly with impressive power, its serrated jaws perforating my skin without hesitation.

'Well, let's find out, shall we?' I snarled through the pain and adrenaline, watching the way Cassius's expression changed.

Opal eyes no longer mocking or satirical, but furious, and something else besides. *Was it fear?* The chimera was drinking, its wings slowly deflating as it took its fill greedily. And it felt strangely natural.

'Stop her!' Livia instructed shrilly.

I didn't miss the fear in her voice either, or the way she was backing away to the exit, and a strange curiosity filled me. As though I were the one feeding on a new source of strength. What was it my blood could do that made them so nervous?

The only known control for Hominum chimera.

Max was hesitating in front of me, mesmerized by the sight of the locked beast, as though it was some kind of sacred act. Then the room started to spin as the chimera's jaws gripped with more strength. It was gulping now, its tiny iridescent scales bulging each time it swallowed. I imagined my blood sliding down its narrow throat, filling its fire-belly, fuelling its fury. I reached out to stroke its spines, which quivered at my touch.

Whatever this madness, there was such a feeling of peace, of

116

wholeness, of home, that I wondered at not having discovered it before. I was conscious of slipping my other hand beneath its stomach, of trying to support it as it drank.

'Seize her!'

I watched, as though from a distance, as one of the guards clamped the beast around its throat, forcing it to release me. Then he lifted the chimera away, which screamed its protest to every corner of the temple.

'Restrain them both!' Cassius raged from the floor, while Livia seemed to have floated further away than ever.

Guards were around me in a second, and Max was pinioning my arms in a fresh vice, but it didn't matter. I was strangely empty of fire now, while the screaming mini beast was purple with rage, its lips stained with blood and face straining from lack of oxygen.

I knew I shouldn't care, and yet I did. My heart ached with sorrow that its young life was going to be extinguished in front of me, and the feeling was more than a moment's amity; it was real.

Black to black. Dust to dust.

I reeled. And at exactly the same moment, the tiny chimera spread its wings and expelled a raucous cry that was in no way final. With a surge of strength, it flapped harder and harder, creating waves of wind through the space that unsteadied us all.

As it began. The chimera was growing before our eyes. Breathtakingly, exponentially. It was the size of a cat, then a dog and now a wolf. I stared, transfixed by the transformation taking place before my eyes. A transformation I had effected – with my blood. The guard holding the growing chimera was forced to release it. It landed with a disgruntled thump and shook out its wings as it drew hoarse, greedy breaths.

There was shouting towards the back of the room as Grey and the rest of the guards under arrest tried to take advantage of the distraction. I was vaguely aware of a fight breaking out, of Max's proximity, of Livia's disappearance and Cassius's infuriated retreat towards the exit.

'Restrain them!' Cassius barked again, and a half-dozen more uniforms closed around me, locking me inside a circle with the growing chimera, but oddly, I knew it didn't matter. I was safe.

More than that, *I was in control.*

A slow thrill spread throughout my body as the creature turned to bare its reddened canines at its first captor, who was slowly backing off, hands held high in submission. The creature, now the size of a bull, turned to look at me, its yellow eyes flashing with raw gratitude.

I understood. It was no longer Cassius's pet. I had set it free and given it sustenance. It was mine to command, and it was the most natural feeling in the world.

'You alone must bear the responsibility, Talia … Thomas hid something in your bloodline … just what is it that makes you so special …'

Whatever the control was, it wasn't just my physical blood, which was the only reason Cassius hadn't thrown me to the strix already. *It was in me*, in my genetic memory and nature. Somehow Thomas's chimera control had become part of my Outsider nature, and that was still something Cassius's Biotechnology Programme hadn't been able to replicate. The thought was intoxicating.

There was another hideous cry as the chimera, now bigger than a molossus hound, rounded on its original captor guard. They crashed to the floor, the guard's chest compressed visibly beneath the weight of its oversized griffin claws. His head lolled to one side, his eyes bulbous and face dark with strain.

'Don't just stand there, I said restrain it!' Cassius roared as the guards around me hesitated.

Max loosened his grip on my arms to make a grab for his Diasord, just as I shot out a hand to still him. The familiarity of my instinct nearly undid me, and I sensed his hesitation. He looked down just as the creature cried out again before sinking its wide, razored jaws around the guard's throat. There was a gurgling noise while his legs writhed and kicked, but I could tell it was already too late.

'Come what may, nature finds a way,' I whispered.

And there it was. A moment's confusion, a tightening across his forehead, subconscious recognition from a place the vaccine had failed to reach. It was fleeting but there, and a flare of hope tore through me.

'Max?' I whispered, just as Cassius bellowed.

'Talia!'

I spun to face him, and he was eyeballing me intently, the snake in a man's skin, the most vile hybrid of all.

'Call it off and I will cut you a deal.'

And even though he was standing beneath the exit, his face was pale, his eyes like pieces of flint and thin lips locked in fury. The recently arrested guards were now forming a tight defensive pack around him. I smiled slowly. This was a first. *Cassius was scared.*

'And why should I believe you?' I responded, scarcely daring to believe I'd stumbled upon a real chance.

It was all there at the forefront of my mind; Max falling with Aelia, the moment we watched Aelia and Eli sink into the glass river, the perilous climb over the North Mountains, the risk I'd carried right into the heart of Arafel, Arafel in flames, Mum taken, the young Prolets, and now, the boy I grew up with, my only other possible ally in this room … no longer knew me.

What possible deal could he make that would turn the clock back? How could I undo that much pain?

The mauled guard went completely still and the creature raised its head, eyeballing the rest, who were already scattering. All except Max. Who, for some reason seemed immobilized behind me. I shot him a glance; his countenance was stony, unlike the rest. He wasn't afraid of death. But then he never was.

We all die in the end, Tal, just not here, not tonight.

They were Max's words, whispered in the treehouse one night

119

when the nightmares wouldn't go away. It was so strange how words could develop a lifeblood of their own.

I lifted a calm hand to the slathering chimera who was eyeing Max with interest, before backing down on its spotted haunches. Its growth seemed to have slowed down at around the size of a small elephant and my thoughts flew to Lake. If I could have this much control over an infant chimera, what influence could I have over *Hominum chimera*, the mother of all mythological creatures?

And was this really what was at stake?

I flung a look of victory at Cassius. Of course it was.

'Vaccine antidotes – for Max, my mother, Prolets, for everyone!' I ground out.

Grey's eyes reached across the space, pleading from beneath his visor and I felt my resolve waver. I gritted my teeth.

'And a pardon for all prisoners of Pantheon ...'

The visor lifted a fraction, enough to convey his silent thanks.

'The end of the Voynich trials, safe passage from Isca Pantheon for whoever wishes it – and your word you will leave the outside alone for the rest of your unnatural days. Grant me these things, and I will spare your life.'

Cassius smirked, though his face had greyed. The promise I'd made to Prince Phaethon floated briefly through my head, and I wondered what would happen if I failed. Would he persuade Eli to return to the icy depths with him? *If he was still alive?* A dozen pairs of lash-less ovoid eyes appeared in my thoughts and I pushed them away. I couldn't think of them now.

'Look up, Talia,' Cassius responded softly.

I cast a swift glance up and cursed softly. There was a high balcony running the circumference of the room, and from this vantage I could see it was lined with more guards, all armed and pointing their weapons down – at me and the chimera that had turned to gorge on the dead guard.

He signalled swiftly and something black flew through the air towards the feeding creature. I opened my mouth but I was already too late, and the creature and dead guard were pinned beneath a mesh so tight it could barely move.

The whole room breathed.

'One more command from me and you and the creature will join your friends in Hades anyway,' he continued smoothly, regaining control. 'And I hope I need not remind you your mother is still my guest?'

I gritted my teeth, furious with myself for not letting the chimera finish him when it could. *And how could I demand anything while he still held Mum?*

'But I have to admit, that is an unsatisfactory outcome for me, and you have demonstrated something very valuable today. You see, I still have some need of you … presently.'

'I know!' I scathed. 'My blood isn't everything is it? Sometimes the science isn't enough. You need me too. The control is in me!'

I refused to look skywards again. If I died now, it would be nothing but a release anyway.

His eyelids lowered and a slow smile spread across his face.

'You are … an insurance, Talia. Chimera control was never Thomas's area of academic research – it was mine. And though he decoded the cipher, and translated the Voynich coding for *Hominum chimera*, his synthesized control was rudimentary to say the least. Who knows how it has morphed and imprinted itself into cell memory through generations of uncontrolled feral breeding? My attempts to make you compliant seem to have failed, but I admire your spirit nonetheless, and as a benevolent Imperator, I am prepared to make a counter-offer.'

He paused to throw the guards on the balcony one of his over-wide smiles.

'Work with my team until we understand the control. And when Lake is located, I will spare your mother and grant you both safe passage from Pantheon. For the love of Nero, I'll even throw in the antidote for your friend. But let's do this the Roman way – a wager first!'

My jaw ached from the strain of trapping my tongue.

'A charioteer's challenge!' he boomed to a weak cheer of support from above.

'Maximus versus a charioteer of my own choice. What's fairer than that? Twelve circuits of the Ludi Cirque Pantheonares and if Maximus wins you will have all I have outlined. Immunity, Talia, imagine that! You will have the protection for your family for the rest of your Outsider days. Come, who can say fairer than that?

'And may all those here today bear witness to my honour,' he added softly.

'And if Max loses?' My voice was brittle, knowing the stakes were going to be so stacked as to be nigh-on impossible. Max didn't know me, I had no idea what Ludi Cirque Pantheonares involved and refusal would mean certain death anyway – for me, Max and the young chimera.

'Lose and you forfeit … everything,' he drawled, his eyes narrowing to slits.

122

Chapter 14

Ludi Cirque Pantheonares Charioteer.

It was such an unlikely title for an Arafel boy with a weakness for apricots. I looked out at the elongated charioteers' track, watching the preparations for the third consecutive week. It was a strange purgatory, with only a small window on the world that was likely to witness the end for both Max and me. Behind the endless rows of tiered seating grew a wall of solid white stone. It glittered beneath Pantheon's bright white lights, contrasting with the gated arches at both ends of the arena, while the large island in the centre housed a series of ominous closed structures. In truth, while Ludi Cirque felt less a feeding pit than the Flavium and Ludi, the arena still looked and felt all too familiar.

I ran a finger down the transparent pane that separated me from the charioteers. It was made from the same substance as my previous holding cell and was deceptively strong. I knew that much because I'd already tried to kick it out.

A shrill alarm pierced the air, as my finger hit the bottom of the window and slid along to the corner. Max would be impressed. There were no gaps or draughts, unlike my old shutters that spilt thin ladders of light on my bedroom floor.

'Detainees, robe.'

I knew the routine by heart. Swiftly I pulled a loose day-robe over my shift. It was soft, white and a vast improvement on the crisp laboratory tunics.

I glanced down the room and sure enough, my cubicle walls were already fading down, revealing a row of similar-looking beds and their incarcerated owners. My gaze swept the unit covertly.

We were all too aware of those who disappeared overnight, leaving only a pile of sterile bedding awaiting a new occupant.

'Detainees, wash.'

The anodyne voice controlled routine in here, and it seemed those of us detained were neither prisoners nor free to leave, but something in between. I picked up my towel and crossed the room towards the row of washbasins at the back.

I was certain Cassius would pit his prize charioteer against Max. But if Max did by some miracle win, what then? Could I really trust Cassius would honour his promise to let us walk free? And for how long when he was planning on redesigning the world as we knew it? What sort of Arafel could survive in a world that no longer resembled itself?

Would it be a worse crime to run away like one of Atticus's rats, when the young Prolets had tried so hard to strike out against Pantheon? What of every man, woman and child who'd been born into Prolet servitude and found their free will violated? What of the dark-tanked room in the laboratories, filled with tiny gelatinous beings? *What if Max should die here on the parade ground?* Cassius still held Mum and there was no answer to my request for access every time I was escorted to his laboratories for testing.

'Detainees, wait in line until wash facilities are free.'

My head hadn't stopped for three weeks. Mum always used to say family came before all else – but how could I trade her precious life for so many others, without insanity following like a curse?

I looked up and nodded at my neighbour, who responded in kind.

During daylight hours they let us mingle, although there was little real interaction. It seemed the point of this particular incarceration was to build anticipation among combatants, because we were all destined for Ludi Cirque in one way or another, and no one was taken in by the faux comfort of our surroundings.

Clean beds, bright walls, good food and warm clothing – these were luxuries compared with my previous situation – but the grand entrance doors were still security coded and guarded by an army of grunting satyrs.

'Zero eight fifteen, breakfast.'

A mutter of interest invaded the room. The orderly breakfast line was always the first open chance to see who else may have joined us overnight. My fellow detainees were by no means all soldiers or gladiators who'd fallen from grace, there was also a steady stream of pitiful-looking Prolets too. Both male and female. It took me a few days to interpret their furtive glances and tangible nerves, but then it struck me.

They were Prolets who'd also voided the vaccine.

It was hope. They were the tiny proportion of the population whose DNA had somehow denied the chemicals trying to claim their free will. Their Prolet-born DNA had to be more like my own, more like Outsider DNA, than I'd imagined possible.

Here in Circus Pantheonares, citizens of Isca Pantheon are given the opportunity to demonstrate their loyalty to the Civitas.

Cassius's rhetoric rang out regularly from the planetary screens, reminding citizens of highlights of the week's Ludi Games. Occasionally we would hear a faint cheer from the Flavium too, and I realized this arena had to be within a stone's throw of Cassius's other source of entertainment.

'Hi.' I nodded a quick smile at Servilia, with whom I'd struck up a monosyllabic friendship. We always seemed to end up next to one another in queues, and through snatched conversations, I'd gleaned the bare bones of her Prolet background.

'Hi,' she murmured, stepping into place, keeping her head low.

125

She was a slight brunette with big darting eyes, and every now and then she would put me in mind of someone, but I could never recall who.

We were ever-watchful of the satyr guards, of their suspicious eyes when a conversation went on too long or grew too animated. And these ink-blue creatures were nothing like the old sentries in Isca Prolet, who once guided me through the underground tunnels. They were part of the new breed who guarded the Prolet work shifts, with bulging arms and iron fists they weren't afraid to use. Even on Pantheonite citizens.

'I've been scheduled for the baths again,' I whispered.

Our schedules varied on a daily basis, and mine had become a mix of laboratory tests, eating and rather unusually of late, bathing.

Servilia blinked in acknowledgement as she leaned in close, filling a bowl with papaya, mango and nuts. The food in here was bountiful, but only emphasized the fact we weren't expected to walk away from Ludi Cirque.

'Me too, our time is coming,' she muttered.

I nodded. Neither of us were deceived. Cassius was fattening his lambs so he could play the benevolent Emperor: the Emperor who fed his people, the Emperor who bathed his people, the Emperor who gave offenders the chance to prove their loyalty – before feeding them to his dogs. It was a carefully orchestrated illusion, maintaining Pantheonite belief in his justice, blinding them to the horror of his violence and making his lies plausible.

And they fell for it every single time.

I nodded under the weighty stare of a nearby satyr, and picked up a crisp bread roll.

***

'Detainees listed for the baths may collect their belongings.'

Servilia and I stood up separately, conscious our breakfast chat

126

hadn't gone unnoticed. I stacked my plastic breakfast bowl, and collected another towel before joining the small group at the bath doors.

We kept our eyes low as we followed the satyr guards from the unit, not wishing to attract any more unwanted attention. The connecting corridors had no exits anyway; we knew that much already.

At first I'd thought the baths an elaborate metaphor. The notion that Cassius would allow any detainee such a luxury was almost too dubious to believe. And when the satyrs had gathered us the first time, I'd protested vociferously, recalling the lizard-skin girl in the laundry. It was only when Servilia intervened, reassuring me of their genuine existence, that I consented to go without being dragged. It had also sealed our unlikely friendship.

'Today's quota.'

The satyr barked our arrival at the Prolet woman who opened the ornate bath doors, and I inhaled deeply, let the fragrances consume me like memories of a forest jungle far from here. Unexpectedly, the bathing house had become a temporary reprieve from the holding wing routine, and I felt my tensions wane as the woman opened the door to let us enter.

'Please follow.'

The richly decorated, swathed bathing rooms always fascinated me. It was the combination of burning oils, silent waiting women and tables, laden with more fresh fruit and juices than you could eat in a week. It felt like stepping directly into one of Cassius's temple frescos, a strange dream world in the heart of Cassius's lair. And though there was always a sense of waiting for the scorpion's sting, the kindliness of the Prolet women who directed us from room to room steadied me.

'Please enter the water.'

It was a bittersweet escape for a forest girl who'd only ever known the ice water of the lake or tepid monsoon rains. My hair knots were worked through, my tingling skin was massaged with sweet-smelling lotions, and my shoulders were wrapped in soft robes, scented like spring grass. It was almost intoxicating – until I recalled that behind it all, was Cassius. Which made the baths dangerous.

Because they made me forget – like the vaccine.

'It's ceremonial preparation,' Servilia whispered over the water fountain.

'It's customary before racing,' she added, nodding at one of the Prolet women, 'to cleanse at least three times. Out of respect for Ludi Pantheonares, the original celebratory Games, and the Imperator Cassius.'

I grimaced. I'd glimpsed him twice through an observation window over the past three weeks, while enduring a painful chimera trial. My unique control was still proving a mystery, and he remained conveniently deaf to my demands that he allow me to see my mother, which made our agreement feel less plausible every day.

I hadn't asked what had happened to the young chimera, though its screeching appeal as it was dragged away still echoed through me. I told myself it was too valuable to be quieted, that Cassius would want to analyse it alive, but I was consumed with such a darkness an hour later I knew I'd only lied to myself.

The same way I'd lied to myself about August. Had he returned to Arafel only to find it an ashen shell? Had he returned at all?

Once our bathing was complete, we were escorted back to the unit to find the long table groaning under the weight of fresh bread, meat and a selection of fruit trifles and cakes. I shot a swift look at Servilia who raised her eyebrows.

Last week, five detainees had been called out following such a feast: four men and a woman with a furrowed brow and hair the colour of flames. They never returned, and their beds were filled the following morning.

'Did you find out any more?' I whispered against the sound of wooden benches scraping the stone floor.

128

Her sharp darting eyes assessed the room.

'Just the winged boy Therry and the Peronicus sisters ... the ones with a pet griffin?'

I nodded swiftly, recalling the girls playing pick-up stones in the tunnels beneath Isca.

'They're alive ... in service ... domestic.'

She looked away, feigning interest in a towering mountain of melon.

Servilia had been making discreet enquiries of the Prolet women working in the baths after I described the children. She was known to most of them, and seemed to have their confidence. It was such a relief to know most of them were still alive, even if their fate had been Cassius's vaccine. I could still picture them all, their faces so thin and pinched you could see the shadow of their bones beneath. I also knew Therry had managed to reject the vaccine, and had so far remained undetected. *But for how much longer? And what did they do with the children who rejected?*

I gazed out at the bright arena, lost in thought, and my eyes settled on the powerful haunches of the new molossers the guards were exercising. Cassius's favourite pack of slathering watchdogs were bigger than the originals, and dark grey with thick wolfish heads and elongated canines. I knew without question they were the result of more DNA mixing, more Voynich experimentation. *Were these destined for the outside world? What kind of world would it be for a child anyway?*

I reached for a piece of chicken. It was moist, tender and fell apart in my fingers, taking me back to Arafel and home-cooked dinners around Mum's cooking pot.

'And Atticus?' I whispered, ignoring the sudden tightness in my chest.

I poured some apple cordial, spilled it deliberately, and leaned towards Servilia as I mopped the table with a paper towel.

'The Commander General Atticus Aquila lives with the Emperor ... has been declared his official successor ... if that ever happens.'

Servilia's whisper rang in my ears as I stared down at my half-eaten chicken, remembering the boy who'd bitten the head off a rat just to prove his loyalty to the PFF, Aelia's Prolet Freedom Fighters.

Where was that fire now? And what had Cassius done to ensure his compliance?

Suddenly, the unit entrance door bleeped. It was a heavily guarded door that only ever opened to admit new or departing combatants, and everyone swung their head in the direction of the unexpected intrusion. It was a doorway that changed things, unlike the exit that led to the baths.

Four satyrs shuffled in with the new combatant pinioned between them. He seemed small yet deceptively strong, resisting his entry with every fibre of his wiry body, while his neck tattoo danced beneath the bright white lights. *Neck tattoo.* My chest began to thump. It was blue and twisted like a river that reached from his dirty collar up his sinewy neck, making three wolfhounds cavort with delight as he was thrown to the floor.

Wildfire chased my limbs, just as a cool hand closed over my own. A warning hand.

'Have caution.'

Servilia's whisper was barely discernible, yet she was flustered too. I could tell.

'He betrayed us,' I returned hoarsely, not caring who overheard me.

And in a heartbeat I was back in the cathedral with Max, staring up at the figure behind Cassius, at the man who'd lived like a rat in the latrines beneath Isca Prolet only to give up his own people the moment his inked skin was under threat. I could still hear the children's screams ripping through the night air as the black aquila dived, still see the waxen sheen creeping across Aelia's face, and the warmth fading from Max's hands. It was just before August and I were taken, dropped to the icy depths of Isca's river, and brought back from the edge of the abyss by the Oceanids.

130

I'd hoped the man responsible for so much pain had been trampled underfoot by one of Cassius's prized griffins – eaten slowly perhaps. But now I could see now he was alive, and if not well, then at least whole. *What had he lost? When the rest of us had traded so much?*

I could feel the rage swelling within me, and swore as Servilia's slim grip tightened. She was trying to protect me, and didn't realize it was already too late. I closed my eyes in the raw hope that when I opened them again, his sprawled figure would be anywhere else.

But he was still there. As was the moment he told Cassius about the cathedral, spilling the blood of so many innocents and people I loved.

He climbed to his feet, looking dazed, before running his gaze along the wooden lunch table and freezing on the spot. His head swung into reverse, lingering firstly on Servilia and finally me. And the flash of sudden fear on his face said everything.

Somehow he'd managed to evade or reject the vaccine. And I took slow vengeful satisfaction as his realization grew through shock into the sly gleam that seemed to be so natural to him.

I was across the table like a forest cat before he had time to prepare. Head first and claws out, I barrelled into his core, the velocity of my attack powering him backwards against the security door. As the guards' swearing filled the air, I ripped him away from the door and forced him to the floor, the speed of my attack giving him no opportunity to react. Then I was astride his back, my napkin around his throat, before he could so much as gasp my name.

'I hope it was worth it!' I hissed, leaning in so it was just him and me.

He gurgled something unintelligible, clawing at the unrelenting pressure around his throat as a jug of cold water doused us both, and rough hands closed around my upper arms. I kicked out with my feet, so determined to end his squalid little life, but I was no match for a disgruntled satyr.

'Release the combatant!'

The satyr's voice was thick, his powerful grip restricting my blood flow and making my arms feel numb.

'Guess you know what makes me so special now,' I hissed as I was yanked away, my dead arms pinned behind me.

He rubbed his neck, which had turned a satisfying shade of purple, as he clambered up. His eyes were fixed on me, and I was satisfied to see the sly gleam was quite gone.

'Thanks,' he wheedled to the satyr, earning a sharp kick from one of the nearby Pantheonite Guards.

'Silence!'

I shot the guard a look.

'You can release her. Cassius wants a race tomorrow not a parade of the wounded!'

It was Grey. *Tomorrow?* I blinked my acknowledgement as the satyr dropped me with a grunt, the hushed room slowly returning to normal.

'Show's over!' Grey barked, reaching down to haul me to my feet as the satyr pushed Rajid towards one of the empty beds. 'Get on with your lunch.'

I threw them both a look of contempt. Did they really think they could leave him in the same unit and not expect consequences?

'There's a plan.'

I froze as Grey's whisper reached through the low rise of clinking plates and subdued chat.

'Just stay alive.'

***

The clock in the ceiling appeared to be speeding up. Only moments ago it was midnight, and now it was close to 06.00. I still wasn't used to the 24-hour clock all Pantheonites seemed to observe like it was in some way intrinsic to their being. In Arafel

132

we rose when it was light, ate when we were hungry and slept when we grew tired.

But here, time was a jailor too.

I rolled over to stare at the opaque wall, exhausted yet buzzing. Sleep was impossible. I sat up and swung my legs off the bed, before forcing myself to look outside at the arena. The Sweepers were already busy cleaning the track, in preparation for Ludi Cirque later today.

A smaller cart trundled by, drawn by two black winged horses. There were two gladiatorial guards up front and a third riding at the back. But it was the guard seated nearest to me, his proud gleaming uniform catching the arena lights, who held my attention. He wore no helmet and his golden Outsider skin was unmistakable. *Max.*

I struggled to take a breath. It was the first time I'd seen him in weeks and though I knew this day was coming, the reality was a real shock. My heart started to thump as the equipage followed a curve around one end of the track, and disappeared inside a black tunnel. *Max was here.* I swallowed hard. *And the race was today.*

Today was the first day of the rest of our lives, or the last.

The alarm sounded, piercing my thoughts as the walls faded back to semi-transparent. It was the five-minute warning. I reached for my day-robe, before swiftly plaiting my hair and pushing any escaping strands behind my ears. If it was to be our last, I wasn't going to be mistaken for anyone but Talia Hanway, feral Outsider.

'And last rightful keeper of the Book of Arafel,' I muttered beneath my breath.

I nodded at Servilia as the walls disappeared entirely, before narrowing my eyes in the opposite direction. The men slept along the opposite wall and Rajid had been given the unit nearest the baths exit. He was seated on his bed this morning, watching the room with an expression that threatened to ruin my breakfast. I

133

dragged my eyes away, Grey's words echoing through my head. Staying alive started with staying away from Rajid.

As it turned out, Cassius's Guard came before lunch to read the official decree, and combatants could only listen in stony silence as several numbers were selected. Mine came as no surprise.

'Citizen MMDCL! You have accepted a challenge from the Emperor Cassius to prove your honour and allegiance to the Civitas.'

'The Emperor awaits your company at 1500h. Your charioteer has selected colours and you are required to make preparations.'

A second guard thrust out a neat pile of what looked to be folded clothes as I walked forward slowly. The tunic was unlike anything I'd ever seen before. It was indigo blue, with rushes of gold throughout, as though the sun had breathed into it as it was spun. And beneath there was a different material – folded calf-skin leather that looked as soft as down, and finished with a thin, plaited golden belt. I stared at the fine Pantheonite clothes as a million ugly thoughts reared their horns.

Was this part of the trap? To strip me of my identity and dress me up as fine as any of Pantheon's caged birds to prove that I was finally under control? Under his control?

'And if I refuse to wear them?' My voice was gritty.

The first guard lifted his eyebrows in amusement as one behind shifted, eyeballing me, trying to dissuade me from causing a scene. Grey again. I scowled.

'It wouldn't be the first time we've assisted with individual preparations.' The first guard smiled too widely.

Grey's eyes were pleading.

I grabbed the clothes, and bit my tongue, suppressing the impulse to throw their precious clothes back in their faces.

'Citizen MDCLII! You have also accepted an invitation from Emperor Cassius to prove your honour and allegiance to the Civitas.'

His second announcement quieted my blood, and I knew, even before I turned.

'You will accompany the challenger in the faction red Quadriga. Collect your uniform.'

Rajid stood up and sauntered across the room, pausing a pace away with a tentative, toothless nod. He was fresh from the baths and yet, somehow, still managed to reek of old leather and sweat.

Shooting me a wary glance, the second guard took a step forward and thrust a matching indigo uniform at him. It included thick leather gloves and a solid helmet, similar to the one August had first worn in the forest.

I stared, barely processing what was happening. Rajid couldn't ride with Max. He was no better than Cassius's pet – a snake's snake – with no respect for anyone or anything. It was a trap!

'No!' I forced out vehemently so there could be no mistake. 'He can't ride with Max. It has to be me … it was always me!'

'Request declined,' the first guard responded with a glint of a smile. 'The Emperor has issued an extraordinary decree for the Quadriga race today.'

I stared at him, feeling colour drain from my face.

'You have received the greatest honour of the Civitas Citizen MMDCL, and are to join Emperor Cassius on his balcony – as his distinguished guest.'

Chapter 15

I surveyed my appearance in the wall-length mirror opposite. In Arafel's twilight forest there had been no mirrors, only shady pools to offer a glimpse of my sandy hair and dirt-streaked face.

Now, for the first time, I could really look at myself, clad in my enemy's standard. And if there ever had been an Outsider rule book, I knew I was breaking every single one. With my hair smoothed and straight, my nails preened, my forest body poured into an outfit that bore no relation to who I was or what I represented, I was no longer Talia of Arafel, one of the last Outsiders. I was a fake and an imposter. It was as though I had been centrifuged and pushed into a Pantheonite mould, so I finally looked sanitized – *like one of them.*

'*I can now confirm the outbreak in the vermin subspecies has been brought under control,*' I mimicked, watching the way my lips formed the words in the mirror.

The Ludi Cirque bugle sounded somewhere outside the thick walls, and for just a millisecond I was back in Arafel, listening to the ibex horn announce the start of the hunter trials. My mind dragged up the image of its charred white handle protruding from the blackened branches that had once protected my people.

The horn's tapered point, dirtied by smog and battered by the

136

onset of monsoon winds, had barely been visible above a growing layer of ash and debris. I knew because it was one of the images played over and over again by the planetary media system.

'It's time, Talia.'

Servilia's voice was low as she finished tying the thin plaited leather belt under the guard's watch. Thankfully, my Prolet ally had volunteered to help when the guards required a dresser, and she was the only reason I was ready at all.

For the past hour we'd been forced to listen to the arena excitement and ceremony fanfare, and it had done little to steady my nerves.

'Welcome, citizens of Isca Pantheon, to this two hundredth anniversary of Isca Pantheon Ludi, and we have an extraordinary Ludi Cirque celebration today. Chosen charioteers have begun making preparations for this special day and your benevolent Emperor Cassius will himself officiate over the special Ludi charioteer challenge.

'Two gladiatorial knights will compete in one race to determine their honour, valour and allegiance to the state of Isca Pantheon. Whose colour will you fly? Faction red or faction blue? Choose your Quadriga carefully, and book your seats now.'

My pale face stared back accusingly, and I knew I'd played right into Cassius's manipulative hands. *How had I ever agreed to this? To watch Max gamble his life? For me. Again. How had I even thought that this could be a chance? That I had any control while he still held Mum?*

I imagined August's iris-blues crinkling with disappointment.

You were meant to save the whole damned world, he whispered.

The Commander General is dead, Grey echoed from elsewhere.

I closed my eyes, forcing all the voices from my head. I couldn't be distracted, not today of all days, when Max needed me most.

I spread my fingers in a bid to release their tension. Even if Max won, which was unlikely enough with Rajid riding beside him, he still wasn't Max. And if Cassius honoured his promise to let us walk from Pantheon if the dice rolled unexpectedly in his favour, what then? How could there be a future with a second Armageddon stirring?

And yet there was no other path but this now. Cassius's scientists had carried out more tests than I could number, but they still didn't understand the control in my blood, I could tell by the frustration written into their faces. He would still need me when he located Lake. Which meant I had to believe in this wager, and that Max and Mum stood a chance.

'There,' Servilia muttered, her dramatic dark eyes wide with awe. 'You look …

'Like one of them?' I finished tersely, staring straight into the mirror.

My eyes seemed wider, bluer against the indigo of my soft tunic top. It was the only part of the forest left. I fixed on them intently; they swam, opening a brief doorway to Grandpa. He was still there.

Feral means free, Talia, he whispered, wrapping me in Arafel sunlight and filling every vein with the beat of the forest.

'Like a warrior.' Servilia smiled, before shooting a quick look at the guard absorbed in his identifier.

'You have only to stay alive,' she whispered, echoing Grey's words and pressing something into my right hand.

I started as my fingers wrapped around a small wooden item on twine that had become as beloved as my old slingshot, long since lost to the Oceanids. She shook her head before schooling her face and turning away. Swiftly I slipped the item over my head and tucked it out of sight, suddenly better armed than if she had presented me with a broadsword fired in the pit of hell.

It was a hand-carved object that would hold no value for anyone else in the world, and yet there was no equal treasure for me – Max's tiny treehouse dart tube. It had been taken from me, when I was under the influence of the vaccine, and I'd given up on ever seeing it again. Now, the feel of its small solid shape against my skin – weapon and symbol of hope in one – lifted my heart. And snug inside the tube, my swift fingers had made out the shape of a single carved dart, weighted perfectly with tiny Komodo teeth.

One of Ida's darts?

I lifted my eyes incredulously. Servilia was fixing a long piece of gold brocade in my hair. I wouldn't let her dress it the Pantheonite way, and had asked her to plait it instead, but on this small adornment I'd relented. She caught my gaze in the mirror.

'How?' I mouthed, hoping she could read the gratitude in my eyes.

'Rajid.'

I lip-read her unexpected response as the bugle sounded again. This time it was joined by a litany of other instruments, creating an imperial fanfare that brought three new guards to the door.

'Tempus movere!'

The words seemed to swallow the room, and as I turned, blood pounding in my ears, I thought I caught a glimpse of double-lidded honey eyes, just watching and waiting.

***

The triumphant announcements grew steadily louder and more pompous as we climbed the wide, marble staircase that led to Cassius's balcony. And with each step, a more complete view of the arena grew through the transparent external wall.

Its elongated appearance was at odds with the circular Flavium, stirring memories of tales about an ancient Roman chariot-racing stadium situated somewhere between the Aventine and Palatine hills of Rome. It was a place where the real Emperors of Rome meted out justice and punishment, dressed as entertainment, and few charioteers walked away alive. I doubted Cassius had more noble motives.

139

I studied the arena as carefully as I could, Bereg's training running through my head. *Hunting or defending, know your territory as well as you can. Lack of knowledge is the first step to failure, Talia.*

And although the Ludi Cirque track moved further away with each step, it was still much larger than had first appeared through my unit window. The tiered seats had to support more than 100,000 souls when all was said and done.

I swallowed the stone in my throat. My new leather boots felt awkward against my skin and restricted my Outsider feet. And yet the tiny dart tube, nestling beneath my indigo tunic, was a real piece of Arafel – a piece of the forest, shaped by the sun and a pair of golden hands who deserved so much more than this. Who deserved so much more than a ghost girl who, for some unfathomable reason, *was still here*, and was now determined to thwart Cassius with every breath left in her body.

The only thing that made sense.

The crowd stirred as a single charioteer, dressed in indigo blue from head to foot, emerged from one of the tunnels and walked directly across to a liveried chariot. I baulked as the world slewed, before running towards the glass wall separating me from the outside, and pummelling my fists as hard as I could.

'Max!' I yelled desperately. 'I'm here, Max! Max, look up!'

But of course, he couldn't hear me, and even if he could there was no guarantee he would actually look. *Why should he when he didn't even know me?*

Seconds later, rough hands seized my arms, bruising them and dragging me away, forcing me on and up the grand staircase that seemed as though it might never end until, finally, we came face to face with a pair of ornate carved doors.

The gods of Mars and Vulcan looked back at me, smiling in that same satirical way Cassius had perfected, and holding a small sphere between them. It was clearly intended to be the world, and above the tiny globe, a fierce draco-chimera with double-lidded eyes threw out her wings.

140

I yanked my arms away from the surprised guards and set my jaw stubbornly. Lake wasn't his yet. And neither was I.

'Think I can take it from here,' I hissed, grabbing the gleaming golden handles and pushing them with a violent thrust.

They melted back into the corridor as a swell of noise reached out to engulf me, suffocating every other sense. The fortified glass walls had cushioned the noise of the gathering crowd, but these rooms were open to the arena, and the excitement below was so vivid as to be tangible.

I stepped into a luxuriously swathed, marble-floored chamber that swept outwards in a circular fashion before tapering back in towards a wide balcony featuring two raised thrones, beside two more chairs at ordinary mortal height.

A contemptuous smile fleeted across my lips as I spotted Cassius and Livia reclining on a wide cushioned daybed to the right of the balcony. It was almost funny. They'd projected so much of their own rhetoric they were really starting to believe it, and as he rose he gestured languidly with hands decorated with precious-looking rings. Briefly I wondered which museums and art collections he'd raided in the Dead City to acquire them.

'Ah here she is, Livia, our guest of honour! And looking quite the prize today if I may say so,' he drawled, his gaze lingering on my figure-hugging outfit. 'Yes, I knew that colour would suit. Something about the overexposed skin tone of your species that befits colour.'

My cells withered as he meandered across the room towards me, closing down the distance and poisoning my air. The difference between Octavia and Cassius was that he really believed in his own deity status. It was a critical difference, that made him far less predictable. He paused in front of me, a curious look in his eyes as he reached out to finger the gold braid running through my hair, brushing the tip of my cheek softly as he did so. His quite deliberate action stirred the very pit of my stomach, and I clenched every muscle I possessed, determined to resist the urge to reach out and plant my knuckles in his gloating face too soon.

Which was when I noticed a glinting white line just beneath his left eye. It was a scar I put there, the day he'd used his son as a human shield, in Isca's ancient cathedral. I smiled.

'The only prize will be your honour, which will be part of the track dirt beneath our feet by the time I'm finished.'

His onyx eyes gleamed with malice. 'Always the fighter, Talia,' he murmured nonchalantly, lifting his hand as though he might touch me again before catching the look in my eyes.

'So full of *wild energy*. Wouldn't it be a relief to put some of that into my hands? When your patched-up forest friend loses against my champion, you will see there was only ever one way forward anyway. Though I must admit you had me thinking you might stand a chance with your little feral stand back in the temple.

'Oh that was indeed your moment, if ever you had one, to push terms. But nice Talia, *noble Talia*, couldn't abandon the young Prolets, or her friends, or indeed her mother … And that, I'm afraid, is your perennial Outsider weakness. Conscious thought, independent will. These are such … draining aspects of original human nature. My trial species will be less troubled by such wasteful emotions.

'But now … time for our wager!'

He clapped his hands imperiously, his lack of conscience so apparent it was terrifying.

'There is nothing like a little bloodletting to raise spirits! And besides, I have a small surprise for you.'

He spun with a flourish of his purple toga, and walked towards the open balcony where the waiting crowd erupted in a cheer. I sucked in another tight breath, trying to steady my nerve.

You are like a black leopard, Talia, Grandpa whispered, *feral and free.*

Though freedom had never felt more like a distant memory than now.

I lifted my head, and forced my feet towards the open balcony, not even glancing at Livia as the outside view rose up to greet me like a page ripped directly from Grandpa's book of mythology.

Ludi Cirque Pantheonares. For a moment I barely breathed. It was as though I'd stepped back through aeons of time and was staring directly at one of Rome's most famous arenas, the ancient Circus Maximus. For all his despotic lunacy, Cassius knew exactly how to build an arena that both intimidated and dazzled with detail. From the precise rise of the occupied seating, to the gleam of burning lavender torches and endless looped track that looked as long as three Great Oak trees laid root to topmost branch, the arena was every bit as imposing as the Flavium.

But the most terrifying aspect of all, was that I wasn't a part of it.

This time, I was an observer of the worst kind, having orchestrated the event and yet retained negligible control. Cassius loved mind games, and what better entertainment than to render the feral girl powerless in a wager that forced her best friend to fight for something he didn't care existed any more?

The triumphant bugles crowed again and this time I could see five heralds, dressed in matching scarlet pageantry, on the opposite side of the arena. Thousands of faces swung towards Cassius, and I could see the conjecture and amazement on the faces of those closest as they glimpsed the Outsider standing next to him.

Cassius threw out his arm in a regal gesture as the crowd hushed, waiting for him to speak.

'Citizens! We are gathered here to witness an inaugural event, a moment in history our proud forefathers would have lauded for celebrating the key pillars of our new Civitas: honour, valour and allegiance!'

I stared out across the sea of listening faces, expecting the usual fanfare of sycophantic cheering and applause, but the arena was silent. The Civitas of Isca Pantheon was listening.

'You will no doubt recall the recent threat to this Civitas in the form of deserter Augustus Aquila? He chose to abandon Isca

Pantheon *after* it nurtured and trained him for senior office, to live with a few weak and infected wildling vermin.

'His disloyalty to this Civitas nearly brought shame and downfall to us all, and were it not for the courage of the Eagle aircraft battalion, who were heroic in their navigation of the North Mountains, the children of Isca Pantheon might not be facing the same bright future they do today.'

I clenched my teeth, every cell bursting with sudden vitriolic hatred. How dare he stand there and justify the razing of Arafel and massacre of my people as some kind of humanitarian effort? My hand reached instinctively towards my concealed dart tube. I could kill him now, in front of everyone. His personal guards would make sure I was dead before his body reached the floor, but he'd be gone, and I'd have fulfilled my obligation to Prince Phaethon too.

But what of Max and Mum? They would be swallowed by Livia and the state left behind, and probably never see the outside world again.

What of August?

My hand faltered.

It wasn't your fault.

His words swam before me, his iris-blues dulling. I'd cut him off, unable to explain anything while the pain was so raw. If I died now, he'd never know the truth.

A good hunter knows when to watch, and when to fight, Talia.

Cassius reached out and closed his hand around my wrist in a showy gesture, unaware of how close he'd come. *The benevolent Emperor-God.* His hold was uncomfortably tight, and a little sweaty, making my skin crawl. I baulked, curling my fingers into a tight fist as he thrust my arm into the air in a mock truce. It wasn't the right moment, but I would take so much satisfaction when it was.

The bugles lifted again, their announcement short and decisive this time. The pageantry was done.

'Citizens of Pantheon, you will recognize before you one of the *persistent* wildlings who, after trespassing inside our Civitas, conspired with Augustus Aquila and rebel members of Isca Prolet to raise an ill-advised rebellion. Thanks to intelligence, the uprising was detected and quashed before it gained any strength, and for that we can only be grateful.

'However, we have been left with somewhat of a quandary. You will all be aware our gracious Civitas has been trialling refuge and rehabilitation with a small number of remaining Outsiders, despite their crimes against us. But this particular wildling has proven somewhat of an exception. Not only has she remained steadfast in her refusal to accept Pantheonite citizenship, she also made threats against my own life only four weeks ago.'

Cassius paused as a predictable gasp swept through the crowd. He extended a hand, as though a father placating his children. I ground my teeth.

'I know, I know … We all know the penalty for traitors. The state of Pantheon is very clear on insubordination, and yet this lone troublemaker …' he paused to smile glitteringly at me '… refuses to pledge allegiance to your most wise and magnanimous Emperor.'

There was another round of hushed gasps, and this time I couldn't help rolling my eyes skywards.

'But! As I *am* a wise and magnanimous Emperor, who believes we can all learn in the end, I've decided to settle this in our time-honoured way.'

Cassius paused as a louder cheer erupted. He held up both hands and over-smiled, his long Roman locks shining blue-black beneath the hot lights.

'As is the nature of my generosity, if the offending wildling wins today, she will gain safe passage for her mother and her champion from Isca Pantheon.'

He paused to acknowledge the shocked murmur with faux benevolence; clearly these were unusual terms.

'But if I win ...' he smiled again, his eyes gleaming with malice '... then she will relinquish all ties to the outside, pledge her allegiance publicly and serve her Imperator graciously and with all the respect due to our most glorious Civitas ... until her dying day.'

He whispered the last words so only I could hear but it didn't matter. I was inside my own fortress, buttressed from the all the lies, deceit and damnation. Waiting for my moment to make Pantheon's death adder eat every last word.

An eerie silence enveloped the arena.

Did they admire or pity me? Did it matter?

'So, without further delay, I give you the Emperor's Charioteer racing for faction red today.'

And this time, the tiered seating fused with colour as thousands of Pantheonites took to their feet with applause that nearly deafened me. Wherever their allegiance, their love for Ludi was not in question.

Every pair of eyes swung to the top end of the arena floor as one of the large black portcullis gates began to lift. Instinctively, I stepped towards the edge of the balcony as four battle-armoured horses pulled out from the shadows, forcing me to swallow a gasp so rapidly it hurt. Because the vision took me back to Arafel's library in a heartbeat. Not to Grandpa's book of mythology, but to a text far far older than all the rest put together.

The four horses of the apocalypse.

The legend drew breath in the beasts rearing below us all now. Their wild, flaring mouths and shining flanks had left their mark the first time I saw them, and now these unearthly animals could be one and the same. Each had skin the colour of old blood, heavily brocaded armour and a single, twisted onyx-black horn protruding from their tossing heads.

Yet these were no faithful horses of myth and legend, these were unicorns of the underworld. *Mounts of Hades.*

The leaders reared, whinnying harshly as a long whip forced them into a canter, and bringing the whole equipage into view.

146

The chariot was the same shade as the animals with high cruel wing-like panels, shaped suspiciously like blades, that tapered into a sharp end seat. It was a chariot built for risk, and the animals were already dangerously excited, tossing their fiery manes while prancing and sidestepping, as though they knew exactly what was in store.

My chest started pounding painfully.

'It's just a game remember,' Max urged from my memory. 'They want a show! And right now that means playing by Cassius's rules, right up until we find his weak spot.'

Gritting my teeth, I focused on the charioteer perched atop the chariot from Hades, the man Cassius had chosen as Max's combatant. He was wearing heavy scarlet armour, a black and red feather fluttering from the top of his helmet, while his profile was stiff and proud. And unmistakable. Slowly, my stomach inverted as the months peeled away until I was left with a stubborn, unsettling boy tearing the head from a dead rat with his own teeth.

I shot a glance at Cassius's exuberant profile. Could he *really* be capable of sending his own son into an arena of torture for his own edification? A strange bitter taste filled my mouth, pungent and earthy. *Of course he could.*

Then the crowd erupted again as the thick black grill groaned upwards for a second time. I could feel the adrenaline sating my body, the blood rush drowning out the crowd as the leaders of the second team pulled out of the gloom. There was a second collective intake of breath.

These animals were blue, the colour of bluebells in the first flush of spring. They too were protected by a thick armour shot through with gold flashes, much like my own tunic, and wore indigo collars that caught the arena lights and trapped them like glittering stars. But unlike the first team, they wore only short horns upon their heads. I scowled. They looked half as ferocious as Atticus's team.

'A fair race, Cassius?' I scathed. 'You choose unicorns and then tip the odds. Too worried to level the game and give the Outsider an equal chance.'

'On the contrary,' he returned lazily. 'Aurochs have proven particularly challenging to breed. I wouldn't dream of sabotaging their species for anything so spurious. Defending champions always have the honour of racing the alpha herd.'

Aurochs ... of course their species name would be different. I had a feeling their nature would be a little different to unicorns of legend too.

My gaze flew back to the track. The second team were a little smaller than the apocalyptical steeds pawing the starting line. Even to my untrained eye, I could see Atticus barely had control over them.

And now the second charioteer was pulling into open view. It was indisputably Max, clad in military armour the same colour as the aurochs and my own tunic, a single brushed indigo feather dancing atop his golden helmet. He was encouraging his team forward with the dependable strength and natural ease he'd always had around animals. And my heart ached.

Max was my best friend, and yet I'd hurt him more than anyone in my life. He was here because of me, and even now he was risking his life because of a deal I'd made. The feral girl he probably wouldn't even recognize. How could I call myself his best friend when all I did was put him in the worst possible danger, *again and again*?

'Max versus Atticus, Cassius?' I scorned in a voice I hoped hid my fear.

Cassius had to be so sure of his victory, to put his only son out there to take the glory. *Did Max even stand a chance? And even if he did, would he even try to win for me – and against a boy? Max was always the underdog champion. Would Pantheon have changed that too?*

I schooled my profile as two more figures ran out from beneath the archway and jumped onto the chariots, which had slewed to a halt before gates that had arisen from the ground, and now stretched across the track. One slight figure was clad in the same Quadriga-red faction colours as Atticus, while the other was dressed in indigo blue, like me and Max. I recognized Rajid instantly, and stifled the protest that flew to my lips. Before I would have assumed he was a backup to ensure Max's very public demise, but since he'd passed on my dart tube via Servilia I'd begun to doubt myself. *I recalled Servilia's agitation when she first glimpsed him; that she knew and trusted him was obvious, but how?*

I pictured his curious, sardonic smile and gritted my teeth – nothing would bring me to trust him again, but I did trust Servilia.

'Yes, Atticus.' Cassius's eyes were gleaming. 'What finer combatant to demonstrate what true honour, valour and allegiance really looks like than the son and heir to the imperial throne, and besides—'

'The stakes are so loaded so as to render the race irrelevant?' I interjected.

'He is not indispensable,' he continued smoothly. 'The true beauty of Isca Pantheon's Biotechnology Programme is that any citizen of worth can be reissued, so long as I deem it advantageous to the state.'

And then he smiled a smile that reached down my throat and twisted my gut so hard I could barely control my hand, which hovered above the thing that could wipe the smile from his obnoxious face once and for all. Atticus was barely fifteen years old, and had a father who attached no value to his life because he could re-create him at will.

Cassius's smiled faded a little, and I turned swiftly to avoid giving myself away. I stared out at the waiting crowd, their excitement almost tangible.

Reissued. It was a soulless word. Where was the room for memory and emotion? How could Atticus, *reissued*, ever be the same boy who stood against his father's tyranny by leading a band of Prolet children away from Pantheon and sustaining them for weeks on rodents and rainwater alone? It was the worst kind of science because it created the illusion of replacing like for like, when the real loss was to humanity. *To originality.*

'What of love and respect, Cassius?'

My words were out before I could stop them, betraying their feral owner. I didn't care.

There was a stir of movement behind us and I didn't need to look to know Livia was stealing up silently, like a wraith.

'Ever the impulsive Outsider, Talia,' she chided. 'One of the analyses from early biotechnical trials was the high cost of emotion to the Civitas. It's an original Outsider trait, no more, a DNA weakness that is better controlled for those whose key purpose is to work and serve Isca Pantheon. The experience and expression of emotion is an area of special interest for me, and quite complex; however, Pantheon's neuroscience team has finally identified the precise area of limbic system responsible. I'm delighted we've been able to trial a new control against this fundamental objective.'

She drew a breath, almost as though she was being modest, while I compressed my teeth until I felt one must crack.

'The new vaccine is somewhat of a personal success, and has had a demonstrable impact on resources.'

I turned back to see Livia gazing up at Cassius, her flat voice unusually triumphant and cold eyes assessing the impact of her every clinical word. I was in no doubt she wasn't simply intending to goad me, she really believed there was a benefit to violating people in this way, to the wholesale removal of their basic human rights.

My thoughts flew to August, to the propaganda in Octavia's research centre and to the way he'd always been able to hide his emotion so far beneath his Equite skin. It was why it had taken me so long to trust him, until that day in the Flavium when he'd ridden out for Unus and I. My heart flared. He'd been an early test subject with the vaccine. It was one of the reasons he'd strug-gled to break his loyalty to Octavia. *Had she also suffocated his emotional freedom?* I knew in a heartbeat she had – and that Livia was reading my thoughts.

'And we've proven through early trials, that emotion, once under control, never quite loses its shackle.'

Her eyes were assessing, dilating with interest as I dragged mine away. Because she'd touched a real and raw nerve. August and I had come so close to sharing everything that night in the North Mountain cave, and the intimacy had opened a door he'd fought to keep open. And yet I'd pushed him away.

I told myself we'd traded our hearts with the Oceanids, in return for our lives. But in reality I'd buried mine beneath layers of fear, all to mask the hurt of losing so many. I'd never felt more of a coward in my life.

It was real for me, Talia.

It felt as though someone was pressing hot needles into the back of my eyes; perhaps Livia actually had a real point. All I did was wreak chaos, because of my weak, emotional decision-making. I'd betrayed Arafel, and failed to protect the Book as well as Mum, Eli and every other Outsider I'd ever cared about. I'd ruined my friendship with Max because I was scared of hurting him, before blindly sending him to his death. And then I'd broken the only good thing to have survived all the carnage, because I couldn't handle the guilt. August's iris-blues swam through my head, chased swiftly by Lake's double-lidded honey eyes.

And wasn't emotion the reason I was standing here right now?

The imperial bugles sounded again and the crowds hushed, tense with anticipation. The animals were prancing impatiently behind the tall spring-loaded track gates, and the combatants' faces were turned towards us, awaiting Cassius's signal.

I tried to catch their gaze but both were locked on Cassius, and then the slight figure seated behind Atticus reached forward to whisper something. He nodded curtly, his helmet locked in his father's direction.

I frowned. We were a good distance away and the figure was

151

clad in Quadriga-red race regalia leaving only the lower half of their face on view, but there was still something disturbingly familiar about them.

I swallowed. The atmosphere in the arena was making me see ghosts.

Cassius stepped slowly across to the edge of the stone balcony, and raised his arms in another stately gesture, savouring the moment. And the tiny dart tube nestled against my chest almost seemed to move, as though it had gained a small heartbeat of its own. I suppressed a grim smile. It was Arafel wood, made by Arafel hands. No wonder it was yearning for blood of the one that turned it all to ash.

'Citizens, let us get this special Ludi day of celebration underway … I present to you, my own beloved son, Commander General Atticus for the state of Isca Pantheon!'

'May the gods favour our ancient pillars of honour, valour and allegiance … Let the Games begin!'

Chest pounding, I moved down the balcony while the crowd erupted in cheers. Though it wasn't enough to distract from movement in the shadows around the room. Cassius's guards were taking no chances. I was surrounded, and never felt more a trapped animal, forced to watch as what remained of my best friend raced to his death. It was the ultimate vicious mind game.

I leaned forward over the cool stone and focused on Max, who met my gaze before looking away again, indifferent. My chest tightened. It cut me every time he ignored me, even though I knew it was unintentional.

'Emotion, once under control, never quite loses its shackle.'

Livia's words were going to haunt me. What had happened to him since the cathedral? *Was it the vaccine or had Pantheon severed his soul and dragged it out? Would he ever be the same?*

All attention was on the charioteers now. Max and Atticus saluted each other curtly before carefully wrapping the auroch reins around their wrists. I gritted my teeth. It would mean a painful dismount if either got thrown. *Did every observance in this place have to be so goddamned Roman?*

Then Cassius threw up an arm in a final stately moment, and all eyes were on a small red cloth floating down towards the arena ground, like a petal forecasting a flower's death.

But it was enough. The roar of the crowd swallowed everything as the gates sprang open and the aurochs jerked forward, billowing up dust as the wheels of the chariots dug into the dirt track. Atticus's team flew into the lead instantly, their larger frames and longer stride making light work of the first section. The crowd's excitement was only chequered by the thunder of hooves circum-navigating the circus arena. It felt like a drum roll, as I fixed my eyes on their retreating forms, hardly daring to breathe.

From this vantage I could see the full length of the course, defined by numerous sets of high-arched open gates, which had slid up as silently as the first and now divided the track at regular intervals. I scowled. There were two more sets to navigate before the track took a sharp loop back on the opposite side, and a single revolution had to be at least two kilometres. The chariots flew through the first gates, one after the other, and as they passed beneath the imposing metallic structure, the whole top bar glowed red.

The gated arches were clearly some sort of counting mechanism.

With the second gate behind them, they continued flying down the first length with Max closing the distance, slipping inside the gleaming black chariot's path as they careered towards the next arch. I clenched my fingers until my nails bit into my palms. *They were too close.*

The crowd gasped and sure enough, seconds later, a nerve-grating sound divided the air. I leaned as far as I dared, my stomach rolling, and caught sight of the high back wheels of the two vehicles locked together, weighing the auroch teams to the left and making Max's leaders rear and spill outside the track. His chariot skewed, the axis of his contraption protesting violently as, somehow, they moved forward at a punishing pace.

The air was thick with anticipation and tiny hairs on the backs of my arms strained as Max tried to compensate, encouraging his aurochs back onto the track. The crowd gasped, before a different sound rattled throughout the tense space. The sound of something large and metallic clanking into place. I inhaled sharply, my thoughts flying to the large metallic maze that had incarcerated Max and I only months before.

Then I realized what had created the noise: the next gate. It was flashing red while it slid inwards and downwards, reducing the space so only one chariot could pass through at a time. I stared, feeling fresh fear scuttle down my spine. They were part of the game – *of course they were.*

Atticus yelled to his team, urging them to break free from Max's equipage as their thundering, rapid hooves approached the flashing gate. I gripped the balcony harder, willing Max to break away. They were too wide, too fast and you could have heard a leaf drop as all Pantheon held its breath. Before the grinding toll of impact. There was the sickening, screeching crunch as the heavy metal of Atticus's front wheel caught one of the arches' metallic supports, and a billow of dust enveloped his chariot.

'Strike one,' Cassius pronounced delightedly, raising his red goblet to the crowd. Red. The colour of blood and hellfire.

Seconds later, there was another sickening groan of metal and Max's team of indigo aurochs pulled clear of Atticus's grounded equipage. A small, instinctive cheer erupted amid the crowd, and I shot a startled look at the tiered seats, as the mood caught and flared in several places before quietening again.

Cassius scanned his offending populace like a hawk, the muscle in his cheek quivering. A sea of Pantheonite faces were focused once more on the track, but the moment had been there and a strange prickling crawled across the back of my neck. Livia suddenly stepped up beside me.

'Don't get any ideas above your station,' she hissed as both teams righted themselves and pelted back down the opposite side of the track.

'It's Ludi so a small number of Prolets have been allowed to attend, as is customary. Clearly, one or two rogue subjects have bypassed security. I assure you they will be brought to account.'

I didn't give her the satisfaction of a response, only made myself a silent promise to show her exactly what a real rogue subject looked like when the time was right. Atticus had recovered and was gaining again, his team's longer stride giving him the edge on the open track. A third arched gate approached, and this time I could tell every pair of eyes was on the ominous metallic structure. I shot a look at Cassius, at the way his heavy eyelids had half-drooped over his gleaming eyes, and another shot of cold fear doused my veins.

Sure enough, a moment later the air was filled with the sound of metallic grinding. I gripped the cold stone of the balcony, air evaporating from my lungs, as a solid horizontal bar at the top descended like a rapid guillotine, presenting the charioteers with no option but to fling themselves to the floor of the chariots and pray. An audible sigh of relief claimed the arena as both teams made it through with barely a hair's breadth to spare.

'Enough, Cassius!' I rattled, eyeing the remaining gates spread out around the track.

'Is the race not enough that you have to subject them to trickery as well?'

He sauntered towards Livia and me, his face jubilant, no shadow of guilt that his own son was enduring the same.

'But those who run with animals must know the nature of a circus … surely?'

And I could see this was his dream moment, to stand with me and prove the iron fist of his Civitas was always stronger than the guttering hopes of an outside world.

'Is your ego still so fragile?' I scathed. 'I haven't forgotten the snake in the cathedral that crawled on his belly and hid behind his son! Do you forget, I still have something you want?' My voice was as icy as a North Mountain storm as the crowd roared again. We both knew that while he held Mum, I was firmly within his grip.

'And I have something you want,' he glittered smoothly, 'so the only question remaining is who wants what the most?'

He turned his attention to the track once more, but his words hung on the air between us. Somehow, I knew he wasn't talking about either Mum or Max this time, and my mouth went suddenly dry.

What or who else could Cassius possibly hold that I might want?

I eyed him with fresh suspicion. There was something in the sardonic twist of his lips that betrayed new excitement. And it sent pure adrenaline haring through my veins. Then the ground started to vibrate. Startled, I swung my gaze back to the arena to see a large black grill was growing swiftly up and around the perimeter of the entire track, separating the watching spectators from the contestants.

Beads of sweat broke out across my hairline. I ran my eye around the whole, resisting the panic climbing my throat. The grill was just the right height for keeping the outside and inside very separate.

Cassius stepped around to enclose me between himself and Livia, before reaching out to place his soft hand over mine, and this time I was unable to prevent myself from jerking it away.

'You see, things are never quite what they seem in Pantheon, Talia; that's the beauty of being the first Imperator.'

His eyes flashed again as the black grill changed direction and slid inwards for about three metres until it ground to a silent halt, leaving only a high central square open to the air. I swallowed down the rocks collecting in my throat. Whatever, or whoever, it was designed to contain, he clearly wasn't taking any chances with his own skin.

But I didn't disguise the look of vile disgust spreading across my face. Of course it wouldn't be just a race with guillotine gates, nothing in Pantheon was ever that simple. There was always an ugly edge, something that personalized Cassius's maligned nature. I scanned the imposing structure, trying to find its weak spot and my fear spiralled again. The structure was so reminiscent of the black spider maze, of *Ludi Pantheonares* and the bellowing bull, and of nearly losing Max once already. Could I really stand here and do the same again?

'Who is it, Cassius?'

My voice was low and hard.

And I was done with his games and surprises. If there was someone else I needed to worry about, I needed to know now. Not later.

'Tstch, Talia, where's your patience … *our little feral cat*?'

My eyes flew to his, onyx-blacks hardening to black water pearls. Laughing at me, relishing every torturous second. And suddenly I knew. He wasn't talking of Eli, or any of the remaining Outsiders.

It was August. He was talking about August.

The bugles blared again. It was a different call, signalling a change in the game, and as both chariots careered towards the second hairpin turn, the walls of the closed buildings on the island began to retract downwards. My breath shortened as the arena light spilled inwards, revealing heavy, entwined limbs that reminded me of Cassius's molossers. It was only as the animals climbed lazily to their feet that I saw they bore more resemblance to cats than dogs. Cats with snow-white-flecked coats. The hot needling behind my eyes returned, only this time it fanned out across my skin.

Cassius was watching me, gripping me in his brutal claws like the dead Aquila, squeezing until my very last ounce of feral will crumbled.

I could feel his eyes darkening, willing me to break. To give in to the pain. A howling black hole of pain. Like the vortex outside our mountain cave. My gut twisted.

'Jas?'

My whisper was hollow, betraying nothing though my head was filled with the moment Jas had leapt for Brutus in the research centre, trying to protect us before she disappeared. To think she'd also been caught and incarcerated here was so hard and yet I knew to break right now was exactly what Cassius wanted.

Give him nothing, I repeated, schooling my face till it hurt. And he was furious. Knowing I was still fighting, refusing to give him the reaction he wanted, refusing to ask if he was talking of August.

'*Perfectus!* Not just your substandard breed of course, but the useful DNA extracted and mixed up with an ancient breed, courtesy of the Voynich, *et non vos!* A new, improved species – one worthy of inheriting a recovering world.'

I trained my eyes back on the arena, forcing myself to think as the biggest snow-leopard hybrid rose and stretched, its long, extended canines glinting in the lights.

'*Machairodontinae* is a particular success of the Biotechnical Programme, thanks to the Voynich translation,' Cassius continued as though conducting a tour, not watching beasts preparing for a killing spree.

'An extinct subfamily of carnivore mammals, they aren't true mythological creatures at all of course – but oh they are entertaining! Unfortunately, we had to void several test specimens, but once we had achieved my specification, it was surprisingly straightforward to breed an alpha pack.'

'Sabre-tooths,' I whispered.

But my erratic thoughts were elsewhere entirely, imagining August riding back to Arafel, only to find it razed to the ground and no one there. *What would he have done?*

Guilt bled through me like a river.

Of course I knew, I'd always known. He would have come straight here, to challenge Cassius and find out what had happened to everyone. To me. We'd parted like strangers. What pain would he have endured when he returned to find the outside he was fighting for just an ashen memory of itself? Its people gone. *His person gone? What would Cassius and Livia have done with him?*

The hybrids were on their feet now, their thickened rear limbs as heavy and powerful as forest bears. But these weren't creatures built for lumbering, instead the rise of their haunches and tilted design were all about speed and power. And they were big, like the heaviest forest tigers. I drew a shallow breath as the creatures gathered at the edge of their enclosure bars, their canines glinting out from their flecked-white coats. It was a colour I'd so long associated with home, with watchful golden eyes, and the courage of a special cat who'd somehow found a path over the treacherous mountains into the Dead City, in pursuit of her beloved Eli.

Where was she now? Where were they all now?

Each thought was a tightening thread bringing Arafel, decimated and broken, to the forefront of my mind. Like Cassius's propaganda on a loop. The image was full of broken bodies and unseeing eyes, threatening to consume everything. *How had it all come to this?* My mother locked away, my brother lost, my childhood friend about to be ripped to pieces and my … whatever he was … incarcerated and probably being subjected to the worst possible torture *while I just stood here.*

'You said a race!' I flung out again, gripping the stone and trying to count the creatures. There had to be at least a dozen.

'And they're racing.' He smirked, gesticulating towards their chariots, flying past the balcony again.

He was leering, slyly savouring my slow unwind. He knew I was close to breaking point.

That I had guessed the truth about August.

The aurochs were now weaving wildly across the track, nostrils flaring and stride lengthening, as they sensed the impending danger. I could tell both Atticus and Max were tiring, finding it harder to maintain control, while their seconds clung to the sides of their chariots. It was as much a game of stamina as anything else.

'How many laps, Cassius?' I ground out.

'Seven.' He gleamed. 'If they get that far.'

I counted silently. The chariots were thundering towards their fourth hairpin bend, approaching the next arched gate at speed. It was an impossible pace for anyone to sustain let alone endure for another five laps. One tiny lapse of concentration would end it all. And all the while, the sabre-tooths were eyeing up the odds, awaiting their moment.

'Call the animals off!' I demanded. 'Surely the prize – freedom – demands the race is conducted with something resembling honour?'

'*Oh e contrario*, Talia! In Pantheon, the bigger the prize, the more dangerous the race!'

He stretched out his arm again, holding a second red cloth and instantly the bugles blared. A slow metallic groan filled the air, and I held my breath as the original portcullis at the top of the arena slowly lifted, releasing another red and black equipage, which spilled onto the track at speed. The blade-door chariot with its prancing aurochs was identical to the equipage Atticus was racing, but the charioteer in control was entirely alone.

A wild cheer erupted through the crowd as Atticus's aurochs swerved off the track and thundered into the black archway exit, his second jumping and sprinting to join the fresh team who barely slowed. But any relief I might have felt for Atticus was sidelined, and I could only watch as though caught up in a nightmare, because every contour of the tall proud Equite tearing down the tracks in pursuit of Max was scarred into my heart.

'He's alive,' I whispered hoarsely, the whites of my knuckles gleaming in the light.

And I was no longer on Cassius's balcony. I was back in the forest, watching the light die in his eyes, letting him say goodbye.

It was real for me, Talia.

'*August!*' I yelled silently, as though everything might change if he knew I were up here, watching.

But he was down there, clad in Cassius's colours, with a two-headed aquila standard streaming from the top of his chariot as he thundered after Max.

Where had he been? Battle-hardened … focused … a gladiator for Cassius? How on earth had he agreed to this? Where were his loyalties now?

'Look at me,' I pleaded silently.

I needed his stony profile to spare just one fleeting glance. So I would know. But his gaze was unwavering, locked forward, and all I could do was watch as his aurochs started bearing down with all purpose on Max's tiring team.

'Never more so,' Livia responded gleefully.

I bit my lip.

'And still quite determined to do anything for a feral Outsider or so it would seem. Which is a fascinating development for his test series. It's a moot point: how far Augustus Aquila has overcome his original trial status.'

I barely heard her crisp, anodyne voice, because my head was compressing with real fear. *This* was what Cassius predicted I would still want, the final dark twist in his plan. I drew a painful breath, trying to order my spiralling thoughts. They were both out there, racing to the death. *Yet this wasn't about them – this was all about breaking me. Controlling me. No matter how high the cost.*

There was another fanfare of bugles, before a new triumphant blast, which the creatures clearly recognized. Their bars slid down and they lumbered out of their shelter, sniffing the tense air. The biggest animal raised its canine-heavy head to the lights and roared. I felt my skin flush ice-cold, despite the warmth of the arena lights.

No snow leopard could roar – Jas could only ever mew – yet this sound was coarse and primeval. It was also hungry.

I leaned further, desperate not to lose track of either chariot through the billowing dust. They had rounded the top hairpin and were slewing down the opposite length again, side by side; the indigo team straining so hard the sinews in their necks were visible, even at my distance.

161

Max was leaning forward intently, while Rajid appeared to have thrown himself to the chariot floor. My eyes flew to August on the outside, shaking out his long reins and roaring at his fresher team while his small second crouched low, using the high blade wings for protection.

What fresh lies had Cassius spun to make August race against Max as though the life of everyone here depended on it?

The small second settled as far back in the chariot as he could. They still looked familiar, and briefly I wondered who could have been tempted to ride as Atticus's second. *Tempted or forced?* Was it one of the Prolet detainees? He seemed familiar somehow, so calm and logical despite his bleak predicament. And my wayward thoughts flew back to a still day with a glass river when my heart crystallized into a million pieces.

It couldn't be.

I was aware my breath had grown ragged as I tried to focus on the crouching figure, to chase the ghost from my thoughts. But the moment was shattered by a succession of blood-stilling roars that reached through to my booted feet. The aurochs' fear was tangible, and the sabre-tooths had noticed. Max threw a look into the centre. I was too far away to see his expression but I knew his lips would be set, his eyes narrowed to hunter.

'Now things get a little interesting,' Cassius drawled, tipping his goblet up and draining the contents, a tiny red drip escaping down his chin.

I had no words left, and could only watch as the scarlet aurochs lurched ahead of the indigo team, their sudden erratic acceleration owed entirely to the predators slinking out from their lair. They lumbered purposefully, every muscle visible and distinct from the rest. The leader was in front, his wide paws padding lazily before he paused to lift his mountain eyes and claim his territory. And I could translate his call perfectly, because I'd heard it a thousand times over, among the predators of the forest. It was a call to arms, and the pack knew it too, closing the distance between themselves and the leader without hesitation.

They were even more imposing as they came together, a silver-white arrow with their leader at the front, their bodies broad and powerful, and their eyes as blue as diamonds. But the master point of their design belonged to the gleaming teeth protruding from their thick jowls. They had to be the length of my forearm. And mesmerizing.

There was another mechanical grinding noise and thousands of heads swung in the direction of the gate responsible. The chariots were most of the way back down the track again, the aurochs' forelocks and backs shining as though wet from the rain. Another archway approached, and suddenly its walls projected what looked to be a hundred sharp spears into the narrow space between.

August's chariot skewed hard left, crashing into Max's equipage, which lurched sickeningly. There was confused shouting, followed by the crunch of thick metal being dragged in separate directions again.

They were both off the track in a heartbeat. I bit my lip hard, drawing drops of blood. They tasted of iron metal and the brown earth beneath our feet, rooting me as I followed the aurochs' frantic swaying progress across the centre of the arena. The eight-auroch conjoined contraption bolted past the watching leopards, and was halfway across the centre, before the axis of Max's chariot buckled under the pressure, throwing Rajid high and clear of the equipage. He landed awkwardly and tumbled through the dirt, a ball of limbs until he came to a sudden, jolting still. I swallowed as the lead sabre-tooth turned his head in his direction.

Then one of Max's lead aurochs stumbled and his whole contraption veered wildly as August's team pulled free and bolted. The injured auroch picked up her hooves, her back matted with sweat, her eyes wide with fear just as the lead sabre-tooth swung his broad head away from Rajid. He drank the air greedily as the remainder of his pack closed in behind, waiting for his sign.

I was pressing so hard into the stone balcony I thought I might fall right through it. Max's aurochs tried to rally, but it was clear the injured animal's exhaustion and pain was too much. And then Max was tying the reins, clambering atop his chariot, and running up the backs of the spooked aurochs. The crowd gasped audibly as he caught the bridle of the frontrunners and leapt neatly astride the healthy animal's back.

And a curious bittersweet tingle ran down my spine. It was old instinctive Max, back in the forest. *Could there be any more?* The crowd hushed again, holding their collective breath as he leaned in close, trying to calm the auroch's violent stumbling. But they were too frantic and skittish, unconvinced by his murmurings of reassurance because less than a tree length away a pack of hungry sabre-tooths were starting to advance. My head felt thick and woolly, and yet the charred remains of one thought turned over and over.

Arafel.

What was left of it was out there, with a pack of sabre-tooths just waiting for the perfect moment to rip it apart. The old Max would never have left me to face these odds alone. *What was I doing?*

Max flashed a look over his shoulder, at Rajid's still body, before pulling a Diasord from his waist and leaning across towards the head of the injured auroch.

This time the crowd roared, beating time with the blood in my ears.

There was a flash as his Diasord sliced the air, followed by the acrid scent of burning before the injured auroch stumbled weakly away, bewildered by its sudden freedom. The crowd roared their delight as Max leaned into the mane of the uninjured auroch, which was still setting a punishing pace, dragging the team and damaged chariot behind it. Cassius glowered and the crowd hushed instantly, torn between their excitement at Max's heroics and their fear of upsetting their Emperor.

'Do you want me to dispatch a guard, Cassius?' Livia asked crisply.

'Play on!' he snarled, rounding on her like an animal himself. 'It's not as though the Outsider will live to realize his luck. And the Commander General has had his orders.'

I suddenly felt clammy and cold. *Why would August accept orders from Cassius now?*

Max was leaning tightly over the lead auroch's head, but I could see it was all too fast, too erratic, and too close to the top portcullis. The auroch veered wildly, making the remaining animals whinny in terror as they all slewed, forcing the equipage onto the rim of its thin wheels. The crowd sucked in a horrified gasp and everything seemed to slow as the leader reared, kicking its hooves high in panic, and throwing Max high into the dusty red air.

Twist, Max, twist, I begged silently.

But whether it was the height, or his confusion, his body only slowed before dropping heavily back onto the dusty arena floor. Then there was only a moment's breath before the teetering chariot fell like a stone, right over him.

The world shrank as the dust cleared to reveal the rearing, panicking animals, and the lone hand of a charioteer protruding from beneath the chariot.

And that was the moment everything stained red.

Every thought, every reason, every face.

I was leaping like a feral cat before I could think, leather boots crunching unfamiliarly on the stone balcony top as I paused to survey the ground in the way an animal might. Detached, focused, hunting.

The only way to beat Hades, was to think like the devil himself.

'Stop her!'

Cassius's furious command was lost upon the crowd, who were too caught up in the drama of the arena to care about a feral girl on the balcony.

There was a tangle of hands, and sudden pressure around my waist and shoulders, but they weren't driven by memories of flames engulfing their home, by visions of broken bodies, of iris-

165

blues losing hope and of lone, still hands. I was flying before they could pull me back. It was the biggest leap of my life, down towards the circus, as though I were one of the animals I grew up with. *Down towards the last of my Outsider blood.*

The cage walls rang like a cacophony of old-world bells as my hands and feet wrapped around their taut, stretched edges. And then they were morphing beneath my fingers, their cold new-world metal turning into young green branches that bent with the breeze as I scuttled along the mesh shelf.

'Detain her now!'

Cassius's furious second command barely reached through the haze. I was assessing the forest jungle, mentally calculating the distance of my final leap and sprint towards the upturned chariot.

'Talia!'

Then I was conscious of the crowd's attention dividing, of an awed gasp as thousands of faces swung between the girl balancing eight metres above the arena, and the small second jumping from the back of August's moving chariot and pelting across the arena towards the crash. And even though the sabre-tooths had swung their heads with interest, I couldn't take my eyes off the sprinting figure because *she was supposed to be a ghost.*

'For the love of Nero, Tal!'

She repeated my name and her voice echoed familiarly, a discord in this circus of blood and dust.

But it was unmistakable all the same.

'Aelia?'

My answer came out a hoarse whisper, as though its very utterance might break the spell. And yet there she was reaching through the dust, fracturing time, and melting the pain that had impaled like tiny crystal shards, since August and I said goodbye on the banks of the glass river.

It was the most improbable thing, that she should be alive, flying across the dirt, slowing her sprint and raising her eyebrows at me as though I were the apparition instead. And then she offered a grin, *of all things*, her head tipped to one side – a look so familiar it ached every muscle I possessed. *And how didn't matter any more.*

I pushed up slowly, defiantly, growing in stature before the crowd, with the strength of an old friend reaching across the floor, firing my limbs with solidarity and life. At last.

'So what are you waiting for ... feral cat?'

They were his words, delivered by his sister, like a brilliant shower of stars, telling me it was still worth the fight, while we lived and breathed.

I rose onto the balls of my feet, assessing the last leap. It was a considerable jump, but I'd jumped further with a hole in my stomach. Aelia turned and began pelting up towards the collapsed chariot and I flashed back to the night at the cathedral, when I urged Max to pick her up and run. I set my jaw. This time I was going to be right there beside them.

In the next moment I was soaring, the breath of the crowd carrying me, until I landed and rolled, a blaze of hot lights on my face and dirt crunching beneath my limbs.

I was dimly aware of August hard-turning his team, and a battalion of guards spread out around the perimeter of the metallic fence. But I had to get to Max, and as I sprinted across the dirt floor, I shot a look up at the balcony. Cassius's outstretched arm reached far above me as he assessed the crowd's mood, before he slowly twisted his fist upwards. I smiled as the crowd erupted in cheers. The show always came first.

The sabre-tooths were between me and Aelia now, and the rear animals turned slowly, eyeing me with interest. Instinctively, I sprinted low and wide around the pack, their diamond-blue eyes following me intently, sizing me up against effort.

They looked even bigger on the ground, as big as Cassius's monster hounds and yet better built for speed, with thickened rear legs and heavy clawed feet. But if their snow-leopard nature was prevalent, they wouldn't attack until their leader gave them the signal, and right now it looked as though he was after bigger game.

'*A good hunter rarely hunts the healthy deer,*' I muttered, skirting around the rear animals and accelerating towards the upturned chariot where Aelia was already pressing her fingers into Max's limp wrist.

The crowd cheered deafeningly as I skidded in beside her crouching form, as alive as the day I met her. I stared at her for a millisecond: pink skin, determined chin, eyes the colour of a forest spring.

Fully fixed, fully in control, fully Aelia. But there was no time for questions.

'How is he?' I whispered, throwing a look over my shoulder. The pack were spreading out, widening their game.

'Unconscious, but alive. Help me lift this so we can pull him free,' she responded.

Without hesitation, I jammed my back against the nearest wing, and heaved with all my strength, clearing just enough space for her to drag Max free. The crowd went wild as the whole equipage crashed back down to the floor, shattering the wing and making the sabre-tooths snarl suspiciously. I held my breath as Aelia leaned over him, her expert fingers searching.

'Lucky!' she panted. 'He must have been cushioned by the frame, I can't locate any broken bones or internal damage.'

She carefully removed his helmet, and his tousled hair and golden face caught me off guard. I dropped to my knees, and my heart flooded with hope as he groaned.

'Rajid?' Aelia whispered, glancing up.

I thought of his curious, sly expression, of his betrayal and finally of the small dart tube resting against my chest.

I gritted my teeth.

He and Servilia had risked their lives to help me.

I jumped to my feet. The sabre-tooths were closing ranks again. The leader's broad head was close to the ground, its canines

168

almost brushing the red dirt as it took a pace forward, the rest of the pack fanning out behind. Clearly, three humans in close proximity, one unconscious, represented better odds than anything else on offer.

I grabbed the Diasord from Max's side and took a couple of paces forward. They were a formidable sight, their oversized tapering canines protruding long below their jawlines, and black and white mountain fur jarring with our reddened surroundings. They were perfectly designed apex predators.

'Oh, Eli, where are you when I need you the most?' I whispered, readying myself.

I was vaguely aware that he would never know how it ended. How I ended. I gripped the Diasord, and flicked out the cylindrical laser. The leader threw his wide head back in a snarl as he slowed to a wary standstill only a few metres from me. I stared in challenge, feeling my breath grow raspy.

They all had her eyes.

But they didn't have her soul, I reminded myself, before snarling my response. They paused, confused, as the crowd fell silent. I was vaguely aware of August driving his aurochs at full pace towards the portcullis gate, of an authoritative command as the animals whinnied in terror and then the resisting creak of metal as the gate opened. I swallowed to ease the burn leaching through my gut, though I never wanted to vent my hurt more.

He was abandoning me? And yet, what did I expect? Hadn't I abandoned him first?

I drew the Diasord through the air in a shaky semicircle, and snarled again the way Jas used to when faced with a predator.

'Take it from me, I don't taste that good,' I added.

But the cerulean eyes boring their way into my own seemed to disagree. The lights burned through the dusty air, creating an eerie hue as the crowd waited. I could feel their nerves, so many hearts beating, waiting for the first strike. And it felt strangely apocalyptical, as though this were an echo of the Great War Thomas had survived.

Was this the reason they'd fought so hard against all the odds to survive?

So I could stand here two hundred years later, the last of my kind, preparing to be torn apart by a pack of Pantheon's hybrid monsters? Or was it retribution for my failure, for sending Max to his death, for denying August, for betraying Arafel, for giving Cassius exactly what he needed?

An Arafel hunter believes in natural order, respect for his place in the forest, and in taking only what he needs to survive.

The leader slunk down, preparing to strike. I squared my jaw. I wouldn't stand aside, not while I had breath left in my feral body.

'Where am I?'

But Max's whisper was lost to the leader's roar as he sprang, his jaws stretched wide and Insider eyes filled with an archaic hunger. And I was vaguely aware of the crowd on their feet, of a different kind of shouting and yelling, of hands and feet scaling the arena fencing and of the bugle piercing the air with a different sound. It was a sound I knew like I knew myself, a call that reached through the air and squeezed my heart until tears of blood rained around my feet.

Because it was the sound of Arafel's ibex horn. The call of the hunters. Singing out across the dead landscape. Bringing the forest. Whispering that Arafel lived still, and had stolen like a ghost, through Pantheon's walls. To bring me home.

Which was all I needed to bring the Diasord up as brutally as I could, before the beast turned my world to darkness.

170

Chapter 16

The world returned as though inflated from the tiniest telescopic pinprick. Like the moment of its own birth. Only this birth had the weight of all the ages on its shoulders.

I was conscious of a rushing, a drawing feeling in the pit of my stomach and then of a tourniquet being applied swiftly. A familiar voice. *Aelia.* Rushing. Pulling.

'It's OK ... you're concussed ... your left arm has a claw wound ... will need cleaning later. But you're OK.'

Her voice was rushed, and kept fading before it disappeared altogether.

I lifted my aching head to see the arena awash with people, and blinked hard but they were still there. *People I knew.* And they were all fighting. Therry dived past followed by Saba, an Arafel friend I thought lost in the fires.

My chest throbbed as I tried to croak her name, before spotting the collapsed sabre-tooth. It was less than five paces away, lying very still, a Diasord rammed in its chest up to the hilt. An acrid nausea threatened to climb my throat. Such a beautiful creature deserved a nobler death than as sport in a circus where all the real monsters were watching.

I stifled a moan as reality returned.

I was half-crushed and everything radiated pain. I sucked in a wheezy breath.

'Max?'

Forcing myself onto my elbow, I tried to ignore the way the arena folded in on itself, and scanned the chaos. Max was nowhere to be seen.

'Aelia?' I yelled fearfully, my vision swimming.

She appeared at a run, her dark hair matted with fresh blood, wiping a short knife on her scarlet charioteer tunic as she knelt beside me.

'I'm here, I'm here ...' she panted, 'you're OK ... nothing punctured, not like last time. You'll be bruised, but you're OK.'

'What happened? Where's Max?' I forced myself up to sitting, lifting my hand firstly to a roughly bound arm, and then my tight chest.

Miraculously, the little dart tube seemed to have survived intact.

She shook her head. 'He's OK ... took off, a moment ago ... Tal, you know Max can take care of himself. We have to get out of here now, for everyone's sake.'

I stared around in abject wonder, so aware the colour of the arena had completely changed in the last few minutes. It was awash with a myriad of Outsider faces and Prolets, challenging the might of Pantheon together.

Hunters, Komodo, Lynx. There was a veritable blaze of outside scoring the bleached interior of the circus. Every cell of my body was convinced I'd awoken in some twisted parallel universe, but my heart soared all the same. And there were more Prolets scaling the wire mesh all the time. *Joining us.* No wonder I'd detected a mood among the crowd. *Had they been waiting for some kind of signal all along?*

I shot a dazed look at Cassius's balcony. He was still there, leering furiously, his face pale and violent as he gesticulated to the guards surrounding him.

And I knew then without a doubt. This was no act of spontaneity triggered by events in the arena.

This was rebellion.

I clambered to my feet unsteadily, as Aelia pushed a Diasord into my trembling hands.

'Y'know you're OK … for a feral girl.' She smiled fleetingly.

I threw my arms around her, burning with so many questions that had to wait, before thrusting her away again.

'Thanks,' I muttered, so conscious of its inadequacy.

But it was all there was time for. Outside the arena, guards were trying to restore order through brute force, appointing sentry positions through the tiered seats, and deploying new guard units to the circus archways.

'The pack are regrouping,' I whispered, sensing the change as the scattered beasts abandoned their kills to respond to the roar of another sabre-tooth.

It was a second leader, taking control. I'd heard Grandpa talk about forest wolves self-selecting a new leader when the old leader died; it had to be a sabre-tooth behaviour too.

'Cassius is opening the guard entrance,' Aelia hissed, ducking an arrow. 'we'll be overrun before we know it!'

'August?' I interrupted, recalling the moment he'd careered from the arena.

She shrugged, her eyes clouding before she ploughed on. 'Cassius won't be looking to take prisoners. Have you seen Raj …'

And just as though he'd heard his name being uttered, Rajid slid out from behind the crashed chariot, his expression so disdainful it was almost comical.

I suppressed a scowl. He appeared to be blessed with the devil's luck.

'How long have you been back there?' Aelia demanded, as we all dived for cover from a shower of arrows.

I looked from one to the other thinking firstly of Grey and

173

then Servilia. *Had they coordinated this together somehow? How many others?*

He looked contrite for a second.

'No matter, we have to signal a retreat! As fast as possible!'

'I like retreats.' He grinned, pulling his white-handled blade from his waistband, his inked Cerberus salivating beneath the hot lights.

Just what makes you so special?

His words had haunted me until Cassius had shared his final bombshell, the fact his brother Thomas had bequeathed me a damned bloodline.

Voynich chimera control.

'Rajid!' I yelled, levelling my Diasord as a guard sprinted in.

Rajid reacted instantly, throwing his knife at lightning speed and dispatching him without so much as a murmur. The guard slid to the ground, his eyes glassy and unseeing while Rajid reached out and retrieved his blade. I exhaled painfully, he was an enigma but he seemed to be on our side for now, at least.

'It's raining,' he warned, tipping his head curiously.

We didn't need another warning, and scattered as a second quiver-full of arrows skimmed our heads, and fell all around us. I watched as three buried themselves in the hindquarters of the dead sabre-tooth.

Each impact seemed to make it twitch.

I blinked. It continued to twitch.

'It can't be alive – you ripped a hole right through its carotid artery!' Aelia whispered, following my gaze.

And as if to thwart every rule of nature we ever held to be true, the creature started shaking, before suddenly rolling over onto its front. Slowly, it clambered back onto its feet, shook out the arrows protruding from its haunches and twisted its broad, blood-stained neck so my Diasord fell out with a thud. Then it bared its gruesome canines at Aelia in a way that left me in no doubt as to its full recovery. And I had the strangest feeling I knew why.

'No!' I forced, jumping to my feet, despite the aches and pains still ratcheting through my body.

The beast hesitated briefly before sinking its head again, its fixed diamond stare telling me it more than remembered our last encounter.

'Stand down!' I added, thrusting out a hand.

Aelia was eyeballing me; I could tell.

'Tal ...?' she whispered, as though I'd finally flipped, and yet I could tell the beast was listening.

It rolled its head to one side and padded forward, pausing in front of me before finally pushing its huge furry head into my hand, the way Jas might have nuzzled Eli.

She gasped, as I took a moment to catch my own breath.

'Chimera,' I whispered, recalling my control over the chimera in Cassius's temple.

I stared down at the purring beast. The animal was a hybrid, not a classic chimera but its multi-genus status had to be enough. *The control was in my blood.* Hadn't I proven it once already?

'It's incredible ...' Aelia muttered, backing off as the creature spun on the spot to face its own advancing pack, its haunches and tail slunk low in clear, protective mode.

I raised my eyebrows and shrugged, aware our odds had just improved dramatically. She grinned as the pack hesitated, confused by the behaviour of their new leader. I scanned the arena rapidly, scores of guards were pouring into the hot battle-scorched dust now. Chaos was breeding chaos, and Max was still nowhere to be seen.

Then a pack sabre-tooth chose her moment, sprinting in, head low and canines bared. Simultaneously, a thundering of hooves forced Aelia and I to dive aside as a loose indigo auroch galloped through from behind, bearing a charioteer.

I knew instinctively it was Max, and watched as the auroch passed us and lowered its head, throwing the advancing sabre-tooth broad side with its horn. The creature whined in sudden pain, before flipping over and landing awkwardly. She retreated to the back of the pack, licking her wound, and I wiped the sweat from my eyes, watching Max slow his auroch in a turn.

Was he assisting us? Or following orders?

Aelia and I were on our feet in a heartbeat, the sabre-tooth's injury creating doubt among the pack. I squared up beside my newly loyal animal, and hissed aggressively.

'Always so reliably feral,' Aelia muttered, before attempting to do the same.

I suppressed a chuckle. 'Says the fireside cat!'

She only had a second to scowl before Therry sprinted past the rear of the pack, tossing something fresh and bloody at the creatures. They turned to give chase instantly, relieved to switch to an easier prey.

I followed his progress anxiously as he sprinted through the dusty crowds, the frenzied pack on his winged heels, dividing the melee. But I needn't have worried; his downy wings spread at just the right moment, raising him above the crowds, and scattering the pack once more.

'Tal.'

Aelia's voice was low and urgent, pulling me back to the moment. And I knew it was Max before I saw him. A look of grey thunder stained his face. Not familiar or with us in any way at all, but furious. My hopes guttered as he advanced, the dust billowing up around each purposeful step.

His Diasord was raised not as a protective homebound Outsider, but as a bloodthirsty gladiatorial combatant, adopted son of Pantheon. Coming straight for us. Horror and revulsion rocketed through my veins, making the arena spin like a winged maple seed.

Then his gaze shifted and a slow smile spread across his face; an ugly smile that took my childhood memories and blackened them.

'August!' Max's demand rose above the din of the arena as a

Pantheonite charioteer wearing a winged gladiatorial helmet, the emblem of the Equite soldiers, charged past us as if we didn't even exist.

'August! Wait!' I yelled in disbelief.

But it was already too late. This was what they'd both been destined for – the charioteer's challenge.

The Commander General has had his orders.

They were Cassius's words, and his twisted game-playing at its finest.

The Outsider against the Insider, each fighting for their unnatural, opposing side. There was such a warped beauty to it.

Dark to dark. Blood to blood.

Their Diasords met in a violent clash of diamond sparks, leaving no doubt as to their murderous intent. And the anarchy seemed to melt away, as every pair of eyes swivelled towards the leaders' challenge circling near the centre.

I threw a glance at Cassius's balcony. His onyx eyes were fixed on our small group, a slow smile of ugly jubilation spreading across his face. And I could almost taste how much he'd pinned on this one vengeful moment. All to avenge a feral girl with a message about the outside. Because it was a truth he wanted to hide come what may.

'No!'

My yell pierced the blood-thick air, but neither combatant flinched. There was another clash of laser on laser, and then another and another, each thrust and parry getting faster and wilder as the fighting took on a rhythm of its own. And a hushed anticipation washed through the arena as thousands of eyes swivelled towards the two men, locked in their own muted world where nothing mattered except their own blind satisfaction.

'August!' I tried again, 'Stop! Max ... he doesn't remember anything!'

But his visor was down, and nothing but determination was written into the set of his jaw and grim smile. He didn't even seem to know me. Terror slid down my spine, the kind that belonged to nightmares.

He didn't even seem to know me?

'Tal …'

There was a slim hand around my wrist, pulling me back towards the upturned chariot where we took shelter from a fresh volley of arrows.

'Maybe … deep down … they've always wanted this?' Aelia whispered.

Her exhausted eyes begged me to understand she wasn't giving up, that she cared as much as I did, but that this was loaded.

I shot a look back at their unforgiving faces, at their circling, violent intent. To believe that on some subconscious level they actually wanted to spill each other's blood was so fundamental. My throat felt tight and raspy, I wanted to deny it. *But I couldn't.*

Could this death combat be fuelled by more than Pantheon, by more than the vaccine?

'That's it, isn't it?' Max fumed from my memory. 'I'm just not him!'

'They didn't take your new dart tube though, the one shaped like a tiny treehouse?' August asked.

I stared into her iris-blue eyes, the same colour as August's, as Max lunged again, giving August the perfect vantage to deliver a stinging blow to his shoulder. Max staggered under the impact, and the air filled with the unmistakable scent of burning flesh as a red welt opened up across the top of his indigo tunic.

'No!'

No more watching.

Shaking off Aelia's restraint, I leapt up and started sprinting towards them as Max reached up to wrestle August to the ground. Then they were rolling over and over, so it was impossible to intervene. First Max was on top, his Diasord rammed so hard into August's neck I could see his vein pulsing to compensate, and then it was August's turn to swing Max over with limb-breaking force.

And in that moment my fear converted entirely to loathing.

178

How could it have come to this? Two people who once meant the world, now eating dirt to kill one another.

The arena around me started to blur with dust, blood and lies. Grandpa had entrusted the legacy to me, and Arafel had never seemed so far away.

Why run when you can fly?

The whisper carried from the roar of the rebellion in the crowd. I spun a look around, at the anarchy outside the arena.

It was still burning.

Pantheonites and Prolets were fighting alongside each other, fighting Cassius's guards. *Fighting back.*

My gaze swung back to Cassius, protected on all sides and yet watching like a vulture, because so long as there was fighting, there was still hope for the outside. Hope, not hopelessness.

This was a war, not a fight.

'Max!' I roared, above the din, 'You're a hunter ... an Outsider ... a treehouse builder ... for the love of Arafel you have to remember!'

Their tumble slowed, and as Max forced August into a head-lock he looked up, and for just one split second I thought I detected *something*.

'Max?' I repeated, willing him to force blood into the quiet forgotten areas, willing him to remember.

And then there was a moment's pause where I dared to let my damned hope flicker, before he reached forward and ran the Diasord directly across August's throat.

A silent kill.

It was the manoeuvre Bereg had taught us both, for use when dispatching an animal cleanly and swiftly. Except we weren't in the forest any more, and as he dropped August's limp body into the red dirt, a hush spread across the entire circus.

I stared as the world faded to ghosts and hatred, to more fighting and bloodshed and battalions of soldiers spilling into the arena without check.

179

Hades was here after all. In front of me, scorching my skin.
Inside me.

And then he turned to salute Cassius's balcony. It was the salute of a charioteer who'd fulfilled his duty, with something else besides.

A smile of quiet victory.

Chapter 17

I pelted straight for my childhood friend, who only stood and lifted his remorseless face towards me.

Cold, bloodied. How could he not know what he had done?

He raised his Diasord as though I would be next and I readied myself, not caring if I was.

And I nearly reached him, before a jolting tackle stole the air from my body, propelling me away until we collided with the upturned chariot. I blinked, trying to clear my vision. Max was holding a fist to the crowd, taking his due, August's body crumpled at his feet.

'He'll kill you too, Tal,' Aelia rushed, strained and desperate. 'He'll kill us both. He can't handle the vaccine. We have to leave now! We'll come back,' she pleaded.

I shot a numbed look around, at the arena awash with valiant Outsiders and Prolet rebels. There were more than I ever hoped for, but we were still no match for the battalions pouring into the arena, for the teams of molossers being unleashed, and for the archers releasing clouds of arrows from the balconies.

The only certainty was that every second I delayed, I risked the lives of everyone remaining.

The last Outsiders. There was still an outside to fight for. Come what may, nature finds a way.

She was white-faced, always the doctor, saving those she could.

I nodded abruptly, before reaching around the upturned chariot to grasp one of the abandoned bugles. It wasn't the ibex, but it would do. I lifted it to my lips, and a moment later, the call of Arafel's hunters was echoing through the arena. Aelia jumped to her feet, and with fire in our bellies, we flew through the bloody chaos towards the top of the fray, towards a pair of two figures barely holding off a pack of guards.

Rajid and Grey? I couldn't quite fathom how it had come to this – running from August and Max, towards men I'd all but hated hours ago. It was brutally ironic.

Aelia didn't hesitate, delivering a short punch into the burly guard's lower back, who dropped with a groan, while I lashed out with a high kick that took another guard off his feet. Then the loyal sabre-tooth sprinted up, and sank his jaws into the shoulders of a third, which scattered the rest instantly.

Rajid and Grey straightened, sweaty, and dishevelled, as I threw a look back over my shoulder. The arena was a hot dust cloud of chaos, but Outsiders and Prolets were emerging from every corner, running towards us. Hope written into their faces.

I threw a look of desperation at Aelia. We were against the arena wall, with nowhere left to run. *What now?*

'Grey!'

Her voice was urgent and gritty as he reached down to grab the broken remains of one of the chariot's sculpted wings. Then he and Rajid lifted it to reveal a slim black hole and, beside it, a round metal plate. It looked like one of Pantheon's maintenance shafts.

'The tunnels,' I whispered, suddenly understanding how so many Outsiders had infiltrated the arena while I was unconscious.

And as I gazed, an ugly realization swirled up inside. I'd sworn never to abandon any of my family again, and even if it was impossible to save Max, Mum was still here.

182

'Stop them! Seize them immediately!'

Cassius's voice boomed through the arena's media system. I glanced up at the balcony, never more conscious of the dart tube resting beneath my tunic. It would never be over until I finished it. I could sprint now, and try my luck. I'd never make it out, but the dart had to be a good one – Ida had made it. And with a little luck Rajid had tipped it with some of his bat poison.

'We leave now!' Aelia hissed, pushing Therry and the young Prolet girl towards the hole.

They jumped without hesitation, and were swiftly followed by an Arafel hunter and Komodo who muttered something unintelligible before dropping into the black. I scowled, urging Aelia forward but she eyed me stubbornly.

'Mum?' I whispered, entreating her to understand.

'She's safe!' Aelia exploded in relief and fury. 'You think we don't know you? We got her first. What do you think took us so long!'

Raw, furious words had never held so much comfort. Yet it was enough. Finally. I took her outstretched hand, and together we dropped into the hole, like two broken halves of an arrow.

Care for the seed and it will care for you.

Grandpa's wisdom whispered around as the black enveloped us. There was a simple poignancy to it. I'd always thought he was talking about the tiny seeds of nature, but now I knew his simple philosophy was much broader. That he was talking about outside life, each other, and the future.

We fell like stones into the abyss, and I would have known the steady tree trunk arms that reached up to break our fall anywhere. *Unus.* He set us on our feet gently, before retraining his pale eye on the circle of light above as another Outsider dropped through. And then another, and another. There were shouts, and even the clatter of the odd arrow as, one by one, the small courageous army that had risked everything to rescue me and defy Cassius, made the leap of faith.

183

Grey never appeared, and as the circular plate was heaved back into place from above, I could feel this was his way of atoning too. So many of us, caught up in Cassius's dark web.

And then at last, silence.

There was little light and the stench-filled corridor was thick with the sound of rapid breathing. No one was labouring under any illusions. We'd escaped one hellhole, but we were now in the underbelly of Cassius's lair. And I couldn't imagine any of his favourite pets were that far away.

I leaned back against the tunnel wall as reality raked down the inside of my gut with gritty fingernails. I swallowed, trying to ease the fireball of pain spreading down every nerve.

Iris-blues smiling, teasing, wanting, protecting ... dying in front of me. At Max's hand? Had I subconsciously fanned the hatred?

It's not your fault.

They were his last words. If I'd known it was the only chance I'd have ... The fireball reached my lungs.

I'd let him leave Arafel believing I didn't care.

It was too much, and I turned and retched against the inside of the tunnel wall, only faintly aware of the slim hand at the base of my spine.

'It wasn't him!' Aelia whispered, the white of her eyes stained pink with arena dust. 'I was deceived too ... but there was ... no recognition or visible scars that I could see ... I'm sure it wasn't him.'

I was so conscious of the tremble in her voice, about how much I wanted to believe her fantasy because it was much easier than reality.

'It was one of Octavia's original test subjects,' she hissed, 'reissued! It wasn't him, Tal. I just know it. He's still out there!'

Her whisper was distraught, needing me to believe so she could believe, and yet perhaps it was a way of getting through too. I could see how sunken and hollow her eyes were, and how all the hurt was writing itself into her face. She'd lost so much too. I'd

184

never been blind to her affection for Max, and now he'd killed her only brother. Probably. It was enough to send anyone into a vortex of denial.

'He's ... not ... dead,' I whispered slowly, 'but *Max*?'

She lifted her jaw stubbornly and I knew her medical brain was trying to rationalize it, to find an explanation for such an indefensible act.

'Some subjects can't ... have no intrinsic ability or resource to reject the vaccine. They can have extreme reactions, a form of induced psychosis.' Her voice cracked.

Her blue eyes were as dark as the indigo sea.

I nodded. It was the only lifeline we had. I stood up to face the small silent army gathering in the tunnel, acutely aware of a fresh responsibility. So many injuries and lives traded, all to rescue a feral girl who was supposed to know how to change it all.

I steeled my nerve, counting swiftly. There were fifteen familiar faces from Arafel and perhaps the same again of Komodos, Eurasians and Lynx. And there was something in their proximity, in the way they stood together, that was new. They were Outsiders, united by persecution, something Pantheon could never understand. And there were Prolets too, at least ten grubby-faced children: Therry, twin girls, the boy with the tiny griffin and more young satyrs. My eyes drank in their solemn, hopeful faces.

Were these all who had rejected the vaccine?

So many were missing. The thought raked my gut anew, and yet there was no time to lose. I ran my gaze over the valiant group, bereft of words. *Thank you* wasn't enough, and this wasn't the place. But the smiles were real, and I hoped they could read my eyes.

'Unus?'

His ponderous shuffle echoed through the darkness as the group divided to let him through. And as he loomed up in the darkness, one of his plate hands reached out and patted my shoulder kindly. Relief cascaded through my body, though a lump the size of a boulder prevented any words from escaping. He inclined his huge head and I knew he understood, and moreover, that there was no time to waste standing here. He turned, and we started down the dank tunnel, his company comforting in a way I'd almost forgotten.

We made steady progress, and although a faint clattering and scuttling proved we were undoubtedly in strix territory, Unus's rumblings kept them all at bay.

'Oh good, bottled bats,' Aelia muttered, as Rajid slipped up next to her, holding one of his homemade lamps, courtesy of Unus.

He smirked, his inked Cerberus dancing in the shifting low light. I nodded. Who was I to judge loyalty, when I wasn't even sure what it looked like any more? I could never forgive him for betraying us at the cathedral, but I could see I owed him some sort of small reprieve. For now. And it distracted from the fact Max had ripped a hole so large I couldn't even think straight.

I felt Aelia's hand touch mine and I gripped back with real warmth. Like a pack of cards, our house had come tumbling down, throwing everything I held to be real and true into the flames. So much lost, so much confused and yet she was here. We were both still here.

'Mum?' I whispered.

'She's OK,' she reassured me, 'she's waiting … with the remaining survivors, in the new camp. Said it wasn't so bad?'

I nodded, unable to smile but feeling a huge weight shift from my chest.

'You all need your heads read,' I muttered.

'Look who's talking,' she retorted, though I could tell the effort was costing her, the same way the effort not to give in to the pain was costing me.

'I suppose you were forced to make that crazy leap into an arena packed with sabre-tooths. Yeah, I mean that's what any sane, rational person would do!'

186

'You started it!' I retorted, nearly choking on a forgotten sensation reaching up my throat. 'You snuck a rebel army into one of Cassius's Ludi arenas!'

'Where have you been … How on earth did you manage …?' I started, my mind clouding with a million memories.

Letting her cold body sink into the glass river, waking up beside Eli, witnessing August's pain when he thought he'd lost her, and the appearance of the rebel survivor army when I needed them most. So many questions I couldn't even begin to fathom while my mind was so clouded.

'Servilia … Rajid … Grey … the Prolets who'd voided …' she responded, reading my thoughts.

'Just stay alive!'

Grey's gritty whisper echoed through my head along with Servilia's friendship, her snatched conversations with the Prolet bath women and then the smuggled dart tube. I'd nearly strangled Rajid, when he'd been brought into the detainees' unit simply to gain access to Servilia and Ludi. So much careful manoeuvring and I hadn't even guessed.

'And the Oceanids never explain, but they always have their reasons,' she alluded.

A tiny smile warmed her pale face.

'Arafel has a lot of friends, Talia … Once Eli began formulating a plan of rescue, it was just a matter of timing.'

'Eli! He's …?' I rushed, finally summoning the courage to ask the question I'd been terrified to ask all along.

'Bossy!' Aelia filled, eyebrows forking.

A river of relief flooded my limbs, making the tunnels waver.

'But how did you organize it …? Get word around on the inside?'

Aelia ghost-smiled. 'Rajid and Grey were slowly building a small rebel army, made up of those few Prolets unaffected by the vaccine. We used the old Roman tunnels to find our way into Isca Prolet, and found a handful of the old PFF resistance there, they were more than happy to help their old General.' She paused to smile.

'We got word to Grey, Rajid and Servilia via the baths' Prolet workers – and used the laundry shifts to access your mum's safe unit. She was anxious, but completely lucid! She made me promise I'd make sure you didn't do anything stupid.'

A dart twisted inside my chest as I felt a second rush of relief and pride. I'd been so terrified Mum would give herself away once she started remembering. It seemed she'd evaded detection until she was rescued.

'And Servilia?' I whispered, remembering how she'd risked her life to help me.

Aelia hesitated before shaking her head. 'She was ... found out.'

My eyes blurred as Rajid dropped his gaze to his feet, and suddenly I knew exactly why Servilia had seemed so familiar. It seemed even unpredictable, Prolet rebels had family.

I sucked in a shaky breath, trying to find some words, but Rajid chose that moment to melt away again, back into the gloom.

'Eli hasn't stopped looking for Lake, the whole time you've been gone.'

I shot a look at her exhausted face, trying to remember how much she knew before the cathedral.

'He told me everything when I got back ...' she whispered.

'I suspected Cassius was experimenting with *Hominum chimera*, but not that he'd made so much progress so fast. Rajid told me about the chimera ward in the laboratories months ago, but that Lake was ... is actually an attempt to re-create the oldest secret of the Voynich.'

'She's possibly the best and worst thing Cassius has ever done.' My head conjured up Lake's fiery will and unforgettable serpentine eyes.

'So why isn't Eli here?' I whispered finally.

I knew of course, my instincts had been telling me for weeks – I just hadn't allowed them to become conscious thoughts.

She threw me a strained look.

'He went out every day with Unus, trying to track her. Evenings were spent planning your rescue. He barely slept. Then two days before we came here, he went out – and didn't come back.'

I swallowed hard. Her words weren't a surprise; they were a confirmation. And while I could tell she was worried, for some reason I wasn't. I knew Eli so well, I'd know if he was hurt or worse …

I sucked in a deep breath. So long as he was on the outside, there was very little that could hurt Eli. He was a trained hunter, and gifted animal-whisperer. Lake could be the one exception, but for some reason I doubted she'd hurt him either. She was complex and volatile, but she was also multi-genus. Eli stood four times the chance of managing her than anyone else.

'There was never any doubt we were coming to get you, he planned it down to the last detail,' she finished.

'And you?' I asked hesitantly. 'Where have you been?'

She hesitated, a sudden shadow in her eyes.

'Do you remember anything about the underwater kingdom of the Oceanids?' she whispered after a beat.

I hesitated before shaking my head.

'I thought as much – memory is a common trade for recovery,' she mused.

I analysed her profile carefully. 'Memory? Common trade?' I repeated slowly, 'I thought …'

I inhaled sharply. I suspected I'd got it all wrong, that August and I hadn't traded our hearts, but everything had become so fogged.

'I thought we traded …'

Aelia looked at me, the sadness in her eyes telling me she knew. 'They're loyal only to themselves,' she added softly, 'but they're not cruel.'

'So do you remember?' I returned, thinking furiously now at last I knew the truth.

It was real for me, Talia.

My skin started to prickle. I'd suspected I was only hiding from my own pain, and now I had confirmation. I'd been cruel to August because I couldn't cope – not because anything had changed between us. Some kind of feral legacy I was turning out to be, when I didn't even have the courage to face my own emotions. Cassius and Livia's trials had never held more relevance and yet, what of the strength that grew from being broken? What of Aelia's fairy-tale hope he might still be alive?

And if he was still alive, where in this hellhole would he be?

'If I stop trying to remember, it comes back,' Aelia began.

'The shadows inside the sea caves, and the sway of the kelp ... their cool healing hands, the soft sound of their harmonies ...'

'... and the gleam of oyster pearls along the pathways,' I finished in a whisper.

And as she spoke, she stirred up near-forgotten memories of dark, deep-sea ovoid eyes silently clamouring for an end to Pantheon.

'You and Eli, did you know each other there?' I added, still caught up in the shadows her words had stirred.

'Eli was always with ... Prince Phaethon,' she responded, eyeing me carefully.

I nodded, recalling the intense night at the lake. Eli and Prince Phaethon – it was so unlikely, and yet Eli's eyes had shone in a way I'd never seen before.

Aelia shot a swift look behind us before leaning closer.

'The Oceanids have existed since the time of the Voynich, in deep oceans and lakes undisturbed by mankind, but there were meetings of the War Council while we were there. Phaethon has been watching Cassius, and his army hasn't seen battle since ancient times, but he's gathering his warriors, Tal.'

I stared at Aelia, the watery echoes of a beating drum reaching through the murkiness in my head.

'He wants Cassius stopped at all costs,' she finished.

'I … made him a promise,' I muttered, recalling my trade at the lake.

She nodded. 'And I promised to help you.'

I stared at her elfin profile in the darkness, at the familiar jut of her proud jaw.

'That was my trade, *come what may*. Course … I would have helped you anyway, just didn't fancy trading my memory,' she added nonchalantly.

I stared at her in amazement.

It was almost comical, Grandpa's words being repeated by an Insider on a mission set by an underwater mythical regent.

'He has an army?' I asked swiftly.

She frowned, reading my thoughts.

'Yes. But the Oceanids don't make promises; they just extract them. He also seems to place the fulfilment of the Voynich legacy above all else, but I guess we can hope he notices if we make a right mess of things.'

There were so many questions on the tip of my tongue as a new noise interrupted the momentum of our feet, making Unus freeze and listen intently. My skin started to crawl as it came again.

'Molossers?'

Therry appeared out of the gloom suddenly and gripped my hand. 'Or the rat-owls. Unus rumble, warn them off!'

I held my finger to my lips, and shot a look at Unus who'd turned his head enough for me to read his grim profile. I recalled only one creature willing enough to take on the strix.

'We stick together,' Aelia whispered, looking pointedly at me.

'Did Eli take anyone with him when he disappeared?' I urged, needing to know everything before I said it.

She shook her head. 'He left early without Unus. Think he knew we needed him more? He took food and blankets though,' she added placatingly.

I nodded, unruffled. It was just like Eli to go looking for a volatile, mythical chimera trusting only to his whispering skills. Somehow I still knew he was OK.

I shot a look down the dark tunnel ahead. *It was silent again but for how long?*

'Lia, you know there's no time for debate,' I rushed, my mind made up. 'We all leave Pantheon now and we'll be running from Cassius for the rest of our lives.'

I gazed at the courageous, exhausted faces gathering around us and felt my words falter. They'd just risked everything, but in reality there may never be another chance.

I drew a deep breath.

'Cassius will be expecting a single escape party, and his attention will be on all the tunnel exit points, not the tunnels beneath Isca Pantheon.'

Aelia's expression was growing darker by the second.

'There's a new camp? Of survivors?' I pushed on, so conscious of time.

'A few, yes. It's on the south-western border of the Dead City ... Your mum is waiting there,' she filled in suspiciously.

'And you're convinced, the charioteer we watched fight Max wasn't ...'

She stared at me, eyes half-closed. 'Octavia's favourites always had a test series. Cassius would have only needed to programme his behaviours in August's absence.'

'Unless he isn't absent,' I filled in meaningfully.

'You think he's here? In Isca Pantheon?'

My breath quickened, as I threw another glance down the tunnel. It was a huge hunch but one I was willing to stake my life on. If August had returned to Arafel to find it razed, wouldn't he have come here? To confront Cassius? *Wasn't that what Cassius had meant about having something I wanted?*

A faint clattering reached through the eerie silence. The strix weren't far away now. Unus reacted instantly, filling the tunnel with a deep rumble that sent the creatures on far enough for the moment.

'Maybe,' I answered grimly, 'he's been gone for months and …'.

'And?'

'I made him feel he wasn't wanted – in Arafel.'

I'd said it, sort of.

Aelia was silent for a moment, filling in the gaps. 'The party of hunters, Komodo and Lynx he journeyed with returned separately,' she mused.

I looked at Aelia sharply. This was new.

'I didn't tell you before now because they said he mentioned one last community to rally. On his own. I took it to mean another Outsider community but the fact he went alone … perhaps he was really talking about one closer to home – if he felt he had nothing to lose?'

'Isca Prolet,' I breathed.

We stared at one another, feeling the truth of it all. It was just the sort of thing he would do, knowing Cassius to be responsible for Aelia's death, knowing he was slowly erasing every free-thinking Prolet that ever existed and *believing I didn't care any more.*

And I have something you want, Talia.

My stomach rolled over. Perhaps, for once, Cassius really had been telling the truth.

Another eerie sound, like end of a howl, reached us through solid rock and this time it was close enough to send the strix clattering, their thick, sharp claws making a hollow raking noise as they panicked. One glance at Unus's hunched shoulders told me we'd done enough hesitating.

I shot Aelia an intense look – a question. Her iris-blues, so dulled by the circus dust, lit up instantly. I smirked, shaking my head.

'We're kinda on a promise anyway.' She shrugged.

'And even if we weren't,' I muttered darkly.

She smiled then and the decision was made.

Two feral heads. Grief fuelled. Arafel, the Prolet tanks, Ludi, Lake, August, Max, everyone we ever cared about … Livia said emotion made us weak and predictable. But she'd forgotten a basic rule of nature, that flesh once torn often binds tighter and stronger than before.

I reached a hand forward to touch Unus's quivering warm arm, indicating a fork just up ahead in the gloom. His whole body was tense as he inclined his broad head towards me.

'Big … dog?' I whispered.

He dipped his great head once towards the right, as another faint howl echoed through the rock walls. It was faint but unmistakable, and this time there was no clatter of strix claws – even they'd had the sense not to hang around.

'Not … far … That … way.'

'And the exit is that way, Unus?' I pointed left.

He nodded again, his large cerulean eye pale with fear.

'Then take everyone that way,' I instructed, 'as fast as you can!'

'Tal … no come …?'

His eye dilated with gentle hurt. He knew, of course he knew.

I shook my head briefly, and wasn't deaf to the collective murmur as my small band of loyal warriors gathered around, their eyes shining like outside stars.

'If I come with you now, Cassius will hound every last one of us until we are dead.' My voice was low and urgent. 'Outsiders will no longer exist. He will win … But if Aelia and I split with you now. There's the tiniest, remotest chance, we can stop Cassius once and for all … and give the outside a real future.'

My voice was surprisingly steady, hiding the grief welling up inside.

Was this the last time I would see any of them again?

And then acquiescence. None spoken, but in the glint of their eyes, and shuffle of their feet. They understood. It was a last chance for all of us.

194

I turned back to Unus and wrapped my arms around him fiercely. He responded in kind and silently, I swore I would wear his courage and friendship like armour.

'I'd like to offer my services? If they can be of use?' a familiar voice drawled.

Rajid loomed forward out of the darkness.

I raised my eyebrows at Aelia who just nodded once. Another pair of hands was always useful, if Rajid could just remember whose side he was on.

'I'll take the rear,' Saba volunteered, 'if Unus can get us through.'

'Yes, now go!' I encouraged, smiling with so much more conviction than I felt. 'Tell the others we're alive, that there's a plan and they must stay hidden at all costs.

'We'll join you – when we're through here.'

Unus rumbled, handing me his bat lantern. 'I come back ... Rat-owls no like dog ...'rember trick.'

I gritted my teeth, refusing to let him see how much it was costing me to be left behind in the flickering darkness with the creatures of my nightmares. Knowing I was saying goodbye to our best chance of getting out of the tunnels alive.

'No don't risk it, Unus,' I whispered. 'We'll find another way out. Just get them out, look after everyone ... till we get back.'

He stared at me, his huge moon-face dulling with sadness as he leaned close to whisper. 'Tal ... have heart of Cyclops ...'nyway.'

Then he turned and lumbered away, and one by one our small band of friends followed.

Leaving the three of us alone in the breathing black.

Chapter 18

There was a strange prophetic irony to it. Stealing through the tunnels beneath Isca Pantheon – inked Cerberus out in front, flesh-and-blood hellhound somewhere behind.

And I still wasn't sure who I trusted less.

Rajid had signed his own death warrant by publicly siding with the insurgents, but the image of him standing behind Cassius in the cathedral would never fade either.

You've the memory of an elephant, Tal, the longest in the animal kingdom.

I could hear the smile in Grandpa's voice even now.

Aelia was a step behind me, her steady breath a comfort among the nightmares. I'd never felt so vulnerable, and the odds were so stacked against us it didn't pay to think about them. And yet, if there was the remotest chance we could tip the balance …

Astra inclinant, sed non obligant. The stars guide us, they do not bind us. He was right about that.

My mind kept replaying the moment August's body collapsed beneath the brutal delivery of Max's blow. Again and again I watched the sinews of Max's treehouse-building arm tightening with intent.

Was it Pantheon that delivered the blow? Or Max? Or me? Had I killed August through words and inaction?

Not dead. Not dead. He couldn't be dead.

'Tal ... Tal?'

Aelia's strained whisper brought me back to the moment. We'd been running stealthily for several minutes now, and had reached another dark fork in the tunnels.

'It's right – we should keep right for the laboratories,' she hissed from behind.

Rajid glanced back, surprisingly calm, as though facing his own gruesome death was an everyday occurrence. But then it probably had been of late.

He nodded, his blackened tooth appearing even more grotesque in the flickering bat-light, before veering towards the right-hand tunnel. I gritted my teeth. The walls seemed to be compressing and space almost airless. The dirty, gaunt faces of the Prolet children ran through my head. They'd survived for weeks beneath the Dead City on nothing but mangy rodent and rainwater run-off. And now they were paying for having dared dream of another life. They spurred me on.

Moments later we approached another fork. Rajid hesitated only briefly before selecting the right tunnel. I shuddered. This one was even narrower.

'OK?' I whispered over my shoulder.

'It's the right direction,' Aelia mumbled. 'Rajid knows these service tunnels better than me, but there's always a risk ...'

'Of running headlong into strix,' I hissed.

'Of not running headlong into strix,' she returned. 'That way we know we're in trouble.'

I glanced into the darkness behind us both. It was quiet, but in Pantheon quiet never meant empty. The hellhound was on our tail, of that much I was sure. The only question was how much tunnel – or wall – stood between us.

'The narrower the tunnel, the harder we are to follow,' Rajid threw back, squeezing past a shelf of chest-height, protruding rock.

I swallowed, recalling the moment Unus and I had faced Cassius's Cerberus in these tunnels. Nothing could have prepared me for the slathering jaws, sinewy necks and blood-lusting eyes. It was a fitting demon for Cassius to call his own, with a tangible hunger that made my skin scrawl with the march of a thousand fire ants.

I closed my eyes and pushed past the same shelf, following Rajid's lead down a putrid tunnel that felt like the fetid entrails of Pantheon's underbelly. By my rough calculation, we had to be directly beneath the central domestic dome, connecting Pantheon to the laboratories.

Which meant we were also close to Isca Prolet. Or what was left of it.

I pressed my teeth together as I recalled the empty shell of an underground world, through which Pan, Max and I had been chased by a swarm of hungry basilisk. Back then the entire Prolet population had been rounded up by Cassius as retaliation for the young Prolets' rebellion. Now Arafel and all Outsiders had all but been exterminated, and with the new obedient Prolet army growing silently in the laboratories, how much longer before the rest of the existing Prolet population were deemed unviable? Rajid and Aelia's people. They had to know the clock was ticking.

Aelia's steady step was doing much to calm my erratic thoughts, even though my arm wound was aching again. She'd always been such a logical, unapologetic rebel. Our friendship had seemed so unlikely at the start and yet here we were together. More than survivors and friends. We were kin.

Rajid paused, holding up a hand, and we all froze, listening to nothing and everything at the same time – the hollow echo of mineral run-off, Aelia's shortened breath, the rub of my fingers. It all sounded overloud and accentuated in this tight, oxygen-less space.

'Strix?' I breathed, almost hopefully.

'Perhaps,' he whispered before creeping forward again, more stealthily this time.

I was too numb to feel scared, almost as though I'd trodden on Eli's Dead City scorpion, and its venom had slowly erased every last nerve I possessed. There was only guilt and a promise, and while I was anxious for Aelia, I felt nothing for my own fate. Or Rajid's.

The air around us had fallen suspiciously quiet. Even the low, uneven rock ceiling seemed to have stopped dripping. And my head was losing its fight against the logical impossibility of passing through these tunnels without detection by its flesh-eating occupants.

'It's too quiet,' I mumbled over my shoulder at Aelia.

Her face was strained, her hollow eyes sculpting the contours of her skull in the low light. 'I know.'

Then we all heard it. A scratching. Beyond the tunnel, but getting louder. It was too consistent to be a pack of strix, and the sound was getting steadily louder. I only knew of one monster with claws powerful enough to tunnel through solid rock.

'It's digging!' Rajid whispered with a curious, fanatical smile. 'It can detect our scent through solid stone wall ... three times the tracking ability of a wolf ... beautiful!'

He reached out, entranced, and placed his palm against the dank, mouldy walls, and as if in answer, they began to tremble. Tiny shrapnel-sized pieces of stone began to crumble off the ravined rock above our heads.

'Your beautiful hellhound is going to bring it all down,' I hissed. 'Move now!'

And at that precise moment the whole tunnel started to cave in.

With fresh adrenaline flooding our limbs we pelted into the darkness ahead. There was no hiding our approach now, but a pack of rat-owls suddenly seemed the least of our problems. Dust, debris and rock showered us as we sprinted, sucking up any remaining air and making us choke and struggle for breath. My eyes streamed amid the dust and grain particles and finally, just when I thought my chest was going to explode, we spilled out into some sort of large underground cavern.

Coughing, we leaned back against the new solid rock wall, taking a moment to wipe our eyes and clear our lungs. It was quieter and cooler in here, with thicker walls all around. It felt like a temporary haven, until Rajid held up the bat lantern.

Prompting a silence of the worst kind.

Because a sea of yellow, predatory eyes were looking straight back at us.

I sucked in a small ragged breath as the bat lantern revealed our mistake. A whole crowd of giant black rat-owls, perhaps as many as two hundred, pressed together in one living, breathing mass of matted feathers and calcified beaks. We'd stumbled straight into their lair, and judging by the way the frontrunners were fixing us with their beady carnivorous stares, they weren't unhappy about dinner presenting itself.

'Don't … make … any … sudden … movements,' Rajid whispered somewhat ironically, his lantern softly swaying from one side of the herd to the other, with a telltale rusty creak. And we might have considered his whimsical advice, had the silence not been broken by low, furious snarling.

'OK … change of plan … move.'

And as hundreds of hard, yellow orb eyes swung towards the tunnel mouth from which we'd emerged, we seized our cue and sprinted along the cavern wall, searching desperately for a recess or exit, anything that might provide shelter from the bloodbath that must surely follow.

A hateful cawing and shrieking started to fill the void, raking over my eardrums and stretching them until I thought they must burst. I shot a look over my shoulder and regretted it instantly. The dim light from the tunnel entrance was slowly being engulfed by an ominous black shadow that was spilling out on the cavern floor before pushing upwards into a terrifying reality. Three looming black wolf-heads, each the size of a molossus dog, with ravenous, bulbous eyes and sinewy, darting necks. Even the strix herd paled next to the hellhound slowly squeezing the last of its muscular haunches out of the tight tunnel, its coarse hair making a hideous rubbing noise. I clenched every muscle I possessed. It looked even more grotesque than I remembered in the dancing bat-light.

'That way!' Aelia panted urgently, pointing through the gloom to a narrow black recess just visible in the cave wall.

I eyed it with blurred misgiving. At the moment there were a dozen strix closer than us, and even if we did get there before them, who knew if it led anywhere, or even if there were more strix inside. And yet, there was no going back either.

The creature's wolfish heads darted from left to right, clearly confused by the sudden choice in meals. Then it slunk low on its huge front paws, its heads lowering simultaneously, daring anyone to move. The strix squared up instantly, lifting their calcified beaks and shrieking in unison, their number of claws and beaks their defence. Desperately, I recalled how the Cerberus chased the strix at the last encounter with Unus, willing it to do the same now, but this wolfhound looked bigger, darker, more malevolent. My limbs tensed, and all I could think as it lifted its heads and howled its slathering excitement to the rock ceiling, was that this wasn't the same Cerberus Unus and I faced at all.

And then, pandemonium.

There was a moment of chaotic frenzy as the Cerberus flew directly at the pack, snapping two sets of glistening jaws around the front screeching rat-owls, and shaking them until the air filled with hideous cracking noises. Then it hurled them across the dark space so their scrawny bodies smacked into the rock walls around us and slid to the floor. Each bone-splintering impact ricocheted through me, as though it were my bones being crushed for sport. The air thickened with the scent of blood and terror as we fought our way along the wall, surrounded on all sides. Thick black wings and claw-shaped beaks snapped and ripped at anything in their way, blinding us, while the Cerberus continued in its crazed killing frenzy. Then a pained scream split the cavern, forcing it into a moment's shocked silence.

'Aelia?' I yelled, a white fear blazing through my veins.

I couldn't lose her, not here, not now.

'Run,' she croaked thickly.

She was close – I shot a hand out in the thick, flapping, putrid-smelling black and somehow found hers. There was another groan about a metre in front as the bat lantern flew up into the air and rolled the centre of the space. *Rajid?*

Then a sharp pain flew up my left arm as a beak made contact with my wound, digging in before retracting again. It was agony. They could smell my blood from the sabre-tooth injury. And it took everything I had not to yell as I battled and kicked the air repeatedly, my arms and legs impacting again and again on the creatures' hard skeletal-muscular bodies, keeping them at bay for as long as I could. If I was going to be eaten alive, I was taking a few of them down with me.

'Hold your wound ... don't panic,' Aelia whispered unevenly. 'They have an acute sense of smell but ... I think they're actually ... blind ...'

I shuddered and clamped a hand over my arm wound. *Blind? Like Cassius's griffins?* It made perfect sense of their incarceration in the tunnels of course – another living defect of his Biotechnical Programme, shut away where their imperfections wouldn't be quite so problematic.

I drew a deep breath and, lowering my head, crept as fast as I dared along the wall, pulling Aelia behind me. We were still knocked and clawed, but Aelia was right, without a noise prompt, the strix had no idea of our precise location.

Rajid's stealthy shadow was just ahead, and it looked as though he'd worked out the same. The abandoned bat lantern in the centre was throwing an eerie uplight across the heaps of broken rat-owl bodies, while their killer was chasing the remaining scat-

202

tered groups with frenzied delight. And now the narrow black inset was no more than a short sprint ahead. I gritted my teeth. We could make it, I was sure we could. And then Aelia squeezed my hand so hard I felt sure she must break all the bones.

'Tal …'

It wasn't so much what she said as how. I sucked in a hollow, jagged breath as I threw a reluctant darting look back.

Six blood-infused wolf eyes levelled at us. *Aware.* Knowing we were making a bid for escape. And this new hellhound could see a million times better than its prey.

It snarled viciously, tired of playing skittles with the strix, as it pulled its muscular body around, sending another group of rat-owls careering into the cavern wall, the dull thud of their bodies their last earthly sound.

Then the three heads fused together to form a solid wall of wolf, as it lowered to level its fireball eyes with ours. Summoning every last scrap of feral will, I forced myself to meet its scrutiny, to look directly into the depths of its voided soul and face the shadows gathered there. It was the coldest place on earth.

This was less a creature than a breathing weapon, moulded by Cassius's darkest intent. Its synthesis was too complex, its nature too artificial, a myth that should never have stepped off the page. And perhaps that was what made Rajid step forward, softly whistling. That or his goddamned variable heart, which seemed to follow every fresh wind that blew.

'Rajid,' I hissed as the hound swung its heads towards the small wiry Prolet, barely visible in the stench-ridden air.

He only smirked and threw a stone so it scuttled along the floor. The sound distracted the wolf momentarily until it rolled to a standstill, and then it snarled violently, swinging its heads back around to face Rajid, its six eyes flashing.

'Beautiful doggy …' Rajid soothed melodically, taking another stone and scuttling it across the floor littered with carcasses.

Its only response was to lift one of its heads and release pure fury in a succession of spine-splintering howls ... It was relent-less. Where one set of wolf-lungs ceased, another other took over until the entire cavern was trembling.

'It's going to bring the roof down!' Rajid muttered curiously, his black eyes glinting in the gloom.

In the next second he was running out and around the Cerberus' monstrous crouching haunches towards the other side of the cavern floor.

'Here doggy doggy ...! No! Over here ... Y'know I'm kind of an admirer ... no its not a chat-up line ... Hey! Fido! I'm not standing around for ever, not with what's left of your feathery mates eyeing me up like an aperitif.'

Aelia and I could only watch in horror as the beast finally gave in and whipped its body around to face Rajid, distracted and furious.

'Well you can either stand around waiting to be dessert, or you could take advantage of my last generous gesture and scram! And, Talia .... get Lia out ...'

His tone was edged with a curious grit that left nothing to question. I stared for a millisecond, spell-bound by the thought that Rajid, of all people, should be the one to rescue us. That he actually had one noble instinct beneath his flippant skin.

I didn't need telling twice.

Grabbing Aelia by the arm, I half stumbled, half sprinted the last few metres to the narrow inset we'd spied, and mercifully it seemed to be another access tunnel. It felt quiet and welcoming, and as soon as we were inside we spun around, desperate to do something, anything, to help. And the scene was astonishing.

Rajid was dancing across the cavern floor, sidestepping and jumping to avoid the beast's lunging, snapping mouths.

'So you got three heads?? You're different ... I get it ... but y'know I'm different too ... in a different way ... I like three heads ... that makes us friends ... sort of.' He grinned, pausing to point to his neck.

204

The Cerberus only fell into a chilling silence, trapping Rajid up against the opposite wall.

'It doesn't need to come between us,' he cajoled, holding up his hands in mock submission, 'and yours are definitely bigger than mine.'

'Rajid, get ready to run!' I yelled, grabbing a heavy rock and scuttling it along the cavern floor so it hit the beast on its back leg. It snarled but gave no ground, standing squarely between us and Rajid.

Then Aelia and I reached down to the rocks and stones at our feet and started raining fury on its haunches, willing the beast to shift just a few centimetres and give Rajid a chance. Its two outlying heads snarled and snapped back in anger, interspersed by a chorus of rough cawing as a few of the rocks impacted on the scattered vulturous strix, just waiting for the chance to finish whatever the Cerberus started.

'Move! You ugly, goddamned son of an under …!' I started as it suddenly rounded on us with a series of vociferous howls that made the rock walls crumble and fall.

'Rajid, run!' I yelled as the earth began to rain her wrath down around us.

'Just remember what makes you special …' came his faded response, only just reaching through the dust clouds billowing between us.

And in that moment, I thought Hades himself had reached up through the heart of the earth. The disintegrating walls gave us no option but to stumble backwards, away from the cavern, and away from Rajid. But just before the tunnel entrance filled up entirely, I glimpsed a last haunting image.

It was of fire-eyes, glowing like embers, and open, slathering jaws as they finally descended around a waiting figure.

***

'It was his kind of recompense … for what happened before,' I whispered.

It was several hours later and we were beneath the laboratories, in the very same tunnel we'd explored with Rajid all those months ago before Ludi. The rockfall had been substantial, chasing us with debris and dust as we stumbled through the dark, until at last we reached a tunnel we recognized. The scent of the latrines brought back memories of chasing Rajid through endless bat-lit tunnels, and Max's indignation when we landed in the decomposing waste. It would have raised a smile another time.

I stared at Aelia's dust-smeared face, and heavy faraway eyes. *Max, August, now Rajid.* Yet we were still alive, still here. She nodded barely perceptibly, but I could tell Rajid's loss was costing her. They'd grown up together, and while his disloyalty had created pain, his courage was far worse. He was someone I'd never have expected to sacrifice his lunch, let alone his life. And yet he had. To save us.

Tal … get Lia out. His last words stained my heart. I'd judged him because of his weakness in the face of adversity. But perhaps I'd been the weak one, for not understanding that one wrong choice didn't make him wholly bad, and for letting his curiousness make me wary. I should have understood his weakness better than most, as an Outsider.

'Do you think the strix were all in there? Cassius will be vexed if we've culled the entire downstairs menagerie.'

Her hollow voice wobbled, betraying her wretchedness, and I reached my arm around her shoulders.

'I imagine he has a few backups,' I muttered drily, 'but with any luck he'll think we've escaped with Unus or been buried alive. Which gives us a small advantage,' I added.

Her eyes flickered past mine to the murky darkness beyond. This tunnel was filled with a friendlier type of silence, the one that accompanied emptiness. We both knew the only reason we were still here was because the strix had been caught up in the

206

bloodbath, and whether marooned or dead, the result was the same.

'Which lessens the disadvantage … a little,' she corrected after a beat.

I nodded, struggling with too many conflicting thoughts.

Care for the seed and it will care for you, Talia.

It's not your fault.

I swallowed hard as August's face swam just above mine in the darkness.

But perhaps it was?

My gaze dropped as the thought nearly overwhelmed me. Because he'd given everything: defiance to his creators, defection from the only home he'd ever known, and a blind trust in a world he didn't really know – even after discovering his own origins weren't as pure as he'd been led to believe. *And for what?* Even if Aelia was right about the charioteer in the circus, the best scenario was that he was incarcerated here somewhere.

I am the Commander General Augustus Aquila, Roman Equite of the Old Order.

I wasn't ignorant or naive enough to deny that most, if not all, of his decision-making was down to my feral existence. *So perhaps it was all my fault?*

My chest felt leaden. I'd been so busy trying to protect my home and people, I'd denied August any place at all. Neither as one of them or one of us. He must have felt so ostracized, and I hadn't given him any reason to hope.

And what if, despite Aelia's insistence, he was dead?

For a moment I was grateful to the darkness, for its unerring ability to cover feelings and swallow shame. Then a slim hand slipped into my own. It was such a simple act; a nuance of kinship, a token of real sisterhood. *Despite the odds, despite our differences, despite Cassius.* I stood up.

'Time to move.'

Protect it with your life, Talia.

I clung to the reedy fade of Grandpa's voice as I looked over at the frayed rope ladder pinned against the rock wall. I'd been this way once before – with Rajid and Max. And though the ladder clearly needed repair, I'd scaled it in a heartbeat, my new determination giving me the fuel I needed to scramble into the dark space above. Aelia was beside me in seconds, and for a few moments we remained completely still, just listening.

Silence.

Your emotions make you weak, and predictable.

A small smile broke across my lips.

It was time to revisit a little science.

'We leave no one behind bars,' I whispered to Aelia.

She stared, her small elfin face slowly lighting up with the thought of my proposal.

And if you're right about August, he might also be here, I added to myself.

Cassius's ego was too fragile to risk a resurgence in popularity for August, and yet I had the feeling he would keep him alive too, alive and close. A disgraced Commander General was an ultimate trophy after all. *The question was, where would he hide him?* There were any number of dungeons in Isca Pantheon, but it was far more likely that he would keep him where he could see him – which meant the laboratories, or his own apartment.

I gritted my teeth and slid back the metallic sheet door, exposing the humming blue world of Pantheon's main laboratory. It was just as I remembered: shadowy, reeking of formaldehyde and whirring with sounds that chilled my blood.

No light or sound reached beneath the close-fitting doors of the internal laboratory. It had to be at least two or three hours since we left the arena, but the darkness of the tunnels was deceptive and without the sun I stood no chance of guessing the time of day. And yet there was no time to waste. Our split with Unus and the tunnel collapse would only distract Cassius until the excavations didn't produce the right bodies. The clock was ticking.

Holding my breath, I climbed out.

Within seconds we were through the disinfection mist, and back inside the main laboratory. The lighting was pale blue, the same colour as my first visit with August, which meant it was still night-time. I exhaled. It was a small reprieve though. I doubted Cassius would let anyone sleep until he had confirmation of whether he was looking for bodies or escapees.

For a moment we stood there, encircled by the bank of tall bleeping desks, level upon level of suspended tanks and cages stretching away as far as the eye could see.

'This place always gave me the creeps,' Aelia muttered.

I rolled my eyes at her.

You just escaped AWOL sabre-tooths, ravenous strix, a frenzied Cerberus and a near suffocating cave-in – and now this place gives you the creeps?

She smiled, despite the trauma written into her dusty, exhausted face. We were such unlikely allies, and yet somehow fate had conspired to place us here. Facing Pantheon and its monsters, with no more than our wits and quick feet. And yet, I felt oddly empowered – as though finally I believed we could bring it all down, if we played the game and chose the right moment.

'Dark to dark,' I whispered, running my gaze around the impossibly high walls, looking for the telltale cameras.

I'd been their victim too many times not to be aware of their existence now, and of Cassius's particular skill for twisting the truth. There were two on this floor alone, and both were flashing a small red light. Seconds later, each one sported a new leather boot, dangling right in the centre of their small screens. I smiled down at my naked Outsider feet, I hadn't realized just how imprisoned the boots had made me feel.

'Feral means free?' Aelia quipped, her eyes gleaming.

Impulsively, I threw an arm around her small shoulders and dragged her into a bear hug.

'Ow, you still hug way too hard for a girl!' she complained, detangling herself.

'In Arafel, all hugs are equal,' I returned pan-faced.

'Yeah I know' – she smirked – 'eat when you're hungry, sleep when you're tired … Don't you people get tired being so virtuous all the time?'

I stared at her until we were both smothering laughter.

'Guess there's no point in doing things by halves,' I managed when I could breathe, starting towards the waiting stairwell.

'Hang on.' She paused beside the circular desk and inspected it before reaching to flick a tiny switch.

'Universal door release, better than struggling with retina codes,' she reasoned.

'Genius.' I winked, as the hum of the security disappeared.

We didn't wait for an invitation.

Together we flew up the floating stairwell, taking the rises two and three at a time, until we reached the first suspended cages.

Aelia glanced back at me.

'No one left behind bars,' I said, glancing inside and remembering the little apricot monkey I'd freed months before.

We both knew that once we started releasing there was no turning back. The chaos would likely bring the guard running, and Cassius would guess it was at our hand.

'No one left behind bars,' she agreed with a broad grin that said she was with me every step of the way.

Come what may, nature finds a way.

Stay with me, Grandpa, I entreated, and as I reached out to pull the catch off the cage I was sure his faded eyes crinkled with approval.

Fire blazed up from the pit of my stomach as a small family of squirrel monkeys regarded me in clear astonishment, before seizing their chance to break out and over the top of the sealed tank. My throat tightened as I watched them take to the air, running and jumping between the suspended cages the way they might in the forest.

Aelia's eyes flashed as she turned to do the same, releasing a pair of lemurs who whooped with stunned delight as they swung downwards through banks of cages towards the floor. We exchanged a euphoric glance. This was a moment worthy of it all, and adrenaline coursed through my veins as we spun and sprinted from cage to cage. It felt as though there were more animals incarcerated here than left in Arafel, and we were giving them back their most valuable possession in the world. Freedom.

Before long the stairs were overflowing with dozens of monkeys, small mammals and rodents. It was the most mesmerizing sight in the world – so much forest life had silently waited for Cassius and his scientists to play creation. And even though we were still in the laboratory, the air was filled with the sound of the outside world. It was the sound of real hope.

Inevitably, just as we reached the larger solid black cages, the air thickened with the sound of a piercing alarm. I yanked open the door anyway, the walkways beneath our feet flashing red intermittently. Clearly, these cages had additional security. I smiled grimly as we sprinted on. Any dispatched guards were going to find the laboratory a little busier than usual.

Then we were back outside the Recombinant DNA: Transgenic and Molecular Species Unit, the ward where Rajid had shown us the small chimera and the Prolets' clones. My heart started to beat faster as I inched open the unlocked door into the sour darkness. It was just as I remembered and we entered cautiously, the silent cages inside contrasting sharply with the excited calls and grunts behind me.

I hesitated. This was the ward of my nightmares, the one in which Max and I had finally glimpsed the world through Cassius's eyes. And as my eyes slowly adjusted to the warm gloom, the silent, hollow-eyed occupants of the cages became visible. I stalled. They were looking our way, gripping bars, their reddened eyes pleading and excited.

Did they know already? Were they waiting for us?

A strange mix of nausea and excitement reached up my throat as I realized that that was exactly what they were doing. They understood. Their feral instincts were still alive – just – and even though they were so much bigger than the animals we'd just freed I couldn't get to them fast enough.

'No one is left behind bars,' I forced out through gritted teeth, yanking back bolts with practised ease.

There was instant pandemonium, but it was the best thing I'd done in a very long time, and I knew the cameras were tracking us now, but I didn't care any more. In truth, I hoped our actions were being relayed, moment by rebellious moment, throughout every domestic cell in Isca Pantheon.

The Prolets were already stirring, their revolt in Ludi Circus Pantheonares had just proven as much. They were at tipping point, and if some of the Pantheonites were also sympathizers … *We just need the right spark, Tal.* Rhetoric or prophecy. It didn't matter. There was no turning back now.

'I don't think we'll come back this way!'

Aelia ducked as two chimpanzees pulled an instruments casing off the wall and began throwing the contents like tiny individual missiles.

I sidestepped to avoid a flying hypodermic needle.

'Natural archers, wish I could stay and watch.' I grinned, spinning on my heel.

The alarms were chasing us through the wards now, but there were still so many left. And then at last we were inside the chimera ward, the last ward Rajid had shown us before the tanks of embryonic Prolets, the room that had finally revealed Cassius's real ambitions.

'Should we free these?' Aelia whispered doubtfully, staring

around at the hybrid life that had known nothing except these four dark, whirring walls.

A menagerie of life stared out at us, indifferent because it had never known anything but this abyss of meaning.

'In a way we will,' I returned quietly. 'Just not yet.'

She nodded her understanding and we stepped across to the room I'd been silently dreading. Aelia shot a look over her shoulder. We could hear the faint sound of drama in the main laboratory now, raised voices and howling molossers, desperate to be free so they could run and chase the chaotic free life in there.

A mischievous light crept into Aelia's eyes and I smirked, imagining the guards' utter disbelief and rage.

'Guess they've found it a little lively down there.'

'Can always count on us feral types to liven things up.' I winked. 'Five minutes?'

'Tops.' She nodded.

I leaned into the heavy door of the incubator laboratory, and stepped inside into its muffled warmth. At first it seemed the same, endless screens and tanks, and a cocooning, womb-like quiet that almost cushioned us from the anarchy below stairs.

Then I caught my breath.

And for a moment neither of us uttered a sound as we digested the enormity of the change.

'They've grown,' Aelia whispered in a hushed voice.

I nodded, wordlessly.

Because they'd grown in both size and number. While Max and I had witnessed tiny embryos, barely bigger than a human hand, and still attached to umbilical cords, the life that slept unconsciously in this room was now full term. The months had done their work, and we were staring at a room full of sleeping infants. Hundreds of them.

A shadow stole across my soul.

'They're babies,' Aelia gasped. 'Prolet babies.'

'They're an army,' I corrected with difficulty, 'a genetically modified slave army.'

'No they aren't,' she breathed, turning around in fascination. 'Not yet.'

And yet, if Cassius had his way, this room of innocent sleeping infants would finish her Prolet people and the last of the Outsiders.

I clenched my teeth.

Emotion makes you weak and predictable, Talia.

'No,' I muttered, feeling the fear rise, 'not this way.'

Aelia shot me a dark, conflicted look.

I was on my own. Aelia was a doctor, committed to saving life, not taking it. Modified or not, this was going to be too hard, too fundamentally opposed to her principles.

Weak and predictable ... we designed it out in the first test series.

Arafel in flames, my mother trusting as the Eagles took her, Eli's pale face when I was caught, Therry and every last Outsider who risked their lives to rescue me. They all flickered through my claustrophobic head. I wasn't weak, I was strong. And this army could finish every last one of us.

Impulsively, I spun and sprinted swiftly to the biggest screen on the wall, deaf to Aelia's pursuit, her passionate entreaties and appeals.

My heart thumped so painfully I felt sure it must leap from my body as I scanned the deck of controls. There were hundreds of different flashing dials and buttons controlling ominous-sounding functions like mineral infusion, hydration, protein, induced sleep ...

Nature and science can have a healthy symbiotic relationship, Talia. A harmonious balance can be struck, if science is a friend to nature.

Faded words pushing through the fog.

Life can take many shapes and forms. Our role is to protect the weak and vulnerable.

214

But how could I protect them all?

Your emotion makes you predictable. It's a weakness!

I gritted my teeth.

And then I saw it. An individual switch beneath a glass case. It looked important.

Life support – universal, Batch XIII

'Tal, wait!'

Aelia was beside me, pleading.

'We have to do this. This army will replace Isca Prolet, endanger every last Outsider. Their DNA will have been modified, their independent will and more removed. They will do his bidding without question.'

I was aware my voice sounded cold and hard. Dark to dark. My thoughts swirled in the oppressive warmth.

The shouting and howling were getting louder. The guards had to be pushing through the main laboratory.

'Or do we become just like him?' she whispered gently.

I lifted my eyes to hers, finger hovering. Her iris-blues saying everything I was trying to deny. Like August, when he left. When I was so scared I'd muted every feeling I possessed just to survive. Iris-blues needing me to open my heart and risk the pain. Because survival was about making mistakes, getting hurt and emerging all the stronger; because life was life no matter how it started; and because compassion *was* humanity.

My fingers flexed.

An Arafel hunter believes in natural order, knows her place in the forest, and takes only what she needs to survive.

Care for the seed and it will care for you, Talia.

And with one almighty, guttural yell I yanked my arm away and spun on my feet, scanning the room for an exit. There was no other door but a small skylight at the top. It would do.

Within seconds, we were scaling the banks of tanks as though they were roots and branches in the forest, reaching the topmost row beneath the skylight just as the door burst open.

215

'Check the life-support deck and search every corner. They have to be in here somewhere.'

Livia's caustic tone was unmistakable, her fury clear through her stiffened posture. Aelia sucked in a tight breath. We were hideously outnumbered.

My chest hammered as I scanned the skylight. There was no latch because no one expected to go outside. A ghost of a smile twisted my lips. But Outsiders didn't expect to stay inside.

Come what may.

Crouching beside Aelia, I scanned the floor. It was overspilling with guards and molossus hounds now. We had seconds if we were lucky, and I would likely never have this chance again. I could feel Aelia's eyes on me as I yanked out my tiny dart tube, and loaded up Ida's sculpted Komodo tooth dart. The tongues around her eyes were dancing, and Rajid's curious smile was widening. We were a long way from the floor, but the dart was solid and weighted, which meant my aim just needed to be true.

This time Aelia made no protest, and with a silent Arafel prayer, I let the tiny piece of forest fly. It was as silent and focused as any new-age weaponry, cutting the air easily and without drama until it found its soft target: the side of Livia's neck. She crumpled to the floor without a murmur.

It was a clinical kill, perhaps one of which even she would have been proud. And I felt nothing.

'You wanna find Outsiders? Look up,' I whispered, grabbing the skylight sill and swinging my legs through 180 degrees, to punch the glass with every atom of rage swirling within me.

Then there was an ugly cracking noise as a battalion of eyes swivelled firstly to Livia's heaped body, and then to us.

'The roof! Now!'

A male voice I recognized rose in abject fury, and momentarily I felt the sweet rush of revenge. It was the peacock.

I swung again as the first volley came, and this time the fortified glass splintered.

216

'Careful, Insiders, it's going to rain!' I yelled, reaching out to punch the mosaic of glass one last time.

The tiny shards of reinforced glass fell like a shower of light from the heavens, knocking the next volley of arrows awry, and bringing twice the load down on the gaping soldiers.

Instantly, the vaulted space filled with agonized shouts, and as Aelia and I climbed through into the vast blinking night, I shot a final glance back at the floor below.

The peacock was standing next to Livia's heaped body, staring upwards with an expression of sheer disbelief as turmoil unfolded around him.

'Citizen MMDCL – at your service,' I muttered, turning my back.

217

Chapter 19

They say there's a roof like the sky at the top.

It was a myth I'd grown up with, but I never expected to walk over it like the gods.

The sweet night air reinvigorated our stained souls, and gave our feet wings as we sprinted over the iridescent surface of the laboratory and domestic domes, towards the rise of Isca Pantheon's main dome.

Briefly, I recalled Max saying he'd done the same more than a year ago, when he escaped Octavia's personal guard. It felt like so long ago, and it was so hard to connect my old irrepressible best friend with the charioteer who'd murdered August in the arena. Pantheon had changed so much.

We'd begun climbing again. It was easy to see now, that the commercial heart of Isca Pantheon was by far the largest dome. *Pantheon*, the oldest, freestanding Dome in ancient Rome. I'd seen pictures in Arafel's history books, and its ancient grace bore no resemblance to the barbaric world beneath my feet.

'Tal ... slow up!' Aelia panted a few steps behind.

I frowned, turning around, and only then realized she was holding her shoulder awkwardly, just beneath the neat collar of her charioteer uniform.

'Glass?' I whispered, my face creasing with anxiety.

'Arrow,' she admitted, lifting her hand so I could see.

I stared, feeling the world recede. There was a perfectly round hole just proud of her collarbone, from which protruded about an inch of hard black wood.

'Diasord arrow,' she clarified, her breathing noticeably hollow now, 'short but a broadhead with expanding barbs laced with a dimethylmercury compound. They're designed to burn slowly, but efficiently so the target is gradually weakened and can potentially be useful before … y'know.'

I gazed at her in disbelief. She was typically matter of fact, and yet her words were like pieces of ice slowly filling my gut.

'What! Why didn't you say? We have to get it out … stop it working!'

She raised her eyebrows in mock horror.

'Pull it out and we kiss goodbye now. There are tiny lines of explosive threaded through the barbs to prevent it being removed. You can cut them out surgically,' she added, 'but it takes a lot of skill, and there's still a risk to both surgeon and victim. Tullius could do it of course, but I've no idea if he's still alive let alone where he is.'

I grabbed Aelia's hand, and pulled her up the steep rise of the main dome.

'How long?' I ground out, my bare feet finding better grip than her boots, and before we knew it we were standing at the summit of Pantheon's sky, looking down onto the planetary system its creator used to perpetuate his lies.

'A couple of hours maybe,' she panted. 'Depends on the strength of the target, to be honest, and the concentration of dimethylmercury.'

From this vantage I could see the giant two-headed haga circling only a few metres beneath our feet, Pantheon spilled out like a distant web, and the Temple of Mars perched like a venomous spider. Just waiting.

219

'Eli could get it out,' I rushed. 'I'll get you to the forest and come back.'

'No!'

Her tone was blunt and uncompromising. My eyes rested on her for a second – taking in the sudden paleness of her face, the tremble of her hands, and the jutting angle of her chin. I tore my gaze away, scared to see any more. She was as stubborn as me when she wanted to be. Aelia always did what Aelia Vulpes needed to do. *But this way she could lose. I could lose.* I looked to the vast inky sky, and it seemed to whisper.

'We finish what we came to do. There's no guarantee we'd make it across to the forest anyway,' she argued impatiently. 'And anyway, I'm not missing out on this, I made a promise too … don't need the might of the Oceanid army chasing my delicate Prolet …'

She winked, but the cost of her decision couldn't be more stark.

Swearing profusely, I tore a piece of cloth from the inside of my indigo tunic top, and ignoring Aelia's objections, pulled open her collar and wound it gently around the entrance wound to cushion the area. My chest tightened as a small involuntary whimper escaped her lips. The flesh around the puncture wound was already turning black.

'Just a scratch,' I reassured her, 'nothing a renegade Prolet General can't handle.'

Then we stole along together, not towards the forest or Dead City, silhouetted in the starry night like a broken picture, but down the opposite slope and towards our target. Octavia's balcony. Except it wasn't Octavia's any more.

'Cassius could be keeping him anywhere – laboratory wards, Flavium dungeons, his new temple …' Aelia panted, as we approached.

I nodded grimly. 'He could,' I agreed, 'and yet cowards tend to keep their enemies close. Yellow-bellied death adders even closer …'

220

She smiled with effort and I didn't vent my real thoughts. That there was another reason I needed to access Octavia's old media suite. That it was the one place I could snap Pantheon's spine once and for all. If it was still there.

The Book of Fire.

The final translation of the Voynich is a glorious moment, and we will be remembered as the Civitas that built a new-world order! Now we can re-create glorious creatures that were victims of man's weak folly; ancient glorious creatures that once graced a richer earth.

With an army of beasts at our command, we will rule as our ancestors did, with honour, valour, and a knowledge that a new era has dawned. The era of Imperator Cassius, last of the Constantinian Dynasty, Protector of Isca Pantheon and Conqueror of the outside world!

Cassius's image, with a writhing medusa of Voynich coding, danced in front of my eyes. This was where I'd first glimpsed the ancient book that should have never survived the Great War, let alone another two hundred years. And if Aelia was right and August was still alive, Cassius might have hidden him here too.

We climbed down the final few metres of wall together, praying Cassius hadn't removed Octavia's lavish stone extension, and I caught my breath as my fingers gripped the slim white rim that ran around the top. I supported Aelia as best I could, ignoring the shooting pain through my arm, but our descent was steady at least.

'Doesn't look so steep from the inside,' she mumbled, scowling.

'That old chestnut.' I winked to cover the anxiety gnawing inside.

She shot me a darkling look. 'What's a chestnut? Anyway, I distinctly remember giving your Outsider feet something to think about when Fabius let the manticore out for a run!'

'Yeah I remember … you were quite fast … for an Insider,' I teased, before dropping lightly to the floor of the balcony.

I gesticulated and steadied her fall as gently as I could.

'I'll have you know ... Rajid and I broke Isca Prolet's rock-climbing record when we were ten!' she whispered breathlessly, as I set her on her feet in front of the floor-length windows, which had given August his first real taste of Octavia's disloyalty.

'Uh-huh ... sure that was hard with a Cyclops on your team.'

She smirked, raised an eyebrow, but the banter was lifting both our spirits.

'OK, let's see how Cassius likes it when we return the favour?' I exhaled, gripping the handles and twisting. To my relief they opened easily.

'Too easy?' Aelia breathed.

'Too arrogant,' I clarified, stepping inside.

***

I peered down the long marble corridor, with a torrent of blood pounding in my ears. It looked familiar, yet different too, and a million memories stilled my thoughts.

This was the place Grandpa had killed Octavia, the place I'd first glimpsed her deception and intentions for the outside. It was also the place I'd said goodbye to August, believing I was leaving behind a new Isca Pantheon, one that wanted a new-world order that valued freedom and peace.

I clamped my mouth tightly, trying not to breathe in the over-sweet scent of wood musk, which barely concealed the formaldehyde anyway.

The truth was I barely remembered the girl who flew from this place on a back of the griffin. And peace was the very last thing on her mind now.

We paused to let our eyes adjust. Gone were the billowing materials and soft luxurious chaises and, in their place, a series of floor-length tanks glowed against dark-veined marble walls.

There was no need for words. Time was short and we approached silently, each step echoing our trepidation. Tanks

222

always contained ugly secrets as far as Pantheon was concerned. But Eli wasn't here, Arafel was gone, Max belonged to Cassius and August was probably dead.

What possible thing could there be left to scare me?

The thought emboldened me to creep close, to know and defy Cassius's new monster as we passed. But I knew I'd made the very worst assumption as soon as I stepped close enough to recognize its profile.

Because this face belonged in the rippling forest pools of Arafel, streaked with red earth and shadowed by dappled sunlight. Not here, clean and terrifying, a sleeping monster just waiting to be woken.

Was this what his team had been working on when I was unconscious?

I took an involuntary step back, nausea rising, needing physical space to buffer me from the violation. And suddenly I felt small and foolish. Cassius always had a way of undoing me, just when I thought I'd reached a place where there could be no more hurt, that there was nothing left for him to take.

'It's me,' I whispered, feeling the raw edge of my words razor every cell.

The logic was so simple really. After all, what was left when you'd stolen everyone and everything else?

'It's not you,' Aelia forced out vehemently, eyeballing the flashing coloured panel next to the upright tank. 'It's a copy. He's been trying to reproduce you because of your chimera control, Tal … Because of Lake.'

'My blood didn't give him what he needed,' I breathed, 'so he's re-created everything to try and understand the chimera bond. So he can replicate it … and control Lake.'

'Because if he controls her, he controls everything that's left.'

I nodded, staring down the line of dark bleeping tanks.

'It's not what you think, Tal!' Aelia interrupted sharply, shuffling closer. 'These aren't grown from modified eggs in the same

223

way as the embryos in the laboratory. They're constructed ... a form of ... unique biotechnology ... Look, they're spares, not new life. It's different,' she panted.

I nodded again, forcing through the shock trying to claim my limbs. Tank after tank returned the same blank, unconscious stare. A forest of my face, sterilized and trapped, and closing in on me.

And just beyond, there were more faces I didn't recognize beside a new bank of flashing screens and controllers.

Think what Cassius is capable of, Talia ... For the love of Nero, he can re-create pretty much anything.

August had tried to warn me, to make me see Cassius had the technology to do what he liked. Why stop at the Voynich when you can re-create or simulate whatever or whoever you liked.

'Emperor Nero ... Emperor Augustus ... Emperor Constantine,' she whispered, 'Tal ... he's begun the Imperial Programme.'

Her voice was uncertain, her breath rasping.

'The senate voted against it so many times, but when Livia took over as Empress ... the mood was clear, voting against the programme would only lead to Ludi ... It's the farthest he's gone ... re-creating Roman Emperors from fragments of ancient DNA.'

She reached out to touch the glass of a tank containing a tall, imposing profile of a figure, aware of how fundamental this was for her. I didn't look any closer. Somehow creating a living memory of someone who'd been at peace for more than two thousand years felt too Pantheon for my feral head.

I looked at her slight, peering figure, so intrigued despite her injury. Always the doctor, saving others, standing alongside me when her own kind had never known the outside. And never would unless we moved.

I reached out for her hand. Time was too short and we'd both sacrificed so much already. Cassius may have stolen my construct, but they weren't me.

'Your wound, Aelia?' I whispered.

'Barely feel it now,' she dismissed, her eyes too bright, her body too stiff.

Panic reached up from the pit of my stomach. I knew the pain of her loss already, though I'd never given up all hope.

This time I could see a shadow in her eyes. It was the same shadow that clouded Ida's eyes the day the Eagles came.

'The Dead City river? We could ask ... the Oceanids?' I rushed, fear suddenly engulfing everything.

She smiled then, and it terrified me. Because she knew too much.

'The Oceanids will only defy nature once, Talia,' she whispered. 'We're all mortal in the end and I'm not afraid to find out what comes next ... Come on ... the only thing I am afraid of ... is not finishing what we came here to do ...'

She ran out of breath as I slid my good arm around her, feeling her weakness. I dug my nails into the flesh of my free hand, and planted the briefest of kisses on her head, making myself a promise to get her to Eli, come what may.

Swiftly, I sprinted over to the door of the old media suite. It was closed – and just as I remembered. I reached out to grip the handle, and momentarily the ghosts closed in around me.

Max in my shadow, August to my side, Grandpa to find and Arafel to protect – everything to live for. But these ghosts were clamouring, not for the past, but for the future. And it was only me and Aelia left.

Resolutely, I pushed open the door. And we were back. Back in the room that held the key to it all: *The Book of Fire*. And it was all exactly as I remembered, the same bank of flickering, moving screens watching everything. Pantheon's spying eyes.

'Tal,' Aelia gasped from just behind me.

And somehow, by the intonation of her voice, I knew exactly where to look. Just beyond the central camera where I'd set up the photograph of Cassius striding through the forest, hoping it

225

would be enough, to the floor – where a single white tank lay. It was identical to the one in which Octavia had incarcerated Grandpa, and inside lay the figure of a tall gladiator.

And it felt as though all the air left the room at once.

I took a step forward. It was too dark to see properly. Cassius had to have an army of enemies, perhaps even more victims. And yet my forest sense, or perhaps it was my fractured heart, *just knew*.

My shaky gasp blurred the room, fuelled by months of suppressed emotion. Denial, desperation, grief and, finally, a burning fury at the injustice of it all.

And suddenly I was back in the North Mountain caves, running my fingers over his Equite skin, glistening in the firelight, anchored by guilt when he knew we needed to escape. *Would he ever be the same? Had I thrown everything away?*

My limbs flooded with life just as Aelia threw out a warning hand.

'Lasers!' she hissed, gesticulating towards the faint red lines criss-crossing through the room.

I teetered on the balls of my feet and narrowed my eyes to glimpse the faint lines. They were everywhere. I threw Aelia an anguished look, recalling August's own warning the last time we were here. She could only look at me yearningly, the hollows beneath her eyes more pronounced in the low light, and my mind was made up. He was her brother before he was ever my … whatever he was, after all.

I was moving before she could stop me, using every tree-flying acrobatic skill I possessed to leap, roll and tumble my way across the room. And somehow, within seconds, I was kneeling beside the canister.

It was him. Proud, Roman and … inanimate – the white scar skating down the left-hand side of his face gleaming beneath the flickering lights of his prison.

I stifled a painful choke.

'It's August,' I whispered back across the room, recalling the moment I'd seen the same scar glinting in the cathedral moonlight.

'The charioteer in the arena … you were right … no scars.'

Aelia's eyes closed briefly.

'Manual override,' she whispered when they reopened, pointed to a flashing box on the wall.

Swiftly I reached up to pull down the switch inside a small red box. The humming noise disappeared first, followed swiftly by the flickering red lines.

She was beside me in a heartbeat. 'August?' she whispered in a raw voice.

For one brimming second, it was as much as we could do to look. And even though his eyelids were still and lips silent – his smile was etched into the fine lines around his mouth and I could picture them whispering my name the way he'd whispered it in the cathedral. *Like a wish.*

Even back then I'd disbelieved him. And now, he lay here like a corpse ready for burial, because of me. Because of my denial that Pantheon could create someone who believed enough in the outside world to forsake their own.

It was real for me, Talia.

His last words reached through the hard Perspex of his tank as though still echoing on his steady breath.

Why did I always end up hurting those I loved most?

Then a noise broke the whirring silence. I shot a look at Aelia, neat adrenaline coursing my limbs.

'Can you do something about this?' I nodded towards the large panel above his head. From what I could see his arms were wired but, mercifully, there was no plate attached to his head.

'I … think so.'

'Aelia …?' I began, my chest constricting at the sight of her trembling hands working the wires back to the panel.

Should have taken her to Pantheon's infirmary? Cassius might

227

have saved a talented Prolet doctor. And yet, she would likely never have seen the outside of a prison cell again.

'Talia, stop with the fretting! You're putting me off ... I've got to recall the correct sequence.'

Her eyebrow forked exasperatedly, and I bit my tongue, praying as she began tapping and sending the levels dancing wildly across the screen. She was the brightest, fieriest, humblest star I'd ever known. I wasn't ready to let the night take her.

I dragged my gaze back to August's unconscious profile; he was so vulnerable now. *Had he given up the fight willingly?*

'Just ... one more ... and that should start ... there!'

There was a sharp click as the top of the tube rolled backwards exposing his shoulders and chest. A shrill alarm filled the air instantly.

'I didn't say it would be quiet,' she rasped apologetically.

'How do we get him going ...' I rattled. 'We haven't got much time left. They'll be here any second.'

And as if on cue, a cacophony of noise from the outside corridor drowned any further exchange. It was the most violent chorus of animal noises, mixed with loud imperial commands and the acrid scent of lasered flesh.

'They're here,' I whispered.

She nodded, her hollowed eyes so wistful and dull.

Clenching my teeth, I stood up and ran towards the cased manuscript.

The alarm was going crazy, but it didn't matter any more. This was the Voynich, the book I'd vowed to burn on a funeral pyre. And it was going to end right here and now.

I reached the reinforced glass and felt around for a way into the box, the open, aged pages gazing back at me all the while. It seemed so small for the world-changing secrets it contained. On the right was a multi-genus animal shape. *Homer's chimera* I muttered, recognizing the classical faded sketch. And to the left, a loose aged page in familiar handwriting, beside an astronomical

228

diagram. My chest tightened. Its creases had been smoothed but I would know it anywhere, because it had lived inside Max's treehouse dart tube for months, until Cassius stole it. It was Thomas's research, containing the tiny double-lidded clue that led me to guess Lake's real identity – the same page that had held the key to the cipher. *REQ.*

Requiem. *Mass of the Dead*. A prophecy in itself. This Voynich page had to be the coding for *Hominum chimera*, the coding for Lake. My blood knew it too. And it yearned with a feral heat I didn't recognize, just as the door burst open.

And the entire forest poured in on the back of one torrential, deafening wave of chaos.

I twisted in shock as the squawking, yowling cavalry spilled inside, filled the room in seconds. There were primates of all size and description, rodents, domestic animals, big cats, birds – every type of forest creature that was able to climb and track had followed us here. And there were hundreds of them.

'Tal!'

August moaned as the doorway darkened with the shape of Cassius's guard.

'They're in here,' one roared.

I inhaled sharply. 'Max ...?' I whispered, staring at the broad gladiator filling the space. He'd traded his charioteer uniform for regular Pantheonite colours but he was still unmistakable.

We locked eyes, and the moment he'd reached down and pulled the blade across the decoy's throat ran through my mind. My fists clenched as several more guards appeared.

'We've got them now,' a low voice sneered behind him, 'and get these lab specimens back where they belong!'

The words had no sooner left his mouth than a large male chimpanzee flew across the room, its eyes bright with fury, and barrelled into the soldiers. A fracas went up as the remainder of the chimps joined their alpha, and a tiny smile of wonder played across my lips. They were Outsiders too, creatures who had suffered cruelly at the hand of Pantheon, and now they were aligning themselves with their rescuers. *With Arafel*. My heart swelled as a large cat leapt past me knocking a small metallic restraint at my feet.

'Thanks,' I muttered, reaching down to pick it up.

The small metallic casement fizzed and sparked as I flicked it on and turned back to the casement. Without hesitating, I held it against the glass and watched as the restraint sent hundreds of volts through the Voynich's case. There was a horrific cracking noise, and the whole room paused, as a million hairline cracks spread through the case like wildfire. Then a second screaming alarm ripped through the chaos, and this time I had no doubt it was echoing through the entire state of Isca Pantheon.

'Stop her!'

'The Book!'

'Tal ...?'

My gaze shot back across the room, in the direction of the voice. A voice I'd longed so hard to hear I'd heard its ghost a thousand times over. And yet this time it was real as the iris-blue eyes, awake and staring back at me, across the chaos.

'Lia?'

August's voice shook, as his sister's elfin face leaned into his view.

'You're ... How can ...? You were ...'

'Dead?' she rasped. 'Yeah ... sorry about that ... here now ... boo anyway,' I lip-read.

They grinned at one another, brother and sister tied and separated by the same screwed-up Civitas.

Suddenly aware of the fracas surrounding us, August pulled himself up and with a surge of strength, began ripping away all the wires still attached to his body. Aelia tried to assist but only fell back exhausted.

I skirted the fray and was across the room in a heartbeat, throwing my arm around her small hunched form. August scowled, pulling his legs free of the restrictive tube. Dressed only in simple cotton trousers, his chest bare save for his glittering Equite tattoo, he looked more the Outsider than Max now.

'He said you were dead …? Arafel … there was no one left … I searched.' His whisper cracked as he suddenly realized Aelia's state.

I could only nod, as she fell sideways into my arms.

August was on his feet in one swift move, just as another violent noise claimed the room. A huge alpha male gorilla, frenzied and yelling its dominance at the top of its voice, had wrapped his huge arms around the fractured casing of the Voynich.

It knew. Somehow. And the whole room watched, silent and transfixed, as he lifted the entire casement high above his straining head, and threw with all his wild strength. The glass case hit the back wall and shattered into a thousand pieces, finally releasing its precious contents, which tumbled to the floor.

'The Book!' I gasped, as the world swung into counter-motion and every living creature started for the fallen treasure.

Guards and animals swarmed like a pack of vulturous creatures, giving chase as the gorilla followed up in a breath, swiping up the book in his leathery hands. He threw a single glance our way, enough for me to glimpse the light of a distant memory in his black eyes, before he lowered his broad head and battered his way back through the room, swatting his opposition like flies.

Despite the fizzing restraints, and burning Diasords, his colossal size made his course unstoppable and, within a heartbeat, he was back out in the long corridor and thundering purposefully towards the open balcony. The whole floor shook with the weight of his progress, as he powered towards the moonlit balcony, his progress just visible in a screen opposite. And I felt his heroic purpose in my blood. Arafel was nothing but ash, and yet it was still within us all. It was within the memory of every new shoot and bud of the old trees that ever held me safe.

He paused only briefly as he reached the balcony – a creature of the forest, holding the secrets of an ancient world within his feral arms. There was furious shouting, a deafening volley of laser fire as the guards regrouped, and a terrifying moment as it ricocheted around him, destroying the walls. But when the dust cloud cleared, he was still standing, like a survivor of the Great War, reclaiming the future. His silhouette rose on his free padded feet, bellowed to the world, and then swung over the balcony with old ease. And then he was gone.

Together with the Book of Fire.

Chapter 20

'Now!' I muttered fiercely, hoisting a semi-conscious Aelia to her feet and propelling her forward.

August attempted to mirror on the other side and stumbled, underestimating the immobilizing effects of the drugs. I gritted my teeth and extended my spare, wounded arm but August's fall seemed to stir Aelia, who rallied gamely. Then, somehow the three of us cut a path down the banks of tanks towards the door, conscious the army of furious forest life cornering the guards could turn tail at any moment.

I scanned the group. Their Diasords were held high and Max was right in the middle.

'I'm sorry,' I muttered, and a feeling of desolation stole through me as August pulled the door closed, and rammed a metal restraint beneath its inconspicuous handle. Yet he would only turn us in, I had to trust his forest instincts and weapons would be enough for now.

August looked down and with a soft raw groan pulled both of us against him, and finally the tissues of my fractured heart mended, pumping warm wild blood where before there had only been ice. His arms tightened.

'Aelia!' I whispered roughly, so conscious that every passing second was depleting her strength as much as it was returning his.

He reached down to pick her up as he might a child. She tried to smile. 'Jeez, Aug, I'll be OK … just don't let her hug me!' she remonstrated, two tiny pink spots staining the contours of her pale face.

'It's a Diasord arrow,' I rattled. 'We have to find Eli or Tullius.'

August paled visibly as he caught sight of the small protrusion from her neck. 'When … how long?'

'I'm not dead yet am I?' Aelia returned, exasperated.

'Max?' August added, gesticulating back.

I shook my head, running towards the door that led out of the apartment. I was conscious of how quiet it was outside, that no more guards had arrived despite the fracas.

'He already killed you once,' I whispered, inching open the door.

The corridor was empty.

I scowled. No waiting guard meant one of two things: one of Cassius's games or there was a bigger problem elsewhere. We had to hope for the latter.

August followed, looking less than impressed.

'Must have been a substandard specimen,' he scathed. 'The last of my test series was supposed to have been destroyed in Octavia's time, and Cassius's second generation work was for the thylacines.'

'Thylacines? He managed it?' Aelia rasped, despite everything.

'Yeah,' he returned drily, 'the Tasmanian wolf is no longer extinct.'

'Or the sabre-tooth snow leopard,' I muttered. 'Except that never actually existed.'

'Unlike the short-faced bear,' Aelia added closing her eyes. 'Which is 2.5 metres tall, 800,000 years later.'

'Yeah, well seeing as it seems we're all absolutely fine with Max murdering August – or a version of him – and there's plenty of time to swap cloning stories when we've got that arrow out, I say

234

we put our energy into getting the hell out of here … Reckon the sky train will be taking passengers?'

'Should be.' August nodded, as we reached the corner of the corridor. 'It's automated so unless the systems have gone down for some reason …?'

I peered around carefully but this corridor was just like the first, eerily empty save for some distant shouting.

And then I realized.

The entire system of Pantheon crashed in Ludi Cirque Pantheonares.

'It's spreading,' I muttered in an odd voice, 'the Prolet rebellion.'

Aelia smiled, the tiny pink dots spreading momentarily. 'Our … plan,' she muttered.

August's bushy eyebrows flew up in shock. 'It's really happening?' he exclaimed sharply. 'How?'

'Just needed … the right … spark,' Aelia forced out with difficulty.

Faint noises were beginning to drift up to us now: guards shouting, molossers howling and Diasords clashing.

'For the love of Nero, it's what we dreamed of, Aelia!' August exclaimed, though I could tell most of his animation was to keep Aelia awake and with us. 'Is Rajid with the PFF? Leading them?'

We crept down the next corridor, listening intently to the faint noises, working out their direction.

She didn't answer.

'Rajid was a hero,' I filled in quietly. 'The Cerberus and strix …'

It was enough. August's face darkened as he glanced at Aelia.

'And from what I saw in the arena, the rebellion is pulling from both sides,' I continued. 'Pantheonites too. It's happening throughout Isca Pantheon.'

'Then we're up against Aquila Command,' August responded grimly. 'He'll dispatch everything he's got to quell the rebellion, including the myth army.'

235

August's caustic words were enough to make my skin crawl. Of course Cassius would have a plan, he had a plan for everything.

'Aquila Command … myth army?' I hissed as we slipped into yet another empty corridor. 'Is it as bad as it sounds?'

'… Worse,' Aelia muttered.

August grimaced. 'It was always Cassius's classified work so I have no idea of its extent, but it's big enough to warrant mention in key defence strategies. And its nature is more Voynich than gladiatorial.'

I nodded. It made perfect, Cassius sense. A myth army in need of its General. No wonder he wanted Lake back so badly.

'Where does he keep them?'

But I knew of course.

'The Flavium,' I breathed, recalling the maze of underground doors Unus and I had bypassed trying to find Max more than a year before.

We'd opened only one, and released a nest of serpents that brought Octavia's games to a standstill.

Who knew how many more monsters Cassius had shut away in case there was ever a moment like this?

I inhaled deeply. Aelia was dying, I'd left Max behind, we had no army, and yet …

Come what may, you will find a way.

'We get to Eli … and then we find Lake,' I forced through gritted teeth.

***

'If we make it to the holding bay, can you override the exit code? We could take a Sweeper … be in the forest within minutes?'

Aelia's eyelids were tightly screwed shut. I could tell her pain was spreading.

'It's too obvious,' August responded as we crept down a silent domestic corridor. 'It's the first place Cassius will barricade, but … if we can get to the guards' stables, we may stand a chance?'

'Bel … lero … there,' Aelia whispered.

'I hope so.' August smiled gently. 'It's the aurochs' training ground and the old exit. It was still usable last time I was there. So no time for any drama till we reach Eli, OK?'

His tone was deliberately teasing, and Aelia smiled but I could feel her slipping through our fingers with every passing minute. I fought the panic and focused on our plan, telling myself there was still time to turn the tables if I trusted enough. I thought of the tips of Arafel's trees, long since lost in the Eagles' laser fire, reaching towards us in the breeze. *Help us,* I prayed silently.

***

'Always wanted to ride first-class.' I grimaced, as we clung to the rails that ran down the top edges of the sky train's capsule carriages.

August and I had each wrapped a protective arm around Aelia's back, as we clung with the other to the rim of the skytrain; its automated coasting from platform to platform the only neat, ordered part of Isca Pantheon left.

And the breathless speed at which we flew, wasn't the reason we couldn't speak. It was the anarchy. There was disorder, fighting and mayhem on every platform we passed through – and for the first time in Isca Pantheon, there was little discernment. Pantheonites, Prolets and creatures ran amok in every direction and the guards lashed out indiscriminately, clean white lines and divisions forgotten.

I stared across into August's furrowed brow, at dark eyes creased with unease.

Pantheon, his world, was in an uproar. It was really happening. We were in the middle of a war, and it wasn't between Insiders and Outsiders. It had started right here – within Cassius's own walls.

I wasn't immune to the irony of it all. To the fact that a feral Outsider afraid of so much, was the spark needed for Insiders to stand together against the biggest threat to the recovering world since the Great War. I tightened my hold around Aelia's limp body.

The Book could be halfway to the forest by now, at the bottom of a river, or torn to pieces and cast out in seven different directions. *It didn't matter.* Cassius's reason was gone, leaving me to deal with the rest – it was time for honouring promises.

We approached the floor at white-water speed, and levelled at the last minute, arriving at the main ground-floor station to the usual, timed announcement.

'Isca Pantheon, *Grande Stazione*. All routes end here.'

I suppressed a grim smile. *Not today.*

'Stay completely still.'

August's whisper was barely discernible but it didn't matter, we all heard them. There was some kind of fracas on the platform: two Pantheonites and a guard with at least one molossus hound, judging by the howling.

'Orders are to remain in your units ...'

'... look around you ... mutiny ... have you even been to the Civitas ...?'

'... every man, woman and child ... evacuation.'

We could only hear snatches of the conversation, but there was enough meaning and after a few seconds the air fell eerily silent. We held our breath, watching the hagas circling far above us. Even they seemed less than interested in the AWOL treats clinging to the top of the sky train.

'It's empty?' I whispered, lifting my head to scan the length of the long white platform, so conscious of passing time.

The sudden quiet was disturbing too, but we had no choice but to move.

August swung down first, his physical strength now fully restored, and I carefully lowered Aelia down into his arms, before jumping down myself. Then together, we cut down through the silent main streets of Isca Pantheon's Civitas, keeping to the shadows as much as possible. It wasn't difficult – the entire city had been plunged into an ashen twilight, taking me back to the shadowy ruins of the Dead City in the gritty blink of an eye. *Except this city wasn't supposed to be dead. Not yet.*

And whether it was the journey atop the sky train or her sheer stubborn will, Aelia was revived enough to stay conscious as we crept through the echoing alabaster streets.

Then at last there was a faint roar of life – from the direction of the grand forum with Cassius's Temple of Mars. It was the type of disharmony that slews everything into slow motion, the way only real trauma can. Shouting, howling, laser fire, crashing, screams overlaying more noises I didn't even recognize – taking me back to Arafel in flames, to ashen hopes and scorched hearts.

It was the sound of hell.

August was white-faced, tight-lipped as he glanced at me and then pointedly at Aelia.

'There's a way around the square,' he whispered, 'through the side streets.'

Aelia roused herself visibly.

'No side streets!' she growled, pulling herself up in August's arms. 'They're my people ... I'm the General of the PFF – they need to see me!'

The set of her obstinate jaw said it was pointless to argue. I understood. It was how I felt when I saw Arafel burning. I would have crawled towards my people on my hands and knees if I could. It was intrinsic to who we were. August and I exchanged glances in the surreal light, before moving down the street towards the noise of affray.

I crept ahead, to the corner where our small side street connected with the top end of the forum square. August was a few paces behind, the effort of carrying Aelia beginning to tell, even though she was light. He placed her down gently between

239

us, as she gamely tried to sit up. I crouched to help her, so conscious of not moving her too much lest it spread the poison further, which was when I saw it.

A cobweb of blackened veins spreading outwards from the arrow puncture wound and extending beyond the buffer of my tied cloth. I forced a reassuring smile, though I could tell Aelia wasn't deceived for one second.

'Make him a … real Outsider,' she whispered so only I could hear.

I suppressed a shiver, as though a cold wind had suddenly blown, before crouching to let my cheek rest gently against hers.

'He is a real Outsider … as you are … Aelia … please … stay …'

And instead of Aelia, it was my father coughing, Grandpa whispering through the trees, Ida's eyes closing, Mum barely recognizing me and Max … Max … I couldn't lose anyone else, especially someone who'd proven such an unlikely and fiery ally.

'You're like the most annoying, frustrating, bossy, stubborn … sister I always wanted.'

She smiled – faintly – but it was there, before she parted her darkening lips.

'Kiss … my …'

Then I grinned even though she ran out of strength, because it said everything, feral girl to feral girl.

August's hand was on my shoulder, gripping it too tight. He'd been quietly observing the rebellion, and when he looked down at us his eyes were full of fresh shock that had me on my feet in a heartbeat.

'They're … executing them?' he whispered queerly, as though he could barely believe his own words.

'Who?' I exclaimed, though I already knew.

I peered around the stone pillar in front of us, and felt my blood drain to my feet.

The square was filled with hundreds of Prolets and Pantheonites,

240

but there wasn't a Pantheonite guard in sight. Groups of well-dressed Pantheonites huddled together, while Cassius's hideous central statue had been turned into a makeshift gallows with two thick ropes hanging in front of a platform. The statue was twice the size of an ordinary man, the drop to the floor more than enough to break a neck. *Which seemed to be precisely the purpose.*

My horrified gaze travelled from the cool white gleam of the statue, to the terrified, blindfolded Pantheonites being marched up to the platform in small groups. On the opposite side, a pack of loose molossus hounds and sabre-tooth leopards were making short shrift of piled skewed bodies, while a crowd in front of the platform heckled as though they'd been watching for some time. It seemed there were far more Prolets who'd voided the vaccination than we ever dared hope for. And now this.

Nausea climbed my throat. The scene needed no explanation. It was fitting revenge on a hierarchy that had reinvented barbaric practices for the purpose of controlling and torturing its people. *And yet.* I glanced back at August, already knowing he was thinking the same. That while these were the same people who'd cheered when Eli had been strapped, half-dead, to the cart in the Flavium, and the same crowd that screamed itself hoarse when Max and I had faced the Minotaurus in Ludi – there was no way we could walk away.

Because that would make us just like them.

'Stay with Aelia!' I hissed at him, before setting off at a sprint down one side of the forum.

The stench of blood and fear filled my lungs as I sprinted past a fountain of Titus, spouting water from his mouth like a grounded Oceanid, and almost directly into a pair of mauling sabre-toothed leopards. I caught my breath, and lowered my eyes as they snarled a warning before returning to the remains of what looked to be a basilisk. I scowled, scanning the floor.

Had Cassius begun freeing his myth army already?

'Tal!'

My eyes narrowed furiously as August caught up and set Aelia gently on her feet, supporting her weight as best he could.

'What are you doing? You'll speed ... use up strength she hasn't got!' I remonstrated fiercely.

'Yeah ... try telling her that!' he retorted, eyeing his sister with respect. 'And besides ... she's right – these are her people more than ours.'

I could tell it was taking all Aelia's strength just to focus, and I shot around to her other drooping side.

The spidery black veins we're inching up her throat now, and one of the sabre-tooths had already thrown us a sidelong look.

'Need to ... talk ... to them,' she croaked, her eyes flickering uncertainly.

I nodded, despairingly.

'Get me ... on that ...'

She was looking at Cassius's Temple of Mars, and I knew then she wanted to show herself because she was the best chance we stood of quelling the bloodthirsty crowd. I sighed heavily. *Why did she always have to be so damned right?*

Together, August and I gently lifted Aelia across the stone forum floor and up the newly stained steps of the temple, which had seemed so grand and imposing before. Now it seemed only the crumbling alter ego of a madman.

'Trust me,' she hissed, shrugging August off and leaning all her weight on me as she forced her feet towards the front of the dais.

I supported her as best I could, a new emotion creeping through my veins as we looked out across all the carnage. Pantheon's clean white lines and oppression had been replaced with a wild, vengeful rage. These were people who had aspired to a better, fairer, more equal life and yet who were now letting their need for revenge taint their blood. And the madness was spreading fast.

Aelia squeezed my hand, and I knew what she needed as though she'd spoken the words aloud.

The cry that left my lips was the rally Arafel hunters used to gather other hunters in the forest. It belonged in the jungle, not here, and yet its meaning somehow transcended its sound. It had the effect of drawing every pair of eyes in the forum towards us.

'Citizens of Isca Prolet!'

Cassius had designed the perfect stage, and my voice echoed authoritatively around the large stench-filled square. I sucked in a breath, so aware of the irony, that we were attempting to stop the Prolet citizens from inflicting precisely the torture that had been inflicted on them for generations. A crowd of Pantheonites, penned in beside the platform, fixed their anguished faces on us.

'And who are you to address us?'

A thick-set male Prolet responded, pushing through the crowd to the bottom of the temple steps. He was flanked by two more Prolets of equal stature, and I scanned for their weapons instinctively. This could turn ugly very quickly.

Fragments of whispers had begun floating up from the watching crowd.

It's her! The one from the outside ... I thought she died in the circus ... or Ludi ...? No, didn't you see her charm the sabre-tooth? But she's with Aelia ...'

The three men had begun climbing the steps, clearly uninterested in negotiating anything.

'She is Talia Hanway!' Aelia's authoritative voice rang out as she lifted her drooping head with what seemed to be herculean effort. 'Descendant of Thomas Hanway ... one of the ... founding fathers of Isca Pantheon.'

I glanced across at her valiant profile. She was using all her remaining strength to project a calm voice that sounded so much like her old self. Only the dark veins creeping up her neck showed how much it was costing her.

My chest ached violently.

'I stand before you all as General of the Prolet Freedom Fighters and swear to you now ... Talia Hanway is the one I told you all

243

about … the one from the outside … we've been waiting for … She is the only Outsider capable of controlling the Voynich's last secret and weapon … *Hominum chimera!*'

She twisted to smile briefly at me, her eyes translucent with the effort of maintaining her show. I tightened my hold on her slipping body as August stepped forward out of the shadows to support her on the other side.

A mutter went up instantly.

'Yes …! The Commander General is alive …' she rallied '… disgraced by this Civitas because he dared to believe in something different … Yet he fought for your freedom … risked his own life … to protect you from Cassius's final plan … And I know this because … he is also my beloved brother.'

Her voice cracked as she turned her face to smile at August and this time the crowd fell silent. A General of the PFF owning a blood relative in the Order of the Equite Knights was clearly a leveller.

'He had Prolet blood?' one of the men on the stairway interrupted suspiciously.

'Yes!' August's voice boomed as Aelia's legs buckled. 'I have Prolet blood just like you, in the same way I have Roman Equite blood … and now I fight as an Outsider … To put an end to Isca Pantheon's Biotechnical Programme, and to Cassius's rule once and for all!'

'For what?' someone jeered from the crowd. 'So you can wear the crown yourself?!'

'Yeah … and we heard about your precious outside! We saw images of your village, Arafel, burned to the ground by the Eagle squad,' another of the men added.

And in that moment I saw how it all looked to them. This was all they knew, and they were seizing the moment to make it theirs. Any way they could.

'Yes, Cassius murdered my people!' my voice grated above the noise of the crowd, never clearer, never more raw.

A strange hush fell over the crowd, as hundreds of surprised eyes swung towards me.

'... as he will murder each and every one of you, if you don't hear us. You think that by executing a few Pantheonites you can bring this house down? You aren't enough! You will never be enough! These people are pawns in Cassius's game, just like you. Right now your Emperor is raising an army far stronger and uglier than even you can imagine. And you are using what little time you have to cut the throats of his pet dogs?' My voice rose in livid anger.

'So what? We are all dead anyway. Why not take a few with us?' One of the burly Prolet men scowled, making a tight swiping gesture with a curved blade.

'No!' I countered in a steely voice that reverberated endlessly around the silent forum.

And finally I knew this was it. The moment Grandpa had foreseen so long ago, that my blood would be a last lifeline between the old Outsider world and the hope of a fragile new one. Images of Arafel crowded my head, so many faces, smiles and hopes. My people had bequeathed a legacy far stronger than any despotic regime. Cassius had called my Outsider emotion my weakness, but he was wrong. It was my core strength.

'There is another way!'

And this time you could have heard a pin drop throughout the entire forum.

'For all of us – but we have to stand together. The world outside is recovering. It survived the Great War, and enabled isolated communities to recover in disparate places. We may all be different, but we are united by one common purpose, ridding the world of a future that is full of darkness. And I believe we can do this, but it will take every man, woman and child standing here now.

'Come with us and fight – as Outsiders! If we die, at least we die as free people. But if we succeed, we will live the way Thomas wanted us to live. A real life between the red earth and warm sun, free from tyranny and pain … A life worth the fight!'

And as my words spilled into the air one of the moving planets far above our heads whirred and clicked into action; it descended at breakneck speed and pulled up sharply just above us before rolling over to display its flat-sided screen.

I knew then that whatever small reprieve we'd won from Cassius was over. So instead I looked squarely into the soulless black screen and smiled, before whispering the words that echoed our own personal war.

'And feral means free.'

Chapter 21

Forty of us. It was a small but vital army. Prolets who'd rejected the vaccine, a few who hadn't but were unwilling to be divided from friends, and a handful of Pantheonites who once freed, decided not to hang around to see whether Cassius was in a good mood or not.

'It's blocked,' I whispered to August.

We were standing at the back of the aurochs' stable, facing August's exit. Or what had once been an exit, and though there was an old faded plaque emblazoned with 'Danger, Waste Disposal Only,' together with a small black figure in an infection suit, there was still only a faint outline in the wall where a door had once opened to the outside world.

'It can't …' August scanned the wall, holding his sister's slumped frame.

He hadn't let her go since the forum, though she'd lost consciousness now and the black veins were webbing across the bottom half of her left cheek.

I'd never felt more helpless. I knew our only hope lay in finding Eli. He wasn't a medic but he'd performed countless operations on the animals he'd helped, and his were the only hands I'd trust other than those of Tullius. But that was assuming we could leave at all.

A few Prolets with clubs and knives stepped up, and tried to find some leverage or small opening, but the doorway might as well have never existed at all.

'Now what?' I asked August in desperation.

His swarthy profile was pale with exhaustion. And the exuberant mood at making it through to the stables was dissipating fast, our new army growing uneasy.

'The Sweeper hold is the only other ...' But whatever else he might have said was lost to the heavy crunch of boots. Boots moving in unison.

My chest contracted with fear.

And before we could assemble any sort of line of defence, a battalion of guards rounded the corner. There had to be fifteen at least, and they were all armed.

'Halt! You are all under arrest, and we have orders to shoot anyone who runs.'

My blood chilled, as I stared at the gladiator in charge. Forest-green eyes that were so at odd with his pristine Pantheonite uniform. *Could it really have come to this? Max, an Outsider, to turn over the last of the feral souls in this hellhole?*

'Max?' I appealed, stepping forward with my hands held out.

'Halt! In the name of the Imperator Cassius I command you to remain where you are!'

'Max!' I entreated. 'You have to let us go ... Arafel ... the outside ... we can try to protect it if you let us go now!'

'I said halt! I have had orders to show no mercy.'

'Tal, he can't ...' August started forward and found several Diasords levelled at him instantly.

Some subjects ... have no intrinsic ability or resource to reject the vaccine. They can have extreme reactions, a form of induced psychosis. Aelia's words echoed through my head warningly.

I gritted my teeth, refusing to believe he wasn't still in there.

248

'Max ... you don't belong here ... you have to remember! Building treehouses ... hunting in the forest ... tree-running trials ... swimming at the lake ... apricots ... this!'

And bringing my hand to my neck, I yanked open my indigo top and pulled out the tiny treehouse dart tube he'd given me, still dangling on its leather.

His eyes dropped to the only piece of Arafel I had left, and there was a heavy silence as his muscles contracted and a fleeting shadow passed across his face.

'Guards!' His voice filled the space finally. 'Take aim!'

And I watched in horror as the guards dropped to their knees in formation and a murmur of terror went up among the people behind me.

'No!' I yelled, running forward. 'You don't have to do this ... You're one of us – an Outsider! Max!'

'The back wall ... fire!'

Then the entire stable filled with the sound of laser fire lacerating the back wall, sending up spirals of grey chemical smoke. And whether it was the power of the laser fire in such a small space, or just Grandpa smiling down on us, the floor of the stables lit up with dancing spirals of real fresh air. *Outside air.*

Several of the large Prolets ran forward, and slammed their combined weight into the wall, pushing until the whole stable wall shuddered and fell outwards, leaving a gaping hole three Cyclops could walk through. And the fresh air that rushed through smelled and tasted as sweet as heaven.

August sprinted to the stabled aurochs and yanked open their door. They spilled out – every colour known to Pantheon – and whinnied incredulously at the new world that presented itself. The sun was just creeping over the horizon, throwing out a soft dawn hue and the outside had never looked so intoxicating. I threw a look back at Max, his hand held high and still, halting any further action by his battalion while we mounted the aurochs bareback. It was clear many of the Prolets and Pantheonites had never so much as sat on a horse, but no one was being left behind. August was astride his winged stallion Bellerophon in a heartbeat, Aelia slumped in front of him.

'For the love of Nero, Tal?' he yelled over his shoulder as I skirted the back of the anxious herd.

'Go ... go on ... find Eli ... I'll follow,' I yelled.

His face twisted with anxiety as he accepted there was no more time, that Aelia's need was greater and this was something I needed to do. He nodded abruptly.

'Yahh! Yahh!' he yelled, as though to muster every ounce of strength he had remaining, and as the aurochs spilled into their first dawn, I sprinted back to Max.

'Come with us? Come home?' I breathed erratically, every Diasord still raised and ready to do his command.

The tiny treehouse dart tube was still dangling outside my indigo charioteer outfit. His clouded forest-greens, eyes that had once meant home, lowered slowly to fix on it. I knew then it was the same as my moment with the girls' leathery back. The vaccine *could* be overcome with the right trigger. And the dart tube he had carved with his own Outsider hands had opened the door a fraction. He was still in there somewhere, in the shadows. My hopes soared.

I could bring him back, I knew I could. If I could just get him out of Pantheon.

'Max, trust me,' I urged desperately, so aware of the emptying stable now, 'you belong with the Outsiders, not here. I can help you ...'

'I ... am a sworn gladiator of Isca Pantheon, citizen ...'

'No!' I hissed. 'You aren't! You're Max Thorn, outside hunter and beloved son of Arafel.'

'I ... just ... can't,' he forced out, as though the words themselves were mountains he had to climb. He reached out halfway, before faltering and dropping his hand.

'Just go ... before I change my mind!'

His tone was abrupt, the familiar muscles around his mouth trembling, as though it was taking every effort to control himself, to resist his conditioning. And to see his torment was more than I could bear. I reached up and kissed his quivering cheek.

'I'll come back for you,' I whispered, 'I promise.'

Raw words, slicing me open, and yet without Lake, none of us stood a chance.

Without looking back, I leapt straight onto the back of the last auroch and out into the sunrise, unable to believe how it ever ended up this way – August on the outside and Max ... being so damned Max.

I leaned low in my auroch's indigo mane, and let her have her head, catching the others with ease. Then we streamed out like one of the old forest herds, Bellerophon and my auroch galloping wide to take the lead, with the runaway army behind us, the thundering of hooves on the dawn soil one of the most glorious sounds I'd ever heard. And I could feel Grandpa's faded smile as we headed towards the start of the mined land separating Pantheon from the outside forest, giving our aurochs' wings.

As the faint healing warmth of the sun reached through my Insider clothing, I focused my eyes on our last challenge. Too many of my ancestors had died trying to cross this stretch of the brown dirt in the aftermath of the war, believing there to be sanctuary on the inside. Now we knew the truth and if I was going to die, I was going to die out here securing a path for the survivors, nowhere near Pantheon.

August threw me a sideways glance as he drew level, his face stony grey in the fragile light, Aelia quiet and still between his arms. We both knew the danger of this last stretch, despite our proximity to the forest. Instinctively, I leaned forward into the mane of my nervous auroch, gleaming like rivulets in the brightening sun.

'I trust you,' I whispered.

She tossed her head in understanding, before pulling ahead

of the herd and slowing to a purposeful trot, her head low and focused. Then the herd narrowed into a single line as we started across the brown dust, a cloud kicking up either side of our progress. It was a test of faith, fuelled by the rhythm of the remaining aurochs and tendrils of amber reaching through the forest ahead.

Which was when I glimpsed her, silhouetted on the other side of the mile-long stretch, her sleek body glowing against the trees.

'Jas?' I whispered incredulously.

My last sighting of her had been when she fought Brutus in the research centre inside Isca's old castle grounds, but it was clear her genes had influenced the sabre-tooths. *Had she been among the laboratory animals we'd released? Or perhaps she'd escaped in the aftermath of Ludi Cirque?*

Either way, her silhouette was as welcome as the rising sun – and then another figure stepped out of the trees behind her, a figure I knew as well as my own.

'Eli!' I yelled in jubilation, and even though there was still a mile of lethal dirt ground between us, and he was too far away to lip-read I could tell he knew me too, that his gentle smile was widening into a grin.

And then Jas was sprinting towards us, taking a circuitous route through the dirt, looping back and forth until her lithe, athletic body was leaping up at my suspicious auroch, and covering my outstretched hands with huge soppy licks.

'Jas, Jas … yes, I missed you so much too … but lead us, go on, girl!' I encouraged, aware my auroch was spooked enough without having an overemotional snow leopard sending her veering off course.

'Tal …'

August's voice behind me was low and urgent. I didn't need to look back at him to know why.

'Go on, Jas … go on … take us to Eli as fast as you can!' I urged.

She didn't need a second telling and bounded ahead, retracing the same looped path she had a few seconds previously. And as we galloped for our lives across the remaining dirt, an animal of the forest and survivor of Pantheon our beacon of hope, I was struck by how alike we all were.

Creatures of nature, creatures of design, Outsiders of the forest, Insiders of Pantheon. Our differences were merely coincidences of creation – of time and place. And yet here we all were fighting tyranny in the pursuit of the same fundamental thing: freedom. The freedom to be who our DNA meant us to be. And I'd never felt more feral.

I threw a look back at the receding silhouette of Pantheon's main dome. It looked quiet and uninterested in our escape. But I knew that its appearance hid a multitude of lies. Inside, a war was brewing, and it was only a matter of time before Cassius brought it outside. To my world. And we had to be waiting.

I'd never been more ready to feel the shadow of the boundary trees spilling over my skin, but their solace was nothing to the comfort of Eli's arms as I slid off my auroch's steaming back. I buried my face briefly in his comforting scent before pulling myself away.

'Aelia,' I whispered, knowing he would lip-read everything into my one word.

Between us we lifted her down from Bellerophon as August slid off behind. Then no one uttered a word as he carried her to the base of the Great Oak just a few metres away. I glanced up into its ancient, whispering branches and felt almost as though we'd come full circle. It was a tree that had known so many hopes and prayers, a tree that had comforted me when Grandpa slipped away, and a tree that watched over us now as Aelia drew faltering breaths.

'Can you help her?' I begged, kneeling beside him and watching his expert hands gently open her tunic, and unwind my blood-stained cloth. The spider web of dark veins had spread all the

253

way across her chest and down her torso. It was a grim sight. And my head knew what my heart refused to accept.

Eli looked back at me, his eyes clouding in the dappled light with an acceptance I didn't want to see. He reached out, and taking a small woollen blanket proffered by one of the Prolets, tucked it around her as snugly as though she were a child going to sleep. Then he closed his gentle hands over August's and mine, before lowering his head.

So we said goodbye, and the grief that cut out my heart and burned it all anew knew one salve. That she'd died leading the charge, as General of her people. She knew it too. It was in the glimmer of her smile when the pink sky beyond the trees told me the angels were already waiting to take the bravest, most natural Outsider I'd ever known, onwards. So when her hand finally relinquished mine, I did the only thing I could. I looked up through the watching trees and vented my anguish. It was a hunter's call; for her courage, for the future she should have known, and for the legacy she left behind.

And finally, when I mustered the courage to face August, I denied the arrows pushing through the tissues of my heart, because I knew she wouldn't want me to cry at all, let alone a river that would drown the whole world.

Chapter 22

We buried Aelia beneath the branches of the Great Oak that reached towards all four corners of the forest. I always fancied the oldest tree was rooted both in this world and the next; that its topmost branches could reach the heavens while its solid, earthen roots grew far into the soil beneath our feet.

It seemed fitting for a girl who made freedom her colour. A girl born with nothing, except the will to change it all. Now that spirit was as free as she always wanted to be, reaching far away into the clouds. And when finally we left, I could already feel her strength flushing through the branches, tingeing the buds and whispering among the spring leaves.

Aelia's loss was felt unanimously, and there were no words or actions that came anywhere close to comfort. It felt wrong to talk, wrong to be silent, and inadequate to be anything in between. Eyes stayed low, as though any casual connection might make the tragedy too real. And yet there was no denying it either. August's face was pinched with a devastation that nothing and no one could mend. Aelia was gone.

We picked up a north-east trail that circumnavigated the forest line, and caught up with the Ludi rescue party, led by Unus and Saba, as early daylight stirred life around us. The soft warming light was so familiar. It was a hunting time of day, the sort of time I used to associate with the start of a shift and the sleepy chorusing of the birds. Today though I resented its resilience.

Talk was brief, but I gathered enough detail to fill in the gaps. Unus and the rest of the rescue party had followed the old Roman tunnels and escaped to the outside just as the rockfall started. They lost one Lynx hunter over the mined land, before Jas spotted them. Eli's journey was still a mystery.

The sight of Mum plaiting wild garlic by the campfire eased my hurt momentarily, and sinking beside her, I dropped my head in exhaustion. She embraced me, smoothing my hair the way she used to when I was younger, after playing among the Baobab with Max. I never envied her oblivion more. Aelia had said she was lucid when they rescued her, but she was clearly back in Arafel now. It didn't matter, so long as there was a chance of another moment.

'You're late, Talia,' she chided indulgently.

I smiled, despite my leaden chest. I wanted so much to unload, to sob until I had nothing left, but those days had passed. I was the rock now, and all the strength, solace and wisdom she'd carved into my heart as a child would have to be enough.

***

Sixty-three survivors – Arafel hunters, Komodo, Lynx, Prolets and a handful of Pantheonites – wound their way wearily through the forest, towards the new Arafel camp. The day was unremittingly glorious, the trees thick in foliage and sun warm before mid-morning, but there was a chill among us that no view could thaw. We may have made it this far, but Aelia was gone and there was no doubt Cassius would be on our tail in a matter of hours, bringing hell in his wake.

I dropped to the back of the exhausted procession, suddenly aware I hadn't yet spoken to Unus. We walked a while in silence, offering each other quiet solace only close friends can, yet when I stole a glance up at his great pudgy face my chest only ached all the harder.

'Lia care … when Unus small …'

I reached out to squeeze his plate hand. 'She was a gifted doctor, a loyal friend … and a true Outsider,' I mumbled, though the words felt inadequate and trite.

I glanced up at August's quiet silhouette up ahead, unsure whether he was within listening distance.

'Lia say … Pantheon control head at cost of heart … but a wise leader … knows strength of both.'

The stone in my throat suddenly moved, and a real smile relaxed across my face. It was just the sort of thing Aelia would say, my fierce, irreverent angel.

Kiss my Prolet arse!

'Kiss mine,' I mumbled.

Unus tipped his head down at me quizzically.

'Thank you,' I whispered before slipping up the line towards Eli.

We still had everything to fight for, and the General of the Prolet Freedom Fighters wouldn't want us to do anything else.

'Tell me everything,' I signed swiftly, 'but first, how did you know we were coming? Across no-man's land?'

It was something that had been perplexing me. His appearance was so opportune. We'd always had a twin connection, but the way he'd been standing there with Jas as we rode across the dirt was a stretch, even for us.

He slipped his arm through mine, pulling me close. It was the first chance we'd had to talk privately.

'Last night, when Jas spotted the Ludi rescue party crossing the mined land without you,' he signed swiftly, 'I thought … It was my worst moment, and yet … I knew you were OK for two reasons.

'Firstly, because I could feel it in my bones, and secondly, because a small army of forest animals had preceded all of you.

257

Some were injured, others weren't, but they were clearly sticking together. They were forest animals, and yet they looked ...'

'Different?' I whispered, suddenly desperate to hear our gallant rescuers had made it too.

'Hunted ... yet, never freer.'

I felt a rush of relief so intense it made my vision swim.

He squeezed me gently. 'I started helping those who would let me, before I realized ...'

'Realized?' I signed rapidly. 'Did you see a big male gorilla? Was he holding anything?'

Eli looked puzzled for a second, before he shook his head. 'I saw a group of gorillas disappear into the bushes, but no alpha males that I recall,' he signed. 'What it did make me realize was that only a feral girl could be responsible for such a wondrous sight.'

I smiled up at him. It lightened my heart to know the animals had made it across the wasteland, their instincts alive and well.

'And what about you? Where did you go? Did you find her?' I signed swiftly, not wanting the others to know how I considered our survival to be entirely dependent on finding Lake.

His eyes narrowed. He knew it too. 'Yes,' he signed, 'in Arafel.'

I stared at him incredulously. 'She made it to Arafel? The village? How did you know to look there?'

'I worked it out.' He frowned. 'After drawing a blank in the Mountains. I started thinking that if Cassius was telling the truth about your blood relationship, she would feel as drawn to you, as you to her. Plus it would be quiet there, after everything. So I went back.'

I drew a breath, aware of how hard and strange that must have been alone. We'd both left so much behind there – friends, our home, and Eli's life's work.

'Where was she? Where did you find her?' I signed rapidly.

He stared at me. 'I didn't have to look far ... and she found me.'

I felt the colour drain from my face. 'What happened?' I whispered.

258

'It was intense,' he signed, lip-reading perfectly, 'like she knew who I was ... knew I was your blood? I managed to climb into our treehouse, thought I might as well try to salvage some books while I was there. And then her head filled the open wall of the living room. She's a titan, Tal ... the size of eight elephants! And kinda beautiful – for a draco-chimera.'

My heart pounded to think of Eli facing Lake alone, beautiful draco-chimera or not, and yet he was still here.

'She's still in her volatile draco form?' I mused slowly. 'She's a responsive chimera so remaining in her most aggressive form means ... she knows a war is coming?'

I searched Eli's face. 'Did you talk to her?'

'I didn't need to,' he signed. 'She understands everything, Tal. Her eyes are ... are ...'

'... hers?' I finished for him.

He nodded.

'Which doesn't mean she's with us,' I warned.

'No,' he agreed, 'I didn't sense any particular warmth, I mean, apart from her acidic steam – and keenness for a meal obviously.'

I frowned.

'Oh not me, thankfully, a couple of nearby deer filled the breach, but I'm not sure she's overly fussy.'

'She's there now?'

'I think so. I think she senses it's your home. Or what's left of it anyway. She's waiting there for you? Cassius? Armageddon? Who knows, maybe a mix of all three?'

I nodded. We both knew our one hope lay within my blood. And for once I thanked whatever curious alignment of stars and science had occurred, to ensure this responsibility had fallen to me alone.

'Then we have the start of a plan,' I signed.

One ancient mythical creature to face a whole army. They were my kind of odds. Outsider odds.

Chapter 23

The Arafel survivor camp was a small cave system set in the side of an old-world quarry, about a kilometre into the dense outside forest. It was a part of the forest we'd avoided most of our lives, partly because of its proximity to the Dead City and Lifedomes, and partly because of the near impenetrable jungle. But it seemed a good choice now, especially since we needed to keep a strict, round-the-clock watch.

We arrived quietly, the jubilation of the survivors far outweighing our own emotions, which were shadowed by the certainty that we'd only escaped the battle, to bring a war to their door.

I cast a swift look around the low-ceilinged rock cavern. The survivors had done their best by salvaging what they could from Arafel, but it made the ghosts more obvious.

There were so many missing.

I swallowed, knowing this was the hardest point, actually facing the loss. And I was so bone-achingly weary.

'Talia! Is it really you? Sit by the fire, all of you ... Bring food, water! Eli, Augustus Aquila ... and new friends! You are, all of you, most welcome ... And Max?' Seth's face lit up with hope before I shook my head. His expression faded before brightening again, and I realized our arrival meant everything, a flame we had to protect. For everyone's sake.

My gaze ran over the mingling mix of people as they were plied with food, drink and a barrage of questions. I didn't ask about Art. I'd seen the blackened roots of his treehouse with my own eyes, and as Seth was the only surviving member of the Council of Elders present, he'd clearly taken on the position of leader. He was young for the job, fifty at most, but it was welcome continuity.

'Thank you,' August muttered, taking a plate of broth and settling down opposite me.

I swallowed to ease the burn in my chest. He'd lost his status, home, friends and now the only sister he ever knew. *Where could we possibly go from here? Would he even stand beside us against Cassius?*

'Talia … Max?'

It was Carah, Max's mother.

She pushed through the small crowd as I stood up to meet her. She was a thin wiry woman, a keen hunter with a ready smile. But the events of the past months had taken their toll, and her face was lined with shadows and anxiety. Max's father stepped in beside her, his eyes darting between mine and Carah's, already guessing the truth.

'He's not here.' I forced a small smile. 'But he's alive and the only reason we made it back …'

***

Our small group of escapees brought the Arafel survivors to little more than one hundred. And it was a lively, mixed community, especially given the addition of various rescued domestic animals plus three teams of Komodos and Friskers the griffin. But we were still nothing like the number needed to take on a myth army.

Could scars make up for numbers?

They would have to.

Seth insisted on an abridged version of our story, and while their shock was evident, it was a relief finally, to share it all.

I wasn't deaf to the whispers. This mixed group of survivors were the first to know the full truth about Thomas's cipher, the Voynich, Lake, and my blood. I could feel their outrage as I related the story as best I could, despite Grandpa's request. But I believed every last man, woman and child deserved to know the whole, if they were to stand beside us, and that Grandpa would have thought so too.

'So where is this Voynich … this Book of Fire?' Seth asked, once I'd recounted everything.

'It's lost and that's for the best,' August filled in quietly.

I nodded, recalling the moment the gorilla had paused to look back on the balcony. I hoped with all my heart he'd taken the book to the topmost branches in the forest, and ripped and scattered its pages to the wind.

'And *Hominum chimera* … Lake as you call her … she's a mythical legend? Re-created from this ancient book?'

It had been the hardest part, describing the blood connection between myself and Lake – something I still didn't fully understand myself, let alone how I knew she was essential to facing Cassius's myth army. Yet most were Outsiders, who'd lived side by side with animals and understood how complex instincts could be. And although this relationship was unique, trust made up for the rest.

'And to think the Book of Arafel – our village book charting every decision since Arafel's beginning – actually hid Thomas's research into the Voynich? Extraordinary!

'Did you ever manage to retrieve it?'

I shook my head.

'Then we start a new Book,' Seth announced resolutely, 'and it will be a record of our second beginning! Not defying the dust clouds of the Great War, but defying the corrupt vision of one man who thought he had the right to rid the world of our kind. Human kind.'

There was a brief silence before a soft harmony began echoing through the cave; and I closed my eyes. It was the sound of warriors – Arafel, Komodo, Lynx, reaching over the stamping beat of renegade Pantheonites and Prolets, and their meaning was clear. We stood together, *come what may*. And whether it was the small cave accentuating the noise, the courage of those present, or the ghosts whispering through the trees, I felt a momentary flicker of belief.

***

August's rush hammock was empty when I awoke. Seth had insisted the new party rest while battle planning continued. No one objected. I'd never felt so weary in my life, we had no real idea when Cassius would come, and none of us were any use exhausted.

Sentries were posted, and shifts set up for food foraging and weaponry, while Seth and August had begun auditing all the weapons we already had between us. There were hunting machetes, spears, axes, knives, a couple of Diasords prised from unwilling Pantheonites, and a pile of agricultural tools that had been salvaged from Arafel. I eyed the small growing heap with apprehension, knowing the number of claws and teeth they would likely have to face.

Toray, a male Lynx warrior, and Saba were swift to distribute airborne weapons to the best archers, together with a small harvest of Black Bryony berries to tip arrows and darts. The venomous bats in Isca Prolet came to mind as a small Prolet group sat and patiently tipped them, Pantheon had its uses.

Arrow-shaping and paring was another swift production line, with Outsider and Insider heads bent together, working furiously.

I could feel Grandpa nodding approvingly, and there was no question that we weren't all one army now. And yet, even though this was Outsider territory and many of us were seasoned hunters, my bones knew we would need every stick, stone, and ounce of courage to face the darkness coming our way.

Which left finding Lake and persuading her to our cause, small words for a herculean feat.

'Did you see him leave?'

Eli was outside feeding Friskers, who seemed blissfully unaware of the impending doom.

'Said he needed a walk to clear his head? That he wouldn't be long,' Eli signed. 'Asked me to make sure you rested your arm.'

My eyes flickered to the new bandage Carah had carefully wound around my wound. I hadn't it paid much attention since leaving Isca, and it was aching less since she cleaned it up. But August's absence filled me with agitation. He didn't know the outside forest, not like me, and it wasn't the sort of place in which you just took a walk.

'I'll find him,' I signed, ignoring Eli's expression. 'We need more berries for the arrows anyway.'

It was mid-afternoon, sentries were changing and dusk wasn't far away. If there was any strike, I was more than convinced it would come at night. Cassius had kept an entire army in the darkness; it made some semblance of sense he would use its cover to set it free.

'You've got the flight of an arrow,' Eli signed, gesticulating towards the sun hanging low in the sky. 'And ... what of Max?' he questioned carefully.

I looked at him, empty of words, never more aware that Max's fate was dependent on the outcome of the battle too. I'd told him briefly what had happened in Ludi Cirque Pantheonares, and we'd agreed to spare Carah the Pantheon vaccine detail. But it wasn't that to which he was referring – we both knew that. He reached out and pulled me into a swift hug.

'What about you,' I responded after a beat, 'have you heard anything?'

I was suddenly acutely aware he hadn't mentioned anyone since our return, let alone an undersea prince who wanted Cassius stopped as much as we did.

'The Oceanids are loyal to no one but themselves,' he closed.

'Well, he'll have me to answer to if he messes with you, Prince or no Prince,' I responded firmly, squeezing his hand.

Matters of the heart were complicated enough without mixing in the unpredictable dating behaviour of a mythological species. He smiled, the way he used to when we were kids. Then I turned and made my way into the quiet forest.

The sun had melted into a scarlet well on the horizon. Time had always stretched out endlessly before Pantheon, sunny days punctuated by meals, sleep, stories and the occasional monsoon storm. Now, it had a crueller edge. It was a keeper of all our fates – Outsiders, Insiders and everyone else in between. No one was exempt from its power, and I kept one eye on the horizon as I walked, not knowing whether it was going to be my last.

The path was freshly trodden, and as a lorikeet dived low overhead I told myself he wouldn't have gone far. There was anticipation in the forest this eve, a tension in the boughs that reached out to brush my skin, as though to warn me to stay alert. And the darting, inquisitive eyes peeking out from behind thickened banyan roots looked unusually apprehensive, as though they too sensed a looming darkness.

'Where are you, Lake?' I whispered, gazing up at the highest point in the North Mountains.

Had she retreated? Did she sense Cassius was gathering his army?

The path narrowed and descended past a burst of wild orchids, spilling out from a tree stump, as though the world wasn't teetering on its smallest axis.

And then I saw him, seated against a large willow trunk, his head resting on his folded arms, the long feathery willow branches

265

reaching down to caress his hunched shoulders. I paused, suddenly feeling an intruder to his grief. He looked so different here in the forest with no uniform, loose Outsider clothing and dark hair ruffled and unkempt.

'I'm sorry,' I whispered, almost regretting the words as soon as they passed over my lips.

He looked up, staring intently, as though I were a vision conjured by the translucent sunlight that could disappear any second.

The old hemp shirt he'd borrowed from Seth's meagre store gaped around his muscular frame, while the open neck fell around the edge of his glittering Equite tattoo, the only visible sign of his Pantheonite heritage. His olive colour could easily be mistaken for belonging here, beneath the sun, while his iris-blues seemed to have acquired a dusky forest veil.

I swallowed, despite everything. He looked as though he'd been born under a constellation, not in a laboratory.

'For what?' he responded finally. 'For doing everything you could to try and stop this happening? For giving people hope? For being stronger than I could ever hope to be? Come what may, Talia finds her way.'

And it wasn't ironic or flattering, it was just broken.

I drew a shaky breath, memories clamouring for space. He'd done nothing but try and protect me, right from the beginning. And I'd fought him in every way possible – in the forest, in the domes, before Octavia, before Cassius. He'd even fought his own nature, to try and make me see we were something stronger than the state of Pantheon could ever be. And I'd rejected him. Believing it was better to shut him out and bury all the hurt and guilt.

When I couldn't have been more wrong.

I barely noticed the soft forest grass beneath my feet as I flew across the clearing. And then I was in front of him, taking his hands and talking. Saying all the words that had got buried and lost along the way.

'*Astra inclinant, sed non obligant*,' I whispered fervently. 'Remember? The stars guide us, they never bind us. We choose our path. We are who we are, who our friends are. We are the choices we make. Everything I've done, I've *only* done because I had loyal friends beside me – and because of the belief of one Insider who saw a different world, and was brave enough to sacrifice everything he knew for it. Despite the storm.

'And I've never wished so hard to be back in our North Mountain cave, so I could show you how I believe, what I always believed deep down ...'

I had no breath left, but when his lips met mine, my words blurred and faded anyway. The soft warm grass became a make-shift bed and the whispering willow a natural curtain that gave us a few precious, stolen moments to say the only thing left to say. And if what happened in the North Mountains had suffocated us, this was breathing again, an answer to the fire that had sparked so long ago in this same forest.

'I thought I'd lost you,' August whispered, tracing a line of tiny kisses down my throat, 'that what happened in the research centre, had ... finished us.'

We were still naked and entwined, and though the willow was cocooning us, time was whispering through the leaves. I reached up and kissed the bridge of his Roman nose.

'I thought we'd traded *us* with the Oceanids,' I whispered. 'That I didn't deserve anything when so many had been hurt. But ... I could never be free now, without you.'

Words that finally made sense of the shadows. Freedom didn't belong to Outsiders or a chosen life beneath the sun, it belonged to anyone with a heart to give.

I scrutinized his face, committing every cell to memory, and this time there was no crushing guilt. Fear and pain made us human, but it didn't define us. Only our choices could do that. Whatever was coming, we would face side by side, Outsider and Insider, *together*.

'We have to go,' I whispered, all too aware our brief escape was over.

I twisted to look at the horizon. August's proximity was intoxicating, and my traitorous body yearned to start over, but we were needed.

'Time to find our alpha,' I whispered, watching a squirrel monkey swing from our willow tree into a neighbouring baobab.

It paused to look back as I slipped on my borrowed Outsider tunic, and briefly I wondered if it was my little apricot monkey, the one I'd set free right back at the start. It would seem prophetic somehow.

August slipped an arm around my waist, pulling me close and setting a gentler kiss on my lips, before dropping his forehead to rest against mine, skin to skin. The intimacy of his gesture made me flush the colour of wild strawberries, despite everything.

'Just in case we *are* fried by a huge, multi-genus, mythological beast, I want you to know I just had the best moment of my life. There. With you.'

I smiled up shyly. Eyes dancing.

'Then just in case we *are* fried by a huge, multi-genus, mythological beast, I want you to know that that sounds like a challenge,' I responded.

He laughed before kissing me again, and then we were running, at hunters' pace.

Chapter 24

The aurochs knew as soon as we moved them up to the eastern forest line. They were nervous, and shied from every shadow as we penned them in. The fencing was secure enough to keep them grouped as a herd, but nothing they couldn't jump from if they really needed. From this vantage we could see both the City of Dust and Isca Pantheon's great dome staining the dusky sky, and the view was stark.

When would they come?

The aurochs were a second line of defence, part of the Lynx cavalry when Cassius broke through the Arafel hunter and Komodo line. And although there were no more than twenty Lynx left, their proud Nordic heritage was an impressive sight to behold.

'A veritable ice army,' August murmured, as he organized battle lines.

After consultation with Seth and Eli, it was agreed we should leave Lake's recruitment until the very last moment, though the occasional ground tremor confirmed she wasn't far. There was enough danger without inviting a hormonal chimera to join us before absolute time. Though we were all aware leaving her too long carried risks too.

'We need to time this perfectly … and you'll need a second when you go – Eli's your best choice,' August muttered through gritted teeth, glancing at me.

I knew he was torn. He wanted to come to Arafel, but our Outsider army was precious, small and disparate enough without a general at its helm. And Eli was just about the best second I could have.

I nodded, showing Therry how to sharpen blades against a stone. Eli was just behind us, penning in the Komodo dragons. They were an impressive group of lizards but none of us were under any illusions. We all knew that the moment Cassius broke the skyline with his myth army, it would take a miracle for us to hold our ground without backup.

'Just what do you think controlling the elements actually means?'

I'd stepped over to help August hide supplies of poison-tipped arrows among the twisted boughs of nearby trees. The hunters, Komodos and mixed Insiders were the infantry, covering as much ground as possible, leaving the agile Lynx to flank the action with arrows and axes.

It was a tough decision to include the children. There were only a handful remaining, but we didn't have any choice. Every child was an extra pair of hands to fire darts and throw knives, and left in a safe-hold they ran the risk of discovery anyway. Unus had already taken the colourful group under his wing, which settled my qualms a little. I knew he would protect them with his life, and they already doted on him.

'No one knows for sure,' August returned, 'but I know how Cassius looks at it. Take nature, imagine that strength and volatility bound up in one legendary being, and call it *Hominum chimera*. It's a kind of physics: every action has an equal and opposite reaction. In nature's case, it's Lake.'

I felt a chill scuttle down my spine, despite the forest warmth. Even without strength of mythical proportions, Lake was a force

270

to contend with. And yet, I had to believe that Thomas had foreseen this day and hidden the only true control within his bloodline.

Would my voice be control enough? Or would it need blood like the infant chimera? How could I let a draco eight times the size of a treehouse feed on my blood without giving everything?

My thoughts grew darker with the night descending around us, conjuring up the starving, fiery child who'd pulled a knife on Max, her double-lidded eyes the only clue to her true genetic heritage. We'd shared a connection from the beginning, but this was different.

Would she even remember me?

***

'It was just after dusk last time,' Eli signed as he helped me climb out of the freezing water tunnel and, together, we turned to look out at the silent valley of Arafel.

I'd always detested the only entrance and exit into our old village but oddly, tonight I didn't mind it. The numbing water felt like a balm, easing the pain of seeing the ashen remains of Arafel for the first time since the day Mum and I were taken by the Eagle aircraft.

This cave and the Ring were the only untouched parts of the village and a wave of nausea threatened to engulf me as I looked out onto what was once a hub of community life. In the twilight, its stark, abandoned appearance was haunting. I closed my eyes and heard Raoul joking as I handed him my foraged goods, caught the faint crow of the cockerel as it heralded the day, and the hammering of the builders working on a new treehouse some-where in the forest. *Max in my shadow, making me laugh.*

An owl hooted as Eli touched my arm, and I jumped. I'd never noticed before just what a mournful sound it was, like a warning.

'You OK?' he signed.

271

I nodded, swallowing hard. There had been no sign of Cassius yet, but every passing minute brought that likelihood closer. We dared leave Lake no longer. He was coming, and it was up to us to be ready when he did.

'Just asking Arafel for her help,' I responded, laying my drying cloth out to dry in the cool air.

Then we stole like young cats through the night, taking to the trees whenever we could, although there were still large areas of ground devoid of any life. The heat had been so severe, most of the old centre was still barren, and more than half the closest treehouses were missing. I kept my eyes on our route, and tried not to look too hard at the shadows.

It was only when we reached the site of Art's wizened old ash treehouse that I slowed. The Eagle aircraft had split this part of the forest, so his neighbour's treehouse still reached into the sky, like the gnarled hand of a survivor, clutching at the air. But its remarkable survival wasn't the reason I'd hesitated. It was because high up among the budding foliage there were marks – deep indentations that looked very similar to the ones we'd glimpsed in the North Mountains.

'She passed by here,' I whispered.

Eli nodded. 'It looks like some kind of territorial marking,' he signed, 'partly warning and partly way-marker, guiding you to her … for a warm bite to eat.'

I rolled my eyes.

He only winked and we pushed on, more watchful this time.

We took to the trees for the last few minutes. There was less damage in this part of the forest, and when we passed the place I'd left Ida, it was covered with bluebells. I smiled briefly. It meant something to see life where her body had lain broken.

Finally we approached our treehouse. While the old white oak itself had miraculously survived the worst of the Eagle fire, our shell of a treehouse home now rested precariously on a broken branch, which forked downwards. One wall of the living room was completely gone, exposing the inside, which now looked weathered and faded, and I could just make out the blackened remains of Jas's bed against the wall I'd painted the colours of the forest. It was a hard scene to assimilate, its broken edges framed by the twilight.

I scanned the bushes. It was quiet. Too quiet perhaps, even for a ghost village.

'Where exactly was she when you saw her?'

But the question died on my lips as a flare tore through the night sky, dividing it in two. It was accompanied by a violent crack of thunder, as though Cassius was shaking the entire world in his greedy, malicious hand.

I reached out to grab Eli. My skin felt clammy, and the trees around us seemed to loosen in their roots.

Was this what it was like when the bombs came for our ancestors? A threat that even the safe, solid ground beneath our feet couldn't withstand?

'Lake?' Eli questioned, the whites around his eyes gleaming and alert.

I shook my head as the violent thundering ceased as abruptly as it had started.

'Cassius,' I signed, trembling. 'It's begun.'

This time I wasn't aware of anything but the whisper of the old trees as we flew. I could almost hear their warning, as if they still remembered the last time, and could sense danger in the air.

And if Lake wasn't here in Arafel, where was she?

To whom was she drawn more?

The ground trembled again as we dropped like arrows into the freezing water, and it took every ounce of control I had to remain calm as the walls trembled, losing dirt and rubble into the black water. Only Eli's steadying hand, pulling me out of the water and into the outside forest, quelled my rising nausea. We both knew there was no room for panic. We had to reach the others and pray Lake was close, if we were to make any stand against whatever he'd unleashed from the depths of the Flavium.

We took the swiftest route back, but there was no need to search for a path. The forest fringe was already glowing amber, illuminating the sky, and before long we were flying against a wave of animals heading away from the threat.

We passed chimps, cats, monkeys, lemurs, rodents, birds of paradise and hordes of scurrying insects, all moving together. And there seemed to be a sense of knowledge in their flight, as though a genetic memory created by the Great War had entrenched itself in their cells, pre-empting their behaviour. A number of ground-dwelling animals had also taken to the trees, trusting to their archaic strength and refuge. It made a chilling sight and Eli and I fought hard against the sudden surge in life and wayward branches, foretelling their own warning.

I paused, face to face with a black panther, her lithe body hunched between a tree fork, her beautiful flecked eyes reflecting the glow of the sky. She yowled softly and then she was gone, her message still ringing in my ears as the first cries reached us. It was a noise that carried me back to the North Mountains, to the nights we'd spent listening to the lonely echo of wolves. Only this howling was deeper, darker and driven less by hunger, and more by blood.

We only slowed when we reached the perimeter of the defence line. It was eerily still here but the faint baying was getting louder with every passing second. I hooted softly and then I saw them: eyes, lots of wide eyes peering through the branches at me. Before a bulky shape melted out from the cover of dense umbrella trees, carrying a huge club.

I dropped to the ground and crept forward.

'Tal,' Unus whispered, his pale eye wary and troubled.

'They come ... August say ... stay back here with young ones ... your mum too ... But how can Unus help here?'

I hugged his huge bulk tightly, so relieved to spy Mum's profile with the children in the trees behind, and not allowing myself to wonder if it was for the last time.

274

'You have the most important job,' I whispered, gripping his free hand and kissing it fiercely. 'Defend them – they're very precious.'

He nodded, his eye glistening, and if it was ironic to leave the future of the outside in the care of a rejected Insider, it didn't feel it. It felt like the safest haven left on earth.

Eli and I stole forward stealthily, our path made much clearer by the emptying trees and the fact the south-east skyline was lit up like dawn, except the sun was still abed.

Finally we reached a tree with a view from Pantheon's no-man's land right across to scorpion plain, where we caught a first glimpse of our enemy's approach.

I sucked in a gasp.

'They're coming from the city,' Eli signed in the murky light.

In that moment it seemed as though the entire ground was moving up to meet us, because we were staring at a line of Sweeper vehicles as far as the eye could see. And above them all, creating a formidable backdrop, were more Eagle aircraft than I could count.

'Looks like Cassius got his house in order,' I whispered though it felt as though the colour was draining from the world around me. *There were just so many. And what hellish abominations were they carrying?*

I lifted my head to the night and released two howler calls. They were answered immediately, barely twenty paces away. Then there was a curious backlight for a second, and the trees around us groaned like foot soldiers hit by a wave of silent guns. The air filled with smouldering acrid smoke before a rain of laser fire followed, sparking too many disparate fires to count, and crumbling foliage to ash before our eyes.

A high volley of arrows responded. Lynx arrows, flaming and silent, falling halfway down scorpion hill into an impressive line. The Sweepers barely checked their progress, but there was something about the unbroken line, lighting up the night and the

275

encroaching army, that looked so damned noble. They sent a message.

We were here and waiting.

I gritted my teeth as Eli and I flew through the remaining trees to join the front defenders August had arced strategically across the forest line. He threw us a strained look – both relieved and troubled as we shook our heads.

'Thought you'd chosen another battle,' he muttered, pulling me into a tight embrace before signalling again across the front line.

'Tempting,' I returned, taking a bow from the stockpile beside him.

'No luck?'

I shook my head, scanning the eerie sky. 'Not in Arafel, but she's close,' I whispered.

It was the truth. I could feel her; I just couldn't see her.

Why was she keeping her distance? She knew I was here – I could feel it. So, why wasn't she coming?

The Sweepers were crossing the arrows, crushing them beneath their heavy caterpillar tracks. It was inevitable but sobering to see our defiance swallowed by their might, and yet it was the moment for which we'd been waiting. August nodded and I tipped my head back in another cry, a wolf howl this time, and a signal to the remainder of the hunters hidden among the glowing trees.

'The Sweepers will likely be the delivery service. The fires are unstoppable but they will create confusion,' August whispered, his Roman face striped with red earth. 'When they come, use everything, don't hold back. We don't have the manpower or resources for a long battle. Our advantage lies in surprise, quick kills and better knowledge of the ground. If we are to stand any chance this has to finish here, tonight. Keep looking, use every means you have to call her … for all our sakes. And, Tal?'

I nodded feeling as though we'd slipped into a parallel universe.

'I love you.'

276

Three small words that stopped time, armoured the soul and set us both free. And though I wished with all my being we were somewhere else, I knew we were the lucky ones.

'I love you too.'

Then we grasped the overhanging branches of a central oak, and pulled ourselves up. I cast a look along our defence line to the shadowy Outsider faces just visible in the neighbouring trees. They were so few, yet real warrior grit and courage was etched into each of their earth-painted faces. My chest flamed with pride, though I was so terrified for them all. So much depended on finding Lake. On me.

Then the piercing Sweeper lights were level with the forest, penetrating the foliage with the same deathly white light as the laboratories. Then the thundering ceased altogether. The armoured vehicles had paused barely half a kilometre from the forest line. There was a silence when every breath was too loud, and their huge side doors began to slide open.

'For the love of Nero,' August cursed as a miscellany of myths spilled into open view.

The entire forest fell silent as Cassius's army finally revealed itself in its ugly, unnatural entirety, filling the brow of scorpion hill. One hundred souls to vanquish an army of mythological abominations; it was bad maths on any day.

And we could only watch and wait. There was every combination of species known to mythkind: giant molossers, distorted griffins, hulking great satyrs, hissing basilisks and two-headed hagas with snapping turtle heads. A swarm of thick marble-skinned cenchris snakes slithered into view, rearing and fighting in their eagerness to get off the Sweeper, their angry tails pointing upwards and small wings enabling them to hover. Coldly, I recalled their story in Grandpa's book, how they were spawned from the blood of Medusa in a desert.

They were followed by a pair of huge lumbering Minotaurus bulls with swinging serpentine club tails, and then a creature three times their size crashed out from a larger armoured vehicle – a three-horned, leathery black beast. I dimly recalled something called an odontotyrannus, a cross between a rhinoceros and crocodile, only this creature was much bigger, uglier and by the look of it, already eating its own army.

And they were all flanked by a squadron of incoming Eagle aircraft, swooping low, firing at will and lighting up the forest as though with hundreds of old Pacha's village lanterns, only these fires were torches of destruction.

'Chimera,' I whispered thickly. 'The myth army comprises Cassius's failed chimera trials.'

There was an eerie moment of silence as our small outside army faced the truth. This was a battle on a scale we'd never imagined, the hideous totality of Cassius's failed experimentation, incarcerated, and now let loose like a nightmare of biblical proportions.

The baby chimera flickered through my mind. I'd controlled it with my blood, so perhaps there was a chance I could do the same here, but how could I turn enough creatures and survive long enough to find Lake? My brief spark died and I scanned the skyline again. We had but one hope.

More Sweepers were opening, spilling out battalions of soldiers, creating an unbroken line of imperial Roman red behind the myth army. They looked invincible, like a wall.

'Now,' August whispered, and lifting my head I howled like a furious she-wolf.

The response was a volley of silent Outsider arrows, only this time they were as black as the night and while their tiny shape appeared inconsequential, each one carried a deadly poisonous tip. I watched with satisfaction as they fell with precision upon both beasts and soldiers alike. Our numbers were small but skilled. August nodded again, and I dropped to the ground to join Eli and Tao, a Komodo warrior, as the sky echoed with pained bellows and howls.

278

Eli reached out to squeeze my shoulder. 'I have an idea,' he signed furiously. 'Stay out of trouble!'

I scowled, but the look in his face told me how much it mattered.

'Hurry,' I hissed, as a chorus of baying filled the air.

It was vile and unholy, the sound of the unnatural world readying itself for blood.

He disappeared into the night as Tao and I dived through the smoking trees to our target and as I looked over the wooden pen at our precious back-up infantry, and now I found their hiss and primordial growl the most comforting noise in the universe.

'Feral means free!' I muttered fiercely, yanking out a rough wooden peg as Tao pulled back the makeshift fencing.

The dragons responded instantly, and whether it was the scent of fresh meat, the lure of open space, or something less tangible, the powerful Komodo dragons that had survived Arafel's razing spilled out and headed straight for the fight. They were an impressive sight, most nearing three metres long, crashing through the undergrowth and hungry. And though they were instantly dwarfed by the army scarring the skyline, I could see the welcoming committee were surprised when they broke the forest line.

'We fire as they move in,' August whispered as I swung back into position. 'Whatever happens ... just ... stay alive!'

Grey smiled from my memory, as did Ida, Servilia, Rajid and my beloved fierce Aelia. So many loyal friends lost; it was time to prove it wasn't in vain. And I'd made a promise too.

I steeled my nerve as I lifted my bow and trained it on the rise of scorpion hill. The Komodo lizards now lined the boundary of the forest, as though they understood they were our front line, and as they lifted their reptilian heads to roar – their tails thrashing in anger – my chest swelled. They could sense the primeval divide. They understood they were facing an unnatural army, and their fury was tangible.

They were answered with a deafening babel of guttural cries, most of which I'd never heard before. The bellowing of a black Minotaurus, the baying of Brutus's giant molossus pack, and the ominous hiss of writhing cenchris were all over lapping and indistinguishable as the creatures lowered their heads and advanced. And the Komodo moved out to meet them; speedily, fiercely and undeterred by the number of beasts bearing down on them. Several of the largest dragons reared high in their first brutal and bloody collision as the two lines closed, one hideously smaller than the first, and the sound seemed to echo through the whole forest.

We pulled our bows back, aiming high.

'Now!' August signalled ferociously as another cloud of poison-tipped arrows cut through the night, taking our hopes with them.

They fell silently upon our enemies, and the roar of pain that erupted was confirmation enough they'd met their targets. I scanned scorpion hill, feeling a fragile elation at every heaped body, outnumbered easily by the number remaining. We were making a difference, but there were just so damned many.

Again we reloaded our bows, releasing a fresh cloud of fire arrows, which this time only served to illuminate the wall of mythological chimera swamping our courageous Komodo. My ears were thumping with painful adrenaline, my limbs wired as the odontotyrannus lumbered forward, its massive gaping jaws resembling an oversized dinosaur.

'Not enough,' August whispered between clenched teeth, 'we need more.'

I nodded, and scanned the horizon feverishly. *Where had she gone?*

And then there was a rustle of big branches breaking, the movement of something large. Only this noise was coming from behind us.

I shot a look at August. *Had Cassius stolen ground when we weren't looking?* He shook his head, his face pale beneath his camouflage. We shifted around to peer through the smoky gloom. My fears began to climb.

Were we surrounded? Was it the end so soon?

Come what may, nature finds a way, Talia, Grandpa's distant voice encouraged.

'But how?' I whispered despairingly.

And then a sight that took our arrows and Komodo dragons and gave them claws and teeth enough to meet any myth army. The advancing body wasn't one huge misshapen mythological creature at all, but a band of saviours – natural saviours. With one familiar figure at the front: *Eli.* I inhaled jaggedly as he waved his courageous forest army forward, their stealthy silence saying everything about our ancient kinship in the face of Pantheon's nightmare.

There was every type of wild creature you could imagine – bears, large primates, tigers, lions, wild cats, horses, hyenas, boar, snakes, even rodents, all approaching as one, and at their head, just behind Eli, was a familiar alpha gorilla, wielding a large club. It was the most painful, noble and welcome sight any Outsider could hope for.

'Thank you,' I whispered, locking eyes with the gorilla, and reading the wildfire there.

August looked at me and we nodded simultaneously. The forest was alive with the cry of the natural world, and now we stood a chance.

We dropped to the ground without the need for words; Outsider and forest beast, shoulder to shoulder, ancient instinct connecting us all. There were no predators or prey, only the earth's natural inheritors, and we were allies until the very last of us dropped.

I tipped my head back to issue the final signal, just as a raucous cry broke the sky in two. And as the moon disappeared behind a monstrous black shadow, every pair of eyes turned skywards.

'Finally,' I whispered hoarsely.

She was there, silhouetted against the anguished sky, like a winged angel of the night, and she was far bigger and stronger than ever I'd seen her. Her spiny draco arrow-point wings spanned the entire width of Pantheon, and her titian body, covered in lustrous scales, shone with reflected starlight, as though to announce her regal status. And as we all watched, a burst of violence, like a sunrise too early, tore across the sky and set the horizon alight.

She was a blue-blooded, mythical queen. Glorious and deadly.

'I'm here,' I breathed, though my blood was already reaching. And I could feel her strength and elemental will answering. She knew I was here too.

Chapter 25

Grandpa used to tell old stories about blood moons. But I'd a feeling he'd never stood above scorpion hill, with the earth beneath his feet staining scarlet in the milk wash of the night.

And the cry that made our enemies stare as we broke the forest perimeter was less my voice and more the sound of the outside world saying it remembered, it bore the scars and it wasn't ready. Not now, not ever.

While our numbers were still fewer, we had something else besides. Wrath at our immense loss – and belief in our fight. For the forest. For Arafel. *For all the ghosts.*

We fought knowing it was our last night on earth. The brow of scorpion hill had never seen so many species together, and for a while we held them back, our diversity a strength. A pride of lionesses squared up to the giant molossers instantly, and even though they were smaller, they had years of hunting on their side.

Eli, August and I stayed close, taking on the guards spilling through the fray, their Diasords picking up where the Eagle lasers had stopped, and all the while I kept one eye on the horizon. *Find me,* I whispered as she circled.

A back panther stretched into a sprint past me, before taking a heroic leap up at the torso of a Minotaurus and sinking her jaws into its thick neck. And something in her seasoned gait made me pull my machete from the neck of a cenchris snake at my feet. *Was she the cat I'd faced in the forest so long ago?*

'Talia, stay in line!' August roared hoarsely, his face stained with blood as the bull yanked the cat from its chest, and threw her as though she were a kitten, onto the writhing floor.

The machete was out of my hands before I could check myself, glinting through the stench-filled air and burying itself in the Minotaurus's thigh. The creature threw its head back and howled.

It levelled its fevered gaze at me, just as a bull lowered its head and charged, taking the creature clean off its club feet with one bone-shattering impact. I pulled out my spare blade and swiped at a cenchris writhing beneath my feet, before the raised tail of an angry scorpion got the better of it.

'First rule of the jungle,' I muttered, *'watch your ground.'*

I scanned the hill grimly. We were holding our line but the background kept refilling from the open Sweepers. My gut lurched. *We were tiring and there were just so many. Black Griffin, Satyr, Minotaurus, swarms of basilisk and cenchris, diving hagas, molossers with jaws reddened by torn flesh, and behind them fresh gladiators, trained to fight to the death.*

How could our courageous but precious few stand a chance against such a force?

Then a new noise reached out across the dead air. A beat – a sonorous ancient rite, that spoke of hidden worlds and forgotten knowledge. And a slow prickle began to creep across my skin as I twisted to scan the forest line. The sound wasn't of the forest, and yet it was coming from behind us.

'Tal!'

August's warning was enough, and I brought my blade up as a diving haga took its chance. It reached for my head with huge claws, its two hybrid heads, a turtle and a bird, crowing with sure victory. Instinct took over and in one sharp swipe it was at my feet. I gazed briefly at its four glassy eyes before returning my attention to the forest line, along with most of the battlefield.

The trees had greyed behind a tall smoky wall, a wall that was separating into individual shapes. It was a fresh army, clad from head to foot in dark grey armour shaped like scales. And at their centre was one helmetless figure, unmistakable in his regency and bearing, flying the standard of another civilization altogether. A civilization who were loyal to no one except themselves – until today.

I caught Eli's smile across the carnage of misshapen, skewed bodies.

Was this why he'd been so quiet about his time with Phaethon? Because he'd also made a promise? I knew at once it was, and the intensity in his gaze left little to imagine. Phaethon had asked me to kill Cassius. But he never meant for us to face the myth army alone. He and his people detested Pantheon's tyranny as much as we did. He knew about my blood tie with Lake, his army were aligning with the Outsiders, and he'd also made a commitment of his own.

Once again emotion had shown itself to be the key, a source of real strength, not weakness. *Was this also part of my connection with Lake?*

I swallowed as more pieces of the jigsaw fell into place. Aelia had mentioned Phaethon was gathering his army. She couldn't have known how serious Phaethon and Eli were, and I had little doubt Phaethon would have made my brother promise not to tell me of his support.

I closed my eyes briefly. My quiet brother who always brought what and who was most needed. If anyone was to survive and lead a new Outsider community it should be him, the most unsung and resourceful of all heroes.

I spun around as the formidable Oceanidic army started forward, the sound of their heavy-armoured march sending new energy through my veins. I side-jumped the charge of a towering satyr before running to the aid of a rearing auroch amid a swarm of basilisk. And as the fresh army swelled our ranks, their barnacled black swords making short shrift of anything they ran against, I felt a fresh surge of hope. And then my eyes locked on a single gladiator I would have recognized anywhere.

I sucked in a breath as he ran towards me, his hunter legs making light work of the uneven, strewn ground, the hound at his side straining at its leash. I sheathed my knife and pulled my bow from my back, conscious the ground around us was trembling again. The quakes had been coming more violently for nearly an hour now, despite the fact Lake had disappeared over the forest line.

Where was she?

'Max?' I exhaled warningly, my hands shaking as he stopped barely three metres away, my arrow aimed at the pulsing artery in his neck. Was it him? Or had the shadows claimed him again? Raoul had taught us all the quickest and kindest way to dispatch one of our kind.

'Tal …'

And the way his lips shaped my name, as though we were back in my room watching the shadows dance, was so familiar that for a moment I didn't breathe. Could he remember? *Could he finally remember it all?*

My bow aim shifted to the hybrid hound at his side, which could barely contain itself. It looked half molossus, half basilisk with a low rear that tapered into an elongated tail that thrashed powerfully.

It lunged then, pulling free from Max's hold and springing directly for the Komodo to my right. The pair clashed and fell into the bloodied earth as Max advanced, his Diasord still high. And there was no time for anything but trust as I readjusted my aim and dispatched the arrow directly into the hybrid's neck.

It stilled as Max reached down and pulled its heavy body off the struggling Komodo dragon, which gathered itself and crawled away.

'Why run when you can fly?'

It was the lightest whisper with barely any volume, but there all the same. And then I knew for sure. I looked up into his harrowed face, at raw forest-greens, just as another body crashed into him, propelling them both into a rapid, blurred tumble. It was one of the grey-scale Oceanids, at least a foot taller, and lightning fast in his movements.

'Max,' I yelled, as a heap of carnivorous basilisks reached up and twisted around my ankles.

I stumbled, trying to free myself, everywhere a sea of misshapen, bloodied limbs.

'Fall back!' August's hoarse echo chased through the violence.

There were so many falling, too many dying. Leaving still more of Cassius's myth army silhouetted against the sky. My scorching eyes searched frantically for Max and the Oceanid soldier, among the heaving ranks of bodies, the dead and wounded alike.

We never needed her more.

'Lake?' I entreated the sky, as an ugly black molossus started ripping down our thinning line, trampling anything in its way.

It was still some way off, but I would know its vicious intent anywhere. Brutus. Part molossus, part Cassius. I drew my bow again, never more hate-fuelled than at this moment, determined to rid the world of one curse, whatever it took. But as I narrowed my sight, I became conscious of the lightest, flecked leopard feet sprinting across the battlefield. A cat with an old score to settle, and more than enough battle-stripes already. I swung my gaze and felt my fears spiral.

'Jas ... no!' I yelled, lowering my bow and sprinting forward for a surer aim, willing my feet over the fallen, willing her to turn tail or fall. I couldn't part with anyone else I loved.

But her snow-leopard legs were much nimbler than mine, and as she rounded into his path, she did what every protective watch-cat would do when faced with a monster that would do her family harm, and threw herself into a brutal collision.

And it was personal. I was within hunting distance now, and again and again I tensed my bow, trying to get a vantage, only for one of them to roll away, blocking the other. It was clear they had unfinished business, and that this time neither was running.

Jas was lighter and swifter, but Brutus had the advantage of brute strength. Repeatedly, her sharp claws ripped through his thick coat, but I could tell she was tiring. I held my breath as I deftly released an arrow, which impaled itself in the side of one of his massive haunches, and as he turned in fury, Jas went for his neck. He roared and I thought perhaps it was her moment, but a cenchris chose that same instant to wrap itself around one of my ankles, and as I fell Jas released her grip. Brutus felt the difference in a heartbeat, and rounding with an almighty roar, sunk his bloodied jaws around her slim neck.

Our gazes connected momentarily, and I saw the colours in our treehouse canopy, a myriad of forest dawns, and Eli cradling her as a tiny cub, reflected in her eyes. Before her light died completely, bringing the sky crashing down around me.

'Nooooo!' I screamed, fighting my way back onto my feet as Brutus let his broken quarry drop.

He sunk low on his haunches, his blood-flecked eyes pumped with victory, as I ran in and skidded to my knees, pulling her beautiful warm head into my arms. Her mountain eyes were empty, just like my fight. And as Brutus's head leered large over mine, his jaws wet with Jas's blood, I found myself wanting nothing more than to leave this raw, painful world far behind.

Which was when I felt her. Which was when everyone felt her, and even the ground beneath us appeared to shake with trepidation. Brutus turned tail and fled with a cowardly whine, while the whole battlefield turned its attention to the night sky – to the shadow of a legendary draco-chimera, slowly consuming the Dead City of Isca.

'She's coming in ... Fall back ... fall back!'

It was a familiar male voice, but he was so detached and far away. All that was real was circling above me – huge double-lidded yellow eyes as wide as my entire length, and as deep and fathomless as the ocean. And as her spiny draco-chimera head dived, her velocity and magnitude made the ground beneath my knees tremble. It was as though the whole world was holding its breath.

Nothing had ever looked more beautiful. If I reached out, I could touch the gold and purple-flecked scales around her eyes, glinting like oyster shell in the dawn light; while her giant fire-skinned claws raked through the tainted earth as though it were sand. She was more than the Voynich's last secret, she was celestial.

Dark to dark, blood to blood.

It was just me and a fiery little girl by the name of Lake. Wasn't it?

'Lake?' I whispered.

The battlefield had fallen silent, while the horizon was beginning to spill an eerie light. There was a sudden rush, the club feet of odontotyrannus thundering towards us, its ugly bellow echoing across the stunned landscape. Lake sunk forward over her thick fore-claws, her amber eyes gleaming and archaic jaws parting. It was already too late, and I dived for cover as the ground disappeared inside a blast of scorching chemical heat.

When I looked back, odontotyrannus was gone.

As was the mood.

Slowly, I put out a hand, trying to re-create the same energy as before but her draco eyes were slices of fury as she swung her gaze back to the rest of the watching battlefield. To the stunned army of mythical creatures and their cowering guards.

'Lake …?'

But this time she took little notice of the feral girl beside her. Instead she lowered her spiny muscular neck and released a single jet of searing steam across the landscape, desiccating everything it reached in a heartbeat.

'Talia Hanway!'

Slowly, I turned in the direction of the voice as Lake released a jet of acidic venom to the sky this time, and though the air was already thick with choking smoke, I was with her. Because he was there, at the centre of a large battalion of griffin-mounted guards, the man who had ripped my life apart, and who I loathed with every cell of my feral body.

And somehow Lake knew.

Her spiny head sank low again, her reptilian jowls pulled back in a vicious expression as a volcanic sound invaded the steaming air. It took only a moment before I realized it was coming from within her.

Hominum chimera is one of the most volatile creatures of the ancient mythical world. It's believed she is capable of triggering a sequence of natural disasters, culminating in the eternal fire of damnation – or the end of civilization as we know it.

August's words ran through my head with perfect clarity, and I knew then she was capable of it all. I had no doubt she had enough power to tilt the natural world on its axis, to start a fire that would engulf the land, to melt the ice and snow, and force the seas to rise enough in fury to drown us all. She could shake the very foundation of Hades if she chose.

Somehow Cassius had rebirthed a legend, the mother of all mythical creatures.

The battalion came to an abrupt halt just far enough away for us to be able to hear through the chilling silence that somehow felt louder than all the chaos of before.

'What a beauty ... my creation ... my Lake,' Cassius crooned, pushing forward through his soldiers on a lavishly armoured griffin to take up position at the front.

His voice was perfectly calm – the voice of a despot who believed so hard in his Emperor-God rhetoric, he'd forgotten his own mortality.

'But how thoughtful of you to bring her to heel for me, Talia. I knew you could do it – though poor Livia had her doubts.'

Poor Livia. The moment Ida's dart buried itself in her neck flashed through my mind and I tightened the hold on my blade, expecting a challenge, but Cassius moved on. *So much for poor Livia.*

He smiled as Lake lifted her draco head, and though she was the most fearsome creature on the planet I could sense her uncertainty. She knew Cassius was connected somehow, and it was making her hesitate.

I cast my burning eyes across the rim of the forest, searching for Eli, but the air was too black and acrid to recognize anyone. And yet, it felt as though the entire hill was watching, the destiny of the natural and unnatural balancing on this one fragile moment.

'Don't listen to him,' I hissed, climbing to my feet. I was acutely aware that her every exhalation could spell death, and yet I wasn't afraid. 'You are the mother of mythical creatures – a living legend – and he is a liar, a cheat and a murderer,' I added, watching Cassius's swarthy face light up perversely.

I could tell she was listening by the narrowing of her double-lidded eyes. Lake, the little girl, was still in there. I could feel her.

There's always a weakness in the life created, Aelia's faint voice explained. *It's why Cassius is hunting for the Book of Arafel – for Thomas's cipher and the correct genetic coding.*

I gazed upwards at the armoured scales, at her eyes, the colour of old gold, and of the power of ages behind each breath. Could it be that she also had a weakness? *Could that weakness possibly be her humanity? Which would explain why Cassius couldn't synthesize my control. It was linked to our humanity – our emotions – the very thing Cassius had tried to design out. My vision swam momentarily and I knew, at last, I was right.*

'Oh but I don't think either of us are entirely blameless on that front, are we, Talia?'

His loaded, twisted words hung on the air as there was a shuffle among the mounted guards. Then a single gladiator was pushed forward and thrown forcibly to the ground in front of Cassius.

'When will you see we're the same, you and I?' He sighed.

'That together we could create a new world, filled with life worthy of the outside. Just think of the glory, Talia!'

But I had no words. Because my attention was on the figure sprawled at the feet of his dark-blood griffin. His helmet was gone, his Outsider skin was cut and smeared with earth, and his forest-green eyes were full of pain as he tried to push himself up. I could see he was badly injured. His left arm swung heavily while the side of his uniform was ripped and congealing with blood.

And yet his old care was there, fully there this time, in the grit of his teeth and thrust of his good arm, warning me. The tiny treehouse dart tube had done its greatest work, and the spark of memory in the auroch's stable had slowly grown. My heart tore, and it took every last ounce of strength I had not to sprint to his side, to give Cassius the perfect bargaining pawn.

'Max!'

My voice sounded leaden in the smoke-filled air, saying everything and nothing at all.

'It's all OK, Tal ...' he responded hoarsely. And I knew then what he was going to say. 'Tell her ... to do it!' he forced, just as one of the guards lashed out with an animal restraint.

'No!' I yelled, but I was too late.

It fizzed as it hit Max, forcing him to collapse to the ground as the griffins side-shuffled in terror.

Bile climbed my throat, filling my mouth. How could one person be capable of so much destruction and malice? Believing himself invincible, untouchable, immortal even.

My dark blood was rising, reading Max's pleading eyes. He did understand. He understood so much and I never gave him the respect he deserved. The guilt in my chest hardened into a cannonball.

'You see, Talia, I still have something you want,' Cassius crooned, leaning forward over his saddle. 'I flatter myself I'm rather good at strategy, as this sort of tactical operation tends to exhaust me. And it's a very simple straightforward choice really.

Do as I ask, and your forest friend will live to see another day. Defy me and …'

He shrugged, as though it was all regrettable, his immortality assured, my hands tied.

Lake's response was to release a jet of pure black flames to the sky, forming a cloud of acidic gas that descended slowly, sucking the oxygen from the air around us. I tried to take short steady breaths, even though my lungs were burning and crying out for relief.

'Pull out while you can, Cassius. Call off your army and we'll finish this between us. Just you and me. After all, what have you got to fear from a lone feral girl?'

There was a moment of silence before Cassius started laughing, his callous mirth carrying to all four corners of the battlefield as movement on the rim of the hill caught my eye.

A familiar knight in Arafel colours, riding bareback across the strewn wasteland, with only a loyal Cyclops for company. My heart throbbed to see them both alive, yet what could they do here except perhaps trade their own lives for the smallest ground? The cannonball hardened further. *You must bear the responsibility alone, Talia*, Grandpa whispered.

Max tried to lift his head and speak, though I could tell every exhalation was costing him. It took all the feral strength I had left not to run to him, to give Cassius exactly what he needed to control Lake. But it was like slowly cutting off my own limbs, and I was near blinded with fear by the one choice I had remaining.

'Cassius!' August's roar cut across the devastation as he galloped towards us, and I felt Lake exhale in recognition.

'This is not what Thomas or Octavia ever intended for the outside world. You know this.

'Thomas had reason to take his chance on an outside life. He saw this day coming, he knew there was no glory in ruling a world that was dead!'

His voice carried clearly, though the air felt poisoned. I inhaled

293

raggedly, trying to fill my lungs though it felt like dragging my lungs over red-hot coals.

'Thomas didn't just take his chances, he abandoned me!' Cassius suddenly raged. 'Taking our research and hiding it for two centuries. So, this dead world as you call it, it is my destiny! And now I will create a new world, filled with life that knows no weakness, and Thomas can watch from whatever hole he is wasting away in, knowing that in the end … I won.'

The pack of griffins scuttled in panic as Lake sank and released a shorter jet of black fire, her draco eyes as deep and unsettled as a storm.

'Yes, my girl,' he crooned, switching attention. 'Just look at how magnificent she is, Augustus. *Hominum chimera*, the one legend Octavia and Thomas believed impossible to re-create, and I've done it. She's mine, as is the control.'

His eyes levelled with mine, pure death adder reaching across the space between us.

'Though she's a little slow to know it.'

He cracked his whip violently in Max's direction as though to make his point, the tip catching him and opening up a deep welt across his cheek.

And just as though I'd been hurt myself, my fury swelled.

'There is nothing I cannot – and will not – do to make this world great again.'

His onyx eyes glittered with a jealousy that had soured his soul for centuries as August charged, his head low and machete ready. It was a sight I could never have foreseen, a free Equite Knight riding against everything he'd ever known, choosing a barefoot girl and a legacy, bound by humanity.

Cassius smiled, pulling his visor down, and indicated to his guards who shifted direction as Lake suddenly released another stream of acidic flames to the sky. I could feel her instability and confusion as culpably as my own. My heart was pumping red, red blood. Arafel blood. Free blood.

A good hunter knows when to fight and when to flee.

I sprinted forward in front of Lake. In this position she could incinerate me with one breath but it didn't matter. Because Grandpa, Mum, Eli, Aelia, Max and August were all in my heart – and the only person who could actually change anything was me. *It was never more time.* For the sake of an Outsider future, between the red earth and yellow sun.

'You want to know why Outsiders survived, Cassius?' I railed.

'Do it, Talia,' Max stormed, telling me he was spent.

He'd managed to push up onto one elbow, showing me the glint of something small in his hand. A dart, he still had a dart.

I nodded, glancing at August, who was slowing as though I were already a ghost. He closed his eyes in silent blessing, telling me he and Unus would take their chance.

'Guards!' Cassius stormed.

'Why run when you can fly?' I smiled, snatching the tiny dart tube from around my neck and scuttling it along the ground and into Max's outstretched hand.

'Guards!'

But Cassius's command stalled on his lips as Max's sure aim found his neck. He wrenched out the small precise weapon as chaos broke around him, his lips staining black with fury. It wouldn't kill him, but Max had bought me valuable seconds.

I was conscious of a confused volley of scattered laser fire as I flew up Lake's outstretched foreleg. And if she was startled by my sudden proximity, she didn't show it. Instead, I could feel our blood connecting, awakening a knowledge hidden there by Thomas when he saw how this would end.

Finally, when I stood at the crest of her enormous draco head, I saw the devastated world the way the gods might. Broken by ambition and greed – and by the selfish desire of a few who took what was real and twisted it until it no longer resembled itself.

But most of all I saw a feral girl, with the future spinning in her hands.

'Gua … rds … stop … her.' But Cassius's voice was nothing more than a pitiful croak, pierced by Max's hunting aim.

His dark eyes blazed with fury as he clenched a hand to his bleeding neck, trying to calm his rearing griffin before he wreaked his revenge on Max.

My eyes sought him out hunched on the ground, his head twisted up to watch, his forest-greens locked with mine. Their light told me he was already among the trees, shadowing me as we flew with the sun at our backs. And I smiled fiercely, holding him tight one last time before I drew my blade across my wrist, releasing a rivulet of blood that fell like tears onto Lake's scales, before trickling in beside her protruding canines. Then I lifted my eyes and whispered the only words left.

'Feral means free.'

They were just loud enough for the angels and Lake to hear, just clear enough for Cassius's expression to twist to terror and just long enough to know Grandpa was smiling – before she opened her jaws and scorched the earth clean.

Chapter 26

We soared together, Lake and I, until the Dead City of Isca was sketched out so far below us it looked little more than a map of old ruins. I could just make out the North Tower of the cathedral standing proud of its crumbling surroundings, and yet there were still too many ghosts.

I was so close to heaven, so close to the tendrils of dawn breaking through the clouds I thought perhaps I could touch them. I closed my eyes to try, but there was nothing but the pounding of blood, ancient feral blood.

For now, at least, it seemed I was still mortal.

Our descent reminded me as much, and as my blood warmed so did the realization that while Lake's quake had devastated as far as the eye could see, Cassius's legacy remained in all its domed glory.

'*Take me back,*' I thought, feeling a ripple of reptilian muscle in answer.

Our communication was silent, a primeval instinct or seventh sense, blood bonded by a unique twist and the one thing Cassius didn't consider, our shared humanity.

We flew down and landed south of the Dead City, the vast walls of the domes dwarfed by Lake's titian magnificence in the early sun.

And as I looked up at their clinical rise, at the pristine walls that had hidden so many secrets, I felt the rise of Lake's fury as keenly as my own. I knew instinctively what she wanted to do, and the reason why she hadn't relinquished her draco-chimera nature yet.

She was barely ever allowed above ground because of her strength and aggression, August's voice echoed, *and when she got there, she unleashed her fury by breaking her chains and devouring the spectators.*

My consciousness had become a stream of images, and I knew Lake was seeing them too: Arafel, Pan, Aelia's sacrifice, Jas, Max's heroism, and Unus, Mum, Eli, August ... How could I even hope that any of them were still alive?

I stretched out a hand, its span not even as wide as one of her iridescent scales, and knew I had this one chance. To avenge them all.

And Lake was ready to do exactly as I bid.

Come what may, nature finds a way, Talia ... Care for the seed and it will care for you ... Hunters take only what they need to survive ...

The ghosts of Arafel began filling my head, filling Lake's head, clamouring for mercy.

For happiness, heart and head must agree.

'But he stole everyone I ever loved.'

I wasn't even sure I'd spoken the words aloud as I looked up into Lake's eyes. The sun was dancing in them, reflecting movement around the curved wall of the largest dome. Behind us. I turned, shielding my eyes as a small figure appeared.

It was a young man, with onyx eyes and a familiar stride.

'Atticus,' I whispered in amazement as a long line of Prolets and Pantheonites appeared behind him, carrying small children and scant possessions.

He paused three oak trees from me, every inch of his proud face asking a question he wouldn't or couldn't actually voice.

I shook my head. He knew anyway – I could tell.

He dropped his gaze to his feet before raising it again. He'd led the young Prolet uprising and helped Aelia, Rajid and Grey to infiltrate Ludi, but Cassius was still his father. He would grieve alone, that much was inescapable.

'Then in the name of peace, I ask for safe passage,' he ventured, 'for myself and for anyone else who wants to leave Isca Pantheon. And I ask if we ... if we ... Is that Lake?'

His voice faltered as his incredulity got the better of him.

And Lake responded by slowly inclining her regal head until she was level with him, her steamy breath whispering in the early sunlight. I pressed my hand against her warm scales, conscious she could still incinerate them all with a single exhalation. But she seemed to remember well enough, and if their old friendship lay among Cassius's ashes, there seemed to be a silent acknowledgement that destiny had led them here.

'There's an end-of-life function,' Atticus volunteered after a beat. 'An emergency measure that seals the domes and slowly reduces life support. Father's scientific team developed it in case life on the inside ever ... grew beyond his control. Let me evacuate those who wish it, and I will activate it. It will finish it all – for good.'

My mind flew to the laboratory of Prolet embryos and to Aelia's fight for their protection, to my own realization that sometimes design had nothing to do with will.

'What of the unborn?' I whispered.

Atticus's face darkened. 'Will it be better for them that they remain so?' he muttered.

A shocked whisper started among the crowd, and Lake's breath deepened. I reached up instinctively, soothing her though I knew what she wanted, understanding that perhaps it was a remnant of her own Prolet humanity.

I closed my eyes. The ghosts were clamouring and the outside was fragile enough without raising Cassius's Prolet army on hope. And yet.

The stars incline us ... they do not bind us.

Cassius and Livia were so wrong. My emotion had never weakened me; it had guided me.

I stared at Atticus's face and could tell he wanted it too. Dark blood could choose mercy.

'They live.'

My voice was strong and there was a tangible murmur.

'But they live and breathe as Outsiders,' I continued. 'And as I stand here now, there will be no mention of Pantheon or Cassius for as long as we all live. They will be raised to think as free people, and through them we will show freedom isn't defined by walls, but by our choices.'

Atticus inclined his head, relief darkening his young eyes. 'I think this is yours.'

He stepped forward, still cautious of Lake's exhalations, and pulled something from beneath his charioteer tunic. It was brown, mottled and conjured images of Grandpa shuffling through a crowd of faded faces. I took it into my hands, and felt its musty scent embrace me like an old friend. *The Book of Arafel.* I inhaled unsteadily. It was such an old, worn collection of pages but their content, Thomas's research, had started it all.

Protect it, he'd entreated. *Protect it with your life, Talia.*

'I tried, Grandpa,' I whispered.

But some secrets were so violent they grew a lifeblood of their own.

Care for the seed and it will care for you.

I scanned the crowd of tense Insider faces. The Voynich was still out there somewhere, perhaps it would never be found, but the Book of Arafel was here in my hands. It was Thomas's cipher, the key to decrypting all the Voynich's secrets. And as its last keeper, this was one decision I could make.

I fanned the pages through my hands, letting their homely, aged scent comfort me one last time before twisting to look up at Lake. Her great spiny head dipped once as I closed my eyes, and then I threw the book high into the air.

She responded instantly, releasing a jet of pure black flames that incinerated Thomas's lifework in a heartbeat. And I fancied the great white oak, still silhouetted on the horizon, whispered its approval.

Chapter 27

We had no choice but to take the long way back, around scorpion hill. The feral girl and the chimera child; small, skinny, still wearing her headscarf and smoke-grey tunic.

Lake had morphed as soon as the Book of Arafel was burned, almost as though her legend had been destroyed along with it. And while she'd shed her reptilian skin in favour of something far less violent, I almost missed her archaic alter ego.

I recalled the skinny, fiery orphan to whom Max and I had offered our last provisions beneath the Dead City of Isca. She was no bigger – that much was certain. But there was a new wisdom in her double-lidded honey eyes that narrowed in the sunshine, and while there wasn't much talk, I could tell she recalled everything. She slipped a small hand through my arm as we walked, our bond sealed, but what lay ahead dwarfed anything either of us could say.

It had turned into the kind of spring day I relished in Arafel. The sky was cobalt blue, the air alive with birdsong and our path alongside the Dead City strewn with fresh blossom. It was undeniably, defiantly spring. I inhaled deeply, trying to carry the life with me, to strengthen me for what we had yet to face.

We traced a circular path with heavy feet. The ground had

become a hardened river of dislodged earth, mud and waste, making progress slow. And I could feel my fear building. There could be no more denial, no more fragile hope. Lake gripped my arm tightly and I drew her near. Drawing strength for whatever lay ahead – no matter how raw.

Then finally, we climbed high enough for our first view of the rise of scorpion hill to its forest brow, where we paused, unsure whether the glinting sun was tormenting us, or if we could trust the sudden euphoria chasing our veins.

Because even though we were still some distance away, the outside forest was *still there*. And furthermore, it was alive!

We fell into an instinctive stumbling run, over the smoking charcoaled ground, towards the precious family of survivors at the forest fringe: Mum, Eli, Unus, Komodos, Lynx, Pantheonites, Prolets – and a Roman Equite Knight who'd never looked more like home.

Come what may, nature finds a way.

Grandpa's whisper gave our feet wings, and I could feel Max smiling as a hunter's cry escaped my lips. Because feral had always meant the freedom to choose a life between the red earth and guiding stars.

And that was worth the whole damned world.

Glossary of Terms

(in alphabetical order)

Astra inclinant, sed non obligant: The stars incline us, they do not bind us (ancient Latin saying referring to strength of free will over astrological determinism)

Aurochs: Hebrew equivalent of 'wild ox' but translated biblically as 'unicorn' in the early Christian church.

Cenchris: One of the many venomous snakes believed to be spawned from the blood of Medusa, and to live in the Sahara desert. Its most obvious characteristic was that it always moved in a straight line, and did not coil or flex its body. Cenchris venom was believed to rot and putrefy flesh, causing lethargy, stomach-ache and death within two days if left untreated.

Circus Pantheonares: Play on '*Circus Maximus*', Latin for greatest ancient Roman chariot-racing stadium and mass entertainment venue in Rome, Italy for *Ludi. It was the first and largest stadium in ancient Rome and could accommodate over 150,000 spectators. The Ludi Cirque Pantheonares is Cassius's own Ludi arena based upon the real Circus Maximus.

Faction Colours: According to Tertullian, there were originally just two factions, white and red, sacred to winter and summer respectively. Later on there were four factions: the red, white, green and blue, and each team could have up to three chariots in a race.

Grande Stazione: Grand Station

Herculean: Refers to Hercules. Hercules was the Roman god equivalent of the Greek god Heracles. Hercules was the son of Zeus, the Lord of the sky and a mortal woman, Alcmene. He was a great swordsman and wrestler, earning his god status.

Imperator Cassius: Imperator appeared in the title of all Roman monarchs until the extinction of the Empire in 1453. *Imperium* is Latin for the authority to command, and the word Emperor derives from this term.

Jupiter: Lord of the sky and supreme ruler of the gods. Known for throwing lightning bolts.

Legatio: Roman envoys were often sent abroad with written instructions from their government. Sometimes a messenger (nuntius) was sent, but for larger responsibilities, a *legatio* (embassy) of ten or twelve *legati* (ambassadors) was organized.

*Ludi: Public games connected to Roman religious festivals. Sponsored by leading Romans or the Roman state for the benefit of the people.

Medusa: Translated from the Greek, the daughter of Phorcys and Ceto who became a Gorgon/ugly snake-headed monster. Perseus beheaded her wielding Athena's shield and wearing Hades' invisible helmet and Hermes' winged boots.

Machairodontinae: A sabre-toothed cat. One of the most iconic predators of prehistoric America. About the size of a modern tiger, but more robustly built, with broad limbs, unmistakable long canines, and a mouth gape range of almost 120 degrees. Additionally it could have reached a body mass of more than 400 kilograms.

Oceanids: From the Greek, 'Clymene' was an Oceanid nymph loved by the sun god Helios. She bore him seven daughters, the Heliad nymphs, and a son named **Phaethon**. The boy was killed when he attempted to drive his father's chariot across the sky.

Odontotyrannus: Massive beast believed to have lived in the rivers of India. According to mythology, when Alexander the Great and his men made camp by a river, they were found by an odontotyrannus coming to the water to drink. It was enormous, large enough to swallow an elephant whole, and black in colour with three horns on its head. When it saw the Macedonians it went on a rampage, killing twenty-six and injuring fifty-two soldiers before it was brought down. Progenitors include the rhinoceros and crocodile.

Oropendola: A large, gregarious tropical American bird of the American blackbird family, which has brown or black plumage with yellow outer tail feathers. The strange and remarkable song of the Montezuma Oropendola is an ascending series of overlapping bubbly syllables, which crescendo to a high peak. The song is often accompanied by a scratchy call that is reminiscent of a fizzling firecracker or the ripping of a thick fabric (Stiles & Skutch 1989).

Quadriga (*Latin quadric and iugum yoke*): a chariot drawn by four horses abreast (the Roman Empire's equivalent of Ancient Greek tethrippon). It was raced in Ancient Olympic Games and other contests. Quadrigas were emblems of triumph and may refer to the chariot alone, the four horses without it, or the combination.

Senatus Popules Que Romanum: 'The Senate and the people of Rome' was written on the standards of the regions. Eagles were the symbols of the legions, which were drawn on the standards.

Servilia: born c.104BC, d. after 42 BC was a Roman matron from a distinguished family. She was the wife of Marcus Junius Brutus and Decimus Junius Silenus, but she is most famous for being the mistress of Julius Caesar, whom her son Brutus and son-in-law Gaius Cassius Longinus later assassinated in 44BC.

Tiger Beetle: Fast-running hunter, armed with heavy-duty mandibles. Often called the 'lion or cheetah' of the insect world.

Titus: Titus Flavius Caesar Vespasianus Augustus was Roman Emperor from 79 to 81AD, and is best known for completing the Colosseum.

Valkyrie: Means 'choosers of the slain' and are believed to show up at battles to decide who will die. Then they escort the chosen souls back to Valhalla where everyone has a good time.

Citizen Numbers (Latin):

Citizen MMDCL (Talia Hanway): 2650

Citizen MDCLII (Rajid): 1652

Want more?

To be the first to hear about new releases, competitions, 99p eBooks and promotions, sign up to our monthly email newsletter.

Acknowledgements

Writing the Book of Fire trilogy has been a challenge and a privilege.

Five years ago, I sat down with a vague idea of a wild girl who saved a dystopian world and Talia just emerged: feral, impulsive, brave, yet very flawed and relatable – save for a few impressive aerial skills!

I tried to make her as believable as possible, while setting her story inside a fantasy world, because she had some real things to say. So if any of her journey has resonated, as it has with me, then I have achieved something more than the adventures of one feral girl and that makes me a very happy author.

In particular, I'd like to extend my special thanks to: HQ Editors Belinda Toor & Abigail Fenton, for their all-round editing wizardry.

The HQ Design team for just the most incredible cover.

Chloe Seager for picking *Book of Fire* off the slush pile four years ago.

Hannah Weatherill (Northbank Talent Management) for support and new friendship.

Catherine Johnson (Author) & the Curtis Brown Creative Team for ongoing support and words of wisdom.

Stuart White & WriteMentor for friendship and new opportunities.

My awesome writing group: The Scribblers for belief, right from the start.

My fantastic readers and followers, who've been a real source of inspiration and support, especially throughout *Storm of Ash* edits.

All the amazing bloggers, vloggers and authors who've given their time to read and review – so important and very much appreciated.

And finally, my fabulous family,

without whom I wouldn't have written a word.

Dear Reader,

We hope you enjoyed reading this book. If you did, we'd be so appreciative if you left a review. It really helps us and the author to bring more books like this to you.

Here at HQ Digital we are dedicated to publishing fiction that will keep you turning the pages into the early hours. Don't want to miss a thing? To find out more about our books, promotions, discover exclusive content and enter competitions you can keep in touch in the following ways:

JOIN OUR COMMUNITY:

Sign up to our new email newsletter: po.st/HQSignUp

Read our new blog www.hqstories.co.uk

🐦 : *https://twitter.com/HQDigitalUK*

📘 : *www.facebook.com/HQStories*

BUDDING WRITER?

We're also looking for authors to join the HQ Digital family!
Please submit your manuscript to:

HQDigital@harpercollins.co.uk

Thanks for reading, from the HQ Digital team

If you enjoyed *Storm of Ash*, then why not try another utterly gripping fantasy novel from HQ?